STARCARBON

By Ellen Gilchrist

STARCARBON
A MEDITATION ON LOVE

A NOVEL BY
ELLEN GILCHRIST

BACK
BAY
BOOKS

LITTLE, BROWN AND COMPANY
BOSTON   NEW YORK   TORONTO   LONDON

First Paperback Edition

The characters and events in this book are fictitious.
Any similarity to real persons, living or dead,
is coincidental and not intended by the author.

Excerpt from "Galaxy Song." Words and Music by Eric Idle
and John De Prez. Copyright © 1983 KAY-GEE-BEE MUSIC and
EMI Virgin Music Ltd. International Copyright Secured.
All Rights Reserved. Reprinted by permission.

Excerpt from "Lousiana 1927" by Randy Newman. Copyright
© 1974 by Warner-Tamerlane Publishing Corp. All Rights
Reserved. Reprinted by permission.

Excerpt from "Cabaret" by Fred Ebb and John Kander.
Copyright © 1966 by Alley Music Corp. and Trio Music
Co., Inc. All Rights Reserved. Reprinted by permission.

Library of Congress Cataloging-in-Publication Data

Gilchrist, Ellen
     Starcarbon : a meditation on love / Ellen Gilchrist.—1st. ed.
         p.   cm.
     ISBN 0-316-31327-0 (hc)
     ISBN 0-316-31462-5 (pb)
     1. Man-woman relationships—Fiction.   2. Marriage—Fiction.
     I. Title.
     PS3557.I34258S73   1994
     813'.54—dc20   93-25130

                 10 9 8 7 6 5 4 3 2 1

MV-NY

Published simultaneously in Canada
by Little, Brown & Company (Canada) Limited
Printed in the United States of America

For Henry and Carolyn and Buiji and Kathleen and Patty and David and Sivagami. "The best actors in the world, either for tragedy, comedy, history, pastoral, pastoral-comical, historical-pastoral, tragical-historical, tragical-comical-historical-pastoral. . . . For the law of writ and the liberty, these are the only men."

". . . and leave you, (inexpressibly to unravel)
your life, with its immensity and fear,
so that, now bounded, now immeasurable,
it is alternately stone in you and star."

Rainer Maria Rilke
translated by Stephen Mitchell

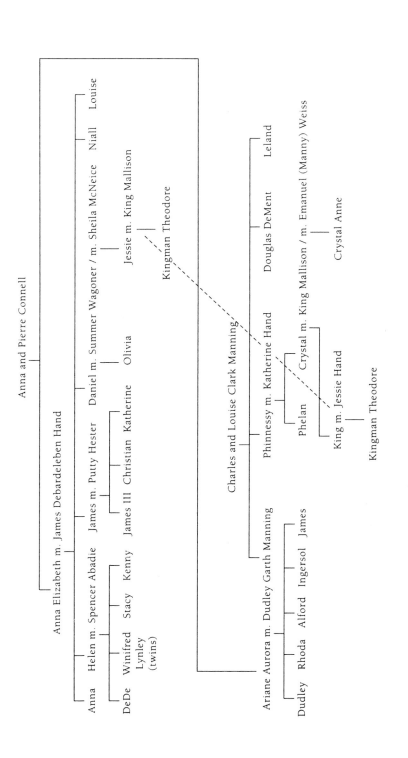

CHIVAS AND WATER

I T was still winter in Boston. The day before, the skies had dumped three feet of new snow on the city, turning it into a wonderland. Helen and Mike were in bed listening to jazz and telling stories. "You all complain about Daniel's drinking," Mike was saying. "But I never see him do anything to hurt anyone. He's always a gentleman around me."

"You don't know what it was like over there at night."

"Tell me." He pushed the pillow behind his head, turned on his side to listen. He loved Helen's stories about her family. They were fraught with danger, passion, glory, struggle. He would wake the next morning with his head full of the stories, completely caught up in them, as Helen's life had been.

"I used to go over there nearly every night to see about the girls. When Olivia first got there and Momma was going crazy worrying about them. She'd send me over to make sure Jessie was all right. The music would be blaring out the front door. Whitney Houston and Madonna, that's all they listened to. And Daniel would be in the den throwing logs on the fire and drinking Scotch. Margaret, or whoever was his girlfriend at the time, and Jade would be cooking dinner and the television would be on, some stupid program. Every Sunday night they'd be watching *Murder, She Wrote.*"

"The telly would be on?"

"And the stereo. Noise all over the place and in the midst of that Jessie would be trying to do her lessons."

"Where would Olivia be?"

"Upstairs in her room. When I came in, Daniel would yell up the stairs and make her come down and speak to me. Then we'd all sit around the den while the girls and the girlfriend fought little skirmishes for Daniel's attention. He'd keep on drinking."

"Doesn't sound so bad to me."

"The tyranny of it, Mike. Because he'd be getting drunker and drunker and it was less and less possible to reason with him or cross him on anything. It was not a proper atmosphere for study. How could anyone learn anything with all that noise? No wonder Jessie had to have a tutor."

"I still don't see why you're so mad at Daniel. He stayed there and took care of them, didn't he? Doesn't that count for anything?"

"It was the atmosphere. That endless glass of Scotch and water."

"He loves them."

"Love isn't enough. Children have to have order. Well, I gave mine order and where did it get me?"

"They'll come around." He pulled her into his arms and kissed her on the hair. "No one could stay away from you."

"Oh, Mike."

"In the morning, light will be all over this bloody snow. The dawn will be so beautiful we'll forget everything else." Now it was his turn to tell a story and he told her about the sun on the snow when he was a boy and went to Norway with his mother.

"He got drunk every night," Olivia was saying to her psychiatrist. "At five o'clock every afternoon he'd start filling glasses with Scotch and water and after that anything could happen."

"What would happen?"

"Usually nothing. Except maybe getting yelled at. We stayed out of his way. Well, he'd make us come sit in the den if anyone came by. Aunt Helen came by all the time."

"Did he ever hit anyone?"

"God, no. Dad wouldn't hit us. He just made everyone do what he wanted them to do. He'd just sit there and we couldn't talk on the phone on school nights."

"So you think that's why Jessie didn't do well in school?"

"It bothered her more than it did me. I was fifteen before I went there to live. I'd known another life."

"What was it like at your grandmother's in Oklahoma?"

"Just like it is now. Everyone just does what they want and no one bitches about it."

"That's how I like it," the psychiatrist said. "That's the way I think life should be."

"Dad loves me so much," Jessie was saying. She was over at her mother-in-law's house watching Crystal and Traceleen making gazpacho for a symphony benefit. The kitchen was full of tomatoes and celery and green peppers and basil and olive oil, the sound of two blenders going full force around the conversation. "So I don't see why he won't come see our house."

"He'll come see you when the baby gets here." Traceleen turned off a blender and cleared a space beside her. "Cut up these peppers for me. The busier you stay the last month, the better."

"He keeps saying he's coming but he never does. He thinks I ought to fly up there. But I can't now. I can't even go out of town in the car. How big do you want the pieces?"

"The smaller the better."

"He's spoiled rotten," Crystal said. "Your grandmother spoiled him. But he was so cute. He was the cutest little boy in the world."

"He's a good-looking man," Traceleen added. "They get spoiled."

"I miss him so much. I worry about him being all alone in that house."

"Call him and tell him to come on down. Keep on inviting him."

"He and King don't get along too well." Jessie began chopping peppers, cutting them hard and expertly on the chopping board. Inside her uterus the six-pound baby boy was listening to their voices. Sirens, he might have been thinking in some watery language. Siren songs.

Jessie chopped harder, her face squinted into a mask of concentration, cutting the peppers into squares for Traceleen to throw into the blender.

In Charlotte, Daniel was drinking Chivas with one of the bankers that he used to buy and sell. The banker was talking about the new golf club that was being built in Clover, South Carolina, just across the state line. "You better join now, Daniel. Get in on the ground floor," he was saying, but he was thinking about how much it pleased him to have Daniel on the ropes, begging for a loan. Good-looking Daniel, who had hogged up all the pretty girls when they were in high school. "Call me when you get an afternoon," Daniel was saying. "I'll come over and walk the course with you. Hell, maybe we can play a round." Daniel smiled and motioned to a waiter. I may have to borrow money from your daddy's bank, he was thinking, but I sure as hell don't have to play golf with you. "Get that waiter over here," he added. "Let's see if we can get him to freshen up these drinks."

BIG DADDIES,
A THANKLESS TASK

CHAPTER 1

CHARLOTTE, North Carolina, May 1, 1991. Mr. James Hand, Senior, got out of his old Mercedes and walked across the soccer fields to the small wooden stands and took a seat by his daughter-in-law. He was wearing a seersucker suit and a starched white shirt and a blue and red striped tie. He was wearing black silk socks and handmade leather shoes. He lowered his tall frame and kissed his daughter-in-law on the cheek. He spoke to several people sitting nearby and stopped to admire a pink pinafore on a three-year-old. He was loved in the world in which he lived. He was trusted and he was loved. He took a seat beside his daughter-in-law. The Trinity Blue Devils' second-grade team took the field. Among them was a chunky blonde with fierce gray eyes named Katherine Elizabeth Hand. She was only seven years old, but already she had the thing that had made Mr. Hand, Senior, an Olympic gold medalist in single sculls. She saw him in the stands and nodded. She did not wave. She was going into battle on the soccer field. No time for frivolity. Mr. Hand watched her with a kind of wonder as he pretended to be interested in his daughter-in-law's conversation. A tear formed in his eye as Katherine took the ball in her hands and marched out to begin the game. "So you've all recovered from your colds?" he asked.

"Not really. She's still on amoxicillin, but she had a fit so I let her come. Have you heard anything from Daniel? Has Jessie's baby come?"

"Not yet. We called last night but nothing's happening. Daniel's going there tomorrow to await the birth. Well, the game's starting. Let's watch the game." He patted his daughter-in-law on the shoulder. She reached up and covered his hand with her own. The argument she had had with James that morning was still running around her head. Her head was like a racetrack where the contending anxieties moved at top speed competing for first place. You need to lose weight. You're too fat. Get someone to clean that garage. She shouldn't be allowed to go to the game. You look ridiculous in those pants. Why did you let her get sick? How can I love you when you look like that. Fat, fat, fat. Do this. Do that. Don't eat.

I'm sorry. So sorry. I'm trying. I'm trying as hard as I can.

Katherine raced down the field, got into position, received the pass with her left foot, and with her right kicked it into the goal. The small crowd of mothers rose to its feet. "Oh, my goodness, gracious me. Oh, Putty, what a child. What a miraculous child. What a good mother you are to give her to us." Mr. Hand, Senior, clapped and smiled. Clapped and smiled. Putty Hand leaned into his tall kind side.

CHAPTER 2

JESSIE'S baby was due on Sunday. On Thursday Daniel Hand drove out to the Charlotte airport and got on a plane and flew to New Orleans to await the birth. He checked into the Royal Orleans and changed shirts and got into his rented car and drove down Saint Charles Avenue to Webster Street and found the house where his daughter lived and got out and stood looking up at the porch. He had not seen her in five months and he had no idea what to expect. His Jessie, the jewel in his crown. His beautiful child, his skater, bike rider, acrobat, swimmer, dancer, about to deliver a child. Well, he was a man and he could take it. He started up the stairs to the house. She came running out to meet him. "Oh, Daddy," she was screaming. "I'm so glad you're here. I'm soooo bored. It's taking forever. I can't wait to get it out. I'm going crazy waiting to see my baby." She hugged him fiercely to herself, and somehow the fact that she was swollen with a baby was irrelevant. She was Jessie, making anything she did look good.

"You need anything?" he asked. "Is there anything I can get for you?"

*   *   *

At four Daniel's son-in-law came home from Tulane and they sat in the living room and almost had a conversation. "Your momma says you're going to engineering school?"

"Next year. We'll have to move to Baton Rouge or somewhere else. Tulane doesn't have what I need."

"You could come to Charlotte. The university there has a program."

"We'll see. I have to finish this year first and get that baby here." Jessie came into the room carrying a small photograph and pressed it into Daniel's hand. "Here's the latest sonogram," she said. "See, you can tell it's a boy. We're naming him Kingman after King but we aren't going to call him that. King won't let me call him that. He's going to be K.T. For Kingman Theodore. I'd name him after you, but I can't. I'll name the next for you."

"The next one. My God, baby, don't do that to me." Daniel took the photograph Jessie had handed him. It was a folded up fetus floating around a womb. It had a discernible penis floating between its legs. It had hands and feet and eyes and a mouth and a wavy-looking umbilical cord. One hand floated near its face as though the thumb had just left its mouth. Jessie stood above him, beaming with pride. She was wearing a pair of white shorts and a long red garment that looked like a pajama shirt. "Isn't he great looking?" she asked. "Isn't he the cutest thing you've ever seen?"

Four days later they were still sitting around the living room waiting for the baby to come, for the "waters to break" or the "pains to start." Crystal was there nearly every hour or so. King came home between classes at Tulane. Traceleen had moved in and taken over the kitchen. Jessie kept walking up to the corner to the drugstore and bringing back magazines and ice cream. They rented movies. They watched television. They went shopping and added things to the crowded nursery shelves. No one was sleeping and nothing was happening and tempers were getting short.

Six days later, nothing had begun to happen and Daniel kissed his child goodbye and got onto a plane and flew on home. "I got to go and save my business, honey," he kept saying. "I sure do hate to leave you, but somebody's got to mind the store."

"Go on, Daddy," Jessie kept answering. "I don't need you here. All I need is for this baby to go on and come SO I CAN SEE IT."

As soon as Daniel was settled on the plane, Jessie's waters broke and she was rushed to Touro Infirmary and K.T. was born in five hours. By the time Daniel had gotten home from the airport in Charlotte the news had come. "Hey, boss," his farm manager was saying as soon as his car pulled into his garage. "Guess what happened while you was flying home? Guess what your momma called to say?"

CHAPTER 3

LITTLE Sun left the office of the tribe geologist with a heavy heart. He had lived eighty years in peace in Tahlequah, Oklahoma. He had raised seven children and only one of them had died and that was almost twenty years ago. In all this time he had made a good living for his family in different ways and had his check from the Cherokee Nation for renting the land his daddy left him and had always been scrupulously honest and taught his children to be. Now he had this secret to keep. "I do not want it known," he had told the geologist. "How many will know this?"

"Before long many will know it. You might as well tell them."

"Then what? My sons will quit their jobs. Everyone will get confused. I don't like it. How much could I sell my piece of it for?"

"I'm not sure. No one thought anyone would sell it. It would be foolish to sell it, after you kept the oil rights all these years. No, I'd never advise you to do that."

"I think I want to sell it. Find out how much they would give me."

"You need to tell your sons."

"No. When will they find out? All the others."

"It's only you, and three more. They won't be drilling for several months. No one lives in Tahlequah but you. The others live in Oklahoma City."

"Don't tell anyone. I am going now. I have to think of this." Little Sun walked the block to his truck and climbed into the cab and began to drive slowly back down Muskogee to the railroad track. A lot of money all at once. That would be the worst thing that could happen to them. How many families had he seen ruined by it. He would tell Crow as soon as he got home but no one else. This was just in time to ruin the homecoming of the little girl.

The others live in Oklahoma City. They won't drill for several months. Summer would come and go and he would think of the best way to keep the oil from drowning all his children. In the evening when the sun left the sky, he would go out and sleep on the earth and ask the stars to help him know the way to go.

He steered the old truck out onto the four-lane and drove along at thirty miles an hour, taking great satisfaction in how unhappy it made the young girls and bucks who wished to pass him.

LOVE FOR SALE

CHAPTER 4

MAY 24, 1991. A long, strange summer is about to begin. For the world, for political history, and for one particular member of our species. One sweet, funny, driven, brown-eyed, nineteen-year-old Scorpio named Olivia de Havilland Hand. She stands five feet four inches high and weighs one hundred and twenty-six pounds. She likes the color blue, rain, American movies, Madonna, rivers, lakes, oceans, baseball, cutting horses, bicycle racing, and is given to writing the first chapters of novels about five-feet-four-inch nineteen-year-old Scorpios who have lost their mothers and are searching for their fathers.

This Olivia, or Via, as she is trying to be called at the University of North Carolina at Chapel Hill, where she is a freshman, is descended on her mother's side from high-strung, extremely sensitive people whose origins are in the high steppes of eastern China and who came across the land bridge when the Bering Strait joined the continents of Asia and North America. From these people Olivia has inherited a latent depressive streak and a way with animals.

On her father's side she is descended from powerful, wary, tenacious, long-lived, blue-eyed blond people who learned to hunt during the long winters of the last ice age. It was an ancestor of Olivia's who drew her hand on the cave wall at Lascaux. Another died in the company of Bonny Prince Charlie.

These are not good genes for sitting around a dormitory room waiting for an SAE pledge to call you on the phone. Still, that is what Olivia is doing as she studies for her last exam of the semester and writes her final paper. The paper is a three-thousand-word essay on Malthus, which her math teacher has assigned to the class as a political act.

"If we had listened to Malthus to begin with we wouldn't be in the trouble we're in now," Olivia is writing. "If we had done what he told us to do there would be a lot less people on the earth and maybe there would be some way to feed them. Personally, that would be bad for me because neither one of my parents would have been born and neither would I. My dad is the fourth of six children and my mom was third of seven. They sure didn't mean to have me, but they were stoned. My half sister, Jessie, was an accident too. So it looks like the population deal is a lost cause. I know this is not the popular argument, but you said to write what we think. I'm sorry people are starving in the world, but a lot of the countries with the worst problems don't even speak English. They couldn't understand Malthus if you read it to them. They think the only riches they have are their children. If they don't have children, no one will take care of them when they are old. They want male children because they can work harder and don't have more babies to cause more trouble. It's a tangled skein.

"Here's the real problem. You can't stop animals from breeding and you can't stop people from having sexual intercourse and if you think young people are going to remember to use rubbers all the time, you're wrong. The only answer is Abortion On Demand. There should be an abortion clinic in every junior high and anyone who gets pregnant can either have the kid or not. But the right-wing idiots just keep lining up to cause trouble at abortion clinics and try to tell other people how to live their lives. No one can tell another person what to do with their body . . ." Olivia paused, chewed on the pencil eraser for a while, stared at her poster of Madonna. It was the famous poster of Madonna with her hand on her crotch which had been used for the West Coast advertising campaign of *Truth or Dare*.

Olivia sighed and scrunched back down over her yellow legal pad. She always wrote first drafts by hand because her aunt Anna had told her that was the thing to do. "It is impossible to understand this problem completely. Would I give up being born to save the world from overpopulation? No. The answer is no. For all we know CHILDREN DEMAND TO BE BORN. They come into the world demanding everything and crying for whatever they want. They might be hot little fires of possibility, spinning around and passing through the earth like neutrinos. Billions of neutrinos pass through every inch of space every second and we don't even feel them. They might be saying, Make babies, make babies, make babies."

Olivia sat back, read over what she had written, then dove back in. "On a personal level, right now I am nineteen years old and have my life before me. I say to myself, why would anyone give up their life to have a child? How could anyone do that if they had a choice? Still, my half sister, Jessie, did it. She had everything she wanted and instead now she has a baby and a husband who won't come home at night. Why should he? He's only twenty years old. He doesn't want to work all day and sit around all night watching television and taking care of a baby. She got pregnant last summer and we all begged her to have an abortion but she wouldn't do it. So the baby's here and they are very unhappy and about to get a divorce any day now. Then where will that kid be? My mother died having me, so I have a jaundiced view. I took her life to get here. I might have been one of those red-hot particles passing through her brain that night in San Francisco, saying Have me, have me. So she did and I had to live almost sixteen years without a mother or a father. Well, I had a good life. My grandparents raised me in Tahlequah, Oklahoma. I am part of the Cherokee Nation, the Cherokee tribe. I can ride any horse you put in front of me and I can shoot and I can run and I can swim. I had a very rich life there and a rich one in Charlotte when I found my dad. I haven't got anything to complain about. I will say one thing for Tahlequah. I didn't have to lock my car or keep my dogs penned up. In Tahlequah dogs go any-where they like as long as they've had their shots.

"I was free in Tahlequah. I wasn't always worrying about whether I was good enough or what someone thought of me. And at least I got laid when I was there, which is more than I can say for this place."

Olivia marked out the last three lines. Then she put down the pencil and took a drink of her Diet Pepsi. She had a habit of getting carried away when she wrote papers. She forgot she wasn't writing a letter. To whom? she wondered now. My dead mother? Aunt Anna, who swore she'd never desert me? The universe? My own lonely soul? My sister, Jessie? Bobby Gilbert Tree?

She got up from the chair and went over to the bed and lay down upon it and hugged a pillow fiercely to her breast. Bond, bond, bond, the neutrinos were saying to her. The world is terrible and dangerous. Find a place of safety, poor little motherless child.

She closed her eyes and remembered Bobby lying beside her in the big king-size bed in the guest house at Baron Fork. His sweet hands upon her back and butt and legs. His mouth on her mouth, on her cheeks, on her breast. Oh, baby, baby, he always said, come to me. Say you'll never leave me. Say you'll never go away.

He didn't have a mother either, Olivia thought. He didn't have a thing but me and I deserted him. I walked off and didn't give a damn if he lived or died. And now what do I have? A mess of porridge. That's what I traded love for. A mess of goddamn porridge and this goddamn snotty school. She sighed and bit her lip. She reached her arms above her head and stretched and stretched and stretched. Somewhere, bright spring sunlight lay upon the grass and trees and water. She was beside the river with Bobby, folded into his arms. I love you, baby, he was saying. You make me so hard. You always make my dick so goddamn hard.

Olivia stood up. She shook her head, finished off the Diet Pepsi. Then she went outside and found her bike and unlocked it and tied the lock around her waist and started riding. I'll do five miles and then I'll eat some lunch and then I'll study for the exam, she told herself. One more day and I'll get in the car and go on home. As soon as I get to Charlotte, I'm leaving for Tahlequah. I've been gone too long. If Dad won't let me, I'll go anyway. Well, he has to let me. I'll go by New Orleans and see Jessie and the baby.

But what is Tahlequah if Bobby isn't there? She was pedaling more slowly now, moving past a row of Bradford pear trees in new summer foliage. Past the carefully manicured lawns of stately Georgian houses. The smell of late spring flowers perfumed the air. Tulips and tulip trees, azaleas and roses, daisies everywhere.

Well, Bobby's in Montana. He's never coming back. He's up there with that Macalpin guy, that writer who raises cutting horses. That's okay. I'm not looking for Bobby anyway. I called him in March and he never called me back. To hell with him. He's probably screwing everything that walks out there. Besides, what would I do with Bobby? I'm in a different world now. I'm not going to live in a trailer with a rodeo hack. He never even finished high school. He never even got an education.

CHAPTER 5

CHARLOTTE, North Carolina. The morning air is full of the sounds of birds. Robins and jays and orioles. Sparrows and larks and chickadees and woodpeckers and mourning doves. Daniel DeBardeleben Hand loves birds. Once, when he was a child, he had been an avid bird-watcher for several months. He had plastered the wall above his bed with drawings and reproductions of every bird in the Northern Hemisphere.

This morning, however, in the ninth month of his forty-seventh year, Daniel was too distracted to listen to the songs that woke him. He had a tractor business that was about to go into bankruptcy, he was suing his older brother over a piece of real estate they jointly owned, his daughter Jessie was married to a boy he didn't trust and was nursing a two-month-old child he had never seen. His daughter Olivia was supposed to be on her way home from college but she hadn't even returned his phone calls to let him know when she was arriving. Also, as usual, he had a hangover.

He got out of bed and began to wander around the seven-hundred-thousand-dollar house he had built when he was a millionaire. He stopped by a bathroom and found a bottle of aspirin and took three of them. He found a bottle of vitamins and swallowed several of them and began to rearrange a row of perfume bottles Jessie and Olivia had abandoned. The names were like siren calls. As he read them he saw his daughters dancing through the house, talking and laughing, getting dressed, making phone calls, flying in and out of doors with their friends, asking for money, dropping jackets and sweaters and shoes behind them.

Giorgio, he read, Spellbound, Roma, L' Air du Temps, Chanel 22. His hangover seemed to subside as he read. It was replaced by remorse. You're a drunk, it came calling. A failure and a fool. You have lost it all, old pardner, lost the women and the children and the store.

Summer was the lucky one. She died when she was young. I wish I'd died that night Hood Morris and I drove Daddy's Cadillac into the river. We were immortal then. But now it's only this. Goddammit, I know I ought to quit drinking. Goddammit, I know it better than anyone, but what the hell, if a man can't even have a toddy in the evening, what's the point? What reason is there to live? Goddammit, I'm sick and tired of a bunch of goddamn women telling me what to do. I gave my life to women and what good did it do me? Jessie's down there in New Orleans with that goddamn King. Crystal's son. La belle dame sans merci. The lady Crystal. She's gone crazy taking everyone to psychiatrists. She had Manny call me and try to get me to have a meeting with this psychiatrist she's got Jessie going to. "She made me call you," he said. At least he had the decency to feel bad about it. "I'm trying one last time to live with her, Daniel," he goes on. "Quit trying," I told him. "I'll fix you up with plenty of women." "I love her," he says, as if anyone needs to be told how pussy-whipped he is. "Let me get this straight," I said. "Crystal made you call me up and tell me to come down to New Orleans to talk to some psychiatrist about the trouble her son has caused my daughter? That's the deal? I should have killed the little son-of-a-bitch when he knocked her up, but she wouldn't let me. How's the baby doing? Is he okay?"

"He's fine," Manny says. "He's all Crystal thinks about. She goes over there every morning as soon as he gets up. She's so happy, Daniel. It's the first thing that's made her happy since King stole those bikes. God, that seems like years ago. You ought to come down here and see the baby. You don't have to go to the psychiatrist. That's just one of Crystal's ideas. How's Olivia, by the way? When does she get home?"

"She's coming tonight. Goddamn, Manny, it's lonely around here with the girls gone. I just knock around the house."

"You ought to get married, Daniel. What about Lydia? I thought the two of you had something going. What's happening with that?"

"She got on my ass about drinking. She got mad and went back to California. 'Let me get you an airline ticket,' I told her. 'I'll take you to the plane.' "

"How'd Olivia do in school this year?"

"She did great. I'm taking her to Switzerland next week. Maybe we'll come by and see all of you before we leave. I want to see the boy."

"You don't want to talk to this doctor then?"

"Nope. I don't."

"She's a nice woman."

"I'm sure she is, Manny. I'm certain that she is."

Daniel turned his head to the side, inspected his profile, his fine thin hair. What's left of my hair, he decided. Well, to hell with that. I can't stop thinking about that phone call. Crystal's son fucks over my daughter and ruins her life and I'm supposed to come and talk to the goddamn doctor. Well, to hell with that New Orleans crowd. I can't do anything about it because Jessie loves the little son-of-a-bitch. I'm going to find Spook and get him to clean off the tennis court before Olivia gets home. To hell with Jessie if she can't even find the time to bring the boy to see his grandfather. I've still got Olivia. She ought to be home by eight or nine. Maybe she didn't get my messages. Crazy little old girl. She's got her mother's craziness. She's got that thing Summer had, that cold fire in her belly. Anna had it too. Well, it was Anna who found Olivia and brought her to me. I might never have even known that she existed. After Summer left me, after she sneaked out of Momma's house in the middle of the night and disappeared, she goes home and has a baby and dies like something that happened a hundred years ago and none of those people out there even write me a note. They said she told them not to. She was proud. You'd have thought she was some kind of a princess the way she acted. That's what those three have in common. Anna, Summer, Olivia. Via, I guess we're supposed to call her now. Well, Summer's dead and so is Anna. We've all got to stop thinking about her. She had cancer and she killed herself and she probably had a right to. She didn't have any kids, that's what Helen keeps saying, when she wants to justify it. Well, Helen's gone off and deserted hers so she's got justifying to do. To hell with it. To hell with all of them.

It's damn hard to believe Anna's dead. Four years and I still can't believe it. That she won't be calling me up at seven in the morning to give me some advice I didn't know I needed. Then she walks into the ocean in November. The doctor she was fucking believes she's dead. I got drunk with him in New York last fall. He cried like a baby in the goddamn restaurant. I was crying too. Then we ended up in some Irish bar. God, that was some afternoon.

So before she dies Anna goes out and finds Olivia and brings her to me. She looks enough like Anna to be her child, looks more like Anna than she does like Summer or like me.

How many times have I gone over this? Summer leaves without telling me she's pregnant. I knock up Sheila with Jessie. Dad gets me an annulment. Jessie is born and it's a miracle. The minute I saw that little face I loved her and I guess I always will. I never could have believed she'd go off to New Orleans and leave me and not even come home to visit. Goddamn a lot of ungrateful children. What time is it anyway? Olivia ought to be leaving Chapel Hill about now. Looks like she would have called and told me when she was getting here. Goddamn everyone you love going off to college or getting married or dying on you. To hell with it. I'm going to find Spook and see if he still knows how to use a broom.

Daniel strode down the hall and into the dining room. He stopped by the liquor cabinet and thought about pouring himself a toddy, then decided against it. Above the cabinet was a photograph of his grandfather dressed up for a fox hunt. In his grandfather's hand was a silver mint julep cup. That was the life, he decided, furrowing his brow and staring up into the eyes of his granddaddy. Get up in the morning, feed the dogs, saddle a horse, ride the fields, come in at noon and eat lunch with the ladies. They were ladies, too, not a bunch of crazy women like a man has to contend with now. Goddamn, it's because we're so spread out. Nobody lives with anybody anymore. Goddammit, I grew up in a house with ten people living in it. Every morning when I woke up there were people all up and down the halls that were kin to me. Worked my ass off for thirty years and gave lots of loving to hundreds of women and what has it got me? Sleeping alone in this big old house without a goddamn soul in it when I wake up. If Spook hadn't agreed to come in from the country and live with me, I wouldn't have a soul within a mile. I got to get some more dogs, that's the ticket. Goddamn girls made me leave the dogs out in the country. That's one thing wrong. Every day of my life I woke up in a house with at least ten people sleeping in it, two or three more in the guest house, and a yard full of dogs, and look at me now. One black man in the guest house, and he wishes he was on the farm, and two little Springer spaniels that have seen better days.

Daniel walked across the room and looked in the mirror over the china press. He looked somewhat better than he had looked in the bathroom. The aspirins were taking effect, his color was coming back. Still, what he saw was worse than what anyone else would have seen. An observer would have seen a tall graceful man with high cheekbones and delicate features and beautiful deep blue eyes. A man who looked like he would never do an unkind or brutal or deeply stupid thing. A gentleman wearing khaki slacks and Italian loafers and an alpaca sweater the color of his eyes.

But what Daniel saw was loss. His balding head, sadness and loneliness and confusion. Failure, he said to his reflection. It's crashing in, it's falling down. I'll be in the poor house any day now.

He thought it was his fault. When he was eighteen years old, his father and older brother James had given him four million dollars to divide up their fortune for income tax purposes. They had put the money in his name and expected him to do what they told him to do with it. But they had not given him the discipline or self-esteem he needed to get a law degree and join them in the firm. He was so different from them they could not understand him. Neither of them could imagine being confused. They were both the eldest sons of powerful women and they got up in the morning and bossed people around and slept eight hours every night. If they were ever drunk or bad it was calculated and controlled. So when Daniel began to "carouse" and "lay out all night" and "be bad," they laughed at him and called him a chip off the old block.

So Daniel got sillier and sillier and more and more addicted to having toddies. And after a while James Hand, Senior, and James Hand, Junior, grew tired of him and turned their attention to their own affairs. He'll grow up, they told each other. He's still wet behind the ears.

Then only the women were interested in him. His mother and his sister Anna and his sister Helen, and for years he could charm and snow them so continually that he almost never had to hear a cross word. On the surface he was their gorgeous son and brother, such a catch, the one all the girls were after. Underneath he seethed and fretted. He wanted to do something, be something, overpower, achieve, but he did not know how to go about it and it grew later and later and later.

One day he grew so frustrated by trying to figure out how to be successful that he went down to the bank and turned all his assets into cash. He took the money into a vault room of the bank and laid it out upon a table and looked at it, trying to believe this unearned bounty belonged to him.

Now, in late May of 1991, he was down to about seven hundred thousand dollars in total assets and he thought of that as poverty.

Also, he was down to three girlfriends, a model in Nashville who was too smart to marry him until he quit drinking, a painter in California who loved him too much to marry him until he quit drinking, and a department store buyer named Margaret who would have married him but she was too fat to turn him on unless he was really drunk.

Fine life, he decided. He poured some brandy into a julep cup and drank it. Fine how-do-you-do. He shook his head, made an obeisance in the direction of the photograph of his grandfather and strode on through the kitchen. He went down the back stairs and out to the guest house where his fifty-seven-year-old black farm manager was living that spring to keep him company. The black man's name was Lucas Dehorney. He was three-quarters Nigerian, one-eighth Iroquois, and one-eighth Scots. He had had as much trouble in his life with women as Daniel had had, but not as much with whiskey. They shared a love of hard physical work, a love of horses, a love of basketball, and an ability to curse that would have shamed Caliban. Lucas's nickname was Spook. He had been Daniel's friend as long as Daniel could remember. Spook had been Daniel's nurse during summers on the farm. They had loved each other then and they loved each other now, although a word of love had never passed between them.

Daniel knocked on the door of the guest house, then pushed it open and went on in and found Spook in the living room, sitting on a straight chair, reading an autobiography of Louis L'Amour one of his girlfriends had given him.

"Listen here to this," Spook said. " 'The dogs bark, but the caravan passes on.' That's this oriental proverb he starts out the book with. What you think that means, Daniel? What you think he's getting at?"

"It means, don't pay any attention to dogs barking. You got to get that tennis court cleaned off, Spook. And get somebody over here this afternoon to cut the yard. Goddamn place looks like it's deserted. No one's hit a lick in weeks. Where's that yard service you got me?"

"It's been raining so much they couldn't get here. This L'Amour guy's got a lot of stuff like that in this book. It's called his memoirs but it's mostly a lot of stories old folks told him that he's written down. How much you think he gets paid for putting something like this together?"

"Shit, how would I know? Anna used to get a hundred thousand for writing one, sometimes less, sometimes more. It depended on how much they sold of the one before. She was always bitching about it."

"I might write me a book, Daniel. I used to be good at writing. My teachers were always praising me for it. I got to find something to do. I'm giving up chasing pussy. That damn Charlene's been calling me all morning. After the way she went off last week."

"You been out to the farm in the last few days? We got to get Vaughn to plant that fescue. It's dry enough to put in a second crop."

"Fescue's in. I told you that a week ago. I don't know where your mind's been, Daniel. You're getting mighty forgetful. You're too young to be so forgetful. And another thing, I got to move back to the farm for the summer. I can't take staying in town all the time. It's too noisy. I can't get any sleep. Airplanes flying over. Traffic going up and down the roads. I heard a truck starting up at five this morning. I haven't been to sleep since."

"You couldn't hear trucks back here. It's a mile from the nearest highway."

"I heard them. I haven't been to sleep since."

"Go on back to the country then, if you want to. No one's stopping you. But I want that court cleaned off today. Olivia's on her way home. She might want to play tomorrow."

"That goddamn Charlene left in the middle of the night last time she was here. Got up, put on her clothes and left. Now she's calling me."

"Take the cover off the pool and turn the pool cleaner on while you're out there. I want things spruced up before she gets home. She's all I got now."

"I'll get it done. Soon as I finish a few more pages of this book." Daniel stood by the door. He had done everything he could think of to make Spook stay. He had bought him a big new Sony and a VCR and gone out and rented a dirty movie and offered to watch it with him. They had poured a drink and sat down to watch. The movie was called *The Houseparty.* As soon as one of the women took off her clothes, Spook got up and turned off the TV. "Turn that damn thing off, Daniel," he said. "I can't look at something like that. If that's what's going on in the world they can leave Lucas Dehorney out."

"I guess I won't ever see Jessie again," Daniel said now, making one last play for sympathy. "It does look like she'd bring the boy to see his granddaddy, doesn't it?"

"They live their own lives now," Spook said. "They don't give a damn about the past."

CHAPTER 6

MAY 27, 1991. Ten o'clock in the morning, Mountain Time. Starcarbon Ranch, Montana. Sunlight is pouring in the windows of the Macalpins' kitchen, a large, square, high-ceilinged room in a hundred-year-old ranch house situated in the middle of six thousand acres of wilderness and pastureland. A hundred yards from the house and down a steep embankment Sliver Creek winds down to meet the Chene River and the western fork of the Missouri.

Biscuits are in the oven. Bacon is frying in a pan. A Boston cream pie with two slices gone is sitting in the middle of a table set with yellow placemats. Beside the pie is a vase of blue wildflowers. The owner of the ranch has been gone for three days trying to renegotiate his loans with the bankers in Billings. His wife, Sherrill, and his trainer, a young man named Bobby Tree, are stirring around the kitchen waiting for the coffee to perk and the bacon to fry.

The sun grows even brighter, comes out from behind the last cloud, and sunlight pours down through the long windows above the sink. Like a laser it turns the air to fire, turns the porcelain to marble, the table into an altar. A blue-and-white teapot in the center seems to dance in the light. "I wait all winter for this weather," Sherrill says. She is smiling her Morning Smile, for which Tom Macalpin has named a sailboat, a Palomino mare, and a book of poetry which won the Lamont in 1984. Her fabled breasts (*Ten Degrees Centigrade,* pages 13 and 74; *Golden Tree,* pages 46, 49, 53; *Haven,* page 92) shake beneath her pale blue sweater as the smile turns into a giggle. "If Tom doesn't get home soon, I'm going crazy. This sunshine makes me horny." She lifts the bacon from the skillet with a fork and lays it on a paper towel. She takes eggs from a carton, breaks them, and drops them into the bacon fat. She is wearing the blue sweater, a pair of skintight blue jeans faded the color of the sky, and a wide leather belt with a buckle she won at the Grand National when she was eighteen. Except for Olivia Hand when she is angry, Bobby thinks she is the sexiest woman he has ever seen in his life. Perhaps the sexiest woman who has ever lived. (Helen, Tom called her in his fiction. Helen Aimee Detroy.) She is also the closest thing to a mother Bobby has ever had. All during the long fall and winter of 1990 and 1991 she has mothered him and bossed him around and made him study, educated him and ennobled him and made him secure. Tom Macalpin had taught him more about cutting horses than he had ever dreamed a man could know and Sherrill was teaching him to believe in himself. Slowly, slowly, he had learned to trust, and then to love them. He had gotten to where he told them anything he was thinking the minute he thought it up.

"Don't talk about being horny. I get so jealous thinking about Olivia down there fucking some boy in Carolina. I've gotten to where it's all I think about, Sherrill. It's ruining my life thinking about it. She's the horniest girl I ever saw in my life. I know she's getting laid. She'd get laid if they sent her to the Gulag Archipelago where they sent that guy Tom writes to. I know she's fucking somebody." He got up, took two mugs out of a cabinet, and stood by the coffeepot while it perked out the last drams of coffee. "I ought to get you a better coffeepot. They got them now that you can get the coffee out before it finishes."

"We don't need a coffeepot. We need you on this ranch."

"I know you do. And I'm sorry I have to leave." He looked down at his feet. Twisted his napkin, turned it into a noose. "After all you guys did for me."

"We didn't do much. You did it."

"You got me set up to go to college. And I won't forget that, no matter where I end up. But I have to go, Sherrill. She's on her way to Tahlequah. I called her aunt Mary Lily and it turns out she's coming home. I have to be there when she gets there. I'd never forgive myself if I didn't try. I want to wait until Tom gets back, but I got to leave soon. It's a long drive."

"You need some new tires on that truck. Get those ones out of the shed that were on that Toyota Callene totaled."

"You don't care?"

"Go on and take them. I'd be glad to see them used for something." Sherrill filled two plates with eggs and bacon and handed one to Bobby. They sat down at the table. They held hands. "Bless this food to our use and us to Thy service," Sherrill said. "Are you going to call her and tell her that you're coming?"

"No. It's got to be a surprise. I'm going even if she told me not to, so I don't see any reason to call her."

"What are you going to do when you see her?"

"Ask her to marry me. Tell her I'll do anything she wants. Tom said he could get me in a college in Carolina. So I'll go there if she wants to stay. Whatever it takes, that's what I'll do. I know if I can see her, I can make her love me again. Well, I have to try."

"Have you got a ring?"

"A what?"

"An engagement ring. If you're going to ask her to marry you you need a ring. How much money do you have saved?"

"Nine thousand seven hundred and forty. Plus the money for the show in Fort Worth if Rose Sally wins. Tom said he'd give me a cut of that. I know she'll make the top ten. She might win. I'm coming down and ride her no matter where I am."

"You can afford a ring. Let's go into town this afternoon and see what Pat Morrell's got in his store. You want me to go with you? He won't rip you off."

"God, I don't know."

"You've got to have a ring. Ride to win, Bobby. If you're going to Oklahoma to get your girl, take some oats."

"Okay. When you want to go?"

"As soon as we finish breakfast. Go turn the two-year-olds out into the pasture and I'll do the dishes, then I'll meet you at the truck. This is going to be fun." She took a bite of bacon, washed it down with black coffee, laughed again. Her breasts rose and fell beneath her blue sweater, sunlight poured through the windows, hope filled the room like snow, possibility, danger, the terror and possibility of love. "Eat, Bobby, I'm not going with you unless you eat every bite on that plate. I'm not going ring shopping with a hungry man. How long have you been in love with this girl?"

"Since I was sixteen and she was fourteen. I saw her walking up the sidewalk to the high school and that was it. She walks like she owns the earth. She walked like that before she even found out her daddy was rich."

An hour later Sherrill and Bobby were sitting in the back room of Morrell's Jewels and Furs, a two-room emporium on the main street of Star City. Spread out on a cloth was a small collection of possible rings. Most of them were antiques, left for hock and never picked up again. There was one diamond solitaire in an old-fashioned Tiffany setting. Bobby was holding it in his hand. "That's the one," Sherrill said. "That's the one she won't be able to resist."

"You're sure? You think she'll like it?"

"Give it here." Bobby held out the ring and Sherrill slipped it on her finger and held her hand up to the light. "She might turn you down," Sherrill said. "But it won't be because she didn't want this ring."

"We can give you a discount," Pat Morrell said. "Since it's for the sake of love. I could knock two hundred off. Hell, if she don't take it, you can bring it back."

"He's got to buy it on time, anyway," Sherrill said. "He's going to college in the fall. He has to save his money."

"I'll take it," Bobby said. "I'll pay you five hundred now and the rest this summer as soon as I get a job."

They all stood up. The ring was boxed in a velvet box and the box was slipped into a paper sack. Bobby counted five one-hundred-dollar bills out onto a counter and was given a receipt and a bill. They all shook hands. Then Bobby and Sherrill walked out into the brilliant noon sun. A perfect day. Sixty-five degrees. Mountains on three horizons. "She might not even remember me," he said.

"She remembers you." Sherrill took his arm, pulled him close to her. "No woman would forget a man like you."

"I hate leaving you guys shorthanded, but the Whitehead twins are home from school. They were over yesterday looking for Tom. They're good. They can do anything I can do."

"We'll be okay. We'll be here if you want to come back. We're not going anywhere. We're here to stay." She pulled his arm closer into her body. He felt her breasts beneath his elbow. He looked down into the blue eyes that had welcomed and disarmed and protected him. "Goddamn, Sherrill," Bobby said. "You could make a man believe in fairies."

When they got back to the ranch, Tom Macalpin was back from Billings and helped Bobby change the tires on the truck. "Go on if you're going then," was all he said. "I'm going to miss you like my right arm. And you be ready to meet me in Fort Worth in December. Don't forget how to ride."

"I'll be there. Wherever I am, I'll be there for that show."

"Sherrill's going to cry. You might as well get ready for that. She's already on the verge."

"I have to go. I'd never forgive myself if I didn't. This is the best deal I ever had in my life and I'm leaving it. I don't want to leave. I have to."

"Remember us. Remember who you are."

"I'll try to. I'm not sure I know."

"You know, when you can remember."

The next morning Bobby packed his gear into his pickup truck and started driving, heading toward Wyoming. That morning, when he had gone out to tell the horses goodbye, frost had been on their withers. The world's made out of water, he remembered. Shit, what do I have to lose? My life's not worth living without her. I got to take a shot at it. He patted the ring box in the pocket of his jacket. He hunkered down over the steering wheel and really began to drive. He was leaving paradise and he knew it, but up ahead were the long months of summer, horse shows and rodeos and long starry nights in the Cherokee Nation.

CHAPTER 7

BOBBY drove steadily down Highway 87 toward Billings. He was leaving behind the unbelievable vistas of the Chene River Plains and he was not immune to what he was leaving. Several times he stopped the truck to look a long time to the north and west. The vast plains, the clear, clean air, in the distance, snow-capped mountains, their cones rising from the vast dark purple of the plains. Nothing could be that pretty, Bobby thought, and dreamed he lived a long time ago and was Crow or Pocatello, Blackfoot or Chinook. He dreamed he hunted clad in furs, half-frozen and dreaming of meat. He dreamed he wore bracelets of Pacific Ocean shells, vests of animal bones, carried walrus oil for lamps. In his dream Olivia waited in a hut made of skins. Wearing deerskin she waited, on fur they would make love. Here is this ring I got you in Montana, Bobby said. You don't have to wear it unless you want to.

The sun slipped past its zenith as Bobby drove and dreamed. The afternoon wore on. Clouds formed on the horizon, purple and gray and green and gold, pink and red and palest lavender and azure, tangerine and dark deep blues. I'm leaving paradise, Bobby knew, but it will always be here. A man could always return to this. Tom and Sherrill would take me back. Cast to the future, that's what Tom said when I was leaving. Find your destiny. Well, I will. I might.

Bobby furrowed his twenty-two-year-old brow and thought about the scraggly pine trees and soft hills of eastern Oklahoma. He saw his dad standing beside the trailer lighting a cigarette, laughing at a joke, telling someone the scores of football games. He remembered a game with Broken Arrow. He had scored the winning touchdown and the crowd was on its feet. His dad stood by the coach applauding loudly, and afterward, when the crowd poured out onto the field, Olivia had let him kiss her in his muddy uniform. She had stood beside the goal-post in her white cheerleading skirt and he had pulled her into his arms and danced her around the end zone. That was before I even asked her out, he remembered. When I was just flirting with her. I got mud all over her skirt right at the place of her pussy and she didn't even care. She brushed if off while I was looking. I knew you liked me, she told me later. Everyone had already told me that.

So I'm going down there and ask her to marry me. That's that. I don't care who she's fucking in Carolina, it won't be what we had. There won't ever be anything as good as that. I guess she's found that out by now. She called me in March and she sounded like she was sick of Carolina. I should have called her back the next day, but I had to go to Idaho with Tom. Then I called up and that goddamn answering machine said she was in Florida. So I got pissed off and pissed that chance away. Well, I'm making up for it now. Everyone makes mistakes. Tom said he'd like to have a nickel for every mistake he made with Sherrill before they finally got together.

She's on her way to Tahlequah. That must mean something. If everything was roses in Carolina, she wouldn't be coming home for the summer. Olivia takes care of number one. Well, that's what I like about her. And if I wasn't supposed to go and meet her, why did I just happen to call her aunt Mary Lily the day she started driving? Tell me that. I don't believe in all that extrasensory stuff Sherrill's into, but I believe in luck. It's time I had some luck with love. It's time I had some luck with her. I could have left a message, but I sure wasn't leaving love notes on a goddamn answering machine while she was off in Florida fucking some fraternity boy.

He pulled the box out of the glove compartment and opened it and looked at the ring. It seemed too holy to touch. He closed the box and sat it beside him on the seat. I need a dog, Bobby decided. If I had a dog to ride shotgun in this truck, I wouldn't be so lonely. He turned on the radio. "Oh, blame it on midnight," a Colorado station was playing. "Shame, shame on the moon." You can't escape it, Bobby decided. Pussy is all anybody thinks about unless they're waiting to see a game or be in one. Well, you think about it then, too. I've thought about her in the middle of a rodeo. I've thought about her teaching a stallion to back, on top of mountains, going down the Snake. Don't rail at nature, Tom says. Well, okay, I'm not railing. I'm just keeping score.

CHAPTER 8

BOBBY spent the night in Billings, got up at dawn, and drove to Sheridan, Wyoming, then down to Casper, where the wildflowers were blooming, then to Cheyenne, then Fort Collins in Colorado. In Fort Collins he crashed for sixteen hours in a Holiday Inn that smelled like bug poison. It was the first time in twenty months he had smelled civilization. As soon as he woke up, he called Tom and Sherrill to tell them about it.

"The whole place smells like poison," he said. "I forgot how to breathe this stuff. I shouldn't have left. Have you hired the twins yet? I'm coming back."

"I wish to hell you would," Tom said. "Blanche Fleur foaled this morning. A little stallion with all her markings. You ought to see this colt. This might be the one to take us to the National."

"Is that the one we got off Sword Breaker?"

"Yeah, but he looks just like his mother. Big neck and short legs. It's the finest-looking foal I've seen in a year."

"Are you losing your nerve?" Sherrill put in from the other phone. "Don't lose your nerve, Bobby. Go on down there and do the deed. You can come back here anytime."

"I'm going."

"I thought about it all night last night," Tom said. "Fuck a lot of young women driving men crazy. Call her up from where you are. If she says yes, okay, if not . . ."

"Tom, he doesn't know where to call her. She's driving, too. She's on the road. He's going to surprise her."

"Bobby, you call the minute you talk to her and tell us what's going on. I want to know the minute you get an answer. I don't want some friend of mine waiting for some little half-baked girl to seal his fate."

"Tom."

"Shut up, Sherrill. If I'd been here you wouldn't have sent my right-hand man off to get his heart broken in Oklahoma. This goddamn colt's got two front socks, golden white, just like Blanche Fleur. Did you ever see the stud?"

"Sure I did. I was there when we bred her. Don't you remember that?"

"He forgets everything now," Sherrill said. "And his chances of getting any breakfast today are getting slimmer."

"Call us collect, son," Tom said. "Keep us posted."

"I got the good drive ahead of me now. I drove Olivia across Kansas once, in the middle of the night. I took her camping in Vail, Colorado, on her fifteenth birthday. She couldn't forget a thing like that, could she?"

"I bet not."

"None of those goddamn pussies she's going out with in Carolina ever took her up to eleven thousand feet, did they?"

"Bobby?"

"Yes."

"Calm down. It's going to be all right."

"Send me a picture of that colt as soon as you get one."

"We'll name him for you," Tom said. "Roberto the Ringbearer. Bobby of the Ring, once more into the Fool's Paradise. Shakespeare coined that phrase, by the way. In *Romeo and Juliet*, the nurse warns Romeo not to lead her little charge into one."

"Tom."

"What, Sherrill?"

"Don't go writing about this. Tell him not to write about it, Bobby, or he might. You have to tell him every single thing you don't want ending up in a book. He thinks every bit of life belongs to him. Once he wrote about my mother's broken ankle. She didn't speak to him for months. He put it on a homeless bag lady in San Francisco."

"Well, I guess I better hang up now. I got to get on my way."

"Travel safely, call again. Wear your seat belt."

"You can write about anything I do," Bobby said. "As long as you don't use my name."

As soon as Bobby had paid the hotel bill and packed up and started driving, the good mood talking to Sherrill and Tom had put him in began to fade. The old defense mechanisms clicked back into gear. Desire and fear, the poles that rule us. She wasn't even that good a cheerleader, he told himself. She mostly just sat around on her ass while the rest of them did the acrobatics. She's too chubby to really look good in the outfit. Susanne Hogan and Phyllis Buchanan looked a lot better. Well, she looks good on a horse. She was made for blue jeans and jodhpurs. Those beige jodhpurs her aunt sent her that time from New York and that big blue-and-gold scarf around her neck. It's no use trying to knock her. She's got my number. She's the one I love. Well, I can be anything she wants me to be if she'll give me a chance. Tom said he could get me in a college in Carolina. I want to fuck her so goddamn much. I want to hold her in my arms.

Bobby leaned down over the steering wheel. He pushed the gas pedal to the floor.

CHAPTER 9

CHARLOTTE, North Carolina, May 27, 1991. Eleven o'clock in the morning. Clouds to the west. A fine, still day. Olivia had rolled in about twelve o'clock the night before. She had kissed her father, told him she was going to Tahlequah for the summer, then climbed the stairs and gone to bed. Since then she had been sleeping. Deep down underneath the beautiful blue sheets of her walnut bed she had been sleeping and sleeping and sleeping. As she slept, she dreamed. In her dream she was wearing a Cherokee wedding dress, a long fringed and beaded dress of the finest buckskin. She stood on a precipice overlooking fields and rivers and pastures. Lined up beside her were the members of her father's family They were talking and joking, gossiping and being charming. They cannot see my dress, Olivia said in her dream. They have forgotten I am Cherokee.

But, of course, it was herself who had forgotten.

Daniel had been up since dawn, planning his campaign to convince her to go to Switzerland. Since ten he had been out in the guest house talking to Spook while he waited for her to get up.

"Can't do nothing with them after they get grown," Spook was saying. "If you can't beat them, join them, that's my motto. Go with her and see Oklahoma. Or let her run. She's a good kid. I didn't use to like her but now I do. She ain't half as wild as Jessie, but you can't see that. You favor Jessie over her so bad it's a shame. Now Jessie's run off and left you and you're going to lose this one too if you ain't careful. You ought to get you a new wife, boss. Get you a young one and start all over."

"I don't want to start over. When did you start liking Olivia so much? You said you never liked her."

"I been liking her. I told you she was lying when she was lying to you, but now she ain't lying anymore. Besides, I've come to see why she was lying. She had to get in with you some way and that was all she knew to do. That's just nature. She was just trying to get by, like we all do. Now I think she's turning out okay. She was the only one that didn't act like a fool last summer when Jessie got knocked up. She kept on saying the truth even after you quit saying it. She said, Get down to the abortion clinic and get rid of it. Instead you caved in and let Jessie go through with it. Now she's stuck, ain't she? So now Olivia wants to go home and see her Indian kinfolks. Well, let her. You don't know what she's up to. Maybe she's got a hankering for some boy back there. That's all they think about at that age, Daniel. It was the same for me and the same for you, only you look like you have forgotten."

"I haven't forgotten. I still think about it."

"Well, you don't do much about it, now do you? Where's Margaret? You hadn't had her over to spend the night in a couple of weeks."

"Olivia's not going to Oklahoma to see a boy. She's worried about her grandfather. He's old and she's afraid he'll die. How come you think you know so much about what went on up in Maine last summer when Jessie got pregnant? You weren't even there."

"I got filled in."

"Olivia doesn't care anything about boys. She's interested in her education. She's hardly gone out with the same boy twice since she came to stay with me. Where'd you get the idea of her wanting to go to Oklahoma to see some boy? Goddammit, Spook, you say the goddamnedest things. Did she say anything to you?"

"I hadn't even seen her. No, it's just a hunch. Well, you go on, Daniel. Believe what you want to believe." Spook went back to frying potatoes, which was what he had been doing when Daniel came out and disturbed his peace. He dug the spatula down under the potatoes and turned them slowly to the uncooked side. He sprinkled them liberally with salt. Daniel leaned on the kitchen counter, taking sips from his coffee. "She's not going to Oklahoma to see a boy, Lucas. What a goddamn thing to say. She's going to see her granddaddy because he's old."

"Then let her rip. You can't afford to be flying a bunch of folks to Switzerland anyway. You need to stay home and help me fix them fences at the farm. Either you got to mend the fences or you got to sell the stock. Your daddy was out at the place the other day. He said he can't believe how you let it run down."

"If I hadn't bought it, it wouldn't even be there. It'd be turned into subdivisions. Dad was griping about it?"

"No, he just said he was glad your granddaddy wasn't alive to see how rundown it was."

"I saved the goddamn place. James wouldn't buy it and Niall's broke and Anna wasn't even in the United States. I paid the taxes and I saved it. Goddamn, he was out there griping about it?"

"Everybody knows you saved it, Daniel. Well, I see your little ole gal is up. She's got her windows open, letting out all the air conditioning in the place." Spook pointed through his kitchen window to the girls' balcony. The windows were open, the lace curtains blowing in the air.

"She hates air conditioning. What's wrong with that? She's a country girl. Well, I'll see you later, Spook. Be sure and turn the pool cleaner on. The pool's still a mess." Daniel left the guest house and walked back across the flagstone patio to the curved stone stairs leading to the kitchen of the main house. He was going to be very unhappy if the bank really made him sell it. He shrugged off the thought, shook his head from side to side and went inside to deal with his daughter.

"Is it because of Margaret going?" he asked. He walked over to his child and kissed her gingerly on the forehead. A hand on an elbow, a kiss on the forehead, a quick hug. These were the only signs of affection he allowed himself where his daughters were concerned. They seemed so holy to him, so mysterious and inviolate. He shook his head, remembering the last time he had seen Jessie. Nine months pregnant and swollen and ecstatic. He had been furious with her ever since, for putting herself in danger, for scaring him to death, for swelling up with a child, and, lately, for not getting on a plane and bringing the boy to see him.

"Is the reason you won't go to Switzerland because Margaret's going? I only asked her so you'd have a woman along. I can tell her not to go. We can go alone."

"No, it's because I need to go home. I'm lonesome for Tahlequah, Dad. I want to see my folks. Besides, there's something there I want to do."

"You need to see Europe before you get any older. Big things are happening there this year. It's the summer to be there."

"I want to go by New Orleans and see Jessie and the baby. We can go to Switzerland next year. Maybe by then Jessie can go with us." Olivia surveyed her dad. His tall frame was bent across the counter. He was a graceful man, with the graceful moves of an old track man and basketball player. In the presence of women he would sometimes lose this grace, become awkward and bent and vulnerable. It was very disarming, and Olivia was disarmed now. "I love you, Daddy," she said. "I mean that. And I really appreciate everything you do for me. I forget to tell you that, don't I?" She had been spooning water over a poached egg. She laid down the spoon and put her arms around her father's waist. Daniel straightened up, allowed his hands to rest on her shoulders. The touch of his children dazzled and terrified and tenderized him past all reason. The marvel, the physical reality of them.

"You got any money left?" he asked. He took his hands from her shoulders and moved away. He didn't push her away, he just slightly distanced himself from her.

"I've got about two hundred left in the bank."

"You came home with money? Isn't that against the law at college?"

"You give me too much. I don't know what to do with all that money."

"It's what Helen said to give you. You don't need to stay all summer down there, do you? Why do you need to go for the whole summer? Hell, we could go to Switzerland in July. I'll call the travel agent."

"Dad."

"Yes."

"I want to go to summer school there. I want to study Navajo. To learn how to write it."

"What for?"

"Because they're coding scientific information into computers in Navajo. My biology teacher told me about it. The government is giving scientific grants based on the security of the computer systems. So a lot of universities are starting coding things in Navajo. If I can learn it, I'll be able to get a really good job anywhere I want. They teach it at Northeastern, this little college in Tahlequah, well, it's a branch of the university, it's not that little. Besides, there's an old Navajo there who's a friend of my aunt's. He married a Cherokee girl in the Second World War and came home with her. He'll talk it with me in the afternoons. I really want to do this, Dad. I've got it all figured out. I told Aunt Lily to get it fixed up for me."

"You got everything you need for breakfast? You want me to call Jade? She's around here somewhere. She could fix that for you."

"I've got everything I want. Sit down with me. Talk to me while I eat. You want some toast?"

"No. Well, I got to think about all this. I wish you'd told me sooner." He sat back, furrowed his brow, looked off into a corner of the room. "We got to go by and see your grandparents this afternoon. And Uncle Niall. He said to call the minute you came in."

"I want to see them, Dad. I love my family here. But I need to go home now. I'm all they have in Oklahoma. All of you have each other here."

"Well, I might go with you then. I might drive you there. At least I'll drive you to New Orleans. I got to go and see that boy. Since it looks like Jessie isn't going to bring him here. Here, let me have that plate. Put some salt and pepper on those eggs. That's all you're going to eat? Goddamn, no wonder all you girls stay so scrawny. You need some milk, honey. Let me get you some milk. I got some fresh milk yesterday at the store." Daniel busied around, getting out milk and a glass, putting honey and jelly on the table. The phone began to ring. It was Jessie calling from New Orleans. It was Daniel's parents wanting them to come right over. It was Daniel's brother Niall, saying he was on his way. It was Helen calling from Boston to ask about her children. It was the Hand family of Charlotte, North Carolina, getting started on the day. "Devotion is knowing how rich we are," it said on a Buddhist calendar Margaret had given Daniel for his kitchen. He leaned his elbow against the calendar as he listened to his daughter talking to his mother on the phone. His elbow dug into the solar plexus of the Buddha of Infinite Compassion as he watched Olivia and worried about how he was going to make his June house payment and how he was going to tell Margaret they weren't going to Switzerland after all.

Outside the windows of the kitchen the Bradford pear trees were in full leaf. The clouds had passed by the city. A brilliant June sun was almost directly overhead. Summer was beginning in the Northern Hemisphere.

CHAPTER 10

BY the time the sun set, Daniel had decided to give Olivia his Mercedes for the summer and drive with her as far as New Orleans. "Hell," he said. "Maybe I'll drive you to Tahlequah. I can fly home from Tulsa, can't I?"

"I can do it by myself. You don't need to take me."

"But why should you?" Daniel laughed his wildest, most generous laugh. He was a generous man. Nothing made him happier than giving something big away, a car or a house or a horse. The day had turned out fine all around. Margaret had been placated by the promise of a weekend at Sea Island and Spook had disappeared out to the farm to actually get some work done and the bank had called and given in on the extension of his loan for another six months.

"You're giving her your car?" Niall asked, when he heard the news. Niall was Daniel's closest brother, a lapsed Jesuit who was the family conscience. Niall had come over with two of Helen's children to have dinner with Daniel and Olivia. "You gave her the Mercedes?"

"I want her in a heavy car. Those roads up there are treacherous. You ought to see those roads. It's like the dark ages. That state's so poor they barely put up road signs."

"What are you going to drive?" Niall reached across the table and touched his brother's arm. Darling lost Daniel, who had lost so much in so many ways. Lost and given away and wasted. Spoiled-rotten Daniel, who had drowned his abilities in Chivas Regal since he was eighteen years old. Chivas or home brew or anything he could get his hands on. Drunk continuously for twenty-five years. At first, to blot out the expectations of his parents and his older siblings. Later, because it was a habit. Lost everything in the process: his women, his inheritance, his business. Now he was about to lose his daughters, his "Jewels in my Crown," as he called them. Losing them because they never knew who they were dealing with. Sober, generous Daniel, or hungover, needful Daniel, or drunk, demanding Daniel. Losing them anyway because he had to lose them. Because they had to lose him to find themselves. Because that's the way it is in the world. Losing them in spite of the fact that they loved him more than they would ever love another man. Because he was their daddy. Their beautiful, golden, charming daddy.

And who wouldn't love him, Niall considered. This tall blue-eyed balding angel, this honey-sweet human, this good-looking father. Olivia and Jessie are doomed to look for his surrogates in the world, to try to re-create him everywhere, to fashion him from whatever they can find: a look, a glance, a way of walking, a deep voice, a wide chest, a way with animals. Doomed to search for and try to own his shadows. This is how we are, Niall knew. This is what we do. Unlucky Jessie, who has found a boy who looks like Daniel and also has his weaknesses. She is stuck for a long time, perhaps forever. Luckier Olivia, who only loved a dream for her first fifteen years. Since the dream was of her own making, perhaps she can go on dreaming, may even be able to love a man of her own choosing one day. It will be interesting, Niall decided, to see if she can ever love at all. I'm pulling for her, that's for sure.

As if on cue, Olivia came into the dining room with her cousins Winifred and Lynley. Daniel called out to the kitchen and the disgruntled elderly maid, Jade, began to bring in platters and set them on the table, muttering about food getting cold and old people about to die who were called on at the last minute to prepare elaborate meals with no help in the kitchen and not much appreciation. Daniel got up and went into the kitchen and began to help. Olivia and Winifred got up, too, and soon the four of them had managed to bring fried chicken and boiled new potatoes and steaming bowls of spinach and cooked carrots and baked squash and homemade rolls out onto the table and apply spoons to the bowls. "Sit down," Daniel said. "That's enough food, Jade. Don't put another thing on this table. Come on, let's say grace." The family held hands around the table and Daniel thanked the Lord for everything in sight, not forgetting to add, in his mind, a thank-you for the bank loan extension.

"I've been missing you so much," Olivia said, beaming smiles at her uncle and cousins. "I'm really sorry I'm going away."

"We missed you, too," Lynley said. "We talk about you all the time, don't we, Winnie?"

"We do. We tell everyone about you. About you writing Aunt Anna and us finding each other. It's like a fairy tale."

"My friend Kevin's in love with you," Lynley continued. "He saw that picture of you at Jessie's wedding and he wants to go out with you. I wish you'd stay."

"I can't. I feel too guilty about not seeing my grandparents. So who's this Kevin? I could use a new boyfriend. I didn't have much luck at Chapel Hill. What a bunch of sissies." She had meant to say pussies, then took it back because of Daniel and Niall. Daniel talked like that, but he didn't think women should.

"Ah, guilt, our old friend," Niall put in. "Probably responsible for ninety percent of civilization. Art, mapmaking, God knows what all. I wonder if there has ever been a culture free from guilt."

"Oh, stop it, Niall," Daniel said. "Stop all that goddamn psychology bullshit."

"Uncle Niall," Winifred put in. "You always make a joke out of everything."

"Go on to Oklahoma and assuage your guilt, Olivia," Niall continued. "Then come back and we'll all go to Sea Island for August. There, Daniel, that's not psychological bullshit. That's a bribe. How about it, Olivia, will you return to us in August and we'll go to Grandmother's house on the beach and lie in the sun and tan our legs and listen to the radio?"

"I sure would like to, but I can't promise until I find out how long summer school lasts."

"She's going to learn Navajo." Daniel had decided to be proud of it. "She says they code scientific information into computers on it."

"Where do you get your ideas, Olivia?" Winifred asked. "You have the wildest ideas of anyone I ever met."

"I listen," Olivia answered. "I find out things."

"We're leaving in the morning for New Orleans," Daniel said. "Maybe I'll drive her to Tahlequah and fly home."

"We're going to go see my momma's grave," Olivia said. "We think she'd like that. Us going there together."

"I remember when she came to visit us, the year before you were born." Niall paused, wondering how much truth he could tell. "She was so beautiful, really startling looking. Her hair was to her waist."

"She got pregnant with me before she came here," Olivia said. "She was already pregnant when she was sleeping in Grandmother's house."

"The round room on the second floor," Daniel put in. "Anna and Helen's old room. That's where we stayed that week."

The room grew quiet. Anna was dead and Helen had run off and left her family for a poet.

"Eat some of this fried chicken," Daniel said. "This is free-range chicken, Lynley. They were running all over the farm before Spook ran them down."

"Oh, Uncle Daniel," Winifred said. "You always make a joke out of everything."

"Momma does, too," Lynley added. "Momma and Uncle Niall are the lighthearted ones. Grandmother says so."

"What do you hear from her?" Olivia asked, pretending to be interested in her lima beans and potatoes.

"Not much," Winifred answered. "She keeps asking us to come up there but it isn't ever the right time. The holidays at Harvard are the same as ours and she and Mike go off places all the time. They went to Canada to see Shakespeare at Stratford and they went to Ireland twice."

"Once to meet his family," Lynley added. "She liked his family. She wants us to meet them sometime."

"I don't think she really wants us to meet them," Winifred said.

"They're just living together," Lynley said. "She never has gotten married to him. She isn't divorced from Dad. That's funny, isn't it? Your own mother up in Boston living in sin."

"Isn't Aunt Helen ever coming home?" Olivia asked, after Lynley and Winifred had left and she and Daniel and Niall were picking up the plates and carrying them to the kitchen.

"We don't know what Helen's doing," Niall said. "She won't even talk to me."

"The kids talk to her on the phone," Daniel put in. "She invited them up there for Christmas but none of them went. Well, talk about something else, honey. That's a sore subject with me."

"She told your daddy not to come see her unless he'd promise not to drink," Niall said to Olivia. "She really hurt his feelings."

"Don't go telling that, Niall. Goddamn, you're worse than Anna to tell everything you know."

"Anna's dead, baby brother. You ought to stop talking about her." Niall put his plate into the sink and began to run water over it. It was unlike Niall to be cruel. It shocked Olivia. She thought of him as an angel who never said a cruel thing. Now he was being cruel to her daddy. She put down her load of dishes and went to her daddy and put her arm around his waist. He looked down at her, grimaced, patted her on the head, then moved away and went to work wiping off the kitchen cabinets with a dish towel.

"She asked if Helen is ever coming home," Daniel said. "And the answer is probably no. Unless that poet gets tired of her, she won't. She's flown the coop. She's got her little love nest and she doesn't want the family messing into it. I don't care what she does."

"You cared when she told you not to come by when you were in Boston. It was uncalled for, and I'm angry about it whether you are or not."

"Let it go, Niall. Have a drink. You want a glass of brandy? Leave the rest of those goddamn dishes and let's get a nightcap. Come on, Via, stop cleaning up. She's calling herself Via, brother. It's her new name at Chapel Hill."

"Except no one will call me that. I can't get anyone to do it."

"I'll do it." Niall put his arm around her waist and began to lead her toward the den. They went down the hall, past the Naguchi statue the interior decorator girlfriend had bought for Daniel, past the Walter Andersons he had inherited from Anna and the statues he had bought in Italy one drunken summer and the trophies from golf tournaments and the framed photographs of Jessie from age one to the present and the framed photographs of Olivia beginning with the first photograph he had ever seen of her. It had been taken when she was fifteen years old at the freshman-sophomore dance at Tahlequah High. Olivia stopped by the photograph now, remembering the photographer posing her for the shot and how Bobby had stood all night along the wall of the gym watching her dance with her date. The next week he had finally asked her to go to a movie with him.

The photograph was of Olivia wearing a pink silk off-the-shoulder dancing dress. Olivia had sent the photograph to her aunt Anna in New York along with a letter introducing herself. Then Anna had taken the photograph to Daniel and begun her campaign to make him acknowledge the child.

I was so manipulative, Olivia thought. I'm proud of that. Of how strong and manipulative I was and how I went after what I wanted. I wanted them to know me. I wanted to have a dad and now I have one and I'm leaving him. "A child will play with a toy for a day, then cry for another and throw that one away." That's what Aunt Mary Lily always said. And she's right. All we want is something we can't have. I guess that's all we do until we die.

"So Aunt Helen just abandoned Lynley and Winifred and DeDe and Stacy and Kenny? That's what you're telling me?" Olivia turned to her Uncle Niall. "She doesn't care what becomes of them?"

"The kids are to blame, too. They've been taking their dad's side in all this. Helen's asked them up there, but none of them will go."

They moved on into the den, took their places on the long white sofas the interior decorator had brought from California. Daniel poured brandies for himself and Niall and a ginger ale for Olivia. "So you're going to abandon us, too," Niall continued. "I'm getting more like Daddy every day. I want everyone on the same block, so I can drop by and catch up on the news. Tribe by telephone, that's what we're developing nowadays."

"I'm too far away from what I am, Uncle Niall. I dreamed I had on a Cherokee wedding dress and none of you even noticed. You know what the Cherokee can do? We can dig down into the ground and unearth thousands of years of our own history. Right here, where we are in North Carolina, the Cherokee have been leaving bowls and beads and arrowheads for centuries. Well, I guess I shouldn't bring that up. Nevertheless, it's true. The rest of the people have to cross the ocean to find their history. I don't know. I just feel like I have to get back there."

"Our dreams are here to guide us. God knows, I believe in that. Well, go on then, but come back to us in August. Don't be like Helen and give up on us."

"I won't. I love you. I love it here. I just don't want to lose the rest of myself. I spent my life in Tahlequah. I need to swim in my own river and ride my old horse before she dies."

"And your grandparents," Daniel added. "She's right, Niall. She needs to see them. Besides, we got to go and see that baby. If Jessie won't bring the boy to the mountain, then the mountain goes to see the boy." He raised his brandy, smiled his most beautiful and charming smile, and proposed a toast. "To good company. And the bonds of blood."

"Amen," Niall said and drank.

"Amen," Olivia added, wondering what all that meant.

CHAPTER 11

EARLY the next morning Olivia and Daniel started driving to New Orleans. They stuck a CD into the CD player and struck out for the Crescent City. "What has happened down here, is the wind have changed," Aaron Neville sang. "Clouds rolled in from the north, and it's started to rain. Rained real hard, and it rained for a real long time. Six feet of water in the streets of Evangeline. Louisiana, Louisiana, they're trying to wash us away, they're trying to wash us awaaaaaayyyyy."

Daniel drove for the first six hours, then gave the wheel to Olivia and climbed in the backseat to take a nap. He pulled his long legs up onto the seat and rolled his jacket under his head for a pillow. They had shipped Olivia's possessions to Tahlequah. She had come home from Chapel Hill with her car so full of stuff she could barely see to drive. A computer with a printer, a portable typewriter, a television set, books and clothes and shoes, and her bicycle strapped to the top.

"Oh, Louisiana, Louisiana," Aaron sang. "They're trying to wash us away. They're trying to wash us awaaaaaayyyy."

"You're not going to Tahlequah to see some boy, are you?" Daniel asked. He had been trying to ask it for six hours and had finally gotten up his nerve. "Spook says you're going to see a boy."

"Spook's a gossip. All he does is gripe about everything and gossip. And I'm not going to see a boy. The only boy I like in Tahlequah doesn't live there anymore."

"Well, if you were, I was going to say you could invite him to come see us. We don't have to go to Switzerland. We could stay in Charlotte this summer. There's a college there. You could see your folks and then come on home. I don't need to go to Switzerland anyway. It's too expensive over there anymore."

"Dad, you don't need to give me any money this summer. I can take care of myself with what I have. Well, I might need some money for books, but that's about all."

"Of course I'm going to give you money. I'll give you the same allowance I've been giving you. I'm not broke yet, honey. I'll let you know when I am."

"If you get broke, I'll get a job. I've worked in every store on Muskogee Avenue. I can get a job anywhere in town doing anything I want to do. Well, go on to sleep, Dad. I can drive."

Olivia swerved to avoid a dead dog, then pushed the pedal to the floorboard. They were in the state of Alabama now, on a two-lane road that was a shortcut from Atlanta to Montgomery. "God, I love this car. I can't believe you're going to let me use it. I'll take perfect care of it, Dad. I won't let it get a scratch."

"Well, don't drive so fast. You scare me to death."

"It's okay. I've never had a wreck in my life. Go to sleep."

"Don't go over sixty-five on this road."

"Okay. God, I can't wait to see the baby. I bet he's so beautiful. I bet he's the prettiest baby in the world with Jessie and King for parents."

"Sixty-five, honey. Sixty-five."

"Okay. I promise. Go to sleep." Daniel closed his eyes, sank his head down onto his chest. Olivia sang along with the music. "River have broken through, clear down to Plaquemine. Ten feet of water in the streets of Evangeline. Louisiana, Louisiana, they're trying to wash us away. They're trying to wash us awaaaaayyy."

CHAPTER 12

SIX hours later they pulled into New Orleans, coming down Highway 59 from Hattiesburg, taking the long slow curves around the lake and past the French Quarter. They got off the expressway at Canal Street and wound their way down Saint Charles Avenue to Webster Street, where Jessie and King were living in a shotgun house painted blue. There was a red swing on the porch. Confederate jasmine covered an iron fence. As they pulled up in front of the house, Jessie came out the door with the baby in her arms. She stood for a moment completely still, then walked down the stairs holding the baby out toward them. "Come look at him," she called out. "I'm so glad you're here. Look at him, Daddy. Isn't he the most beautiful thing you've ever seen in your life?"

They hurried out of the car and surrounded her. A holy moment, hushed and uncertain. There he was, a baby boy, a whole new thing.

"Jesus," Olivia said. "A baby."

"Mighty nice," Daniel added. "Mighty nice baby, honey. Nice as he can be."

"You want to hold him?"

"In a minute. Let me get used to him first." A car drove down Webster Street taking a lawyer home from work. Another passed full of teenagers on their way to the Quarter to get in trouble. A kid rode by on a bike. A dog barked. The bells of the Saint Charles Avenue Presbyterian Church began to ring. "Come on in," Jessie said. "Come see our house."

They went up the wooden stairs and across the porch and into the small high-ceilinged living room and sat down upon a sofa. The baby's father, King Mallison, Junior, came out from the back of the house and shook hands with his father-in-law. "He weighs eight thousand four hundred and five grams, dressed," King said. "Look at those ears, Olivia. Aren't they something? He looks like a Volkswagen with the doors open."

"Oh, King," Jessie said. "Stop saying that to people. You're just jealous of all the attention he's getting. This woman I go to, Doctor Kaplan, says men are jealous of babies when they come. They think they're going to get all the love. It's like this darkness of jealousy we all have in us all the time but it comes out when something like a baby happens."

"Oh, God," King said, and laughed out loud. "If I was going to be jealous of anyone it would be Doctor Kaplan, since that's all you and Mother talk about."

"You got any whiskey in this house?" Daniel asked. "It's been a long drive. I sure could use a toddy."

"What do you think of him, Daddy?" Jessie asked. "Say you think he's cute. Don't you think he's darling?"

"He's some boy, honey. He's a beauty."

"There's a bar on the corner," King said. "We could go down there. Jessie won't let me keep it in the house. I quit, didn't you hear about that? I haven't had a drink since K.T. was born. If I get drunk, she's going to kick me out." He laughed again. Suddenly, he looked like a grown man. Olivia and Daniel turned their attention upon him. "I quit drinking, Daniel. I don't even miss it. But I'll go down the street with you. I still like to watch people drink. I can get a Coke."

"I got a bottle of Chivas in the car." Daniel stood up. "Just get me a glass and I'll go get that. You don't care if I bring it in here, do you? I'm not going to the psychiatrist. So I'm going to keep on having toddies if nobody minds."

"Manny and Crystal want to see you as soon as you get here," Jessie said. "They want us to come over there if you want to." She stood up. "I'll call Manny for you, Dad. He'll have a drink with you."

"Good," Daniel said. "That's a good idea. I like Manny. I'd like to talk to him." Jessie walked over to her father and put the baby into his arms. "Hold him," she said. "I'll call Manny and let you talk to him."

Daniel looked down at the baby. I tried to get rid of you, he was thinking. Well, I'm glad I didn't. Not to mention the two Charlotte aborted and the one Margaret got rid of last year. Well, she did that behind my back. I didn't even pay for that. So I'm glad you're here and I wish you luck with all these people.

The baby made a sound. Ohhhhhhh, it said. Very small, very nice sound. Oh, oh.

"Dad." It was Olivia at his elbow. "Let me hold him. I want to hold him. I haven't held him yet." Daniel very carefully transferred the baby to Olivia's arms. What a deal, Daniel decided. Girls having babies and not a woman in sight. Where are the grandmothers and the great-grandmothers? Where's the plan in all of this? Where's the blueprint?

"Here's Manny," Jessie said, handing him the phone. "He wants to talk to you."

"Manny. Hello, it's Daniel Hand. You all get on over here. The god-damn kids won't even let me have a drink. Come on over here and have a drink with me."

In a few minutes, Manny and Crystal Weiss and their daughter, Crystal Anne, age ten, came running in and joined the party. Manny went into the kitchen with Daniel, and the rest of them sat in the living room worshiping the baby. Crystal Weiss had once been the wildest girl in Mississippi. Then she had been the wildest old girl, then the wildest old, old girl, then had the wildest midlife crisis. Now, at age forty-four, she was beginning to settle down. Grandmotherhood had settled around her shoulders like a cloak. From the minute she learned Jessie was pregnant she had been changed. The oldest son of her only son. These first few months of his life were a time of almost unadulterated joy to her. Every day when she woke up, she seemed to know exactly what to do and the largess of her happiness spread out to cover anyone she met. Of course, there were days when she got out of hand. The day she replaced all the glass doors with Plexiglas. The day she sent five thousand dollars to the Society to Prevent the Abuse of Children without asking Manny. The day she bought Jessie a diamond bracelet.

Mostly, however, her transformation had been smooth. She had ordered several little washable knit dresses in bright colors and had taken to wearing them everywhere. "So he can spit up on me," she told her friends. Also, she had started recycling and begun to worry about the sale of jets to Arab countries. "You're making up for being too young to be a mother to King," her psychiatrist told her. "You've been given a second chance."

Manny Weiss had flourished with his wife. What made her happy, made him happy. What lifted her, lifted him, and he forgot the trauma of his law practice and the constant struggle to make money, and began to really enjoy his wife and daughter. He loved Cyrstal's wild spoiled relatives. They represented something his careful background would never let him become. Their self-indulgent escapades never failed to cheer him up, as though he were reading in the *National Geographic* about a tribe of savages recently discovered in Zaire.

"Goddamn, Manny, thank God you're here to have a drink with me." Daniel got out glasses and began to pour. "We been on the road for two days. Olivia's going to Oklahoma for the summer. You ever live by yourself, Manny? It's a bitch. Get up in the morning. No one to have breakfast with. I brought my farm manager in from the country. Lucas Dehorney. His nephew's Salva Dehorney on the North Carolina team. You ever seen him play?"

"Of course. I saw the Blue Devils play when I was in Charlotte last winter. I should have called you to go to the game, but it was a last-minute thing because my client had some tickets."

"Spook would have been better than that if he'd been given a chance. I don't know about our black buddies, Manny. I don't know if they'll ever get their share. They're not mean enough." Daniel handed Manny his drink. "What do you think?"

"You know what the Jews say, don't you? It's a joke. You can give the whole country to the blacks and the Jews will get it back in ten years."

"Yeah. Well, Spook could run G.E., but he doesn't give a damn. I tried to get him to go to business school but he quit. He doesn't care about money. I never could figure it out. You couldn't bribe him to take his feet down off the table if he didn't want to. Well, I didn't mean to get off on race and politics. Little old boy looks pretty good, doesn't he? Mighty good."

"Crystal thinks of nothing else. It sure has made my life better. I've never seen her so happy."

"How about Jessie? You think she and King can make it?"

"I sure hope so. We're doing everything we can."

"I know you are, old pardner, and I appreciate it. Here, let me freshen that for you." Daniel reached for Manny's glass and added Scotch to it, then "freshened" his own.

"Daddy, come here." It was Jessie, coming to find him. "Come and see him. Olivia's getting him to laugh so much. He loves her. He won't let anyone else hold him."

"We're coming, baby. We'll be right there." He reached out and took her hand. Their fingers interlaced. Fathers and daughters, Manny thought. Will Crystal Anne and I be that way? Will I learn to protect her, even from myself and my desire to never let her go? I wish Doctor Lacey wouldn't keep telling me that stuff. I don't want to hear all that dark unconscious stuff. Can't a man just love his children anymore? Can't we just do the best we can?

"Well, no," the doctor might have told him. "New ideas are rising in the human psyche. New ways of being trying to become manifest. For example, we will teach fathers not to seduce their daughters' minds, not to buy them off, not to bribe them for attention, not to want to be the primary man in their lives."

"How's that boy treating you?" Daniel asked, pulling Jessie closer to him. "Is there anything you need? Anything I can get for you?"

CHAPTER 13

BOBBY drove into Tahlequah at sunset and stopped at a 7-Eleven and called his dad. "I'm in town," he said. "I thought I'd come over and spend the night, if that's okay."

"Sure," his father said. "Come on. You can have the trailer. It's right out in the yard. Hell, you didn't know I moved into a house, did you? Sharrene made me get a house. We're over on Plum Street, right down the block from the trailer park. Come on over. It's 993 Plum. I'll be out front waiting for you."

"I might stay awhile."

"That's great. Come on. We're glad to have you."

Bud Tree hung up the phone and turned back to the men sitting at his kitchen table. "You boys clear on out of here," he said. "My kid's in town. I don't want him knowing about this."

"Sure thing," the oldest of the three said. They didn't want to get in bad with Bud. He was the pilot. Without him, the whole deal fell through. "We can talk some more tomorrow. Come by my place."

"I'll call you tomorrow. Go on. Clear on out." Bud stood by the door and the three men marched out and got into their car and drove away. Then Bud went into the bedroom to find his girlfriend. "Bobby's here," he said. "Put on some clothes, Sharrene. He'll be here in a minute. Come on. Get dressed." He patted her on the shoulder to make it easier and then went out and stood in the front yard and waited for his son. Bud Tree was a good man. He had never cheated at a game or hurt a horse on purpose or been mean to women. He had done the best he could for forty-two years with what he had to work with. Now he was down to running dope for a bunch of Chinese gangsters from Kansas City and he was sorry he was doing it. Two more runs, he promised himself. Then I'll buy a farm and start raising horses. Two more runs and there'll be fifty grand sitting in the bank and I'll have a stake.

Well, shit, Bobby's coming home. If Sharrene doesn't like it, I'll run her ass off.

Lights were coming down the street. Bud held his arms up in the air and began to wave.

Bobby turned his truck into the unfamiliar driveway and felt his throat constrict at the sight of his dad. His coach, his old partner, who had never beat him or made him do a damn thing and had never had to. He loved Bud Tree the way he loved Olivia Hand. Blindly, perfectly, steadily. If Bud saddled a horse that had never been ridden and smiled in Bobby's direction, Bobby climbed up on it and broke the son-of-a-bitch. If Bud got drunk occasionally and cried on the kitchen table, Bobby stood by and hid his own tears. If the score was twelve to twelve in the last quarter of a game against Broken Arrow and Bud Tree was in the stands, Bobby found a way to lead the Indians to victory. It was just that easy to love someone and want to please them, just that easy to take the pain yourself and let the other person go.

I missed him so much, Bobby thought, watching the tall spare figure. He turned off the lights and climbed out of the cab. I can smell him from here. Then Bud was beside him and pulled him into his arms and the smell was right, cigarettes and horses and something that always seemed like the whole truth and nothing but the truth. "How you doing, Dad?" Bobby said. "How things going? So she made you get a house. You didn't tell me. What if I'd written you a letter? It might not have ever gotten here."

"I can't afford it. That's for damn sure. Work's scarcer than a chicken's brain. What brings you home out the blue? Not that I'm not glad. I'm about sick of living with a woman and no man to talk to."

"I came home to see my girl. She's coming here in a day or two. I'm going to ask her to marry me."

"Nothing stops that when it starts. You won't get any arguments from me about the heart. I'll just stand by to pick up the pieces. Is this the same girl that ripped you up a year ago? The little short stout one?"

"Olivia. The only one I ever had. Don't act like you don't know her name." Then they were laughing together and Bud had a suitcase and a duffel bag over his shoulder and they were starting down the path to the house, which was dark behind overgrown shrubs.

"Sharrene better be up and finding something for you to eat. Damn. I sure was glad to hear your voice. I didn't know I'd been missing you. The old trailer's right over there by the drive. You can clean it up and move in tomorrow if you like. I was thinking about selling it. Damn, I'm glad you're here." They went into the living room and the old table they had made together out of railroad ties was by the sofa and Bobby leaned over it and read the things they had carved on it during several winters when he was ten and eleven and twelve. "It's only a mountain, I can move it." "Shit happens." "No Cats." Including a tic-tac-toe game that had taken place during a snow-covered Christmas when Sharrene got mad and it was just the two of them for four days while the snow fell. Bobby had won the games but he always thought Bud gave them to him.

CHAPTER 14

IT was Saturday night. At Jessie and King Mallison's house on Webster Street in New Orleans, the grandparents were babysitting while the young people went to Tipitina's to hear the Neville Brothers and hook up with Andria Brown, a half-black, half-Norwegian prima donna who was the niece of Crystal Weiss's housekeeper, Traceleen. Jessie, Olivia, King, and Andria had spent the past summer together on the coast of Maine. Olivia and Andria had been privy to the secret romance between King and Jessie and the begetting of Kingman Theodore Mallison (K.T.), and they thought of themselves as participants in some great and tragic drama.

Jessie, King, and Olivia made their way into the crowded noisy heat of the dance hall bar. "Way down yonder in New Orleans, in the land of the dreamy dreams," Charles Neville was singing. "There's a garden of Eden, that's what I mean."

Andria emerged from a crowd of young people near the stage and pulled them to a table she had been saving. "God, I'm glad to see you," she said. "How come you didn't answer my letters, Olivia? You get them?"

"I was having a terrible time. All I've been doing is trying to pass a goddamn physics class. We've got this teacher who's a lunatic. He had a sex-change operation. I'm not kidding you. Besides, I knew I'd see you sooner or later when I got down here."

"Jessie said you were coming. How long can you stay?"

"Just a day. I'm on my way to Tahlequah. I've got to see my folks."

"You getting laid?" Andria lowered her voice.

"No. Are you?"

"Hell, no. I wouldn't let anyone stick a dick in me with all the stuff that's going on down here. Everyone in Louisiana has AIDS. And every other goddamn thing. I'm trying to keep my scholarship. That's all I care about. I got a job for the summer with a radio station downtown. An oldies station, but it's pretty good money. All I have to do is announce the news and do a few ads."

"Quit telling secrets," Jessie said. "When are you coming to see the baby, Andria? You haven't seen him since he was born. He's twice as big as he was then."

"I'm coming. He was big then. I thought he looked real good."

"Let's dance," King said. "We'll turn into pumpkins in an hour." He pulled Jessie up from the chair and led her out onto the crowded dance floor. The Nevilles were playing "Angola Bound," a song that had been King's favorite in the days when Tipitina's belonged to him. It was at Tip's that he had taken the famous twenty-seven hits of acid that had fixed his reputation as the wildest boy in uptown New Orleans. He led the equally mysterious Jessie out onto the dance floor and the crowd moved back to give them room.

"They look like they're doing okay," Olivia said.

"Aunt Traceleen said they'd all quit drinking, the whole family of them."

"Jessie never drank anyway. That time last summer was the only time I ever saw her drink anything. She hates it."

"Aunt Traceleen said King gave up all that shit. Of course, she always thinks the best of everyone. Look at them, you got to admit they look good together." The two young women gazed out onto the dance floor. Jessie and King were twined around each other.

"She's devoting her life to him," Olivia said. "Can you imagine that? She's only nineteen years old. Give me a break."

"Fucking A. Still, they do look nice together. You'd never know they already have a baby." The band had moved into an old Allen Toussaint song, "With you in mind, with you in mind." King and Jessie were even closer now.

"It disgusts me," Olivia said. "You wouldn't believe this house they're living in. It's so Yuppie it's unbelievable. I guess Crystal gave them all that furniture."

"Boring," Andria said, and sat up straighter. One of the younger Nevilles was heading their way. "That's Carter Neville. I went to school with him at NOCCA. He thinks he's so cool. They almost never even let him play." She wet her lips and gave him a profile. "So tell me about the University of North Carolina," she said in a loud voice. "You haven't told me about your classes."

Later, much, much later. Andria and Olivia and the young Neville and two of the Lewis triplets were sitting on Jessie's porch talking politics. A quarter moon was sinking in the west. Stars moved in and out of vision in the dense, moisture-laden sky.

"I should stay a few more days," Olivia was saying. "I've hardly seen my nephew." She leaned back and gazed up at the sky. She decided the Lewis boys were half in love with her already. "Why am I leaving this great city?"

"Because you got that fortune cookie at the Chinese restaurant." The dominant brother moved nearer to her on the porch.

" 'You are on a mysterious journey,' " Olivia quoted. " 'The destination will soon become clear.' "

"A computer writes them," Andria said. "My Mass Com teacher said it's just a bunch of bullshit."

CHAPTER 15

THE next morning Olivia woke up in a small high-ceilinged room painted white and blue. Its windows looked out upon a garden with hollyhocks and gardenia bushes and morning glory vines upon a trellis. Along a fence were six azalea bushes in full bloom, red and pink and fuchsia. The windows were open. It had been cool when Olivia opened them at three in the morning. Now it was hot. Hot, hot, hot, hotter than hot. The languor and humidity of New Orleans had invaded Olivia's soul as she slept. How will I ever drive all the way to Oklahoma? she wondered, and put her feet down upon the floor and began to think of coffee.

She walked barefoot across the room and opened the door. She heard the baby making noises and followed the sound and found Jessie in the living room with the baby at her breast. "He is my gene-bearer," Olivia announced. "I thought he was a bad idea, Jessie. I'll admit that, but as soon as I saw him, I changed my mind. He's really wonderful. He's fabulous. How does that feel? Does it hurt to do it?"

"Of course not. It feels good, to tell the truth. Besides, you get full of milk and you need to get it out."

"I guess he's sessile, isn't he?"

"What?"

"I mean, he's like a tree. He has to stay attached. I mean, he looks like that's where he ought to be."

"I like him so much. I can't believe I like anything this much. I want to be such a good mother to him. I don't want to be like my mother was."

"Are you going back to school?"

"Not until he's a lot bigger. They don't want you to leave them, Olivia. They don't want to be taken care of by maids."

"I did okay, and I never saw my mother."

"Well."

"I mean, I know I can't stay in love with anyone and all that, but at least I know it. So you're going to a shrink?"

"I love to go. I love her. She's a woman. She's teaching me so much. She's teaching me to be happy."

"I quit seeing that woman they sent me to in Chapel Hill. She had an agenda for me. Well, it was nice in a way, but in the end I got mad at her. I had this accident on my bike and she said maybe I wanted to get hurt so I wouldn't have to think about things that bother me."

"Like what?"

"Oh, I don't know. Sorority crap and stuff. I don't want to talk about it. Well, look, I've got to get packed. I want to leave by one or two at the latest. Is there any coffee made?"

"Dad wants to drive you part of the way."

"Well, I don't want him to. I'm nineteen, Jessie. I don't need people driving me places."

"He's always that way. He used to drive me to camp every summer, even after I was a counselor. He doesn't like people on the road." Jessie moved the baby from her nipple. His eyes were closed and milk was running out of his mouth. Olivia stared down into his sleeping face. It was too much. It was too terrifying and too fabulous and too real. A real live baby made of flesh and blood. First Jessie and King were sneaking off to spend nights on the beach and then K.T. was in the world. That's all it took. Some guy you loved and a beach and you were on the couch with a baby stuck to your tit.

Daniel appeared in the doorway, dressed for the day. He looked down at his daughters sitting side by side on the sofa holding his grandson and thought he should run out on the street and give some money to someone. Ought to hand out hundred-dollar bills or fix someone a drink.

"Sit down, Daddy," Jessie said. "Sit on the chair and I'll let you hold him."

"I'll just watch. Don't go moving him around so much in the morning. I don't think it's good to get him all stirred up."

"I want to leave this afternoon and drive as far as Little Rock," Olivia said. "There's not a single reason for you to go with me. You can stay here and be with Jessie and I'll call you every four hours from the road. I'll call from Jackson and I'll call from Little Rock. You don't need to go with me, Dad. I can drive up there alone."

"Let her go," Jessie added. "She'll be okay. She knows what she's doing. Besides, you need to get to know K.T. He's your gene-bearer, after all."

"What?" Daniel said. "What are you talking about? What are you saying now?"

At one that afternoon Olivia climbed into the Mercedes and started driving to Oklahoma. She passed over the Bonnet Carré spillway, across the marshes and the lake and headed straight up into the state of Mississippi. It was the second day of June. The world was at peace, for the most part. Four hours earlier, the United States and the U.S.S.R. had settled their differences on a treaty to limit conventional weapons. In Angola, a new government was being formed. In Albania, the people were on the streets demanding freedom.

Olivia heard some of this on the radio but it did not seem to have any bearing on her life. When the disc jockey came back on and began to play a love song, she listened more closely. "Oh, blame it on midnight," the song was playing. "Shame, shame on the moon."

Twelve hours and I'll be home, she was thinking. I'll go to the river and take off my clothes and swim like a fish. I'll go out to Baron Fork and get a horse and go riding. The new colts will be running around everywhere by now. I'll sleep in my old bed. I'll eat Grandmother's corncakes. I'll get that goddamn Chapel Hill out of my soul. Bobby might come home. If he finds out I'm there, I bet he'll come. I don't care how many Montana cowgirls he's been fucking. He can't forget what we had. If it got any better than that, nobody would ever get out of bed.

CHAPTER 16

TAHLEQUAH, Oklahoma. June 1, 1991. Wild geese flying in formation above the limestone cliffs. Small farms and small neat pastures and grazing cattle. Stockades with horses, winding creeks. Woods with maple, spruce, oak, locust, and scraggly pines. Limestone formations. Tiny huts built into the sides of hills by masons from Ireland.

High wooded bluffs. Upon their ridges eagles nest in tall wind-sculpted trees. Everywhere the songs of birds: robins, orioles, sparrows, chickadees, crows, blue jays, bluebirds, larks. The long sad notes of the mourning doves.

Brown houses with scraggly pines, gangly colts born in the spring, winding two-lane asphalt roads, stones, barbed-wire fences. June 1991. The Tahlequah Little Theater is playing *The Crucible* by Arthur Miller.

On Muskogee Avenue the store windows are filled with manikins wearing fake Indian clothes. T-shirts printed with bastardized Indian designs. Jeans and braided belts and cheap leather boots. Sexy underwear in red and black and gold.

Town Branch runs through the town. It rises in limestone and ends in pasture. Northeastern Oklahoma State University looks down upon the town. Its music department is talked of in the area.

On Muskogee Avenue the town's movers and shakers have gathered for their morning coffee at The Shak. They will pool information, gossip and surmise, wait for the day to deliver its surprises.

A block down the street is the Cherokee Museum. Between two and four on any weekday you will find Eagle Kingfisher holding forth on Cherokee history. He is telling someone now about the Five Civilized Tribes.

"Cherokee, Chickasaw, Choctaw, Creek, and Seminole. Some of us have lived to tell the story. I have no resentment toward any man.

Once we tamed the horse and dog. Once we knew the secrets of the sacred fire. Once we worshiped the light as it lies upon the water. Someone must tell the old stories. If you hear them, you must tell your children, you must seal them in your heart."

Doctor Georgia Jones, M.D., Ph.D., is driving to Tahlequah, approaching from the east. She is on her way to spend the summer teaching anthropology at Northeastern. There is a package of rice cakes on the seat beside her. She is drinking coffee from a plastic cup, eating the rice cakes, and composing a letter to her lover. He is the first man in years she has allowed herself to love. This is a very scary deal for a forty-six-year-old control freak.

Dear Zach, To think that the possibility of such tenderness exists and we don't use it all the time, throw it away, squander it.

I'm sorry I ran off like this, but I had to. This is the reaction. The catharsis. Sure, you made love to me yesterday afternoon. Sure, when the heat was on, when you knew you had fucked up, you came through and made me come. About time. After all the blow jobs I've given you when you couldn't get it up. Is it my fault they had the Gulf War? Did I discover nuclear fusion? The last straw was when you started faking orgasms while being fellated. So I'm getting away for the summer and hoping you will get your act together and come to your senses and have a life. So I can share it. I've done all I can do. The ball is in your court.

After you left me yesterday afternoon, and that's typical, that you would leave right after the best sex we've ever had, to GO BACK TO YOUR WORK. Which is what, Zach? Sitting all day in front of a computer screen talking to other people who think we're doomed? Anyway, after you left, I slept a long time and when I woke up I decided not to go after all.

Then I started thinking. At the rate we've been going I figure I'm getting one orgasm for every six thousand dollars you borrow from me to give to your causes. That's pretty high. Not as much as Donald Trump is paying for his pussy, but too high for a woman with a good-looking body. You've got to admit I have a gorgeous body.

Well, I signed a contract with Northeastern and I need to get away so I'm going. I may go back to practicing medicine in the fall. Meanwhile I am going to stop worrying about you and take care of myself. I am going to rent a house, get it comfortably furnished, teach, meditate, give up coffee, and write you a lot of letters which I may or may not mail. Love, Georgia.

I will be happy. I will be happy. I will be happy. "What a piece of work is man, how noble in reason, how infinite in faculties, in form and moving how express and admirable, in action how like an angel, in apprehension how like a God! The beauty of the world, the paragon of animals . . ."

The world is a feast. A fabulous, rich treasure. Okay, eat a rice cake, look out the window, it's summer and you're autonomous and you're free.

Georgia stuck a tape of Beethoven's Sixth Symphony into the tape player. Autonomy, she decided. That's a lot of bullshit. There's no autonomy anywhere in nature. Nowhere in the physical universe, in animate or inanimate matter, not one case of autonomy exists. Everything is connected to everything else. God, I am so sick of being lonely and alone.

She drove into town and went directly to a real estate office. Two hours later she was moving into a partially furnished house near the campus. By five that afternoon she was at the Wal-Mart buying supplies. Dearest Zach, she composed as she drove home from the store. There is still light in the sky. Your favorite time of day, your favorite time of year. Tahlequah is pretty sad and dead. There seems to be a little theater of sorts. Signs of culture include T-shirts in store windows with imitation Indian designs. Lots of sad-looking fat people.

I'll take Northern Europeans, thank you. I know, you hate that about me, but I don't give a damn. I come from the culture that built Chartres Cathedral and gave us Milton and Shakespeare. I still think that's better than eating dogs and making war on your neighbors every spring. Okay, we did that too, but at least it was to conquer territory.

The human race has taken so many dead ends. Cannibalism,

Victorianism, communism, the present-day refusal to take AIDS seriously. At any moment the virus can mutate to live in the presence of oxygen and then it's over.

Why do you think I quit practicing? I couldn't protect an entire operating field and do my work correctly. I wasn't thinking about risking my life for a bunch of dope addicts. Who needs it?

Of course the end was the child torn up by the bull mastiff. The owner of the dog was in the waiting room with the parents. They're friends.

Excuse me, I'm not perfect. I miss you. The best thing for both of us is to quit seeing each other for a while. You're going to have to choose between me and Armageddon. The good thing about me is that I'm here, now. Armageddon might not happen for five, ten, maybe fifteen years. Love, Georgia.

CHAPTER 17

GEORGIA'S morning. *This is a feast?* Gets up at six. Makes coffee. Writes letters. Drinks coffee and eats two rice cakes. Takes two teaspoons of C Aspa Scorb dissolved in orange juice. Does yoga. Lifts five-pound weights. Cleans face. Puts on Chanel Refining Mask. Sits in meditation while mask hardens. Gets up. Cleans face. Applies Chanel Super-Moisturizing Mask. Sits in meditation while skin absorbs sheep estrogen. Achieves union with universal consciousness for fourteen seconds. Starts thinking about Zach. Wishes to tell Zach about universal consciousness. Manages to stop thinking about Zach. Wishes for resumption of communion with universal consciousness. Thinks about going back to Memphis to practice medicine. Sees child dying of dog bite wounds. Gets up. Washes off mask. Gets dressed, decides to go downtown and find somewhere to eat breakfast. Starts out door. Goes back in. Calls Zach.

"Where are you?"

"In Tahlequah. Where I told you I would be."

"You couldn't have been hired that fast. You must have known you were going to do this for months."

"Well, I was. These people are crazy about me."

"How much are they paying you?"

"I don't see how that's any of your business."

"What did you call me for, Georgia? What do you want me to do?"

"Nothing."

"Nothing will come of nothing."

"Don't do that, please."

"All right."

"What?"

"I said, okay, whatever you want. Look, Georgia, why don't you drive over here on Friday night and let's talk this over."

"It's Tuesday morning, for God's sake."

"Well."

"You want to wait until Friday night to talk about this?"

"You're the one who left."

"This really hurts me, Zach. This is killing me."

"It hurts me too. What do you think it does to me?"

The line was quiet. For almost a minute no one spoke.

"Okay," Georgia said at last. "I'll come over Friday. If your kids won't be there. Will they be there? Can I stay at your house with you?"

"They won't be here. Yes, you can stay with me. I want you to stay with me."

"Okay. I'll come Friday then. As soon as I can get away. It might be six or seven before I get there."

"I'll be waiting."

"I might send you a letter. I've been writing letters to you. If you get one, read it very carefully."

"Oh, oh."

"What?"

"Nothing. I mean, yes, of course I will."

"I love you, Zach. That much is true."

"Good. I want you to. I love you too."

*   *   *

They hung up and Georgia went out and got into her car and drove downtown looking for a place to eat breakfast. The Shak, it said on an old-fashioned-looking restaurant in the middle of Muskogee Avenue. "Where Tahlequah Meets and Eats."

CHAPTER 18

OLIVIA turned off the highway onto the gravel road that led to her grandfather's house. It is always strange to return to a place where you have lived as a child, strange and compelling and sensate. Every leaf on every tree is the progeny of leaf and bole and tree that fed Olivia oxygen when she was one and two and three and seven and ten and twelve and fifteen. When she rode this way on her first bike, or on her spotted pony. When she drove Mary Lily's old Pontiac up and down, the year she learned to drive. It was a mile from the highway to the house, an unbroken stretch of maple and locust and elm and oak and cedar and pine and wild dogwoods.

How could I leave this? Olivia wondered. Where in the world have I been? She speeded up, leaving a trail of dust in the gravel, and turned by the mailbox and parked in the yard.

There it was, her home, the small house nestled beneath maple trees, the barn, the corral, empty now except for one old mare leaning against a post batting its eyes against the flies. Olivia got out of the car and went running toward the house. Crow and Little Sun and Mary Lily were on the steps before she reached the house. They had been watching for her out the windows. Lines from a poem came to her. "The piled grief scrambling like guilt to leave us. At the sight of you looking well, and besides, our questions, our news."

"I'm so sorry I was gone," she said. "I missed you so much. Where are the animals?" She hugged them fiercely, and everyone began to cry. Aunt Mary Lily wept stingy old-maid tears and Crow wept laughing grandmother tears and Little Sun wept manly unashamed tears and

Olivia wept until she choked. Then she turned to the corral and the old mare standing by the gate.

"Bess," she screamed. "It's me. Olivia. I'm home. Oh, Bess, don't you know me?" The mare lifted its head and whinnied, and Olivia ran to the corral and climbed the fence and kissed the horse on its nose.

"That cat Desdemona's in the house," Mary Lily said. "And your dog too. They stay in the house half the time and Bobby Tree called last week. I told him you were coming home."

"What?" Olivia said. "What did you just say?" She climbed back down from the gate. "What did you say about Bobby?"

"I made you a cake," Crow put in. "There's a chicken cooked and peas and potatoes and snap beans in the pot. Come inside and let me feed you."

"He just was looking for you. He called up from Montana." Mary Lily turned and started toward the house.

Then they went into the kitchen and Olivia had baked chicken and boiled new potatoes from the garden and fresh peas and carrots and biscuits warmed in a new microwave. "What did he say when he called?" she asked Mary Lily several times. "What all did he say?"

"He just wanted to know where you were," Mary Lily answered. "He didn't say much of anything."

"I can't believe you got a microwave. I just don't believe it."

After Olivia had eaten every bite she could eat and drank three glasses of iced tea, they all went out to the yard and sat on wooden yard chairs and talked about the future and the past, about dogs they had had and horses they had owned and how Wilma Mankiller was a great chief and how many tribes had come to the powwow in Tulsa and how many reporters were there and how many stupid questions they were always asking Little Sun when he wore his ceremonial dress. "Veterans of all the wars came," he told her. "They wore combat uniforms and carried rifles. They danced the Navajo victory dance. It was powerful medicine, and it was put on the television and broadcast everywhere, but I do not think they know what they were watching. It was a celebration of victory. The reporters think it was against the wars." He laughed and let his eyes rest on his granddaughter. He had not allowed himself to know how much he missed her.

"I'm going to Northeastern this summer," she said. "I'm going to study Navajo. I want to find Mack Crosses and get him to speak it with me. Is he still around? Is he out at his old place?"

"I see him around," Mary Lily said. "But he's mostly drunk. He's been drunk ever since his wife died. I wouldn't fool with him if I was you. He's just a drunk now."

"I want to see him anyway. I have a funny feeling about him. I think there's a reason I have him on my mind." She put on her knowing look. In the Wagoner household intuitive feelings were taken seriously. The Wagoners believed the world was full of things waiting to reveal themselves. They believed the world was full of messages waiting to be delivered.

"You should go to Flaming Rainbow," Crow put in. "That's where they have the languages. Mrs. Harness is teaching there. I saw her last week at the farmer's market. She told me everything they're teaching."

"I forgot about Flaming Rainbow. Maybe I will. I'll go by there tomorrow and see what they have. It would have to transfer to North Carolina. I'm not sure Flaming Rainbow would."

"I will call Mrs. Harness. We'll see what she says." Crow disappeared into the house to make the call. As soon as she was gone, Little Sun put his hand to his mouth to mean This is a secret, and said, "She's always talking about Flaming Rainbow. I think she wants to go herself."

"Then she should go," Olivia said. "Lots of older people go to school now. Why shouldn't she?"

"Maybe she wants to." Little Sun smiled. "You ask her. See if she'll go with you."

"It's just for Indians," Mary Lily said with a sigh. "They won't take it in North Carolina."

"I'll go by there tomorrow." Olivia got up, went over to her aunt and hugged her fiercely. Mary Lily had been her mother since the day she was born. Had been her keeper, nurse, intermediary, companion, slave. "I'm sorry I didn't come home sooner," she said. "It was awful of me. And I didn't write enough or anything."

"Young people go to seek their lives. It's what happens now." Little Sun made this decree and Olivia and Mary Lily nodded and accepted it. "Let's go in now," he added. "Your grandmother will talk on the phone for an hour. Let's go and listen to her."

"Let's go to bed," Olivia said. "I can't wait to sleep in my old bed. You better not have changed it. You didn't change it, did you?"

"It has new sheets." Mary Lily laughed. "It was a surprise. Sheets with animals I got at Workman and Stone at a sale. I was saving them for you."

They went into the house and ate the rest of the biscuits and Crow reported that Mrs. Harness said anything from Flaming Rainbow would transfer anywhere, even Harvard University. Then the lights were turned off and Little Sun and Crow went into their room and began to whisper.

Olivia went into her room, which was exactly as she had left it, only the crepe paper from a Homecoming dance was faded now and drooped where it was strung along the frame of a photograph of Olivia with the Tahlequah Indian cheerleaders. The bed had been painted a fresh new ivory color and was made up with beautiful sheets and a cover with jungle animals in a wild design. "I love my bed," Olivia said. "It is so beautiful. Sleep here with me, Aunt Lily. I want you to. There's room enough for both of us. Come on, get in."

"No. You are too big now. I have my room. I'll see you in the morning." Mary Lily stood in the door. Looking very old and very young.

"I want you to sleep with me. I want to hear you breathing in the night, so I'll know I'm really home. Come on, get on your gown. Get in with me."

"Okay. If you want me to." Mary Lily smiled, a wild bright smile that only happened once or twice a week. Then she disappeared down the hall.

Olivia put on a gown and climbed into the new sheets. She snuggled down into her bed. I was born in this house, she thought. Mom died and I was born. All that's left of her is in this house, in Mary Lily and Grandmother and Granddaddy and me. I am always safe here, with the ghost of Momma and Mary Lily and Little Sun and Crow. It smells so good. It smells like wildflowers. It smells like home. Can you believe she got these sheets with lions and tigers on them? I can just see her down at Workman and Stone picking them out. Oh, Jessie, I wish you could be here for a day or two and know what it's like to be loved. I wish Dad could come sometime. I wish he wouldn't drink so much, but there's nothing I can do about it. I'm here now. I don't have to do a thing. Oh, God, I'm so glad to be home.

Mary Lily came to the door wearing her old gray flannel gown. "Are you sure you want me to stay in here?" she asked. "Are you sure there's room?"

Olivia opened the covers and smiled mysteriously. "Come into the lion's den, come and see my shining tigers. Come on, Auntie, I'll protect you. Nothing will harm you in this jungle bed."

Then Mary Lily turned off the light and lay her big heavy sweet body down beside her niece and they hugged and kissed and went to sleep.

The next morning Olivia was up with the sun. She went out into the yard and fed oats to the mare and scared up the chickens in the pen and walked down toward the orchard to see if the apple trees were bearing. On her way back to the house she saw Little Sun come out and stand in the sun. He looked powerful and tall, standing by the well in his soft brown shirt, his chest so fine and wide, his powerful face lifting from his neck like a chieftain in a painting. He turned and listened. He was looking for her but he couldn't see that far away. He's getting old, Olivia decided. Real, real old. I think I got here just in time. "I'm over here," she called out. "I'm by the barn. I'm coming. I'm on my way."

He waved and turned in the direction of her voice. "The moon's still up," he called out. "Look over your shoulder." Olivia turned to the southeast and saw the full moon sinking below the horizon. It was very white and perfectly defined. "Copernicus went to jail for saying we are moving," she called back. "That's one thing I learned this year." He laughed out loud and held out his arms and she ran to him and hugged him fiercely to her breast.

"Crow is making pancakes," he said. "She sent me to bring you in. And Kayo called from Baron Fork. He said to tell you to come and ride the Connemaras. New ponies they got from Ireland last week."

"That's all he said? Just to come and ride? How did he know I was here? Did you tell him?"

"He said he heard you were coming."

"Then Bobby told him. No one could have told him but Bobby." She took her grandfather's arm and they walked into the house to eat the pancakes. Mary Lily was up and dressed. She was the assistant manager of the new Bonanza Restaurant and had to be there by eight every morning. "Where did I learn to walk?" Olivia asked. "When I was in the yard I remembered you showed me a place where I learned to walk. It was right by the old garden, wasn't it? By the oak tree?"

"You let go of my hand and walked away," Mary Lily said. "Three steps, a very brave walk. I ran into the house and told them to come and see, but when they came you would not do it again. Two days went by. On the third day you walked again. Since then, there is no stopping you. You go wherever you wish to go."

"I remember doing it," Olivia said. It was an old game she played with Mary Lily. Mary Lily would tell her things she did when she was an infant and she would pretend to have total recall of them. "You had on a blue-and-white-checked blouse and your Nocona boots."

"When I come home this afternoon I will take you to see the new waterfall," Mary Lily said. "They built a dam in the park and it made a waterfall. Everyone goes there now, to see the waterfall and watch the sun go down. Would you like to see it later?"

"If I get back. I have to spend the day getting registered for school. If I come back in time, we will." Olivia felt guilty. Already it was starting. If she loved them, they wanted to have her every minute. "I don't know when I'll be back," she added. "It might take a long time. I have to go to Northeastern and to Flaming Rainbow."

"Flaming Rainbow is the best," Crow put in. "They write about it all the time in the paper."

After breakfast Olivia dressed in her best skirt and blouse and walked out to her car to leave for town. Little Sun walked with her to her car. "This is a fine car you're driving," he said. "I haven't seen one like this."

"It's a German car, Granddaddy. It's my dad's car. He just let me use it for the summer."

"How much does this car cost?"

"Too much. You wouldn't want to know."

"Well, drive it carefully then. You have a rich life there. He gives you this fine car to drive and plenty of money."

"He doesn't want me to get hurt in a wreck. I have a nephew, Granddaddy. Did I tell you that? My half sister had a baby."

"You have a rich life there."

"I have a rich life here. I'm rich in riches. But they don't hug and kiss like you do. Their whole family is that way. Like they're afraid of each other."

"Maybe they are busy."

"They are. They lead a pretty hectic life."

"They are your people if they are busy. You are never still."

"I hope I don't forget how to love people. Well, I have to go. I really have to leave." She got into the car, and drove off with him watching her. But I have forgotten, she decided. All I do all the time is be jealous of everyone and everything. All I do is think bad things about people and be glad if they make bad grades or break up with their boyfriends. I don't want King and Jessie to be happy. I like to think they're stuck and can't get out. Well, I'll do better now that I'm home. I'll learn Navajo and maybe Spanish or German or French. Olivia stuck a CD of Madonna singing the score of the Blond Ambition tour into the CD player. She threw back her head and sang along as she cruised into town in the Mercedes.

It was nine-thirty when Olivia got to town, and the registrar's office at the college didn't open until ten, so she decided to go by The Shak and see what was going on. She parked the car a few doors from the restaurant and got out and stood on the sidewalk searching in her purse for some change for the parking meter. As she lifted her head to put the dime into the meter, she saw Bobby. He was walking toward her with his hands in the pockets of his chinos. He was wearing a blue shirt and he was smiling at her as if no time had passed since the cold November afternoon when they had sat in his car by Lake Wedington and she had broken his heart. Ruthless, and cold as ice, she had sat beside him and told him she was leaving. Now he was walking toward her as if the sadness and disappointment of that afternoon had never happened. *As if he loved her.* (Of course I would love to hurt him, she would know later. Of course I have to pay back anyone I love for my mother's death, wound them because she wounded me. Eye for eye, wound for wound, karma for karma. So if I take off my clothes and lie down beside a man and he makes me love him, then I must hate him for that love, despise him for making me need him, want to kill him because it would be easier to kill or die than to put up with being deserted. I CANNOT BEAR TO BE LEFT ALONE IN THE UNIVERSE, the baby Olivia was wailing, I CANNOT STAND TO BE ALONE, TO BE LEFT HERE TO DIE, TO BE DISSOLVED, TO GO BACK INTO NOTHINGNESS. WHERE ARE YOU? MOTHER, MOTHER, HOW COULD YOU LEAVE ME?)

"The piled grief scrambling like guilt to leave us," Olivia said to herself again as she saw Bobby. It was part of a poem her English teacher had given them the year before. It had struck her like an arrow to read that poem. She had read it over and over again. Had memorized it without trying.

Then he was there beside her, so close she could hear him breathing.

"How's it going?" he asked. "You look great, baby. You really look fine."

"I thought you were in Montana."

"I was, I came here because I heard you were coming. Listen, baby, I tried to call you back in March. I tried three or four times, but your machine said you were in Florida and I got pissed off and didn't leave a message. I figured you were with some guy. Anyway, I want you to know that."

"Okay. How was it in Montana? What did you do up there?"

"I told you when I talked to you. This guy Macalpin and his wife practically adopted me. We've been training cutting horses. He's got a big spread."

"Aren't you a little old to be adopted?"

"Not me, baby. I need all the help I can get. Hey, you want to eat breakfast with me? I'm starving. Come on, let's go eat." He reached down and took her elbow. He looked down into her eyes and the old stuff started happening. Right there, on the sidewalk in front of The Shak, with everyone who walked by watching, and the June heat falling all around them. In a moment, in the time it takes a nineteen-year-old heart to beat, Olivia was not alone anymore. She had been sixteen when she left Tahlequah. Now she was almost twenty and Bobby was twenty-two and nothing had changed between them. When he touched her arm it was hot hot light all along her arms and up and down her legs and in her pussy and in her breasts. It was all the moments they had spent alone on beds or in Bobby's car or in a tent beside the river or upon a blanket on the summer's grass. Am I awake or sleeping? Olivia wondered. Is this waking up or going back to sleep?

Bobby took her arm and led her into the café.

"So how are your rich relatives in Carolina?" he asked later. The waitress had brought them waffles and bacon and syrup. Fresh-squeezed orange juice and thick black coffee. Olivia poured syrup over her waffle and watched it soak in. "They're crazy," she said. "They all drink too much. My sister Jessie had a baby. She keeps breaking up and making up with this guy she married. He's our third cousin. She never should have married him. He's not a bad guy, he's just spoiled to death. They had this real cute little baby. They call him K.T. I just saw him. I went there before I came here. They were getting along okay this week. To tell the truth, it made me jealous. You look great, Bobby. You really do. You really look good."

"I'm doing great. This guy, Macalpin, and his wife were really good to me. I told them all about you. They knew your aunt, the one that killed herself. She and Macalpin used to teach together. They used to go someplace to teach in the summers. Some writer's camp." Bobby stopped, took a bite of his waffle. Then very very politely he lay his knife and fork across his plate and reached for Olivia's hand. "I miss you, baby. I been missing you every minute of every day. It's like missing you was part of my life."

"Don't tell me that. You've had fifty girls since me."

"No, I haven't."

"So what do you want to do?"

"I want to lie down with you."

"So do I. What time is it? Don't you want your waffle?"

"It's ten-fifteen. You want to go?"

"Okay. I've already eaten breakfast anyway. I just got this to keep you company. Where can we go?"

"We can go to my place. Dad moved into a house. He's living with this lady that runs the tourist bureau. Sharrene Barrett. You might know her son, Jimmy. He was in your class."

"He was a linebacker."

"That's the one. Olivia." He wiped his mouth with his napkin, then folded it and put it beside his plate. Everyone in The Shak was watching them but they didn't know or care.

"Yes."

"Let's get out of here."

"Okay." They stood up and Bobby put a ten-dollar bill on the table underneath the salt shaker and turned and spoke to the owner, who was standing beside the cash register. "We're going, Bill. I left some money on the table."

"Nice to see you," the owner said. "Glad you're back in town."

They walked out onto the sidewalk. The sun was blinding now, pouring down hydrogen and helium upon the earth, filling every corner with its bounty. Olivia and Bobby got into her car and the seat belts clamped down upon them and they began to drive down the sun-drenched streets, sunlight pouring down upon them and old sun burning in the engine of the car. "The old trailer's out in the yard beside the house," Bobby said. "I cleaned it up. I've been sleeping out there most of the time to stay out of Dad and Sharrene's way. You want to go out there? There isn't any air conditioning, but I've got a fan."

"That's fine. It doesn't matter. Anywhere you want to go. Tell me where to turn. Where are we going?"

"It's over behind the high school on Plum Street, over where Cindy Witt used to live. Go down Hill."

"I can't believe you're here. God, I was so glad to see you. I couldn't believe it when I saw you on the sidewalk."

"So what have you been doing in North Carolina?"

"Well, I haven't been fucking anybody, if that's what you mean. Have you got a rubber?"

"Yeah, I do." He reached over and put his hand on her thigh and he kept it there while she drove down Hill Street past the high school to Plum Street. "Hey, baby," Bobby said. "Remember that night we broke into the school and fixed that stuff on the computer? That was a night."

"I don't want to think about that, Bobby. That's behind me. This psychiatrist I went to told me not to worry about it. I was just doing what I had to do. I don't do anything like that anymore. I live intelligently now."

"That's it, baby. That white house with the truck in the driveway. See the old trailer. It looks pretty good, doesn't it?" Olivia parked the car behind the truck and turned off the ignition. Bobby got out and came around and opened the door for her and helped her out of the car and took her arm and they walked to the trailer and he opened the door and held it open for her. "Your pleasure, madam," he said. "What can we do to please you?"

In the back room of the trailer there was a mattress on the floor covered with quilts and piles of clothes and a suitcase and a saddle and a pair of boots with spurs. "I'm sorry about this mess," he said. "I was going to clean it up later."

"Who cares about that?" Olivia began to put the clothes in stacks on the floor. Bobby took the rest of the things and threw them into a corner and straightened up the quilts. He pushed the saddle to the side and set the boots beside it. Then he took Olivia's hand and they lay down together and began to remember how to love each other. Give in to it, Olivia told herself. It's only Bobby and he loves me. He has always loved me and he always will. He won't die or go away or think bad of me. It's Bobby and he belongs to me.

No guts, no glory, Bobby told himself. She couldn't hurt you any more than she already has. You might as well forget it and get laid. "I haven't been with anybody else," Olivia said. "I bet I forgot how."

"You'll remember. I love you, baby. I'll always love you. I'll love you till I die."

"How'd I do without this? How'd I leave you? Have you been all right? Are you okay?" She was stroking him with her hands, exploring every bone and crook and muscle of his body, finding all the places she had known. "Oh, Bobby, I'm so sorry. I've been so unhappy. I've been so lonely, so far from home."

"Hush up, baby. Let me come into you. Let me love you. Just let me love you."

"It's been so long. Oh, God, it's been so long." It had been a long time. Once she had done it with an SAE who took her home afterward and never called her up again. And once with a boy who got scared and couldn't get a hard-on after they took off their clothes in a hotel room. After that second try she gave up on sex and decided to devote herself to school instead. Only she hadn't been able to devote herself to school. All her passion and nineteen-year-old wonder had turned into jealousy and nervousness and spite.

"So what do you want old Mack to teach you? How to talk Navajo or how to write it? I know how to talk it. I could talk it with you. Kayo had a hand out at Baron Fork who was Navajo. God, he was a tough bastard. He was a cuttin' fool. He could back a horse with his knees." Bobby was sitting on the side of the mattress looking down at her. He was trying to figure out a way to give her the ring but he couldn't decide what to do. I could wait until tonight, he was thinking. Until it's dark. Chicken!

"I want to learn to write it. You should, too. It might really be a high-paying job one of these days. They want to translate scientific ideas into Navajo and hide them in computers."

"It sounds pretty stupid to me. There're thousands of broke Indians who speak Navajo. They could get any one of them to tell them what it says. It's the biggest tribe. Didn't you ever go to the powwows in Tulsa? There're more Navajos than any other tribe." He pulled a cigarette out of the pocket of a shirt lying on the floor and lit it. The smoke curled up to meet the ceiling of the trailer. "I got my G.E.D. Did I tell you that? I'm going to college. Can you imagine that? Old Bobby signed up to be a college student."

"I'm glad. That's great. That's wonderful."

"Yeah, Tom and Sherrill talked me into it. Hell, I did great on the tests. I was so busy rodeoing when I was young I didn't pay any attention to school."

"Bobby?"

"Yes."

"Put that cigarette out and get back in bed, will you? I'm not through with you."

"You aren't?"

"No, I'm not. And I don't want to die from lung cancer if you don't mind too much. I want to die from making love to you." Then she pulled him back onto the mattress and began to count his vertebrae with her fingers. "Uno, dos, tres," she began, "quatro, cinco, seis, siete."

"You going Mexican on me?" he said. "You turning into a señorita? First Navajo, and now Mexican."

A long time later they woke up in each other's arms. It was four o'clock in the afternoon. "I have to go by the university and register for my classes," Olivia said. "Get dressed. I can still make it if I hurry."

"Maybe I'll sign up, too. Hell, I've got to start somewhere. You think they'd let me?"

"Sure they will." She pulled on her underpants and skirt, then began searching for her bra. She found it, then sank back onto the bed. "Well, I've got two more days. Wait until tomorrow morning and we'll do it then. If you're serious. We'll go in the morning and I'll show you how. Besides, you'll have to send for the papers. You have to have your birth certificate and all sorts of things."

"Maybe I shouldn't do it."

"Of course you should. It's a wonderful idea. Do you have any money?"

"I've got plenty. I need to get a job for the summer, though. If I'm going to stay here. I thought I could get something in construction. They're finishing the turnpike. It's going to be great. Have you seen it?"

"No." Olivia sank back into a pile of pillows. Inside them was an old brown shirt of Bobby's. It was so soft and old and dear, so much a part of him. She pulled it onto her chest. The heart was going out of the day. Fear was beating on the windows. Fear was seeping in. "Bobby, what's going to happen now? What's going to happen to us?"

The fear slid around the room, curled up around the ceiling, traced the faint smell of cigarette smoke, doused the light. "I guess we'll be together for a while and then you'll break my heart." He was dressing now. Pulling on his pants and then his socks and boots. He bent over to undo the spurs and remove them.

"I don't want to break your heart. I want to love you." Olivia put her face down into her hands and began to cry. He sat back down on the bed and patted her on the shoulder. Then he pulled her into his arms and lay down upon the mattress and held her while she cried.

"There's nothing to cry about. You got me, baby. Anything you want I'll do it. I'll go to school or work. Anything you want. I told Tom when I was leaving. She's got me, Tom. I'll do anything for her. I'll let her call the shots."

"Just love me." She wept into his shoulder, but it was subsiding. "The world is a terrible scary place. People lie and cheat and steal and shoot each other and blow each other up. This psychiatrist I had for a while last fall. She's this wonderful lady. I shouldn't have quit going to her but I was worried about Dad spending all that money. She's like the best mother you could ever imagine having. I would just walk into her office and sit down on the floor and start bawling. Well, I still call her up. I might call her up this afternoon. Anyway, I told her about you and she said it sounded like a healthy relationship. She was surprised I'd leave it to come to Charlotte and try to get Dad to love me. She said it was terrible not to have a boyfriend or ever get laid. She thinks people ought to have love. No matter how hard it is to get or how much trouble it is to keep it. I don't want to leave you ever again. I don't want to leave you now. I'm afraid to even leave this trailer."

"Well, we better go over to the house and call your Aunt Lily. I don't want her getting mad at me the first day we're together."

"Are we together?" She sat up now, still holding on to him, pulling him up with her. "Are we together, Bobby? Is that what this means?"

"I'm yours, baby. If you want me, you can have me." If I can get her in the house I can get out the ring, he was thinking. If I can ever get her out of this trailer. He moved to disengage himself from her, but very very carefully and slowly. He had seen Olivia get sad before and it scared him. He had spent too much time on horses not to take it seriously when an animal got frightened.

They left the trailer and went into the house and Olivia called Mary Lily and told her she was with Bobby and that she would be home by dark. "I guess I better go back and spend some time with them," she said. "You can come eat supper with us if you like."

"You want me to?"

"Yes, if you want to. They like you, Bobby. My folks think you're great."

"You think they'd let you sleep here with me? We could tell them we have to go to college in the morning." He laughed. He was putting a piece of sliced cheese between two pieces of white bread. He added mustard and mayonnaise and held it out to her. "Eat this. You haven't had anything to eat all day."

"I guess I better stay out there tonight. But listen. Tomorrow night I probably can. I'll tell Crow and Little Sun I'm staying with a girlfriend. Mary Lily doesn't care, but they do."

"I hate for you to lie to them. Don't go lying to them, Olivia."

"Well, it's not really a lie. I mean, they know I'm lying. It's just to be polite."

"Whatever you say. They're your folks. Go on, eat that sandwich. I'll make myself another one." They took the sandwiches and two Cokes and went out and got into Olivia's car and she drove back downtown and left Bobby at his pickup and he followed her out to the farm. Every few minutes he would look inside the glove compartment at the sack that held the box that held the ring but he couldn't get up the nerve to touch it. Tomorrow, he decided. I'll give it to her tomorrow night.

Later that night, after they had gone out to the farm and eaten with Olivia's folks and then sat out in the yard talking to Crow and Little Sun while Mary Lily did the dishes. After they had kissed goodnight a dozen times and Bobby had driven away and left her. After he was gone, promising to come back at nine in the morning to drive her to the college, after he was gone and she was alone with the night and the stars and her sleeping grandparents and Mary Lily reading a *New Woman* magazine she had bought at IGA. After all of that, the fear returned and Olivia picked up the phone and called the psychiatrist at Chapel Hill. "I hate to call you at home," she began. "But something important has happened. Something happened I have to talk about. You told me if I ever got the idea in my head that I wanted to be dead to call you up. Well, I've got it. I was so happy today that when I stopped being happy I was so unhappy. I'm at home, in Oklahoma. I saw Bobby. I spent the afternoon with him. Now it's night. I don't know what to do, Doctor Carlyn. I don't know what I'm supposed to do next."

"Keep talking to me. I'm glad to hear from you. I was sorry you stopped coming, Olivia. I was hoping you'd come back."

"I couldn't. It cost too much. Dad's so worried about money, Doctor Carlyn. He won't admit it, but it worries him to death."

"Start at the beginning. Start talking. Where are you exactly? Tell me where you are."

Then Olivia talked for sixty minutes, telling the doctor about her year in school and Jessie's baby and coming to Tahlequah and what it had felt like to enter the house where she had lived and seeing Bobby and making love to him and crying afterward and how terrible it was when they were eating dinner with her grandparents and how she kept knowing he was about to leave. "Ever since we woke up this afternoon, I kept thinking, Now he's leaving. Now he'll die in a car crash. Now he'll go back to Montana. I bet he'll never get into college and he'll get mad at me for that. It's starting to rain," she said at last. It was eleven-thirty. They had been on the phone for an hour. Three times Mary Lily had come into the kitchen to see if Olivia was all right. Go away, Olivia had said to her. This is an important call. Leave me alone. Go away. "It's probably going to rain all night. I can hear it on the trees. I hear the raindrops hitting every leaf. I used to believe trees were alive. These trees around this house. These trees know me. They were here when I was born."

"Does the rain bother you?"

"Sometimes. When I'm alone. I think it hurts the horses to be out in it. I think they will be cold."

"Your mother died, Olivia. You think you will be cold and disappear and die. When you get upset or when it gets cold or wet, you think you are alone. You think you will be absorbed back into nothingness because your mother wasn't there to hold you when you were born. But you aren't alone. You have me and you have Bobby and your family there and your folks in North Carolina and your sister. You're talking on the phone to me and you're in that house where you were kept safe for sixteen years. Listen to me, honey. You're okay. It's only raining. Rain is fine. We're made of water. Olivia."

"Yes, ma'am."

"I want you to call me back in the morning. Go get a pencil and write down some numbers I'm going to give you. I'm going to find you someone to see up there. I have a friend in Tulsa you can see. A good man."

"Okay. I got a pencil. Tell them to me." Doctor Carlyn gave her the phone numbers, then she spoke in a very quiet voice.

"Is your aunt Mary Lily there?"

"Yes."

"Is she still awake?"

"I think so."

"Go tell her that you love her. Thank her for loving you. You can learn how to love, Olivia. You can learn to be in charge of love. When you're the one who gives it, you have an unlimited supply. Could you believe that, honey? Just for tonight."

"If you say so. If you want me to. Only I can't see how I can stay with Bobby. It seems like so many things can happen. How can we figure all this out?"

"That's what time is for, Olivia. This is only the beginning. Go tell your aunt you love her. Sleep with her again if you like. You have my permission to be twelve years old tonight."

"Okay. I will, that's good. Thanks an awful lot, Doctor Carlyn. Thanks for talking to me." Then Olivia hung up the phone and went into Mary Lily's room. Mary Lily was curled up on her side with her face toward the door, wide awake and worrying about her. "Scoot over," Olivia said. "I don't want to be alone tonight. I don't ever want to sleep alone again until I die. I'm sick and tired of being all alone." Mary Lily rolled over and Olivia got in beside her and put her arms around her and kissed her on the forehead and mouth and cheeks and then curled up beside her and fell asleep. Outside the rain was falling harder. A long wet front had moved in from the west and was pouring rain down upon the part of Oklahoma called Green Country. The parched earth and rocky soil and moss and tree roots and rusty-colored fields and creeks and gardens and rivers began to fill with water. Behind the clouds the moon moved ever eastward through the sky.

Every living thing begins with water, Olivia was thinking. Perhaps water is like time — it's our metaphor for time — only time isn't real and water is — water carries the earth and serves it — makes the earth live.

She fell asleep thinking things she had learned in this house — things she had forgotten in the schools of North Carolina.

CHAPTER 19

GO over this again," Bobby said. It was the next afternoon. The ring was still in the glove compartment. Bobby and Olivia were barreling down the highway in the truck. They had given up on Flaming Rainbow and gone on and registered at Northeastern. Olivia had signed up for classes in Navajo and anthropology and they had started the wheels in motion to have Bobby registered as a freshman. Tom Macalpin had been on the phone all morning to the registrar and the chairman of the English Department and Bobby was going to be able to start on Monday as a special student until the paperwork was done.

Olivia had called Dr. Carlyn again and had the name of a psychiatrist in Tulsa. "Be sure and call him," Dr. Carlyn said. "It won't be easy to get an appointment, so go on and make the call. You'll like this man, Olivia. He's a friend of mine."

"Okay. I will. I really will. As soon as I have time."

"Do it today. Call and get an appointment set up."

"Can I call you too? Can I talk to you again?"

"Of course. But make an appointment with Charlie."

"I will. I really will." Olivia hung up the phone and felt for a moment strangely dissatisfied, as though she should not have hung up, as though there were things yet to say. Charlie, she decided. Charlie Coder. Charlie. Well, I will call him. It isn't far to Tulsa. We could go and see the Drillers play and get some ice cream in those little hats.

"Come on," Bobby called. "Come on, baby, let's get out in the country. I got to break into this school business easy. Let's get out to some fresh air."

Then they had eaten sub sandwiches for lunch and gone out to Olivia's farm and dug her old boots and jeans out of a storage chest. Now it was three in the afternoon and they were on their way to Baron Fork to go riding. "Go over that again," Bobby was saying. "This doctor told you because your mother died you're afraid to sleep by yourself? That's good luck for me, isn't it?" His hand was on her thigh. She was sitting so close to him he could hardly drive. The glove compartment was twelve inches from his hand. All he had to do was open it and reach inside. No, he decided, you better wait. "You got the softest skin in the world," he said. "I love you, baby. I been missing you so much. It's like part of me was cut away. You know what Tom said? He said I was the most in love of any man he'd ever seen. I told you he knew your aunt, didn't I? A long time before he married Sherrill."

"Do you think he was her boyfriend? There's a cowboy in one of her books that has an affair with the main character. He sounds like that guy."

"I don't think so. He wouldn't have been talking about her in front of Sherrill. Sherrill's the most jealous woman you ever saw in your life." Bobby patted Olivia's thigh. Olivia leaned her face into his shirt sleeve. If happiness had a smell, she decided, it would smell like this, soap powder and ironed starch and the sweet smell of Bobby's skin. "I want you so much it hurts," she said. "Stop this truck and let's do it on the highway."

"On the four-lane?"

"Yes." He pulled the truck over to the shoulder of the road and turned off the ignition. He pulled her body into his and kissed her on the mouth. For several minutes he kissed her as hard as he could. Then they both started giggling.

"It's probably against the law," Olivia said. "We might get arrested."

"I can just see it in the paper. 'Ex-fullback and cheerleader caught on the highway in the middle of the afternoon. Olivia and Bobby are at it again.'"

"Her psychiatrist said it was okay. Listen, Bobby, you can go on now. You can start driving." She slipped back over to her side of the seat and

adjusted her blouse. She rolled down the window and stuck her arm
out into the soft June air. "We're spinning through space," she began.
"Oh, God, I saw this movie in Carolina. Called *The Meaning of Life*. It's
hilarious. This English guy climbs out of a refrigerator. He's trying to get
this lady to donate her kidneys. They've already killed her husband taking his. It's called 'Live Donor Transplant.' It's hilarious. Anyway, he
climbs out of the refrigerator and starts singing this song. Jessie and I
memorized it last year. It goes, 'Just remember that you're standing on a
planet that's evolving and revolving at ten thousand miles an hour. It's
orbiting at ninety miles a second, so it's reckoned, the sun that is the
source of all our power. The sun and you and me and all the stars that
we can see, are moving at a billion miles an hour.' " Olivia was singing
at the top of her lungs, so happy she could barely contain it.

"I bought you something in Montana," Bobby said. "But I'm afraid
to give it to you."

"Why?"

"Because I'm afraid you won't like it."

"What is it then?"

"I wish I hadn't brought it up." He held on to the steering wheel
with both hands. He looked straight ahead. "Okay, look in the glove
compartment. It's in the sack in a box. See that package there?"

"Morrell's Jewels and Furs?"

"Yeah. Go on. Open it. I don't care if you don't like it."

Olivia took the ring box out of the sack. Then, very, very carefully
she opened it. "Oh, Bobby. Oh, God, what is this? I don't believe it.
This is for me?"

"If you want it. It's to ask you to marry me. Will you marry me? I
want you to marry me. I'll work for you and go to school. I'll take care
of you my whole life. It's all I have to offer, Olivia. Just what you see.
Well, what do you think?"

"I think it's the most beautiful ring I've ever seen in my life. I love
it." She lifted out the ring and put it on her finger.

"Do you want to marry me?"

"I want to. You know I want to. But I don't know if I can. We're not
old enough to get married. People our age can't get married, just like
that."

"If they love each other, they can."

"I'll be engaged to you. Is that enough? Because I love you, Bobby. And I love this ring."

"Then keep on wearing it. Hell, it cost a month's wages, but if I win the Futurity in Fort Worth it'll pay for that and lots of other things. I'm going to ride this great mare of Tom's. I trained her. She's good enough. I promised Tom I'd meet him there in December. Hell, you can go with me and meet them. They'd love to meet you. When you get time you ought to read Tom's books. I've got them all in the trailer. He gave me a whole set of them."

"I want to wear this ring, Bobby. And I want to be your girl. But I don't know about getting married. It's going to be a long time before I want to do that. Does that make you mad? Are you mad at me?"

"No. Hell, no. Come over here. Come over close to me." He pulled her to his side and they drove the rest of the way to Baron Fork plastered to each other's sides. Every now and then Olivia would hold the ring up into the air and look at it, then fold her hand back down into her lap. She felt guilty for wearing it, strange and compromised and guilty. Dad would die if he knew this was going on, she was thinking. Andria'd have something cynical to say. Get out of the Romance Novel section. That's what she says about anyone who's in love. But I don't care. He's mine, he's my boyfriend. I love him. I'm sick of being lonely. I'm sick of being alone all the time. I bet Andria'd change her mind in a heartbeat if Bland Neville asked her to go steady. She's just waiting for someone with some money. Well, Bobby will have money someday. Money didn't do me any good in Chapel Hill. That's the most miserable I've ever been in all my life.

They turned off at the entrance to the lake and drove down a gravel road to the high white fences of Baron Fork Ranch, a six-thousand-acre horse farm owned by an absentee landlord from New York State. The place was managed by Bobby's uncle Kayo, and, ever since they were young teenagers, Bobby and Olivia had had the run of it. The first time they had made love was in the master bedroom of the Baron Fork river house on the Illinois River. "What's this horse you want me to see?" Olivia asked.

"Studley. He's a beauty. He's part Thoroughbred. His great-grandfather was Native Dancer. Kayo wants to show him next month in

Oklahoma City, so I've got to start working with him. Hell, Kayo'll have a fit when he finds out I'm going to college. He might not let me ride in the show if he thinks that would stand in my way."

"You've got enough time to do both things. If you don't go out drinking beer at night, you'd have time to do everything you want to. You can't drink if you want to succeed, Bobby. I got into drinking a lot the last couple of months at school. Well, I'm through with all that. All I want to do is get a future going for myself."

"I hope it includes me."

"It does. I've got this ring on, don't I?"

"I want you to meet Sherrill someday, baby. I think you'd really like each other. She won the women's reining last year in Denver. Well, no one's better than you when you want to be. You could have been a star if you'd stuck with horses."

"I still like horses. You just wait. I didn't lose anything. You get me a horse to ride and we'll see. Is Straw Girl still out here?"

"She sure is. I bet she'll go crazy when she smells you. You two always did get along."

They had come to a voice-activated gate that led to the barns and Bobby called out a code and the gate opened and they drove through. Spread out before them were the pastures and hills and white fences and barns of a small empire. They parked the truck by the first barn and went inside to find Kayo.

Half an hour later they were in an indoor ring with four steers and a radio playing country music. Olivia was sitting on the fence, her boots tucked under a rail, and Bobby was on the stallion, Studley, teaching him to work the cows. Uncle Kayo was astride a mare, backed into a corner to be out of the way.

"Watch him, Bobby," Kayo was saying. "See how he keeps trying to get on top of the cow. Don't let him do that. Ride him hard. He can take it. That's a boy."

"Give me a turn," Olivia said. "I want to ride."

Kayo walked the mare over to the fence and dismounted and adjusted the stirrups and gave her a leg up. Then Olivia pulled herself up into the saddle and began to laugh. "Goddamn," she said. "I haven't been on a real horse in two years. You ought to see what they ride at my dad's." She pulled herself up out of her waist and dug in with her knees. Then Bobby moved to the side of the corral and Olivia began to work a cow.

"That's cuttin'," Kayo said. "Goddamn, I'd forgotten how that girl can ride. Shit, Bobby, let's let her ride Studley in Oklahoma City."

"Stop buttering me up," Olivia giggled, and backed the mare into a little pirouette. Then made her kneel.

"Try reining," Kayo called out. "Let's see if you still know how to rein."

Olivia went through a reining technique, then rode over to Bobby. "It's too pretty to stay in here all day. Let's ride down to the river. Can we take them on a trail ride, Kayo?"

"You can take the mare, but leave Studley here. If he got hurt it'd be hell to pay. His great-grandfather was Native Dancer."

Bobby saddled a gelding and they left the corrals and rode back into the fields behind the barns. As soon as they were out of sight of Kayo they began to gallop toward the river. Olivia forgot everything now, now it was only horse and wind and sky, blue flowers in the fields, crystals, starcarbon, oxygen, and flying. A thousand times she and Bobby had ridden these fields together. Down the pastures to the woods and through the paths to the river.

When they got to the main river house, they tied the horses to a post and went up onto the porch and lay down on two of the dusty recliners. "How did I go and leave you?" she said. "If I did it once, I might do it again. Aren't you afraid of that, Bobby? Aren't you afraid I'll break your heart?"

"No guts, no glory. Well, maybe you will. At least I have today."

"How did I use to keep from getting pregnant. I shudder when I think about the things we did."

"You used to make me take off the rubbers. You always made me take them off."

"I had that stupid cream I got at the drugstore. Who knows, maybe I'm one of those people who can't get pregnant."

"Don't say that. I want us to have some babies. Someday we'll want some babies."

"Well, it won't be until I'm thirty years old, I can tell you that. At least thirty. I'll go to Planned Parenthood tomorrow and get some pills.

It's easy to get on the pill. I should have gone today." She sat up. The sun was getting low in the sky. They needed to be starting back.

"You know what I was thinking about," Bobby said. "I was thinking about this story Tom told me about this guy named Aeneas. He was this hero who wants to find this golden bough so he can go down to the underworld and come back safely. Well, he goes through all this stuff to find the golden bough and when he gets it, you know what he wants it for?"

"No. What?"

"He wants to go down there and get a girl and bring her back with him. All this stuff he was doing was just for a girl. This golden bough is so special that the only one that can pick it has to be a hero, like a great quarterback or a pitcher."

"Or a Junior Cutting Champion. Like you, Bobby. Someone like you."

"I don't know about all that, but I knew that story was right on. This guy Virgil that wrote it lived about three thousand years ago, maybe more. But it was the same way then. The way I feel about you."

"You are the most romantic person I've ever known. You know that."

"Romance me this then," he said and lay down on top of her and pinned her to the chair. "Romance me those pants off."

"Let's go inside then. I'm too old to make love on the porch. Let's go in the bedroom if you want to get serious about romance. It means Roman, by the way, did you know that? It's about being Romanesque. It doesn't have a thing to do with fucking."

It was late when she got home that night. Mary Lily was sitting in a chaise reading a Harlequin Romance called *Possessed by Love*.

"We went on and ate," she said. "I didn't know where you were and some woman's been calling you from the school. I wrote the name down on the pad. A Mrs. Jones, she's going to be one of your teachers. They changed the place where they're going to have the class."

"Bobby asked me to marry him."

"What did you say?" Mary Lily put the book down on the table and heaved herself up into a standing position.

"Well, you want to see the ring?"

"He gave you an engagement ring?"

"Here it is. Look at it." Olivia held out her hand and Mary Lily took it and looked a long time at the diamond. "It's pretty," she said. "But it's sort of plain, isn't it?"

"I might marry him some day, but, don't worry, it will be a long time. Anyway, I'm going to wear the ring and he's going to college with me. I want to be happy, Auntie Lily. I haven't been happy in a long time. I've been so lonely. I've been very, very lonely and sad. I had a horrible time up there, to tell the truth. I can't believe I stayed." She turned a long thoughtful face to her aunt, the hand with the ring still outstretched before her.

"Oh, honey, don't tell me that. We missed you so much. We suffered to have you gone but I did it because I thought it was the best for you."

"We don't know what we're doing half the time, do we? I think most of the time we just knock around and don't know what the hell we're doing. You want to sleep with me again? Come and sleep with me. I'm tired of being alone. I want someone to be in bed with me."

"If you want me to. Go on in. I'll be right behind you." Then they turned off the lights and put the animals outside and climbed into the jungle sheets and went to sleep.

The earth held its orbit. Gravity and electromagnetism and the weak and strong forces and the vastness of dreams held Tahlequah in its place and the night passed.

CHAPTER 20

BOSTON, Massachusetts. Helen had found a story that morning in a box of letters and receipts for repairs Anna had had done on her house in the mountains the year she left New York. The year she got sick, Helen thought, brushing her finger across the date on the story. The endocrine and the immune system are the same. That's what Doctor Jains told us at that party. Anna knew all about medicine and science but she didn't know about herself. Why didn't she marry Philip? Why didn't she go on and be happy? Because happiness can't be based on someone else's misery, but it can. I'm happy and I'm making Spencer unhappy by being here. No, I'm not. He's happy as he can be down there in Charlotte hating me and being a martyr and having everyone on his side.

"What are you reading?" Mike had come in without her hearing him. He threw his coat over a chair and leaned down and kissed her. "What'd you find?"

"This story. It was in a box of things for the income tax. You want to read it?"

"No. Finish it. I want to take a shower before dinner." He kissed her again and disappeared down the hall to the bedroom. Helen settled back down against the soft pillows and kept on reading. Ever since she was in the first grade she had been reading things that Anna wrote. Everyone had thought it was a joke when Anna made her the executor, but Anna had known what she was doing. Helen was her oldest fan, the one who knew where the dreams came from.

She began in the middle of a paragraph.

So I got on the Concorde and flew to New York that morning and went to a hotel and waited for him. I had all the luggage from Greece and the box with cowbells and the rocks from Delphi and all the notebooks. I put on the orange dress I bought in Athens and when he came we ordered wine and made love and were sad. What else is there to say about love? It makes you sad. It isn't like friendship or knowledge or fun. It isn't fun, even when it pretends to be. It's about conquest and being conquered, about pregnancy and the death of the self. The Procrustean bed. Nothing is forever and relationships don't work. That's how cynical I have become. And none of this will change a thing. I found my true love and I cannot have him. It's as simple as that, and Sappho knew it and Millay knew it and Emily in her tower knew it and when that happens, it's over. There may be a personality type that longs to inhabit a tragedy. So be it.

So it was over, but I got on the Concorde and flew to New York and fucked him anyway.

"This is unhappiness she is describing." Helen had followed Mike into the bathroom and was sitting on the side of the bathtub watching him shave. "Nothing but unhappiness. I used to think Anna's life was so exotic. I used to think she was living in some perfect world and that I had been left in Charlotte to do the work. Well, it was work, being married to Spencer. It was work trying to cheer him up. Listen to this." She looked down at the papers she was holding.

I had plans to hear the London Philharmonic that night. They were playing the ninth. Robert was going with me, I think, or maybe Mick. Anyway, I said, maybe I'll come by New York on my way home. I'm thinking about it. And he said, Come here, Anna. Please come here. So I got on the Concorde and went to meet him. As soon as I got on the plane, I began to drink champagne. I was drunk by the time I got to JFK and took the free helicopter ride into the city. What a stupid thing to do. It was crowded and uncomfortable and I ended up standing out on the street for thirty minutes trying to catch a taxi.

What else? It was a gorgeous day. A fine fall day. I can't think when the city looked so beautiful to me, although, now, the whole city was only him. He was every inch of pavement. Every molecule, animate and inanimate, was my love for him, his love for me, our tragic affection and scattered dream.

He came to the hotel and we lay down on the bed and I gave him one of the bells. One small bell from a chain of them. The rest of them are hanging in the apple trees in the mountains. Somewhere, if the leather hasn't shredded yet, those bells are ringing, Greece and those lovely weeks in the Peloponnese and coming home and touching him.

"She could wield the language." Mike put up the razor and stepped into the shower and turned on the water. "Get in. Come in with me."

"No. I'll get my hair wet. Well, I'll go put this up." Helen walked into the breakfast room. She stopped for a minute to inspect a vase of lilies that were losing petals. They might do another day. She leaned into the center of one, the vibrant red of the stamen. If you get it on you, you are stained for life; she had read that somewhere in Anna's papers. What am I doing here? Helen thought. How dare I be so happy? Living in Boston, Massachusetts, with an Irish poet, as though it were a perfectly normal thing to do, as though I have a right to do it.

The phone was ringing. Helen let it ring four times, then picked it up. It was her son, Lynley, calling from Charlotte, wanting to know where she had put his fencing foils. "I think they're in the attic," she said. "I put all that stuff up there because you said you weren't going to use it anymore. Ask your daddy. He helped me carry all that stuff up to the attic. The ornate swords are in the umbrella stand. You said I could leave them there for the little children. You know, the ones with pretty handles. Where are you, Lynley? How are things? I've been missing you."

"I need the foils for a play they're doing at the Little Theater. Molly Harrison called and asked to borrow them."

"Are you going out with her again?"

"No, she just wants to borrow the foils. Well, I better run."

"I miss you, Lynley. I've been hoping you'd call."

"I'm fine. See you later then." He hung up the phone without giving her time to reply. Helen bit her lip, then picked up Anna's story and carried it into the crowded bedroom that was her office and put a paper clip on it and dropped it into a box marked "Unpublished, Don't Know What to Do With." Then she went back into her bedroom and took off her clothes and climbed into the gray silk sheets of her adulterous bed and waited for her lover to come to her from his bath.

It was later that afternoon.

"My New York agent called today to tell me about an offer." Mike was ladling Hungarian goulash onto a plate for Helen. He had been cooking it all afternoon, teaching her how. The table was set, candles were lit, the fading lilies threw their shadows upon the wall.

"What was it for?"

"A novel. I haven't written one in years. Seems an editor at Random House found an old one of mine somewhere and wanted to see if he could stir me up to write another."

"For a lot of money?"

"A hundred thousand maybe." He handed her the plate and she smiled, then she giggled.

"That's a lot of money."

"I would do it if I knew a thing to write about. It's such a tedious undertaking. If I took it on, would you mind?"

"No, of course not. I don't care what you do if you keep on loving me. And if you cook." She giggled again. "I cooked so many meals for so many years. Now I am forgetting how. How long have I been here, Mike?"

"It will be two years soon. It doesn't seem like it, does it?"

"No. It would make up for not letting them make that movie out of Anna's stories. It's almost the same amount of money, isn't it?"

"I might do it. If I can think of a story."

"I think you should. How would they pay you?"

"Fifty for signing. Sight unseen. Not bad, huh?"

"Lynley called me again. He didn't apologize for hanging up and I didn't say anything about it. But it was better, I think."

"What did he want?"

"He wanted to tell me he ate dinner with Daniel and Olivia and Niall last night. Olivia is home and she and Daniel are going to New Orleans to see the baby. Daniel's pouting because Jessie won't bring the baby there but I guess he's giving up now. Anyway, Olivia is going back to Tahlequah to spend the summer with her folks. My family! When I'm there I take it for granted, the things they do, the nutty things they do, and their tempers and their red hair. Now, when they call me up, I think it's some sort of soap opera. I used to help do it." She looked down. "Only I'm a lead character now, I guess. Even if I stopped getting pregnant every day."

"They have a lot of energy."

"They never sit still. There are only two or three people in the whole family who ever sit still. I can sit still. I am very proud of that. At least I don't get up and pace around the room."

"You pace, in your head."

"I do, don't I?"

"Yes you do. Best to keep you busy. We could get over to the university in time to see a movie if you liked. There's a Chinese film I've been waiting to see. *The Yellow Earth*. Everyone says it's spectacular."

"Maybe it would give you an idea for a novel."

"It might. You can't tell where such things will come from."

The auditorium was packed. Helen and Mike found seats in the back and settled down. All around them students were climbing over each other and stacking books on the floor and handing each other cookies and bars of candy. Finally, the lights went out and the film came on. A movie about pre-Communist China, about deprivation and courage, about arranged marriages and dangerous love, about a world as tight and old and destructive as the ones in which Helen and Mike had been raised. The panoramic views of the yellow hills of central China dazzled the eye, then the camera turned to the huts of the Chinese peasants, with their shining black hair and their shining eyes, their desolation and dark culture and religion-ridden lives. Helen's hand found Mike's. She held on to him for dear life. Her body had been sold like that, into marriage and endless childbirth, into the death of possibility. She looked around her in the darkened auditorium. The spoiled young women of the 1990s were all around her, in their messy clothes, with their backpacks and their dissatisfactions. I was having my third child by the time I was that age, Helen thought. DeDe, Kenny, Lynley. They hate me now. They think I'm insane. I guess I am insane. I ran away from my responsibilities. Nothing will save me now and I don't care. Great lovers lie in hell. I'll lie in hell with him. I'm never going back, not for a moment. They can do anything they want to. They can steal everything I have. They can do anything, if only my children didn't hate me. I don't want them to hate me. I wish they'd come and visit.

"Are you okay?" Mike whispered into her ear. He pulled her arm closer to his. She was going down. He could feel it across a room, when the enormity of what they had done dawned on her. "You want to leave?"

"No. I'm fine. Shhhhh, they'll get mad if you talk in here." She lay her head upon his arm. The movie continued. The lovers were caught and then destroyed. The landscapes claimed their victims. The lights came on. The students gathered up their backpacks and their books and toggle coats. They began to file out of the auditorium. Helen and Mike filed out after them. They walked out into the cool night air and began to walk in the direction of the apartment. When they were out of sight of the students, Helen took his hand and held it as they walked.

"It was a beautiful movie," she said. "I can't believe they have cameras that can make the mountains seem like they are in the room. Even on that little screen."

"The youth group of the Chinese Communist Cinema Production Company made the film. It was beautiful, wasn't it? Disturbing."

"It was like that in Charlotte. Just like that."

"It was like that in Dublin. It is like that in most of the world."

"Will things ever change?"

"If the young have their way. My students are a pretty canny lot. They see through most of the cant, but they have bought another load that's almost worse. Most of them live off their parents until they're thirty years old. It never ceases to amaze me. Still . . ."

"Still what?"

"They're just striving to find a way to live like all people do. Trying to figure it out and find some safety and a place to love."

"Do they find it?"

"Not many of them." They had come to their apartment building and went inside and went up to their apartment and Helen made hot chocolate and got out vanilla wafers and they ate and drank and then went into the bedroom. "I love you," Helen said. "It's the first time in my life I have even begun to know who I am. Some days I know. I look around and all the Helens I used to be seem like counterfeits and I can't believe I inhabited them. On other days it's this Helen who seems a dream."

"Come here to me. Get closer. It's only tonight, Helen. We don't have to live in any other moment. Only this one, you and I together." He began to move his hand up and down her soft back, past the roll of fat around her waist and the soft hips and the loins that had given birth five times and still were beautiful and tender. He took off her gown and her underpants and turned off the light and began to move his lips across the skin of her stomach. She was so responsive. He had never touched a woman who was so responsive. He could make her come in thirty seconds and he gloried in it and he did it.

*   *   *

In Charlotte, Helen's brothers were discussing children.

"The hostage factor," Niall was saying to Daniel. "Giving hostages to fortune."

"I've never really understood that," Daniel answered. "Explain that to me."

"Well, as far as I can tell from observation, it's this. You can bear misfortune or bad luck or even death. You either fix it or you bear it, but when it is your children, or in my case, my brothers and sisters, it isn't that easy. When they suffer, you can't fix it and you can't bear it, and you are doomed to watch it."

"Niall, you know what's wrong with you?"

"What's that, baby brother?"

"You say *doomed* too much. It's from reading those goddamn musty books when you could be watching television."

"You're probably right. No one on television is doomed. Doom is not a word they understand, or even death, really, unless it's caused by murder."

"Let's get a brandy and go sit on the porch for a while."

"Why not? If you insist, I might. E. A. Robinson."

"And quit quoting poets, while you're at it. Use your own words when you want to make a point."

" 'The bird is on the wing,' the poet said, and the poet was right. That's also called getting the last word. Pour the brandy, since we're doomed to drink." They took the brandies and went out onto the porch to watch the constellations in the cool night air.

CHAPTER 21

TAHLEQUAH, Oklahoma. Olivia's classes began at ten. On the third day she got out of bed early and tiptoed around trying not to wake Bobby. "I went to The Shak for breakfast," she wrote in a note.

Meet me by the statue of Sequoyah at twelve-fifteen and don't worry about anything. You'll get a job and you'll be great in school. There are free tutors in everything. Go meet them. It creates jobs to use them. It keeps graduate students off the streets. Love, Olivia.

P.S. Remember I have to go to Tulsa tomorrow afternoon to see that shrink. You don't have to go unless you want to. I act funny when I've been talking to shrinks. You might not want to be around me right after I talk to one. Doctor Carlyn used to tell me jokes, these stupid jokes I can't stop thinking about. About cows, for God's sake.

It was eight-thirty when Olivia got to The Shak. There was a new car parked by the front door. A red MG with Arkansas license plates and two straw hats piled in the backseat. The fender of the car was plastered with bumper stickers. Every politically correct stance of the last five years was represented.

I bet it's someone from Fayetteville, Olivia decided. Someone coming to write about the Cherokees. This is the time of year when they start showing up.

She opened the door to The Shak. It was very crowded. Every table was full. Olivia spotted her new anthropology professor sitting at a table by the window. A tall blond woman with rimless half-glasses holding a small stick between her fingers and reading a stack of papers as she ate. Ms. Georgia Jones, M.D., Ph.D. "Ignore this stick," she had told the class the first day. "I'm trying to quit smoking. I think the feel of the cylinder is part of the obsession."

The woman spotted Olivia and smiled and waved. "That's a nice car," Olivia said. "Is that your car? That MG?"

"It's my boyfriend's car. I traded with him. I wouldn't put a bumper sticker on a car for all the tea in China. Sit down. I'm almost finished. Go on. I'd like some company." Georgia gestured toward the empty chair. Olivia sat down in it. "I was told everyone in town came here," Georgia continued. "Well, I'm glad to see you. I've been afraid there won't be enough students for the class if anyone else backs out. So let me buy you breakfast. I don't want anybody else dropping the class." She laughed as though that were the funniest thing in the world. "What else are you taking?"

"Navajo. I'm trying to learn the language this summer. But I want to take your class too. I won't drop it."

"It's going to be a crip. Anthropology. What a joke. The whole discipline's a joke. Everything's a joke except literature, music, painting, and pure science. Mathematics. I'm a medical doctor, did you know that? I quit two years ago and decided to teach for a while. I taught last year in Fayetteville and now I'm teaching here." She stuck her legs out into the aisle between the tables. She was wearing long silk slacks. On her feet were brown leather sandals. Everything she was wearing looked rich. "Actually, as soon as I got to Fayetteville, I fell in love. Wouldn't you know it. So I'm here to rethink that."

"What's wrong? What happened to it?"

"The war in the Persian Gulf. My love affair is a casualty of the war. Actually, it wasn't perfect before that. Now it's really a mess."

"He had to go?"

"No. He led the protest. The war's over and he's still protesting. He's a nuclear physicist, if that makes it any clearer. He was working on a superconductor, happy as a clam, making a new tool for mankind. Then he went crazy when they started the war. He's this gorgeous guy. He's unbelievably beautiful. I'm a fool for beauty. He's got this dazzling smile, gorgeous nose. Fabulous in bed—at least at first. I thought I had it made. We were spending every night together. Then that war. Next thing I knew he started dragging in every night at two or three, too tired to fuck me. Fuck the war, I told him finally. Let them have the war. Let the nukes proliferate. What difference does it make if you can't even find time to make love to me. That helped for about a month. Then the war ran out and he started in on the environment with the same group that had been protesting the war. So I came over here. Let him miss me. Let him see if his little politically correct half-educated friends can keep him warm. It looks like a waitress would come and at least take your order, doesn't it?"

"That's okay. I guess you just have to love him like he is, or break up with him. This psychiatrist I went to in Carolina said wanting to change someone is just trying to control them. If you can't like them like they are, you might as well quit. How old is he? Maybe he's having a midlife crisis."

"I thought of that. He's forty-nine. I'm forty-seven. I've already been through mine. Unless you could call what I'm doing now the last wave of it. Until I go back to Memphis and, as we say, resume practice, I guess I can't talk. But I didn't get out on the streets every night. With my face painted white. I didn't carry a cross everywhere I went or wear black armbands. He's a tenured professor of physics, for God's sake. It's too much."

"So are you broken up?" Olivia was leaned halfway across the table. She had completely forgotten she was talking to her professor, much less someone she had never spoken to before. Georgia's every word was so intense she swept Olivia into her obsession.

"No, we're still supposed to be in love. I don't know, sometimes I think I'm an emotional coward. I can't stand to be in love. It drives me crazy to be happy. It drives me crazy to love this man."

"I guess I better order breakfast," Olivia said. "What time is it? Your class starts at ten."

"It's nine-fifteen. Listen, I'm in here every day. Eight-thirty. Come find me. I have to have some structure in my life, so this is it. I'm going to eat breakfast at the same place every day. In the first place I don't like to cook and in the second place I have to have some structure in my life, so this is it. I'll eat breakfast at the same place at the same time every day. The rest of the time I'm free."

"To do what?"

"I'm not sure yet. Stay away from Fayetteville, I guess. Try not to barter the self for the relationship, as we say."

"To do what?"

"The central problem of romantic love. To maintain autonomy while getting bonding energy. It may not be possible. If it was easy I wouldn't have had to go a hundred miles away for the summer. Actually, I'm going to see him Friday." Georgia was gathering her papers, getting up. A waitress appeared to take Olivia's order. "I'll see you in class," Georgia said. "I need to get on over to my office and put some of this stuff away. Don't hurry. Eat breakfast first."

"I read the assignment," Olivia said. "It was really interesting."

"Yeah, Dyson's hot. Next I want to give you some of Robert Coles's studies of children. That's the bitch about this subject. There isn't a decent text. I have to xerox everything I need. Well, see you in a while."

Georgia was gone, weaving her way to the door, smiling back at Olivia over a stack of books and papers. Why do I need to see a shrink? Olivia wondered. When I have this woman for a teacher.

The waitress appeared with Olivia's muffins. "I heard you and Bobby made up," the waitress said. "I sure am glad. Everybody's glad."

"Where'd you hear that? Well, I forgot. The Tallequah grapevine. Yeah, we made up. I'm glad you're glad. Bobby and I are too."

"I heard you got a ring."

"Yeah, I did. You want to see it?"

"Sure. Where is it?"

"In my purse. I don't wear it all the time."

"Why not?"

"I don't know. I don't know what it means, I guess. Anyway, here it is." Olivia took the velvet box from her purse and removed the ring and put it on her finger and held it out to be admired. The waitress, whose name was Castell Carter, marveled at it. Then the other two waitresses, whose names were Jayne Anne and Emily, also came over to admire it. Food service stopped at The Shak. Jayne Anne had been a cheerleader with Olivia and Castell had been on her soccer team. "I always knew you and Bobby were meant for each other," Castell said. "We all thought it was a shame when you left him."

"She had to go," Emily said. "She went to meet her dad."

CHAPTER 22

H E has been captured by his anima," Tom said, putting down the phone. "She reminds him of his grand-mother. His grandmother, Sherrill. Can you beat that?"

"In what way?" Sherrill was ironing a red silk cowboy shirt to wear that night to a benefit at the grade school. A neighbor kid was being taken into the National Honor Society and she and Tom had promised to come to the ceremony. Sherrill was never without a child to love, sometimes two or three. Tom could never figure out where she got them. Suddenly a new boy or girl would appear, taking riding lessons, washing windows, borrowing books, being dropped off for the weekend while their parents went away.

"He said when she walked away she looked like his grandmother dancing. His grandmother was a German settler who remembered how to waltz."

"Then he isn't full-blooded Cherokee."

"Almost no one is anymore, I think." Tom poured a cup of coffee, added sugar and cream, sat down at the table to watch his wife. He should be worrying about Bobby Tree's anima, when Sherrill looked enough like his mother to be her twin. "What do you see in me?" Sherrill was always protesting. "I'm nothing special. You're a famous writer and all I do is ride horses and cook and you act like you're lucky to have me. I think there's something fishy about that." And she would wiggle around beneath his hands and curl her legs around his and plant little childlike kisses on his ear. "The Fisher King," Tom always replied. "I was wounded in the thigh until I met you. In the heart and hand and thigh."

"I won't fuck you if you talk about things like that, sad things. You were not wounded. You had just won the Pulitzer Prize and you were in the papers every day. I was scared to fuck you, you were so famous."

"Why did you change your mind?"

"I don't know. Because I did. I can't even have you a baby. What kind of life is that? You ought to leave me and get a younger girl. Like that young writer that came out here. She'd marry you."

"Finish that shirt," Tom said. "I want to go upstairs with you. I want to bury my face in your breasts."

"We have to leave at six."

"We'll be on time. If I make you late I'll buy you that new saddle you've been wanting. If I make you five minutes late, it's yours."

Sherrill took the unfinished shirt off the ironing board and hung it over a chair and went to him. She took his face into her hands and sat down upon his lap across the straight chair. She began to desire him as soon as her hand touched his cheek. "Oh, baby," she said. "I love you so much. Don't do it to me. It's too much. It's too much to bear on a weekday afternoon."

She has a way of going feminine on me when I'm mad that disarms me completely, he had made a character say in a book that morning. *I'm all set to start a fight, all overtaken by a mood and in despair and want to fight it out with her and finish up my whole world while I'm at it and she'll turn around and put on a peignoir or start making cornbread or just get gentle and turn those damned blue eyes on me. Hell, man, she overwhelms me. She outfeminines the witch that's chasing me. She outwomans the anima. It's Helen Detroy I'm talking about, for Christ's sake. Who did you think I meant? My wife, the lucky thing some god let slip through the lines one watch when he was asleep.*

"It's like being in grandmother's bed," Bobby had said on the phone. "When I was a kid the only place I wanted to be was in bed with my dad's mom. I called her Tottie. She had the softest, sweetest bed with these clean, white sheets and she had a feather bed for winter. She'd cuddle me up and I'd sleep like I was dead. She'd snore sometimes, just the softest little snore, like a horse's whinny. She'd be having sweet dreams, I guess, because I was there. We were always trying to get off and have some time together. Because Dad would be off rodeoing and everyone else was always arguing or worrying about something. Not Tottie and me. No sir. We'd get the papers or books she took out of the library and we'd go get in her bed and she'd put on her specs and start reading. I'd go to sleep sometimes with the light still on. Sometimes she'd turn it off and we'd cuddle up and she'd tell me stories, like pretending she thought the voices in the radio were little people who were locked up in a box and couldn't get out or pretending she was some little weak person and I had to guard her with my sword.

"Yeah, Olivia and me were in bed the other night and we both had our books we were studying. She's reading this book for her anthropology class and I was reading my history book for World History and I thought, Christ, it's like being with Tottie. No wonder I'm in love."

"Don't tell her that," Tom said. "I wouldn't tell her she reminds you of your grandmother if you can help it."

"I can't even remember Mom so she can't remind me of her."

"Don't be too sure. It's a dangerous maze, crossing the romantic love terrain. Look out for sinkholes. So forth. So she took the ring?"

"Hell, Tom. I don't know what I'm doing. I just get up every day and face the morning. What can I do? I got a job and I'm signed up in college and I got you to talk to and she says she loves me. What the hell? I don't think my dad's doing too good, but I can't do anything about that."

"We'll be in Billings over the weekend. Call me Sunday night when we get home."

"If I can. If I remember."

"Hold on."

"Same to you. Thanks."

Bobby hung up the phone and went outside to watch the last red rays of sun falling down through the trees on the horizon. Behind him, a full moon was in the still light sky. We think the moon is a lady, he was thinking. Silvery and coming out of nowhere to surprise us and keep us company at night. His dick started getting hard at the thought and he looked at his watch to see how long it was until nine o'clock when Olivia was coming over. He scratched his head and started walking toward the high school, thinking he might go run a mile or so around the high school track before he studied algebra.

CHAPTER 23

A GLORIOUS morning in Tahlequah, Oklahoma. Georgia is dressed for the day. She is writing a letter. Her books and the pop quiz she is planning on giving are stacked neatly by the door. Her bed is made. The dishes are done. "Have you registered to vote?" is the first question on the quiz. "Name five justices of the Supreme Court" is the second. "Tell me everything you know about DNA and the human immune system" is the third. For extra credit there is a fourth question. "What is Macedonia?"

"My darling Zach," she is writing.

> The thousands of moves and countermoves, decisions and revisions, loves and destructions and trusts and betrayals. Not just in our two

lives but in all the lives that made us. The ice age, the discovery of America, your career, my career, my leaving my career. The way my first husband made love to me and the way he laughed at me and the way your last girlfriend ran off with your car. Well, now I'm driving your car. Maybe you try to get women to take your cars. Maybe you want us behind the wheel of your phallic symbols.

What do you want with me, Zach? Well, I know. You want me to be your momma and love you no matter what you do and eat dinner with you and sleep with you at night and tell you that you're right. Well, you may not be right. I know you are right about nuclear proliferation and the need for diplomacy and peace.

But the Japanese and the Europeans and the white Africans are going to eat our lunch, dear heart. We aren't as fierce as they are anymore. Our people aren't scared enough to work in factories. We want day care. Read Philip Levine, for God's sake. He'll tell you what it's like to work in a factory in Detroit. No wonder they started letting the forklifts drop the Chevrolets on the concrete. How would you feel if you had an IQ of one hundred and thirty and were on the line and saw in the paper that your CEO had just given himself a salary of twenty-seven million dollars?

Zach, it's the fifth of June and I slept by myself last night. Is that my fault? Well, yes. I'll see you Friday. I just want to come to your house and walk in the door and get into bed and start making love to you.

I met an interesting little girl. Her name is Olivia and she has come back to Tahlequah to go to school. She's got some wacko idea about learning Navajo because knowledge will be coded in it into computers. I didn't really understand what it is about but I'm sure I'll hear more later. I eat breakfast in the mornings at this downtown café where everyone gathers. The Scene, as it were. Until Friday. Love and more love. Whatever love means.

Zachery Biggs, Georgia's lover. Here's a study in modern history, a lesson in contemporary mores. Here's a good boy, an oldest son, an Eagle Scout, a dean's list, dean's darling, Momma's angel, finally gone all the way around the bend.

For the first forty-five years he never broke a rule or a law, never missed a meeting or a class, came to the bell and Momma was supposed to love him, wasn't she? He had dreamed of giving all the mommas a super gift, a superconductor that would allow them to transmit clean power and save a lot of energy and money. Did the mommas appreciate it? No.

Three women had left him for greener, more exciting, less obsessive pastures. The first one had left him with a pair of twin boys, so alike no one could tell them apart, sometimes not even Zach. The second wife had left him a shed full of her dark, undistinguished paintings and the third wife had left him heavily in debt.

He was doing the best he could with all of this. He loved the boys and kept them on weekends and in the summers. He had six of the paintings hanging around his house although it depressed him to notice them. He was doing his best to pay off the debt and save enough money for the boys' education. He was always broke. He liked being broke. He liked never having a new shirt or a pair of running shoes. It made him know that he had suffered for a momma. If he suffered, surely he was good and would be loved somewhere in the world.

He had heard about Georgia before he met her. "The dean's hired a medical doctor to teach in the Anthropology Department," a colleague told him. "She told the dean she didn't want to use a text and he hired her anyway. She completely snowed the old fool. She's going out with him. He took her out to dinner the night she got to town. You need to meet this dame. Then you'll know what we're up against. I couldn't even hire one more graduate student and he goes out and brings this loony here from Memphis because he wants to date her."

Zach's subconscious perked up. A brilliant, loony, single woman. His main mommy had taught the Great Books seminar when he was a boy. She had smoked while driving a convertible. She had read Anaïs Nin. He was programmed for Georgia, ready and waiting. "The male perceives the female anima as wary, unstable, changeable, illusive, seductive. The female perceives the male as the gray wolf coming over the continents to penetrate the barriers of the sacred kingdom."

"I'd like to meet her," he had answered. "I'll look forward to that."

He met her three times before he could get her to remember his name. "I guess I wasn't wearing my glasses," Georgia always said later. "How could I not have noticed you?"

*   *   *

Now, two years later, on a Friday afternoon in June, Zach is waiting for Georgia to arrive from Tahlequah. He has straightened up his house, put all his books and magazines into stacks in corners and under tables. He has fed his dog, run the vacuum sweeper over the middle of the rug, called the Handicapped Housecleaning Service and let them wash the windows and clean the refrigerator and mop the kitchen floor. He has put clean sheets on the bed, gray and white striped sheets he bought the year he was at Princeton.

He goes over to stand by a window and look out upon the earth. Only yesterday it had been the gray leafless landscape of winter in the Ozarks. Then spring came barreling over the hills and turned it green. Earth and clay, he mused. The great conductors. I have to tell Georgia that. She's always wondering how the messages get through. She thinks they're traveling in ether. It's clay, I'll tell her. The great conductor with no loss of heat. She'll say, Oh, Zach, you're so brilliant. No, she'll say, That's bullshit. Earth's too slow. We're slow, I'll answer. Landlocked and slow.

There's nothing slow about Georgia. What a hot little show she's running. She's hot, the hottest woman I ever fucked and the strangest and the best.

He looked at his watch. Six after six. If she left at four, she ought to be along within the hour. He went out into the front yard and dug up a ball of earth from under a persimmon tree and held it in his hand. It's something we've missed, he decided. One element, some balance, something I already know. If she drives up now and sees me like this, she'll think, the mad scientist. I think it was because I put the white paint on me. That's the thing that scared her. They don't want us to be fierce or crazy. They reserve all that for themselves. He squeezed the ball of clay. He looked up the street toward the main thoroughfare that ran along the south side of the campus. Maybe it would be enough to grovel and admit his need and say he loved her.

He heard the last notes of the chimes on Old Main. He heard the cheers rising from the baseball diamond by the track. A postseason series against the Texas team, a doubleheader. The Razorbacks had two men on base and no outs in the bottom of the third. Cheers rang out across the valley, traveled across the track and soccer fields, past the high school and into Zach's low-lying neighborhood. If he had not been waiting for Georgia, Zach would have been at the game.

As she drew near his house, she saw him, standing in the yard holding something in his hand. He's trying to look like a scientist, she decided. God, I love him. He's so goddamn silly and transparent, such a dope. Zach, my love, it's me. I'm naked underneath this dress.

She parked the car and he came walking toward her, still holding the ball of earth. "The street looks great," she said. "Your house looks fabulous with the trees in leaf. You look wonderful. I've been missing you."

"I've been missing you. Come in. I have to do one thing. A student is bringing me a paper, then we can do whatever you want to do."

"What kind of a student?"

"A boy in one of my classes. His father died and he couldn't get the paper in. He'll be here by six-thirty."

"He better be. I have plans for you that can't be interrupted." She took his hand and they walked together into the house. They walked past the swing that his last girlfriend had painted red and past the half-dead potted plants and into the living room and down the hall and into the kitchen. Then they stopped and Georgia began to unbutton the buttons of his shirt. "I love this shirt," she said. "This shirt reminds me of my grandfather. He used to wear shirts with little lines on them like this." She finished with the buttons and began to undo his belt.

"What if my student comes?"

"Leave him a note on the door. Tell him to leave the paper. Tell him to go away."

The doorbell was ringing. Zach fastened his belt and went to the door and had a few minutes' conversation with his student. Then he shut the door and locked it and came back to where she was. He stood near her with his glasses falling far down on his fine thin elegant nose. "Would you like to go to bed with me?" he asked very formally, in his most precise and professorial voice. "I would like to take you there."

Several hours later Georgia woke up in the gray and white striped sheets. She was plastered against Zach's body. It was dark outside. The

sound of crickets and tree frogs and the last three notes of the chimes
on Old Main counted out nine o'clock.

"Given," she said. "I love you and I think you love me."

"You're right about that."

"Is that baseball game still going on?"

"We could go see. It's a doubleheader."

"Okay, get up. Did you notice I was naked underneath my dress
when I came in?"

"No. I'm sorry. Come here, Georgia. Come back to me."

"Again. Twice in one afternoon?"

"I'm not dead yet."

"Will you love me till you die?"

"If you want me to."

When they got out of bed, they walked over to the baseball field
and caught the last two innings of the second game. The Razorbacks
had won the first game and were tied in the bottom of the eighth in the
second. They had two men on base and no outs and the crowd was
going wild. Georgia and Zach stopped at the concession stand and
bought hot dogs and Cokes. Carrying the food, they climbed high in
the stands to Zach's seats beneath the press box. A five-foot-five-inch
Razorback batter who was a great favorite with the fans for his tenacity
and passion came out onto the field. He hit a foul ball into the parking
lot and the loudspeaker registered a high-volume crash of metal and
glass breaking. The crowd roared its approval. On the next pitch he
got a double and streaked for second base. The crowd roared. Georgia
and Zach giggled and squeezed mustard onto their hot dogs from a
plastic tube.

Two men crossed home plate and the Razorbacks were ahead. A
breeze blew in from the south. Georgia and Zach ate the hot dogs and
drank the Cokes, which were watered down with ice made from chlo-
rinated water from a river polluted by chicken offal. Test of the
immune system, Georgia thought to herself, and sucked hers down
through a straw.

The Razorbacks held on to their lead in the ninth and the game was
won. Georgia and Zach walked home through the victorious crowd,
holding hands and not talking. He didn't say, You picked a fine time to
leave me, Lucille, and she didn't say, Why can't it always be like this?

Why don't you shoot those kids or send them back to their momma? How could I live with you? How could I tolerate the confusion and mess of your life? They walked home across the darkened campus, holding hands and keeping their mouths shut.

The twins were on the porch when they arrived. Surrounded by five or six other scroungy, pimpled, teenage boys. Two motorcycles were propped against the porch. Beer cans were in the yard.

"Hello, Taylor," Georgia said. "Hello, Tucker, long time no see."

"Can we borrow the convertible?" Taylor asked. "Since she brought it back."

"We need some money, Dad," Tucker added. "You got any cash on you?"

CHAPTER 24

ON Monday morning Olivia was waiting at The Shak when Georgia got there. "So how did your weekend go with your boyfriend?" she asked. "Did you have a good time?"

"If you call having nightmares a good time."

"You had nightmares?"

"All night Saturday night. I was in a strange city with a teenage child strapped to my back. One of Zach's twins. It's a manifestation of anxiety, Olivia. We all have a certain amount of free-floating anxiety, waiting to attach to something. Anyway, I was walking down this street with the child on my back. Actually, the street is one on which a female psychiatrist I went to for a while actually lived. I did my residency in New York in a city hospital. It was the pit of hell. To think anyone could survive something like that and then quit the profession. So I delivered this parasitic teenager to Zach and Zach got mad at him for being on my back. Zach has teenage sons by his first wife, I don't know if I told you that. She's an emotional cripple of the first order, so there's a message and a warning."

"A warning?"

"From my subconscious telling me not to marry him. I would marry them, too, those dreadful needful bad destructive boys. They scare me to death. One of them has his hair dyed blue."

"Do they live with your boyfriend?"

"God, no. Thank God for that. They live in Fort Smith and come to visit. They stay three months in the summer. It's hell. Well, I left. I won't be in Fayetteville when they're there. The yard stays full of beer cans. Their friends call at all hours of the night. It's chaos. Do I need this?"

"I guess not. Are you going to marry him anyway? I mean, if you love him, I guess you have to put up with some stuff."

"Here's the main thing. In the dream the boy was on my back. I could have shoved him off, but I let him ride. He isn't bigger than I am, not yet. And when we got to Zach, Zach got mad at him for riding on me so I guess my subconscious perceives Zach to still be on my side."

"Against his own child?" Olivia looked down, then raised her eyes to meet Georgia's. "Listen, my dad has lots of girlfriends, but he doesn't like them as much as he does us. I mean, he was taking me to Switzerland this summer with his girlfriend Margaret, and when I said I didn't want to go, he said he'd tell her not to go. It's always like that. He always picks Jessie and me over his girlfriends. I hate to tell you that, but it's true. I mean, I wish he'd be nicer to Margaret. She's the best one he has. I wish he'd marry her so he wouldn't be thinking about us all the time."

"You turned down a chance to go to Switzerland?"

"I wanted to come home. I haven't been here in two and a half years. I was worrying about my grandfather. I started dreaming he'd die. Cherokees take dreams seriously. Well, I guess you do too since you were telling me yours."

"Here's the rest of it. Then this little girl appeared. She was about five or six and she said, Let's go up this street. The street forked. It was this really ugly dark industrial city. Then Zach became physically smaller, very small, like Charlie Chaplin, and he showered money on her, a shower of dollar bills. She went up one street. Zach stayed at an intersection but I followed the child and she got us lost. We were lost in a terrible dark city. We went into alleys and were threatened by ferocious dogs. We went into halls and lions stalked us. Finally I was in a small house. A nice boy let us in but it turned into a den of thieves. All this time I was carrying a billfold with my credit cards and money. It was a symbol of my entire financial structure. All the money I have in the world, all the possessions and so forth. Then it was lost and all I had was myself and this evil little girl. Still, I had to protect her. I had to keep her safe."

"That's a terrible dream. That's a nightmare." Olivia lay her hand flat down on the table. She was getting bored with Georgia's dream. She had wanted to tell her about Bobby and show her the engagement ring. It looked like anyone would notice it. There it was, lying in the sunlight, on the blue-and-white-checked tablecloth. The waitress appeared with their plates. Georgia poured syrup over her waffles and continued to talk about herself.

"Well, I didn't abandon her. I decided not to worry about losing my entire fortune. I just took her by the hand and dragged her down the street and finally I saw the world headquarters of the Episcopal Church and I went in and found a labyrinth where some men in suits were having a meeting. I told them the names of all the important people I knew. I thought they could tell by my voice that I was upper middle class and well educated. I went to Wellesley. I thought that would protect me. So they agreed to call my cousin, who's a broker on Wall Street, and then I knew I was home and would be safe."

"What do you think all that meant?" Olivia had given up on showing Georgia the ring. "So you went to Wellesley. That's a long way from Oklahoma."

"I don't know what I've been doing for the past few years. I have to go back to practicing medicine but I don't want to do it for another year. Well, I think it means I've gotten too far from my power base. That if I keep on loving Zach I'll end up with some goddamn teenage boy on my back and I'll be broke. That's pretty dreadful, a dreadful dream, a dreadful message."

"So why do you keep on going with him?"

"I like to fuck him. I know he doesn't have AIDS or, if he has, it's too late now. I don't want to find another lover. Besides, it isn't the personnel, Olivia. Who you love isn't important, it's that you love."

"God, that's the truth. That's what I like about my boyfriend. When

I'm with him, I forget myself. He gave me an engagement ring the other day. You want to see it? I'm wearing it but I don't know if we should get married. All I know for now is that I love him. I'm going to start going to a psychiatrist. I guess you know that doesn't mean I'm crazy, since you went to one."

"We're all crazy. The whole culture. Who are you seeing?"

"A man in Tulsa. The psychiatrist I went to in North Carolina got him for me. I quit going to her but I shouldn't have. So, do you want to see the ring?" Olivia held out her hand.

"Very elegant," Georgia said. "Who's this boyfriend? He must be nice. I didn't know young people had good taste anymore. I thought it was all blue hair."

"He's special. He's a rodeo star. A real star. Well, he used to be. Now he's trying to go to school."

"Well, I'll be late for class." Georgia put her knife and fork down beside her half-eaten waffle. She stood up. "Thanks for coming to join me. This is good. Keep coming here. We'll support each other. I believe in support systems, I believe in friends. You never have night-mares about your friends. Did you ever think of that? I think you must be good at having friends."

"Well, one or two at a time. I don't like to have a lot of people in my life." Olivia looked down. Georgia asked too much too fast. It was hard to keep up with her.

"Did you read the Robert Coles?"

"I loved it. Sure I read it."

"Good, probably no one else did. Ask some questions. Show off." Georgia walked over to the cash register and paid for both their break-fasts without letting Olivia know she had done it and tipped the wait-ress and swept out of the café. She had just had half an hour of the divine pleasure of talking about herself and arrived at her office still thinking about the conversation. She's a good listener, Georgia decided. I could make a doctor out of that girl if I had time. Well, I'll have to meet this young man she's fucking. I have to be a real older friend and not buy into her perceptions unless I share them. That's always been my problem. Wanting friends so much I go along with everything they say. Then a few months later I say what I should have said to begin with.

Three students were waiting outside her office. Georgia ushered the first one in and began to listen to his problems. She had decided to be a great teacher if she was one. A teacher and a friend.

CHAPTER 25

WE ought to kill her," Taylor was saying. He and Tucker were sitting on the back porch of their father's house smoking and drinking Cokes and eating Nacho Cheese Flavored Doritos for breakfast. Taylor was in the swing with a wireless phone he had stolen from Wal-Mart putting in calls to their friends in Fort Smith. He was getting ready to call his old girlfriend when Georgia called looking for their daddy. "We don't know where he is," Taylor told her. "We don't know when he's getting back."

"Do you think they're going to get married?" Tucker asked. "I don't think they're going to. I don't think he really likes her."

"We could blow up her car. It's easy to do. All you do is put a bomb in the motor and when she turns it on, shazammm. I hate her so much. That dyed hair and all that crap she's always talking about the culture. Who gives a damn? We could do something to her car. But it's Dad's car. He gave her the convertible to drive as long as she wants to."

"He won't marry her. Mom says he'll never be able to live with anybody. He's too messy."

"He's got us. He wants us to live here. If we stay here, he won't marry her because he'll have us."

"What about Mom? She wouldn't have anyone with her."

"Yeah."

"We don't want to stay here, Taylor. He can't even cook. I hate it when he cooks."

"He takes us out."

"So does she. Besides, I don't want to change schools. Maybe he and Mom will get married again. They were nice to each other last night."

"If she calls back, I'm telling her he's gone out with Mom." Taylor reached down into the sack and took out a handful of Doritos and munched them up. "There's some light beer in the refrigerator. You want to drink one? We can split it."

"Okay. You get it."

The phone rang. Taylor grimaced, let it ring twice, then answered it. They knew it was Georgia. She always called two or three times in a row when she was looking for their dad. "He's not here," Taylor said. "He took Mom out to breakfast. We ate up everything in the house last night because Mom's staying here with us. Yeah, I'll tell him. We're going to barbecue for dinner tonight. You ought to come over. Okay, I'll tell him you called." He hung up the phone, laughing so hard he could hardly breathe. He staggered over to the refrigerator and pulled out a beer and opened it and handed it to his brother. "You should have heard her. She was going crazy. Where is Mom, by the way? Where'd she go?"

"Out to the mall. She's coming back here before she leaves. You shouldn't have done that, Taylor."

"Why not? It's true. She did stay here."

"He let her because she's broke. He was just being polite. She told me she appreciated him being polite. Now you got him in trouble."

"I wish she'd drive off the road. If he marries her I'll never speak to her again. Oh, oh, there he is." They heard the motor being turned off in Zach's ancient Land Rover. Heard the front door slam. They made no effort to hide the beer.

"Hello, Dad," they said together when he came in. "We opened a beer. Don't worry. We only took a sip. We didn't drink it."

"Did Georgia call?" he asked. "Did the phone ring?"

"I don't know," Taylor answered. "We saw a snake out in the backyard. I think it's a garter snake but I'm not sure. Have you got a snake book? We want to look him up. It might be poisonous but I don't think so."

Zach snapped to attention. If there was one thing he liked to do, it was look things up in reference books. He embraced his sons. He ran for the encyclopedia. He sang through the house.

"She'll call back," Tucker said.

"Not while I'm on the phone." Taylor dialed a number. A reservations clerk at Delta Airlines came on the phone and Taylor walked back out to the porch and sat down on the swing and began to ask for information about flights to Berlin and Moscow and Hawaii.

Zach came tearing back into the kitchen, his arms full of encyclopedias and nature books. "Where did you see it?" he was asking. "How big around was it? What were the markings? Was it orange and black?"

Georgia hung up the phone from talking to Taylor. She pulled on some slacks and sat down on the unmade bed to tie her running shoes. Good, she decided. Perfect. He has to have a mommie. If I quit on him he goes out and finds a substitute. Dallas Anne shows up to see the boys. Be my mommie, he screams in pain. Sure, she says, and moves in. Might as well manipulate him a little if there's nothing else left to do, no Sufi dancing classes, no white witch covens, no belly-dancing classes, tai chi, left-wing causes to espouse, why not hang around and fuck up Zach's head. Help the boys steal something, maybe. Jesus Fucking H. Christ, I have to go back to Memphis and get to work. I have to leave this swamp. Why did I ever get involved with him to begin with? To hell with it, I'm going to The Shak and get some breakfast.

Well, it's because he's powerless, she decided, driving to The Shak. He hasn't even got the power to keep her from staying at his house. I can't live with a man who can't handle power. What in the name of shit am I doing in this crazy country? I'm the one who's mad. I've gone completely mad. I will not call him back. I will not call him back.

She parked the car and went into The Shak and ordered breakfast. When the waitress brought the plate, she thanked her and asked, "Where do people go around here at night? Where do they go to meet other people or to dance?"

"At the Teepee," the waitress ordered. "It's on Sequoyah Street. They play music there. They have bands. There's a really good one there tonight. The Vidalias from Broken Arrow. They're real good."

"What time does it open?"

"The music starts at nine. But it's open all day."

"Thanks," Georgia said. "I'll be there tonight. Come and sit with me. I'm looking for a boyfriend. If Olivia comes in, tell her I'm on the rampage. Tell her to come and find me."

CHAPTER 26

DALLAS Anne came back from the mall in a good mood. She had run into an old boyfriend who wanted her to go camping with him and had told her she could take the boys. She packed them up, promised Zach to bring them back by Sunday, and took off in her old Datsun. "Are those tires good?" Zach asked. "They look mighty slick."

"I'm not into tires, honey," she said, sticking her head out the window. Taylor and Tucker were in the backseat, beaming at their parents, their long legs already too big for the small car.

"Where are you going?" Zach asked. "Who's going with you?"

"Just some friends. We'll be back by Sunday." Taylor prodded Tucker in the ribs with the cordless phone. He had it in his jacket pocket. It was buzzing. It was Georgia trying to call Zach but all she got was the answering machine Taylor had programmed. "I'm away on a desert island," the tape said. "I probably can't answer your call for a week or two."

Zach walked back across the yard thinking about his sons. I have to love them unconditionally, he repeated like a mantra. They have special problems because they're twins. If Georgia would get to know them, she would like them. She always leaves when they're around. How can she love them if she never sees them? I don't know why she hasn't called. I guess I ought to call her. No, I'll wait for her to call. She's such a strange woman. Sometimes I think all she wants me for is an audience.

He went walking off down the street in the direction of his office and his laboratory. He had thought of an element they had never had time to try in the workup. His mind was filled with formulas that said that it might work. It was beautiful. A beautiful hypothesis. A beautiful, beautiful day.

CHAPTER 27

FOUR in the morning, June 15, 1991. In the Philippines a volcano called Mount Pinatubo began a long series of eruptions that would devastate the surrounding areas and cause beautiful sunsets in Tahlequah for many months.

At the private airport out by the ancient restored Cherokee Village, Bud Tree climbed into the cockpit of a 1976 Turbo Cessna with a flying range of 1,200 miles and took off for Iowa City. The back of the plane was loaded with 400 pounds of prime Razorbud marijuana, cleaned and packed in airtight containers. There was also a small plastic cooler filled with ten kilo bags of Peruvian cocaine. The plane had been stolen the week before in Little Rock, Arkansas, but no one had bothered to tell Bud Tree. All he knew was that he was to load the plane and fly it, for the successful operation of which he would receive twenty-five thousand dollars in unmarked one-hundred-dollar bills. The offer had been for fifteen thousand dollars but he had turned that down. "Hell, man, I could make fifteen busting my ass in a rodeo."

"Except you can't rodeo with your leg."

"I could rodeo."

"Okay. Twenty-five. There'll be a plane waiting. File a flight plan the night before and call and tell Reno when you get there. You sure you want to do this? Don't do it if you're getting hesitant."

"I want the job. I'm not hesitant as long as I get paid."

"You'll get paid. Leave as soon as there's light. We want you there before ten. If there's a head wind it could slow you down."

"I know the wind, man. You worry about the Feds. I'll worry about the weather."

*   *   *

"Slip the surly bonds of earth," Bud said as he eased the plane out onto the runway. It was a saying he had learned in Vietnam from a guy who died. "Pass the peanut butter crackers."

At five-thirty Bobby woke up in the trailer and slipped out of bed trying not to wake Olivia. He had been in college for twelve days and already he was obsessive about the math homework. If I didn't fry my brains doing speedballs to rodeo, he kept thinking when anything got hard. But hell, Tom said he never saw anybody do figures like I can. Hell, how would he know. I had to show him what the book meant. Still, hell, you got it, he told me. Don't get scared. Going to college is just like breaking a horse. You keep on until it gets easy. Ride to win, that's what Sherrill says. Okay, I'm doing great. I'll make some coffee and leave it out for Olivia. She likes it when I do things for her. Well, she's my baby. Goddamn, she makes my dick get hard.

He turned on the coffeepot he had set the night before and carrying his books and notebooks walked out of the trailer into the fine summer dawn. His dad's car was gone and the house looked quiet so he went over to sit on the front porch and read. He could do the math and then try to read the physics again. He had had a hard time with physics the first week until Olivia's teacher had explained it to him one morning when they met for breakfast at The Shak.

"It's just a complicated game," she told him. "An hypothesis. The only reason it's valuable is that it lets us manipulate physical reality. The words and symbols are a closed system. A set of rules. The amazing thing is that this probably flawed knowledge works. Of course, nuclear weapons are a mixed blessing. Still, forty years of peace. We haven't used them in another war."

"It's hard to believe in them." Bobby had been sitting opposite Georgia. He watched her as she spoke. She was so nervous. Trying so hard to please, to be liked.

"My boyfriend teaches physics. I'll let you meet him when he comes over. He's a great teacher. The students voted him their favorite teacher last year. If you get in trouble he might help you. And use the department tutors. They have to stay there all afternoon. They may as well be helping someone."

Bobby drank his coffee. He propped his feet up on the porch

railing. He finished the math and began to read the physics book. "Nature and heaven's laws lay hid in night: God said, 'Let Newton be! and all was light.' "

> The difficulty arises because a physical phenomenon has associated with it a vast number of facts . . . if the task of physics is to find some order in natural phenomena . . . then clearly some observations will be more significant than others . . . the problem is that in the early stages of a scientific inquiry one does not yet know what the theoretical framework will be . . .

Bobby settled down into the chair. He could hear Sharrene sigh in the bedroom behind the porch but he didn't care. He looked toward the trailer, thinking of Olivia. I want us to get married, he was thinking. I don't want any of this living together shit. I love her, that's for sure. She fills me out. She makes me believe it's all worthwhile. Two people make a channel for life to run through. That's what Sherrill said. It's true. Together we're bigger than when we're apart. I'll be good enough for her. Hell, she's Cherokee too. All the rich relatives in the world don't change that. So the Cherokee are dead. So we don't even have a brave for a chief. Well, hell, Wilma's a good woman, don't go knocking Wilma. Study the goddamn book. You got to learn this stuff before you go to class.

He sank deeper into the chair. The sun was climbing the wooden stairs, beginning to heat up the bottom of his legs. He stretched his feet out to meet it and began to think.

At ten that morning the editor of the *Tahlequah Reporter* received a phone call. "Yeah, I know him," the editor said. "He's a good man. His kid's the best barrel racer in the state. Why, what's happened now?"

When he hung up the phone he walked over to the copy editor's desk. "Bud Tree's been arrested for running dope in a stolen plane. Will it ever stop?"

"Oh, shit."

"I used to worship that man. I've seen him ride a horse, you thought he was part of it. It'd make you believe in centaurs. I've seen him lift a horse from the earth and fly."

"Bobby's better than his dad. He's back in town. I saw him the other morning at The Shak. He's with that little Hand girl that used to do back flips at the games."

"Well, his dad's in deep shit. You don't know where I could find Bobby, do you? I'd hate to have him read about it in the paper."

"I'll go look. You want me to go look for him?"

"Yeah, go on."

The copy editor got up and put on his seersucker jacket and wiped his hand across his jaw and squinted up his eyes and shook his head. "Okay, I'm going. I think he's out at Northeastern. He told me he was going to get him a degree."

"I hope to God he isn't mixed up in this."

"Bud wouldn't mix his kid up in something like this. He worships that kid."

"I hope you're right. Shit." The editor buttoned his jacket, squared his shoulders, ran his fingers through his hair, checked his reflection in the glass of a framed photograph on the copy editor's desk. "I hate this kind of shit. We've got to get some industry in this part of the world, Warren. We've got to save our kids. We got kids running off to make a living following powwows. What kind of life is that? Dancing for tourists. I know how you feel about industry, but you're wrong, Warren. People have to have something to do. There's nothing to do around here but steal. Goddamn, Bud Tree. I've seen him lift horses from the ground. We've got to save the kids. We've got to get some industry in here."

"You can't save people, Bob. Nobody ever got saved yet. Life just hands out its stuff and you roll with the punches or you die. That's it." He pulled a cigarette out of a pack and lit it, looking guilty. "He was better at football than he was at rodeoing. He could have played in college if he'd kept up with it."

An hour later the copy editor gave up looking for Bobby and left a note on the door of the trailer. "Call me at the newspaper office when you get home. Your dad's in trouble. Bob and I want to help if we can. We'll be there all afternoon. Yours sincerely, Warren Brown."

*   *   *

At twelve Olivia met Bobby in the student cafeteria and they bought sandwiches and went to sit on the concrete tables that overlooked the quadrangle. "I don't feel very good," she said. "It's like something was hovering over me all day. I woke up on the wrong side of bed, I guess."

"You want to go over to the trailer and turn on the fan and study together?"

"Sure. I don't have to do anything else here." She covered his hand with her hand. Ran her hand up and down the soft smooth surface of his arm. "Who is at my window? Who? Who? It is the old cuckoo, mulling the same song over. The old song is about fear. About tomorrow and next year."

"I'm getting lost in this physics. I was thinking this morning it reminds me of this Jewish guy, this poet, that Tom had out at the ranch last fall. He wanted to learn cutting and he couldn't get the horse to do anything. He'd get up every morning and want to try it again. I was getting sick of it because we had other things to do. It was right when it started getting cold and we had to get things squared away for the winter, but every morning we had to waste half the day with this guy in the ring. One morning he forgot how to use the reins. He panicked and let go and we had a hell of a time catching him. Anyway, after a long time, one morning he got it. He just got it and after that he stayed a week and helped us out to make up for wasting all our time. We ought to go up to Lake Tenkiller this weekend and camp out. You want to go? Dad's got a good tent."

"Sure. Okay, finish that sandwich. Let's go lie on your mattress and turn on the fan. When I get through fucking you I might even study." She gave him a fake seductive look she had learned from Madonna. It was a look that said, It's nineteen ninety-one and I'll pretend to be a whore, but we know better. I'm in charge of this operation now. I might even run for president. Don't fuck with me, Bobby. I am a new woman in a new world.

CHAPTER 28

OLIVIA and Bobby drove to the trailer without talking. Bobby was thinking about jobs he could apply for and Olivia was thinking about going to get some birth control pills. Then Bobby was thinking about the Futurity in Fort Worth and how much money he'd get if they won or placed and Olivia was thinking about Chapel Hill and her sorority sisters and what they'd think if they could see her in this truck with a cowboy. Then Bobby was thinking about how much he liked to make her come and Olivia was thinking about her father and his beautiful house and her grandmother Anna Elizabeth Hand and her aunt Helen and her uncle Niall and how they would never be able to meet Bobby and like him. Nothing would make them understand or like Bobby. He was white trash to them. And I am white trash too, she decided, if I fuck him all the time in a dirty old trailer like a whore, but what choice do I have? I couldn't get anyone to like me at Chapel Hill. That guy never even called me back after he fucked me. I bet he told everyone I was a whore. Well, to hell with Chapel Hill. I don't need a lot of snotty rich people telling me what to do. Doctor Carlyn said for me to find out what I want and she'd help me learn how to get it. Well, what I want right now is to get laid and then I want a chocolate milkshake or at least a frozen yogurt. I've been starving all day. All day I've felt like the sky was about to fall. Chicken Little to the max-i-mum security. That's what my big sister in Zeta used to say. Chicken Little supreme with some anxiety on the side. Anxiety. I wonder what it means. Why do all these shrinks keep telling me that? You're anxious about it. They all say that to me. Of course I'm anxious about it. What do they think I'm in there talking to them for?

Bobby stopped the truck near the trailer door. He could see the note. He thought it was a notice of an unpaid bill. His dad had been worrying about money. Ever since he got home from Montana, all his dad did was talk about being worried about money and lecture him to have a bank account. Hell, if it was a bill collector that would embarrass Olivia. She liked to act all the time like she was rich. Well, she said her old man was going broke. So they had that in common too, didn't they?

He walked to the door and took down the note and read it and wadded it up and stuck it in his pocket.

"What is it?" Olivia said.

"It's nothing. Just a note from Dad. I've got to go and pick him up. Shit, there goes our afternoon. I'm sorry, baby." He turned to her and she knew he was lying.

"Let me see it. Let me see the note."

"I can't. You don't need to see it."

"Then it's from a girl."

"It's not from a girl, Olivia. That's not what it's about."

"Then why won't you let me see it?"

"It's about Dad's business. It hasn't got anything to do with you. Everything in the world isn't about you."

"Take me back to the campus, please. I want to get my car." She was climbing back into the truck, getting madder every second. He took a deep breath, bowed his head, tried to think. You had to be so careful with Olivia. But he had studied her, hadn't he? God, he had studied her. Had watched her like a colt he was fixing to break, had watched her skittishness and quick, unannounced moves, had seen her eyes narrow, had seen her grow still and then bolt, the quick terrible rage she was capable of, the quick terrible joy. I know you, he said to himself, I know who you are, baby, and now I have to make a choice. If I tell you, then you won't love me anymore. You can't stand white trash stuff. It drives you crazy.

And if I don't tell you, then I lose that way too. Because you know I'm lying and that is crossing you and you can't stand to be crossed or lied to or told you're wrong or called on anything.

The thing to do is hold her, he decided. If I can just get hold of her I can decide what to do.

"Please come inside awhile," he said. "Come lie down with me. Something bad has happened. I want to talk to you about it."

"What happened? Go on and tell me."

"Come inside and sit by me and I will."

"Okay, go on in." He went into the trailer and sat down on the bed and she followed him.

"Dad's in trouble," he said. "I got a note from the editor of the paper. But I already know what it is. I've been expecting this to happen."

"What did he do?" She was edging away from him, already scared of the contagion.

"You know he was flying for J. B. Hunt last winter but he quit because they kept making him get up in the middle of the night and he's too old to fly like that. He can't rodeo anymore and it's hard to get a job flying up here. There isn't any work here. You know that. Anyway, I think he's been running dope. The guys he's had around here are into that. I think Sharrene did it to him. She's a gold digger if I ever saw one. She's got two rooms full of new clothes in there. She just shops all the time. Anyway, he quit J.B. because he couldn't stay up all night and keep her happy too. She's a party animal. She likes the bars. Anyway, he's up to his ears in debt from all the stuff Sharrene charged to him and I think he's been running dope. I've been thinking so." He took the note out of his pocket and showed it to her. "So I got to go on over there and see what they say. You can go with me if you want to."

"No, you go on." Olivia was getting up, smoothing her skirt down across her stomach. She was backing out of the room. "Call me later. Tell me what they said. Come on, take me to my car. I want to get some studying done if we're not going to stay here."

She was out of the trailer, out into the fresh air. Get me out of here, she was thinking. Get me away from this goddamn trailer park.

CHAPTER 29

OLIVIA'S appointment with the doctor in Tulsa was at three o'clock in the afternoon. She walked into the waiting room and sat down on the sofa and began to get nervous. She crossed and uncrossed her legs. She looked disapprovingly down at her blue jeans and shoes. She stood up and tucked in her blouse and frowned at a fireplace filled with half-dead plants. On the mantel was an odd assortment of vases, most of them with figures carved on them. Greek, Roman, Indian. The wall above the fireplace held a copy of a painting of a small fat man flying above a town. He had a lovely smile on his face. Olivia seemed to settle down as she looked at the painting. I used to dream I was flying all over Tahlequah, she thought. And Bobby dreams he's flying all the time. Well, now his dad's going to jail and if Dad finds out about all this, I'll never see any of them again. They aren't going to have anything to do with criminals. I don't know what to do. I don't know why I came to this place.

A stereo system was playing New Age guitar music. Then the music changed. A piano began to play long deliberate notes like a keen lullaby. Olivia got up and went to stand by the CD player, trying to get closer to the music.

"Hello," a voice said, and a short, good-looking man in a brown coat opened a door and came into the room. He held out his hand and she shook it. "I'm Doctor Coder," he said. "You are Olivia?"

"That's me. I couldn't have come on a better day. Boy, do I have some problems."

"Come on in," he answered and held the door. "Sit down and talk to me."

Forty-five minutes later, Olivia was still talking. "So if I tell Dad I'm involved with Bobby then that's the end of that. Even if he isn't rich anymore, still it's my only chance to ever get any money, and I like all of them, well, not the people at Chapel Hill. I bet I hardly had a friend there, well, except for Cornelia Bosworth, this girl from Charlotte I knew in high school. I like her, she's really great but she went off to London with her folks for the summer and Jessie's in New Orleans with this baby sucking on her tit. You know what she told me the other day on the phone? She said every two hours he sucks out all the milk in both of her breasts. She's so tired she can hardly make up the bed. Well, Crystal will get her about ten more maids. I wouldn't have a baby for all the tea in China. That's what this woman, my teacher, Doctor Jones, says about everything. She says I wouldn't do that for all the tea in China. Well, I have to go over to Planned Parenthood and get some pills. I keep meaning to do it every day. Well, if Bobby's dad stays in jail I sure don't have to worry about that. He wouldn't even fuck me yesterday. He just sat around all night worrying and being so cold to me. I mean, he couldn't even get interested. He thinks it's going to make everyone hate him. He's worked all his life to make people think he isn't white trash and what good does it do? His father was the first person in their family to even know how to drive a car. They were really country people. They didn't even live in town. They lived out on the Illinois by Clear Creek and trapped and fished for a living, raising chickens and pigs. He took me out there once and showed me where he came from. Oh, that was so long ago.

"So what do you think I ought to do? I can't give him back this ring when he's already so worried he can't even fuck me. Can I? I came down here to learn Navajo. Well, all I want to do now is go home and see if Dad will still speak to me. I tried to call him four times last night but I didn't even get an answering machine. I guess he's gone on to Switzerland with Margaret. He wanted to go eat asparagus and drink hot chocolate. He told me they brought the hot chocolate out in two pots — one with melted chocolate and one with hot milk — and then they bring you three kinds of sugar and you mix it yourself. I was a fool not to go. I should have gone with him. What am I doing back in Green Country with a bunch of jailbirds? Bad blood. It's just bad blood. I'm like my mother. She was just a whore. She was hitchhiking across the country like a homeless person while she was pregnant with me. That's why she died. If she had stayed in Charlotte with them she'd be okay. Why are you looking at your watch? Is it time for me to leave?"

"In a few minutes. I'd like to see you again tomorrow afternoon. Could you come at three?"

"I don't know. It's an hour's drive. I get out at twelve. Well, okay, I told Georgia I'd come and have tea at her house but I can do it later, I guess. She goes to shrinks. She was all for me doing this. I have to call Dad and make sure he can pay for it. He thinks he's rich but he isn't anymore. Grandmother told us not to make him spend money on us."

"I talked to Doctor Carlyn in Chapel Hill. She said your father was very eager for you to see someone."

"It's because I changed my grades on a computer at the school when I was a sophomore. He thinks I'm a criminal. He thinks he's just lucky every day I don't steal something. That's what Doctor Carlyn said. She said it would make me sick if all I did was work that scam. So I try not to spend any of his money if I can help it."

"Would you like to call and talk to him about it? Or have me call?"

"Would you do it? I've been trying to get him but he doesn't answer."

"If you like."

"What are we going to do in here anyway? I mean, what are you trying to do with me?"

"I'm not trying to do anything with you. I want you to find out what it is you want."

"I want to get out of college and get a job and be on my own. Well, I want someone to sleep with at night. I can't stand sleeping by myself. I could sleep with Aunt Mary Lily but she's so big and she snores and she worries about sleeping with me. She's afraid of lesbians. She thinks people will think we're queer if we sleep together. Well, to tell the truth I want to sleep with Bobby. I like to touch his skin. I like to lie around and be next to him. Is that so terrible?"

"Nothing is terrible except fear. Ignorance and fear. Well, I'll see you tomorrow then. We'll work out a schedule of appointments." He stood up, came around the desk, held out his hand. He was standing very still, a powerfully built muscular man with kind eyes, dark brown eyes set deeply into a kind face. Olivia met his eyes and smiled, then looked away. It was too nice, too tender, she could not bear that much intimacy. That much love.

"Okay, I'll see you tomorrow then." She turned at the door. "What should I do about Bobby? Should I give him back the ring?"

"I wouldn't do that yet. Not while he's unhappy. Don't do anything you wouldn't ordinarily do. I'll see you tomorrow afternoon."

She left the building and got into her father's car and strapped the seat belt on and turned on a radio station playing country music. She drove through the city of Tulsa listening to music and thinking about Doctor Coder. Maybe it wasn't so hopeless after all. Maybe she could have Bobby and keep it a secret from her dad. I ought to go and get some pills, she thought. I'll do it tomorrow as soon as I get out of class.

Bobby lay stretched out across his bed in the trailer. It was five in the afternoon and it was hot. The fan blew across his naked shoulders. His calculus book was propped up against a saddle. He studied the figures. He dove deep down into the calculus and forgot the heat and his father's voice on the phone from the jail cell in Iowa City.

"Forget about me," the voice had said. "I got what I deserved and I got caught. If you break the law, you get caught. Take care of Sharrene if you feel like it or don't even talk to her if you don't want to. She's going to Oklahoma City to stay with her folks in a few days anyway. You can move into the house when she's gone. I got the rent paid for the rest of the month and there's enough money in the bank to pay the utilities. You take what's left of it and use it for yourself. I'm going to call Bunk Halliday and tell him to let you take out the money. They said I could use the phone to call him. So you go see him tomorrow."

"Can I help you?" Bobby had said.

"No. Hell, no, I'll be all right. Hell, they got the jails so crowded with criminals they may not be able to find a place to keep me. Don't worry, son. I'll be all right. There's a spade in here who used to rodeo in Kansas City. He's all right. He's turning out to be a buddy. You go on and get your education. It's time a Tree got a college education. Well, I got to go now. They don't want me talking all night."

"I love you, Dad. I sure am sorry about all this."

"Sorry never bought a meal, son. I took a gamble and lost. You stay clean, you hear? Do your schoolwork. That's what you can do for me."

The phone went dead and Bobby went back out to the trailer and took off his shirt and lay down to study the beautiful calculus of Newton.

He had been studying for two hours. One more hour and then I'll get washed up and wait for her to get back, he decided. I'll take her out to the lake and we can go swimming and get some burgers and have a picnic. Hell, she knows who I am. She's got the ring, doesn't she? Not that she'd ever marry me anyway, much less now. Her rich kinfolks will be coming down here to collect her any day. Well, I knew that was coming. Who have I been fooling?

"Bobby." It was Sharrene outside the window of the trailer, calling out in her little nasal country voice. "Bobby, come in and talk on the phone. It's your friends in Montana. They said to call you to the phone."

He got up from the bed and pulled on his pants and walked out of the trailer and went on a run across the yard to the house. "Thanks, Sharrene," he called over his shoulder. "Thanks for coming to get me."

"What's happening?" Tom Macalpin said. "Why did I dream about you last night and again this afternoon?"

"What did you dream?"

"I dreamed you ran into a room quoting Dante. You aren't studying literature, are you?"

"I don't know what you're talking about. But my dad's in jail for running coke, so if you dreamed I was in trouble you got that right."

"Sherrill, his father's in jail. See, it was a message. She said it was a message and I pooh-poohed her."

"What did I say in the dream?"

"You came running into the room and said 'Dante,' then you spread out your arms like wings and started quoting.

> *'The day was departing and the darkening air*
> *was taking the creatures that are on the earth*
> *from their daily toil, and I alone*
> *was preparing to endure the hardship*
> *both of the journey and of the pity*
> *which unerring memory will relate.'*

It's Beatrice's opening canto on Good Friday. The sun that cheered Dante is going down."

"Well, it's sure going down for me. I don't know what's going to happen. I know I've got to find someplace to live and I've got to go out tomorrow and find a job."

"Get one that will let you stay in school."

"I'll find one. They're building the turnpike around here so there's plenty of construction work, or Kayo'll give me work at the ranch. I'll be okay. I may not have a girl by the time the day is over. She's in Tulsa talking to some psychiatrist. I guess he'll tell her to get rid of me."

"Why do you say that?"

"Because she's haughty. She can't stand for things to go wrong. She cares what people think of her. She won't stay around me when people know my dad's in jail. Hell, Tom, I know her. I been studying her for years."

"Then you have to stop loving her. You can't throw your heart down on the ground for her to trample on."

"She isn't mean, she's just how she is. She's proud."

"I thought you told me she got you to sneak into the school and change her records on a computer, so she's not the soul of honesty and virtue, now is she?"

"That was a one-time deal. It was a long time ago."

"Remind her of it."

"I couldn't do that. Well, I better go get cleaned up. She'll be back soon. She said she was coming by here but I don't think she'll do it. She'll go home and wait awhile, then call me up and make some lame excuse."

"If I was as proud as you say she is, I'd act better than that before I started judging other people."

"She's just like she is. She didn't ask me to come down here."

"But she's got the ring."

"She's got it. She doesn't wear it much, but she keeps it."

"Bobby."

"Yes."

"Take care of yourself. Protect your flank."

"Maybe you ought to fuck somebody else." It was Sherrill getting boiling mad on the other phone.

"Sherrill, not now."

"Hey, Sherrill, thanks for calling."

"Go out with somebody else if she doesn't come by. To hell with her. I've had it with this girl, Bobby. I'm about sick to death of this goddamn snotty little Miss Hand. Her aunt was the snottiest broad I ever met in my life. I never did like her. Everyone was always sucking up to her at writers conferences and talking about her humanity. I thought she was a snob. This girl sounds just like her. Come on back up here with us. We need you. We're shorthanded and Tom's hurt his back."

"Hang up, Sherrill. Don't start all that."

"To hell with this little bitch chewing on his heart. You could have plenty of good fine women, Bobby."

"Hang up, Sherrill. Let me finish talking."

She slammed the receiver down on the phone and Bobby started laughing. "Now you've done it, Thomas. Now you won't get any for a week."

"Trust your instincts, Bobby," Tom said. "If you want her enough to put up with all of this, maybe she's worth waiting for."

"She is to me. She's what I want. And I'm not giving up on her, not yet, if she doesn't give up on me. But she might."

CHAPTER 30

OLIVIA drove home from Tulsa in a driving rain. Hard, straight, gray rain that filled the valleys and woods with mist. Long trails of pale gray mist swirled upwards from the trees, mixed with the dark gray falling water. By the time she was ten miles down the road from Tulsa, it was dark from horizon to horizon. She turned off the radio, tightened her seat belt and tried to pay attention, remembering a night she and Mary Lily had turned the Pontiac around in the middle of the road coming back from a rodeo in Springdale. Goddamn this rain, Olivia was thinking. Now I'll be late and Bobby will think it's because his dad's in jail. Well, I don't have to solve his problems. That's what Doctor Coder said. He said, Don't try to solve other people's problems. If you try to remove the impact, you'll get shit all over you. He was talking about trying to fix a blocked intestine in a fat man when he was an intern. He said, Remember this, Olivia, if you try to remove the impact, you'll get shit all over you. Well, I wonder if he's going to tell me things like that all the time. I can't stop thinking about it. God, it must be awful to be an intern. I'll have to ask Georgia when I see her. I'll go eat breakfast with her in the morning and tell her what he said. Look at this rain, will you. Look at all this goddamn rain.

Olivia slowed down even more and drove steadily down the curving highway. There was hardly another car on the road. I guess no one's fool enough to drive in this, she decided. I'm getting off at the next exit and wait for it to slow down. Well, it's Green Country and we're in Tornado Alley. Weather gets together from the whole country here. Gets together and gets wilder. Powwow. Tornado Alley, that's about par, that's about what they would give the Cherokee when they ran them out of Carolina.

She pulled off the highway at Locust Grove and went to the doughnut shop and called Bobby. It took a long time for anyone to answer the phone but finally Sharrene answered it and said she'd look for him. In a few minutes she returned and said he wasn't there. "What's going on with Mr. Tree?" Olivia asked. "I'm stuck in Locust Grove, Sharrene. It's pouring rain. Is it raining there?"

"It sure is. It's been raining all day. Bud's in big trouble, honey. I'm going to Oklahoma City to stay with my folks. He sounds okay, though. He sounds pretty good. I guess he's in for a while, though. The plane was stolen, but no one told Bud about it. It had papers. He thought the papers was good."

"Were good. Never mind. I don't want to know about it. Listen, Sharrene, you have to leave Bobby a note and tell him I called. I wish you'd go find him, but I guess that's too much trouble, isn't it?"

"I don't know where he'd be."

"Try the pool hall. Call and see if you can find him. Anyway, leave him a note, okay? Tell him I'll call when I get home."

"Okay, honey. I'll find him if I can." Sharrene hung up the phone, got a beer out of the refrigerator, opened it, and sat down to write the note. She made a couple of beginnings but she couldn't spell Olivia so she got frustrated and tore up the notes. She tried to call the pool hall but the line was busy so she went back to the note.

"Dear Bobby, your girl called and said she was in Locust Grove." She looked at the note for a while but she still didn't like the way it looked, so she tore it up and started one more time. "Dear Bobby, your girl said she would call you when she got home. Love, Sharrene." She looked at that for a while and decided she liked it. She was searching for an envelope when her brother called from Oklahoma City to say they would come the next afternoon to help her move.

"You take plenty of furniture," he was saying. "Don't come out of this empty-handed like you always do, Sharrene. Me and Dad aren't going to support you this time. We want you to come home but you got to carry your own weight. I got plenty of people to take care of without adding you to the list."

By the time she finished talking to her brother, Sharrene was so mad she had forgotten all about the note. She opened a second beer and went downtown to go shopping, leaving the note still attached to the pad and lying on the table.

Olivia stayed at the doughnut shop long enough to drink two cups of coffee, then she got back into the car and pulled back out onto the turnpike. The rain was slacking but it was still falling.

It's possible to be alone and not be lonely. That's what Doctor Coder had said. She could love Bobby without needing him so much that she'd give her life to him. Nothing's draining all the lifeblood out of me every two hours, she decided. Then what will we do? Be like Georgia and her boyfriend and never have the courage to live together? Why should it take courage if it's such a good idea? Tell me that. Did I ever see anybody who was married who lived happily ever after? No. The minute they get married, the honeymoon is over.

So what do we do? I asked him. Get smart, he said. If you want to be happy you have to work for it. You have to tell the truth, the whole truth, and nothing but the truth and you have to take chances and you have to talk.

So when I get home we're going to talk about it. I'll say, Bobby, it bums me out that your dad's in jail. I don't want to be mixed up in that. If my dad finds out he'll never speak to me again. No one in the Hand family will be mixed up with criminals. So then what? So go with me to North Carolina in the fall. Oh, yeah. Well, first you have to meet my dad.

She shook her head and drove on home. There weren't any answers to any of this. Just problem after problem after problem.

It was late when she got home and she was tired of thinking. She kept meaning to pick up the phone and call Bobby but she couldn't get herself to do it. Finally, at ten-thirty he called her. "I decided to call you," he said. "I figured that shrink told you to get rid of me."

"It bums me out that your dad's in jail. I can't be mixed up in that, Bobby. If my dad finds out he'll never speak to me again. No one in the Hand family ever had to go to jail. My granddaddy is a lawyer. I don't want to say this to you. Why'd you call me up? If you hadn't called me, you wouldn't be hearing this."

"I knew that's how you'd feel. What can I do about it, honey? I didn't do it. Maybe I ought to go up to Montana and go back to work for Tom. Hell, I don't know what to do."

"What'd you do all day while I was gone?"

"I got a job, for one thing. Driving a bulldozer for Jay Knight. Three hundred a week and I can do it in my spare time."

"Good. That's good. I'm glad."

"You want me to come out and talk to you?"

"Tonight?"

"Yeah."

"No. I have to think about it. I have to go to the shrink again tomorrow."

"Twice in one week?"

"I'm going to go three times a week. Maybe four."

The line was quiet. He's a man, Olivia was thinking. He never whines. He knows how to wait. "We'll go somewhere day after tomorrow," she offered. "I have to think about all this. And I have to tell the truth about how I feel, Bobby. If we start lying we'll never figure out what to do."

"I know what to do. I don't have any choice."

"I'll see you day after tomorrow in the afternoon. Maybe we can go to the lake."

"I'm yours. Whatever you want to do." He glanced down at the table. Saw Sherrill's scribbled note. Thought about how poor and mean the world he lived in was. Looked off into the living room. He couldn't love a thing he saw, and yet a huge strange thought was in his heart, the thought of Olivia in a home with him.

"I'm sorry I'm this way," she said.

"The way you are is fine. I'll see you in two days then." He hung up the phone and went out into the yard and watched the last of the clouds moving across the moon. The trees were dark and wet, the world was saturated with water. The huge strange thought was in him still. It would carry him through the night.

CHAPTER 31

THE psychiatrist kept Olivia waiting the second day. She spent a long time looking through old *New Yorker* magazines and getting up and looking out the window. Finally, he opened the door and she went in and lay down on the sofa and began to cry. She told him about her aunt Anna and what it had been like to wait for her father to call her up and say he wanted to see her.

"He didn't know Momma had me. Why didn't she tell him? What a mean thing to do. I think she was mean. Everyone says she was mean. I hate her for dying and leaving me and for not telling Dad. I think he's mad at me because he didn't know. Maybe he's just mad at me for being here. All the time after I wrote Aunt Anna and she came to see me, all the time I felt like a beggar, like I was begging my own father to admit I was alive. And Jessie is so perfect, well, she's a fool but she looks perfect. She's so beautiful people go crazy when they see her. It didn't change a thing for her to have K.T. If anything she's prettier than she was. I miss her. I loved having her those two years we lived

together at Dad's. I don't know what to do. I don't know who to love."
She put her face down into her hands and wept deep hard tears. When
she looked up the psychiatrist was waiting.

"What do you want to do?" he asked. "What do you need?"

"I want to get in the car with Bobby and drive down and see Jessie
and King and K.T. I want to take Bobby to Tipitina's to hear the
Nevilles and introduce him to Andria and eat beignets in the French
Quarter. I want to have a good time for God's sake. I'm sick of
Tahlequah already. Sick of school. Bobby's better than King. If they
high-hat him, I'll never speak to them again."

"Have you talked to your sister?"

"Yes. She invited us to come. It's a thirteen-hour drive but I've got
Dad's car. We could leave on Friday and go down and come back
Sunday night and drive all night and get here for our classes. It looks
like I could have a good time some time, doesn't it?"

"Then why don't you go?"

"Maybe I will," she answered and felt like sunlight had just come
out from behind the clouds. "Maybe I'll do just that." She paused,
looked at his old brown shoes propped so neatly on the desk. "Then
just keep on going, drive to the Grand Canyon and Yellowstone
National Park and see the geysers. Find a mountain town and get a job
in a café and be a part of life. Chapel Hill isn't part of life. It's like some
expensive camp. You know what else?" She turned to him. "I figured
this out in Charlotte. It isn't the rich people who go to places, who
have fun. It's the people who work there who have a good time. Bobby
and I could work anywhere. We don't need an education."

"Wait a minute." Doctor Coder had been with her all the way until
she started that. "Education's okay. I'll admit there's a lot to be said for
practical knowledge, but books have their place. English and history
and science and math."

"That's what Georgia says. This doctor who's a friend of mine. She
teaches anthropology but she says it's just a pseudoscience. She said
most of what they teach in school is crap. Somebody's opinion or their
ax to grind." Olivia sat up. She looked at her watch. An hour was
almost over and she felt like she had only begun to talk. "I don't want
to leave," she said. "I never want to leave here."

"I'm going to see you Thursday," he answered. "Thursday afternoon. By then, who knows what will have happened in the world." He smiled at her, the kindest, most open smile Olivia had ever seen in her life. It reminded her of something, then she remembered. Anna. Her aunt Anna had looked at her like that, as if she knew all the way into Olivia's heart and knew the deepest secrets of her mind. Where did people learn such things? Olivia returned the doctor's look and his heart turned over at the intelligence and searching and goodness of her face. A truth-teller, he told himself. An intuitive. Yes, this one will be worth teaching. This one will want the truth enough to find it.

The next afternoon, as soon as their classes were over, Bobby and Olivia piled into the pickup and took off for Beaver Lake. They drove out past Eureka Springs to where great granite bluffs overlook the lake and make a series of steps down into the water. They set up camp with the tent and ate submarine sandwiches they had bought at a store and made love in the tent and then put on bathing suits and got into the soft dammed-up river water and began to swim. They swam out four hundred yards into the lake and turned and were resting on their backs, letting the current rock them.

"I think I'm studying the wrong thing," Olivia said. "I think I ought to go to medical school. Georgia says she thinks I have a scientific mind. Well, that's because she likes anyone who doesn't believe in God. She says God is the silliest idea in the world. You know what she said? She said, imagine a creator who would hold the creation responsible for itself. Like my dad. He created me, didn't he? Him and Mom. So whatever I am, they made me this way." She was dog paddling, watching Bobby, trying to decide if he was smart enough for her to love, when he said something that surprised her. "I think about God a lot, but not a God like that. Like the mountains in Montana and the way skies seem so beautiful to us. Only people know how beautiful things are. I study the beauty of the world, not to know what it means, but because it's there for us. I wish I had more to offer you, baby, but I don't, just as I am, as the old hymn goes. Well, look, you want to start back now? I might want to dive off the overhangs." He smiled at her then and turned in the water and began to swim, slowly at first, waiting for her to catch up, and then, suddenly, he took off and swam very fast back to the shore and climbed up on the steps and began to climb.

A rocky path curved up the bluff to where three wide outcrops overlooked the water. It was a place where young men from Eureka played chicken. The first step was about fifty feet above the water, the second about a hundred, and the third, which was almost to the top of the bluff, two hundred and fifty feet or more. Olivia had seen plenty of boys dive from the first step and once had watched Bobby dive from the second step, but she had never seen anyone dive from the third step (although there was a story that a boy high on psychedelic mushrooms had jumped from there and landed on the rocks and broken half the bones in his body).

Bobby passed the first overhang and kept on climbing. Olivia was out of the water now. He's going to the top, she told herself. I have forgotten who he is. All these weeks I've been fucking him and bossing him around and treating him like shit and I forgot who he is. His dad can go to jail and he can be broke and live in a trailer and it doesn't matter. He's a hero. He was a hero when I met him and he'll always be one. He's going to the top and when he gets there, he's going to dive. Nothing's going to stop him so I might as well just watch. Besides, he won't die jumping off that cliff. If he did, it doesn't matter to him like it does to people who are always on the second team.

A hawk left its nest and hovered above the path where Bobby climbed. Bobby climbed more slowly now, as the path was steeper. Small birch trees grew here and there beside the path and scraggly juniper bushes. At one point Olivia lost sight of him as he climbed. He had passed the first overhang and kept on going. He walked out onto the second ledge and threw a stone into the water and turned and smiled at her. Then he went back onto the path and kept on climbing. The hawk circled the bluff. A bank of clouds like a huge glacier was moving slowly across the eastern sky. Bobby disappeared again and reappeared on the third ledge. He threw a second rock into the water and watched it sink. Then he threw another further out and waited until the ripples from it split the surface. Then he turned and looked in Olivia's direction and saluted her with outstretched arms. He turned back to the ledge. He walked out to the edge of it and dove. His body arched out into the trajectory of the third rock and entered the flat brown water. He surfaced thirty feet from the point of entry and turned and began to swim slowly back to where Olivia was standing.

*   *   *

They spent the night in the tent. First they built a fire and cooked hot dogs and ate them and then they got into the truck and drove into Eureka to go to the Blues Festival in the park. "Knife in the Water" was playing, a Muddy Waters imitator from Fayetteville, and they listened to that for a while, then wandered around the crowd talking to people they knew and flashing Olivia's ring. "Bobby dove off the third step at Spider Creek," Olivia told a couple of girls she knew. "Can you believe him?"

"You're lucky," one girl replied. "I bet he's the only boy in the Ozarks who wants to get married. All the boys are acting like horse's asses. I'm about to quit going out with them."

"Yeah," the second girl said. "Me too."

The next morning they woke at dawn and packed up their gear and drove eighty miles an hour back to Tahlequah. They got to the trailer at eight to find that Sharrene had packed up and gone, taking half the furniture in the house and all the kitchen utensils and pots and pans. She had even taken the kitchen phone. The note she had forgotten to give Bobby was on the table with another one beside it. "I'm at my folks in Oklahoma City. Keep in touch. Give me a call if you need me. Love, Sharrene. I took the phone because I got it for him. I hope that is okay."

They stood on either side of the kitchen table and smirked. It was too embarrassing to laugh at, too stupid and greedy to be regretted.

"We don't have to stay here," Olivia said. "When summer's over we could leave all this behind. We could get into your truck and start driving. I told the shrink I wished we could go to Colorado or Montana and leave everyone behind and start all over again. Just the two of us, and you know what he said?"

"What did he say?"

"He said we could if we could get hold of certain things inside ourselves."

"Like what?"

"Knowing we are part of everything. All the clouds and everything there is. Like you diving off that cliff. Like knowing there isn't anything to be afraid of. I'm always so afraid I won't have any money. It's all I think about. As much money as Dad gives me, and I don't even spend it. I'm afraid it will run out."

"I'm going to be making three hundred a week working for Jay. I'm not broke, Olivia. I've got nine thousand some odd dollars. Well, I owe a little bit more for your ring." He looked at her hand. She was wearing it. She had put it on when they left for the lake and except when they were in the water she'd been wearing it all the time.

"Well, right now we've got to do something about this house. Let's walk around and see what all is left and make the living room look good and one of the bedrooms. We can get some pans out at Grandmomma's. She'll give you enough stuff to cook on. Come on, let's get started."

"We have to go to class first. We can do this when we get back." He came around her side of the table and pulled her into his arms and began to kiss her very softly and sweetly on the mouth. "The good thing is we've got a house to live in. I think I'll just go burn that trailer."

"Would you do that?" She giggled. "Let's blow it up. Let's blow it all to hell."

When she got home that afternoon her father had been calling. "Your dad's been trying to get you," Little Sun said. "You must call him. He hasn't heard from you and he's worried."

"What did he say? Is everything all right?"

"He just wants to know how you are. He sounds like a nice man, Little Flower. A lonely man. He said that he is lonely with you gone."

"What did you tell him?"

"I told him nothing. I told him you had been at school all the time. He said to call when you came in. No matter what time it was." Little Sun stood in the kitchen by the table he had made and painted blue. He was still very tall for an old man, very straight, with only a small stoop to his back. His face had changed in the time Olivia had been gone. Had become thinner, younger looking somehow. The skin stretched tight across the jaw and cheekbones, and become translucent. But the eyes had remained the same. The same brown eyes that met your own and held them. He never had to tell a lie to anyone, Olivia thought. Like Doctor Coder is trying to teach me. Do not lie in thought, word, or deed. Don't let anyone make you want something enough to lie for it. Well, he had his government checks. He could quit anything he was doing if he didn't like it. I want Bobby and me to have a life like that. But then I'd have to give up Charlotte, because all anyone does in Charlotte is think some kind of lie all day.

"I ought to call him and tell him to stop drinking. Then he wouldn't be so lonely." Olivia smiled into her grandfather's eyes. "What if I called and told him that?"

"Maybe you could find a way to say it that would not wound him."

"He needs wounding. He needs to see what he does to people. Well, I'll call him. Let me get the phone." She walked over to the wall by the table and took down the phone and dialed the number. In a minute Daniel answered. "I'm sorry I didn't call you," Olivia said. "I've been busy with school. It's hard to go every day and I'm going to this psychiatrist. Are you sure you can afford it? It's costing six dollars' worth of gasoline to drive over there and back. I don't think I ought to spend this much money. Is it okay?"

"Don't worry about that, honey. There's plenty of money for what you need. But your grandmother's having a fit because she hasn't seen you except for that day. Why don't you fly up here for the Fourth of July. Everyone's coming home. Helen's coming from Boston and Louise is going to be here. We can get you a plane ticket. How about it?"

"I don't know." Olivia turned and looked at her grandfather, who was wearing his please-be-kind look. "Okay. I'll come. Aunt Louise will be there? I haven't seen her in so long. How about Jessie? Will she come and bring K.T.?"

"I invited them. I hope they'll be here. Well, let me hang up and call the airlines. I'll call you back. Will you be home now?"

"I guess so. Sure. I'll be here. I love you, Dad. I've been missing you." Olivia sighed. That wasn't a lie. She did miss him. She had missed him all her life. Her beautiful tall wonderful father. Her divine golden father. The end of the rainbow. The pot of gold she had gone to seek. Memory is a dance. The face of her grandfather smiling at her for being kind. The voice of her long-lost father, whose voice she had finally heard one day when she was sixteen years old on this very phone. The room six feet away where her mother had died giving birth to her. The light dying in the west and the purple glow upon the table and the shadows of the leaves, the death mask Little Sun's face was becoming. Death waiting for them all, everywhere, and, in the meantime, everyone all scattered out. "Oh, Dad, I want so much. I want to be there with you and also here. I want to see Aunt Helen and I want to show this place to you. You've never even been here. I was born here. A few feet from this phone. You should come and see it sometime." Olivia was going to cry. It was going to happen. There would be no preventing it. Tears began to run down her face. Only yesterday she had been at the lake with Bobby, young and alive and free. Now she was back into all this mess.

Little Sun took the phone from her hand. "I'll call the airline, then I'll call you back," Daniel said.

"She is crying," Little Sun said. "I think she misses you very much."

Olivia ran into the bathroom and washed her face and got mad at herself. You pussy, she scolded her reflection in the mirror. You goddamn pussy. I thought you were going to be strong. Where's strong? I don't see any strong.

She put on powder and lipstick and combed her hair and went back into the kitchen and ate vanilla wafers until Daniel called again. "Two-thirty on Wednesday afternoon," he said. "You can go back on Sunday. Is that okay? Can you get to the plane in Tulsa by two-thirty?"

"Yes, listen, Dad. Tell Jessie to come, will you? I want to hold K.T. I'm dying to hold him in my arms."

"You tell her. Call her up tonight and get her to come. Hell, I deserve a look at my children once every couple of months."

"How's your business doing?"

"It's rough, sugar, but we'll make it. I may try to sell it as soon as things smooth out in the economy. Well, I'll mail you the ticket tomorrow then. What else is going on?"

"Not much. I went swimming at the lake yesterday. If you came you could go. I bet you'd like it. It's a huge lake made from the White River. I bet you'd love it."

"I'll come someday. Well, study hard. I'll send the ticket tomorrow."

They hung up. Olivia had not told him not to drink and she hadn't told him about Bobby. But I got taken by surprise by his wanting me to come for the Fourth of July, she told herself. That's what happened. If I'd thought up calling him I'd have been the one to set the agenda.

"Let's go for a walk and watch it get dark," Olivia said. "Come on, Granddaddy. Go for a walk with me."

Then the two of them went out into the yard and walked back across the pasture to where the old corn patch had been. Not talking about anything, just walking and not even touching. Just walking side by side as the sun took its light away and left the earth in darkness. By the time they got back to the house stars were everywhere. A moonless night, millions of stars shone down upon the house. They went inside to eat their dinner.

Very late that afternoon, Georgia was sitting in zazen. She was doing a sutra called The Blue Flower Meditation. She was sitting on a prayer bench looking at a blue lily. She traced the stamen down into the stem.

She settled down, tried to stop her mind from thinking. Slowly, her cheeks began to relax, her jaws went slack. Then, very slowly, she reached out her hand and began to open the petals, spreading them out, unfurling the flower.

The possibilities, she decided. That's what I've lost. The width and breadth of the world, the lavish vast unexplored regions, oceans and rivers and canyons and roads and mountains and towns and cities. "Where are the other places?" a philosopher once asked. "I have got my own self, but I have lost them."

Georgia stroked the flower with her finger. Golden pollen fell across her hand. Shower of gold, she said to herself and went into her deepest impregnation fantasy. Against her will, in a harem, she was being impregnated three weeks after giving birth.

She went into the bathroom and put on lipstick and powder and plugged in her heated rollers and went to the phone and called Zach. "So did you sleep with Dallas Anne?" she began. "If you did, just tell me and I won't like you anymore."

"She didn't stay here," Zach answered. "Why do you keep saying that?"

"Taylor said she stayed there. They hate me, Zach. Can't you feel it? Don't you even know that?"

"They like you, Georgia. They don't hate you. They're fucked up. I'll admit that, but it isn't about you. They just haven't grown up yet. They're coming along."

"You didn't fuck her?"

"She didn't stay here. I swear she didn't. I can't believe Taylor told you that. You must have misunderstood him."

"No. I know what he said."

"Then I'll ask him about it. As soon as he gets back. They've gone to Fort Smith for the week."

"They're gone?"

"Yes."

"Then I'm coming over. Tomorrow afternoon. I'm horny, Zach, I want to fuck you. I'm tired of all this rigamarole. All I want to do is fuck you. I'm tired of our lives getting tangled up. I didn't make your past. I didn't have those twins. You didn't fail to love me when I was two. To hell with it. Could we just go back to being in love? Do you remember how lonely and neurotic we both were when I met you? Well, I remember."

"When can you get here?"

"By four. Come home early and be waiting for me."

"I will. I'm glad. I love you."

But of course he isn't waiting for me, she decided. It was four-fifteen. She was standing on the porch watching it begin to rain. She had been at Zach's house since three-thirty. She had been getting mad since two after four. She went back into the house and put a CD in the CD player. *Heavy Weather,* by Weather Report, a CD she had given him for Christmas. She went back out onto the wooden porch. The sky was growing darker, the wind picking up in the dense trees that filled the yard and lined the street. I hope it pours, she thought. I hope it floods the town. She sat down in the porch swing, began to gently swing. The wind blew her hair into her eyes, blew her scarf around her neck. She forgot her anger for a moment, caught up in the sight of a pair of five-year-olds across the street. They came out the door in their little cotton underpants and walked down their steps and out into their yard and turned their faces up to the falling raindrops. They began to giggle, touching hands and shoving each other. Then the boy began to run and the girl began to chase him. Their screams rent the sky, began a long sound that ended in thunder. Life held me green and dying though I sang in my chains like the sea, Georgia thought, slowing the swing with her sandals. Why can't I be like that now? Why am I jealous of his children, his completely insane ex-wife? I wouldn't talk to her if I met her at a party. Why would I be jealous of anyone like that? What's wrong with me? I know what's wrong with me. It's the same reason I was jealous of Sybil or Aurora when we were young. If Momma or Daddy gave them a stick of gum, I got jealous. Oh, God, we're hopeless, all of us. Birds in a nest, give me, give me, give me. I want, I want, I want, me too, me too, me too. Pitiful, pitiful, like me the most, like only me.

Disgusting. What did I tell Olivia the other day? I said, *The central problem of romantic love is to get bonding energy without bartering the self.* But that's not true. That's only the beginning. The problem is to learn to love without bonding. Bond with the universe, with lightning and thunder and rain and flowers and oxygen-giving trees. Keep love clear of bonding crap and it might work. I'm bartering this very minute. Where is he? What did he find to do that was so goddamn important he wasn't here after I drove all the way over here?

She picked up an old straw hat sitting on a chair and put it on and walked out into the yard. Small hot drops of rain fell on her hands and arms, the sky was black now. A long network of lightning filled the air to the south. She walked to a bed of purple iris and picked two of them, then picked a third one and went into the house. She went into the kitchen, found a vase, put the flowers in it, and began to meditate upon her every act. Every act must be in the spirit of Zen, she decided. Every moment is Zen. Let the earth be beautiful. Let me go in there and make up that bed and get ready for my lover.

Who is probably standing beside his desk letting some little pubescent coed tell him her troubles. Her folks are getting a divorce, her mother has cancer, she doesn't know what to do for the summer, she lost her textbook.

What defense do I have against that? I can't act like I need him. I don't need him to solve my problems. I just need him to come on home and fuck me in the rain.

She went into his bedroom and made up the unmade bed and threw his dirty clothes into a pile on the closet floor and dusted off a table. Rain was pouring straight down from the sky now and Georgia was getting into a fabulous mood. She reached up under her skirt and took off her underpants and threw them on the pile with his clothes. She walked back out onto the porch and stood by the door. He drove up in his car. She smiled and waved and the frantic look left his face and he parked the car and came running toward her.

"She made you do it?" she was saying later. "Go over that again."

"I had the operation because she wanted me to." He moved away, not much, just an inch or so, just an almost imperceptible little defense.

Don't fuck up this afternoon, Georgia told herself. Don't start a single sentence with "you did" or "she did" or "you should" or any of that stuff. Say "I am," and "I want," and "I need," and "I love." That's it. Stick with that. I am a goddamn little needful bird in the goddamn endless nest saying I need, I need, I need. Oh, to hell with that.

"You got cut because she wanted it? Well, maybe you wanted to also, Zach. Maybe it wasn't just for her."

"No, I didn't want to, but I didn't want her to leave. I don't like to be left, Georgia. I think you know that. I think that's why you do it."

"Maybe so. If so, I'm sorry. Are you sorry that you did it, got cut, I mean? Well, don't answer that. Come here, get close to me. I want to plaster my arm to yours. I needed to be near you and here I am. I drove eighty miles an hour to get here. And what I want now is to hold you as close to me as I can for as long as I can stand it, considering the fact that I'm starving."

"I could cook you some fettucine."

"I'd adore fettucine." She put her lips very close to his neck. She breathed in the smell and life of him. For almost three minutes they were almost happy. Then the phone started ringing. It was one of the twins, saying they had had an accident in Hope, Arkansas, and would Zach talk to the police and tell them what to do with the car.

CHAPTER 32

YOUR mind has been very far away," Little Sun said. He and Olivia were sitting in the wooden yard chairs facing the barn. Day was dying in the west, huge fabulous clouds moved across the horizon, orange and red and pink and mauve and purple and gold and every shade of gray and white and blue. Dust from Mount Pinatubo was moving across the surface of the earth, breaking sunlight into colors for the human eye. A hummingbird moved its beak in and out of the lilies, drawn by the infrared patterns of the petals, the maps of love, the Landsat photographs of the hummingbird eye. A garden tiger moth spread its wings and landed beside a fallen oak leaf. Summer was fully come to Oklahoma. Each new season was vital and charged with meaning for Little Sun now. Five more summers, he would say to himself. Maybe seven summers, then fields where the ancestors sit in counsel with the elk and deer. Who knows where we walk when this time on earth is over. Poor Crow, she knows when I think of death and spoils the biscuits and will not lay her body against me in the dark. I must not think of this anymore. I have work to do and I must go tomorrow to see the lawyers again. All this money is going to start being in the bank and I must guard my children from it. I will not have my sons ruined by this money or my daughters either. Mary Lily is happy getting up each morning to go to her new job. When she finds out about this money, she will want to go on vacations to Kansas City and will get fatter eating candy.

The moth fanned its wings. The hummingbird moved on to other flowers. Little Sun reached across the wooden loveseat and put his hand on his granddaughter's arm. "Is love the cause of your troubled face?" he asked.

"Do I have a troubled face?"

"You have not smiled in many days. Who is this doctor you are driving so far to see?"

"Probably a mirage. Oh, Granddaddy, I don't know what to do. I want to stay here with all of you and I want to stay with Bobby and maybe marry him someday. But I don't want to give up my family in North Carolina either. I like them and I like all the money that they have. Is that so bad? I can't help liking it. But I can't introduce Bobby to my dad. His father just got arrested for running drugs in a stolen plane. I know you read it in the paper. I know you know about it, don't you?"

"These are hard times for everyone. But that is no excuse for being a bad man. For doing things against the law. So this is about money. You believe your father will know of this dishonesty of his father and throw you away for that?"

"Yes. I don't even know if I want to go back there. I didn't even have a boyfriend in North Carolina. They didn't like me. I was nobody there. But they have so much money. Well, Dad doesn't have it anymore but he still lives like he does. The rest of them really have it. It's so beautiful and rich. Their houses are so beautiful. They just get anything they want. But they aren't happy. You ought to see my cousins, Granddaddy. They don't know what they want to do. They're really nice but they just keep sucking off their parents and they never have a career or anything. Mooching, that's what Spook calls it. I don't want to be a mooch. I don't know. Sometimes I wish I'd never written to Aunt Anna and started this. Then I'd just be happy being here."

"When you have learned the Navajo language and graduated from college you will have a career. Then you will have your own paycheck like Mary Lily and it will make you happy. You won't be taking money from your father then. How much money does it cost you to go to college in North Carolina?"

"A lot. And I didn't even have a boyfriend or anything to make me happy. All that money he was paying and I was so unhappy I couldn't sleep at night, much less learn anything. I don't think I learned a thing last year except maybe some books I read that I liked. I could have read them by myself." Olivia twisted the ring around her finger. "What's wrong with being happy, that's what I'd like to know. I want to get a good education, Granddaddy. I want to be able to take care of you when you get old. I might build you a bigger house. One that's easy to live in and has a new kitchen."

"We would like that." Little Sun laughed, thinking of a conversation he had had with Crow that morning. "It is time to tell them," she had insisted. "May Frost needs a new washing machine. I wish to give her one. She is driving the clothes to the washateria every morning. I want to call them to a meeting and tell them there will be money in the bank."

"Not yet," Little Sun said. "You must wait one more month."

"I will buy her a washing machine." Crow had gotten up and was putting on her teddies. She would not look at him. "She has to take the baby in the car to the washateria. I want to go to Sears and get a new washing machine for her."

"Then go do that."

"Then Roper's wife will say, Why did she get a washing machine for May Frost and not one for me?"

"See, it has already started, the trouble money brings."

"I will buy her one. I will say I won the money at the races in Oklahoma City."

"Now the money makes you lie to your children?" Crow would not answer that. She smoothed the teddy down across her hips, gave him a cold look, then slipped a housecoat over her body.

"I will go to Sears today and pick out the machine."

A long pink cloud dissolved into a purple one, a streak of orange opened along the horizon, the purple became black. "Do you not love your father that you went so far to find?" Little Sun asked. "Is that not the truth of your worry, not this about money?"

"I love him. Of course I do. Only it's hard to love him because he's so nervous and everything always has to be his way. First he gets mad at us, then he gives us money. Well, not mad. I don't know what it is. It's like nothing ever pleases him. He always wants something else. He wants some life that isn't true anymore. Aunt Anna told me that. You know what he really loves? When both of us are all dressed up and we go somewhere with him, like to church or over to his mother's house. Or out to dinner where people see us. He never has time just to sit around and talk to us. Besides, his girlfriends are always there. Mostly it's Margaret now, and she's not so bad. She's fat and she likes to have fun. She laughs at him."

"Bring Bobby Tree out here to eat dinner with us tomorrow night. I will see how he will seem to your father. Tomorrow I will catch fish and Crow will fry them and make hush puppies and we will have vegetables from the garden. If his father is in trouble, we must be kind to him. If you love him he must be a good young man. I have no doubt of that. I think you are borrowing trouble with your frowning thoughts."

"You know what he did yesterday?"

"Tell me."

"He dove off the very top of the bluffs over Spider Creek. He just spread out his arms and dove right in. He has no fear of anything, like you are, like Dad. Dad isn't afraid of anything. If he didn't get drunk at night he'd be so wonderful. Bobby dove off that cliff to say he loved me. It made me drunk to watch him. I thought, I had forgotten who he is. He isn't some criminal's son. He's Bobby Tree. Afterwards, it was like I was drunk. I was like someone I had forgotten how to be. I wasn't afraid of anything either because he was brave. He isn't a bad person. If anyone is bad, it's me." Olivia began to cry, weeping into her hands, and her grandfather held out his arms and she went to him and sat across his lap and wept her tears. "All I do is cry all the time," she said. "Talk about a baby. I'm the biggest baby in the world."

Crow came out on the porch and saw them and came tearing down the stairs and across the yard. "What's the matter?" she demanded. "What's going on? Why are you crying? What did you say to her?" She sat down beside them and began to rub Olivia's arm. She pushed her hip against Little Sun, glad of an excuse to touch him after she had been cold to him all day.

"I am going into town tomorrow to buy a washing machine for May Frost," she said. "You can come with me to Sears and help me pick it out."

"A washing machine." Olivia sat up. "How can you buy a washing machine? What will you pay for it with?"

"She's been playing the horses." Little Sun laughed. "Your grandmother has become a gambler."

Later, after the sun was all the way down and they were in bed, Little Sun and Crow took up their argument again, although softer now, as they were in each other's arms. "In two weeks we will tell them, not a month," Crow said. Little Sun was stroking her back. She had been a fool for that for sixty years and she was a fool for it now. "Two weeks," she repeated. "And tomorrow I'm getting that washing machine. May Frost has to put the baby in the car every morning and drive to the washateria. Our pasture full of oil and May Frost has to pack up the baby and drive to town to wash the clothes."

"Where do they use so many clothes to be washed every day? Perhaps she likes going into town to see her friends."

"What difference is it whether it's two weeks from now or a month from now? If Roper quits his job, he quits his job. He doesn't like being a mechanic for the Ford Motor Place. He doesn't like having grease on his hands. He is breathing bad air in that little garage. JoDean said he was coughing in the night from breathing all the things they fix cars with."

"He is coughing from the cigarettes he smokes." Little Sun moved his hands down Crow's stomach and found her soft vagina and sighed as his fingers slipped into the small wet heaven he had loved so many years. He touched her very softly, as if she was a small weak thing that might break. He had held her hand while she delivered May Frost and Summer Deer and Creek. He had never been able to imagine that her body could become such a heavy animal. She was always fifteen years old to Little Sun, skinny and nervous and trembling beneath his hands. He sighed again. Maybe she was right. Two weeks or a month. This change was coming over them and he was powerless to stop it. "He smokes because he is unhappy with the Ford Motor Company," Crow went on. "You think he will stay in town and drink beer but he might go out into the country and fish instead. Who are you to keep the money from our children? We don't know everything. We are getting old." She turned closer into his arms, then moved over on her back and let him touch her. A squirrel dropped a walnut on the roof above their head. Somewhere in the same tree the garden tiger moth found the leaf she wanted and began to lay a neat line of eggs along a vein. A waxing moon came out from behind a cloud and poured its borrowed sunlight upon Tahlequah. The Cherokee Nation lay bathed in silver.

CHAPTER 33

EARLY the next afternoon, Olivia was in the crowded waiting room of the Planned Parenthood Clinic in Broken Arrow filling out the patient questionnaire. She had driven over as soon as her classes were out for the day, giving up her chance to help pick out the new washing machine for May Frost. She smiled to herself, thinking of Crow with her new idea.

"Does anyone in your family have cancer?" the questionnaire asked. Olivia thought it over and decided to leave out her aunt Anna since they might not give her the pills. She circled no.

She finished the other questions, then opened her Navajo grammar book and tried to study it. It was so boring, the examples were like something out of a children's book. Where is your house? How do you get to the library? Do you like to go to the mountains?

She closed the grammar and looked around the room. A pregnant girl sat in a chair, looking remorseful. A young woman with a child tried to amuse him with a stuffed toy. Two pimply-looking teenage girls gossiped behind a magazine. Maybe I should put on my ring, Olivia decided, and slipped it out of her purse and put it on her finger. She had met Bobby at noon and told him where she was going and asked him to come out that night to dinner. "How are things going with your dad?" she asked.

"I think he'll go to jail, maybe for five years, maybe more." Bobby straightened his shoulders and looked down at her. "I wish we didn't have to talk about it. There's nothing I can do, is there? What time do you want me to come out there?"

"Around six o'clock." She put her hand on his arm, sorry she had asked it, feeling spiteful and mean. I'd rather have a pit viper for a girlfriend than me, she thought. I'm supposed to love this guy. I knew better than to bring that up. "Granddaddy wants to see you. He's going to catch some fish."

"I'll be there, baby." Bobby smiled, forgiving her. "I can't wait to eat Little Sun's fish. I'm honored he'd want to see me. Hell, I might even shine my boots."

"He wouldn't know the difference." Olivia laughed. "But Grandmother and Mary Lily will."

Thirty minutes later she emerged from the clinic with a package of birth control pills in her bag and began to drive to Tulsa. I'm getting to where I live in doctors' offices, she decided. I'm turning into some kind of hypochondriac.

Doctor Coder opened the door to his office and Olivia walked in and went to the couch and lay down upon it. "I got these birth control pills, but I'm afraid to take them," she began. "Why should I put chemicals into my body just so Bobby can fuck me? We can use a rubber or I can get some jelly or we'll do something. I don't need to take hormones that might give me cancer. And I don't want to marry him either. I'm taking off this ring. What does it mean, wearing a ring like a noose around your neck, like a harness or a bit. I'm not a horse. No one's going to ride me or hobble me or breed with me. I wouldn't have a baby for all the tea in China. I haven't talked to Jessie for a while. I can't tell her about Bobby because she'll tell Dad. I don't know what to do, Doctor Coder. I'm not getting a thing done in school. I cut a class this afternoon to go get those pills. All I'm doing is driving around the country seeing doctors."

"Do you know the old Indian legends about people's spirits being captured by their enemies?"

"Sure. Everyone knows that."

"Well, I'm going to tell you something, Olivia. Your spirit has been captured. Because your mother died. Your need for bonding is so strong that you'll sacrifice yourself for it. But it does no good. Grown people can't get the stuff that little babies have. All you do is trade in your adult life for something that is doomed to failure. No one can complete you and make you happy but yourself. Is this making sense?"

"Oh, God, that's what Georgia says. That's all she talks about. She keeps saying the same thing over and over. Don't ante the self for the relationship. She's got this big sign on her refrigerator. She's always talking about that."

"What's the main thing that's worrying you today?"

"Telling Dad about Bobby. Yeah, and what he'll say when I don't pass a thing in summer school, which is where I'm heading."

"Then call him up and talk to him and tell him what's on your mind."

"I can't do that."

"You can try. Then you could go on to the big stuff. This business of worrying about what your father will think of Bobby is just a cover for your real problem. *The anxiety arises from the intimacy.* Put that on *your* refrigerator. It's what you feel for Bobby that's driving you crazy. You think if you bond with someone, they will disappear. Until you understand that, all your relationships will be doomed. It's the intimacy you fear."

"I didn't have any intimacy at Chapel Hill and I was worse off than I am now. What am I going to do, Doctor Coder? How am I supposed to know what to do?"

"Start by understanding. Watching, thinking, finding out how you tick. Think of your life as a broad field. If there are holes, fill them in. If there are dangerous weeds, cut them out. Patrol your fences. Until it is time to pull them down." He suppressed a sigh, thinking of how long it took to begin to plant the hope that became the will that made real independence and health. He thought of a painter in Colorado he had cured of a neurosis. Now her brilliant lighthearted paintings were being bought by museums. He lavished the memory upon the room and dug into the problem of Olivia.

"You sound like this nutritionist from Washington they had come talk to the Zetas last year. She said, Get up every morning and pull the weeds out of the garden of your life. We were all cracking up listening to her."

"She was right."

"That's all you're going to tell me?" Olivia was sitting up now, thinking what a waste of money Doctor Coder was.

"Lie back down, Olivia. Close your eyes. Tell me what you see."

Olivia lay back down on the couch. She pulled off her sandals and lay down and tried to be still. She closed her eyes. "Okay, the first

thing I see is colors, red like blood, shot through with lightning. Gold
and so forth. Then Dad's sitting in the kitchen waiting to get mad at
me. My waist feels fat. I'm fat. Spook says something. Except it's the
kitchen here, in Tahlequah. Grandmomma and Grandaddy are up to
something. I can't figure out what. Grandmother's buying a washing
machine for my aunt May Frost. I don't get it. Well, Aunt Mary Lily
slept in town twice last week. I think she's having an affair with the
assistant manager at Bonanza. Bobby's coming out to dinner tonight.
I don't know when to start taking these pills. I'm afraid to take them.
I might get cancer if I do. I don't feel like getting laid anyway right
now. It's too complicated. I've got too much on my mind. I just want
to get Bobby and run away. Only I don't even have my car. I have
Dad's car. Nothing I have belongs to me. It's all someone else's stuff.
So what do you think? Am I worth fooling with? What do you want
me to do?"

"Take the pills." Doctor Coder sat up and put his elbows on his
desk. He had done his first training analysis with a strict Freudian and
still was able to shock himself by his methods. "You won't get cancer.
What's the dosage?"

"Three point six milligrams."

"You'll be okay. Take the pills. Start with that."

"You want me to go on with what I'm thinking?"

"Yes."

"I'll be in a coffin in a wide place beneath some trees but the top's
still off and they haven't put dirt on me. I'm just lying there and there's
a big cross by the tree. Three crosses. But it's nice in the woods and I'm
not scared. Then I get up and walk away. It's hard to walk through the
mud by the coffin but I make it. I say, I'm not doing this. I'm not getting in this grave."

"The dream of death is not about real death. It's about dying to one
life and finding another. It's about growing up."

"You've got an answer for everything, don't you?" She sat up again,
mad at him for belittling her dream. "What time is it, anyway?"

"You have a few more minutes."

"This is the longest hour I've ever spent in my life. Okay, I'll try
some more." She lay back down and got back into the open coffin and
tried to think about what it meant. In the fantasy a bluebird landed on

the cross. It picked a few bugs from under its wing. Then it began to sing, a crazy, larky little melody.

CHAPTER 34

WHEN Olivia got home the family was gathered. Five of Little Sun and Crow's children were there. Sam, Roper, Creek, Mary Lily, and May Frost. Plus Roper's wife, JoDean, and their teenage sons, Tree and Jimbo, plus May Frost's children, May Light, May Morning, and the baby, Field. Plus Sam's wife, Little Sugar. Creek's wife had stayed at home because she had a stomachache.

There were cars all over the yard and along the side of the road. Mary Lily's Pontiac was parked underneath the maple tree. Roper's jeep was beside it. Sam's pickup was in the driveway and his wife's El Dorado and Creek's Chevrolet. Roper and Creek were standing by the steps smoking. Little Sun was on the top step with Mary Lily. May Frost and two of her children were in the glider. Crow was holding May Frost's baby.

"What is going on?" Olivia asked. She had parked the Mercedes by the El Dorado. She walked over to her grandmother and May Frost. "We're rich, honey," May Frost answered. "They found oil in the Craylies' pasture and it runs under ours. We're rich as Croesus. Come here and speak to Olivia, May Light, come show her your new dress." A little black-haired girl wearing a pink denim dress came over to her mother and hid her face in her legs.

"It's okay, May Light," Olivia said. "I won't look at it if you don't want me to."

"It's because we went for the washer," Crow added. "The clerk told May Frost he heard they'd found oil and were fixing to start drilling. Your granddaddy's known about it for weeks. He wouldn't tell them. So now they know."

"Come have a beer," Roper called from the steps. "Come celebrate with us." He threw his arm around his brother's shoulders and waved a beer bottle in Olivia's direction. He was the oldest of the Wagoner children, almost forty-seven years old. In those forty-seven years he had never known a day he liked as much as he liked today. The only thing wrong with it was that he had to wait until eight o'clock tomorrow morning to quit his job. "I'll tell that little son-of-a-bitch to stuff it," he kept saying. "Stuff it, you little bastard."

"Get your severance pay," Creek kept saying. "Don't be a fool, Roper. Make him fire you and collect severance pay and get some unemployment. Goddamn, it might be weeks or months before Daddy gets money from the well. It might be a year."

"Stuff it," Roper kept saying. "Stuff it up your goddamn ass." He waved his longneck in the air. His wife, JoDean, was inside the house watching television with their teenage son. She came to the back door several times to see what Roper was doing. Then she'd go back in without saying anything.

"Momma and I were going to cook fish and vegetables," Mary Lily kept saying. "But Denise and Arleen and them want to order pizza. What do you want to do, Olivia?"

"Bobby's coming to dinner," she answered. "Did everyone forget that?"

"Let them order the pizza," Little Sun decreed. "We might as well spend some of the money." He held out his hands to Olivia. "Come here by me. Don't be afraid of this. It will not change the world. Only Roper gets to quit his job and now he's getting drunk."

"I'm not getting drunk, Dad." Roper took his arms from off his brother's shoulders and turned to his father. "I don't have to put up with crap from you. This land belongs to all of us. It's a trust. We all get to share whatever comes of it. You can't be in charge of it."

"It is for all of us. Good and bad. Go help them order pizza, Olivia. Go around and ask everyone what they want."

"I'll drink all the goddamn beer I want." Roper walked up the steps and called to his wife and son. "Come on, JoDean. Goddammit. I'm leaving. If you want a ride home, come on out."

"We'll stay here." His wife came to meet him. Everyone in the yard had grown very still. It was the same thing that always happened if

they got together. Roper got drunk and left. So what, they were probably all saying. Who gives a damn.

Bobby drove up and parked behind Olivia's car and got out and
came walking toward them. Roper passed him without speaking and got
into his truck and backed out of the yard and drove off down the road.

"What's going on?" Bobby said. "Is all this for me?"

"We're rich," May Frost said. "They found oil in the pasture."

CHAPTER 35

O N Friday Olivia packed a bag and drove to Tulsa. She saw
Doctor Coder, then went straight to the airport and caught
the plane to Charlotte.

"Just be careful," Doctor Coder had told her. "Watch what happens
and don't judge it and have a good time with your father. If he asks
you what you've been doing, tell him. Try treating him like a friend.
He wants to be your friend, Olivia. He doesn't want to be your enemy."

"He wants to tell me what to do, but he knows he can't do it. Now
he really can't do it."

"Then why are you going to see him?"

"Because I love him. He's my dad. I didn't have him and now I do. I
don't know. I don't know why I'm going there. Bobby won't have anyone to go out with on the Fourth. Maybe I shouldn't go." She sat up on
the couch, turned around. Thought perhaps she would just walk out
the door and go get Bobby and head for Montana.

"You can go to Charlotte and come back here. You don't have to
choose between the people that you love. You have to find your own
center. Then you are safe anywhere."

"That's easy for you to say. Where did you come from?"

"Let's stick with you."

"No. I mean it. I want to know about you. Where did you live when
you were little? Tell me. I want to know."

"Are you going to get mad at me? Did I create your confusion?"

"You make it worse. You bring it up. You make me think about it. I was doing just fine about this weekend. You're the one that said I had to know why I was going."

"Why are you going?"

"I don't know. To tell Dad about our oil, I guess. I want him to know that. So he can stop looking down on my mother for the first time in her life."

"Your mother's dead, Olivia. What is going on, right now, this moment, in this room? Tell me the first thing you think of, quick."

"Georgia says it's all energy, electromagnetic fields, all swirling particles and light and we are held together, God knows how, by some sort of pattern we call the genes. Also, we are thinking and talking and thinking has weight. Dad's thinking about me right now, I bet you he is. And if Jessie knows about it she's jealous we're together. And you're making a hundred dollars an hour by letting me talk about myself. And what else? I think I'm going to miss the plane."

"Very good. Anything else?"

"Blood and nutrients and all sorts of chemicals and messages and God knows what all are going in and out of the cells of your body and my body. Georgia says the cell wall alone is worth weeks of meditation. She said she shouldn't have been a doctor because she can't stand the sight of blood running out. She likes it all inside. She's in love with this physicist and she won't live with him. She thinks being in love with him is some dangerous mission she's on. God, I hope I don't end up like that. I hope I know how to love Bobby."

"You're doing a pretty good job."

"What time is it?"

"Almost time for you to go. I hope you have a good time with your father, Olivia. Just love him and watch him and tell him about your life."

"I don't want to tell him about Bobby."

"But it's the most important thing to tell." He got up from behind his desk. He looked at her, in all her fabulous health and youth and dark brooding sensibility and confused dreams. Focus, he was thinking. Keep your head in the game. "Olivia, tell your father the truth. If you suffer for it, call me up. I'll be on call all weekend. If you suffer one real pang for talking to him as you would to a friend, I want you to call me up and report it to me. Will you do that for me? Will you try it my way?"

"You're the worst psychiatrist in the world." She stood up, starting to laugh. "You're not supposed to be bossing me around. You're supposed to be making me cry and remember bad things that happened to me."

"I want good things to happen to you. I want to see you really start to use that mass of ganglia we call the brain. I want to see it running on all its cylinders in some direction that makes you happy."

"Then why am I flying to Charlotte, North Carolina?" She stopped at the door.

"Maybe you are going to find out. Then you can tell me."

"Maybe I already know. Maybe we know the future. Maybe we read each other's minds. Maybe there'll be a plane wreck and you'll be sorry you were mean to me." She smiled her widest smile and left the room and closed the door. Doctor Coder looked down at his deskful of papers. A small carved bear a patient had given him was on a stack of magazines. He picked it up and began to stroke its small, cold, round, marble back.

Olivia slept on the plane to Charlotte. She was still half asleep when the plane landed and she gathered up her things and walked down the ramp and into her father's arms. He seemed so tall and strong and perfect. He seemed the father any girl would dream of in any world and she hugged him fiercely and loved him too much for any words or any sense. "I missed you so much," she said. "Oh, Dad, I've got so much to tell you. They found oil on our place. We're rich. All my aunts and uncles. And guess what, I'm in love." Daniel looked down into this strange daughter's face. In many ways there was no way he could ever love her as he loved Jessie, whom he had always known and never feared, and who resembled him. This lost and found child, this child with his sister Anna's power and will, this dangerous child, had a different hold upon his heart, half guilt, half fascination. Fascination with the idea that he could have helped create something so interesting and uncontrollable and unique. Sometimes he looked at Olivia and saw only trouble, trouble brewing, trouble in the making, trouble to come. Other times he looked at her and saw possibility. She might grow up to be anything, might be like Anna and amaze them all. Already she had the power to make the other children in the family jealous and to draw them near. She had imagination, the most seductive of all gifts. She used it in her own life and she had the power to evoke it in other people. It was this gift that reminded the Hand family of their lost Anna. In her generation it had been Anna who dreamed up and proposed the games the Hand children played. In this generation it was Olivia, who had dropped into their lives through a series of events the stodgier children in the family found fabulous and exotic. They whispered about her among themselves and repeated things she said.

"Let's get your bags, honey," Daniel said. "Grandmother and Granddaddy are waiting for you at their house. I promised I'd bring you by the minute you got here."

They drove down into the beautiful manicured neighborhoods where the Hand family lived. Olivia was sitting primly in the passenger's seat. She had dressed in a white linen suit for the trip, a suit she had bought on sale in Tulsa one afternoon when she went to see Doctor Coder. It was the only money she had spent all summer that was in any way frivolous. " 'Beware all enterprises that require new clothes,' " Georgia had quoted when she saw the suit, then added, "On the other hand, it looks divine."

Now it was wrinkled from being worn all day and the new white shoes had black stripes on the heels from being kicked around on the plane. Still, Olivia looked like a lady; she was even wearing panty hose.

"Jessie couldn't come," Daniel said, "but she sent some pictures of the boy. They're on the dash in that envelope if you want to look at them. I should have bought you a camera to take to Oklahoma. You got any pictures of your folks back there?"

"Well, not with me. I have a lot of pictures of Bobby, that's my boyfriend, from when his picture used to be in the paper. He used to always be in the paper when he was in high school."

"Well, you remind me and I'll get you a camera to take back when you go. How long can you stay?"

"Until Monday. I'm really liking using your good car. That was so nice of you." This isn't talking, Olivia thought. We aren't really talking. I don't know what to say to him that would be real. I don't know where to begin. "Dad, did I ever tell you I had a picture of you when I was little. It was in a box of Momma's things they kept for me in Granddaddy's safe. Listen, it was a photograph of the two of you in San Francisco. I used to look at it for a long time. I treasured that. It was the only thing I had that meant I wasn't just an orphan."

"Oh, honey." He stopped the car in his parents' driveway and turned around. His brow was furrowed. He did not have the vaguest idea how to begin to cut through the terrible guilt Olivia produced in him. "I wish I'd known you were there. I sure do wish it hadn't taken so long to find you."

"It's okay. I guess it scared you to death when Aunt Anna told you about me, didn't it? I guess you thought I'd come up here and get all your money or something, didn't you?"

"I don't know what I thought. I shouldn't have made you wait. I thought about that a lot. Is that what you talk to that shrink about?"

"No. He wants me to tell you about my boyfriend. He wants me to learn how to talk to you. He said it didn't even matter if you learned how to talk back. As long as I was always telling the truth."

"What's the truth, then?"

"That I was really mad because you wouldn't come to see me. That I think you don't love me because of what I did that time to the school computer. That you think I'm some sort of criminal about to erupt." She kept on looking him straight in the eye as she talked. She did not let him escape.

"Oh, honey." Daniel sighed a great huge sigh, but he returned her look. He didn't chicken out of this thing that she had started. He didn't back away. "If I think so it's probably because I'm half a one myself. I'm in so much trouble with the IRS right now the only way I can sleep is reminding myself that the jails are full of armed robbers and maybe there's no room for me. So you may be right. But I love you. You're wrong about that. You're my little girl and I'm damned glad to have you." He reached out and laid his hand upon her arm and patted her as he would a pet. Very soft little pats with the fingers of his hand upon her forearm.

"Okay," Olivia said. "That's enough for now. Let's go inside and see

Grandmother. She's probably wondering what we're doing out here."

"Don't say anything about that IRS business to anyone. Just keep that under your hat."

"Who would I tell? I don't have anyone I'd talk to about your business."

They got out of the car and went together into Daniel's mother's house to talk to the old Victorians who had caused a large part of the mess they were tentatively trying to clean up.

"So who's this boyfriend you were supposed to talk to me about?" It was the next morning. Daniel and Olivia were in the kitchen making breakfast. Spook was sitting on a bar stool listening. Daniel was having the conversation in front of Spook to give him his due. He had been right. It was a boy she had gone to see. Well, let him gloat. Let him say I told you so.

"A boy I used to go with in high school. He's from a terrible family but he's a wonderful person. He was the Junior Reining Champion of Oklahoma and he was the best football player when I was a cheerleader. Every girl in Tahlequah wants him but he always liked me. I don't know why, but he does. I thought he'd gone away. He came back because I was coming there. My aunt told me. He loved me a long time before he found out I was going to be rich."

"You going to be rich?" Spook laughed delightedly from his stool. "That's good news."

"Her granddad struck oil. They've got oil in their pasture."

"You can lend us some," Spook added. "So your dad will fix the fences before every horse and cow we've got is loose in the county."

"Shut up, Spook. Go on, honey. So what is this paragon's name?"

"His name's Bobby. His mother's dead and his dad isn't worth talking about. I want him to go to Chapel Hill with me next year. He has enough money. He's been working since he got out of high school and he saved a lot of money. Well, now I said it, and you don't look like you're having a fit, so Doctor Coder was right and you can talk about things if you have to."

"Are you wanting to marry this boy?"

"No. I don't think so. I don't think I ever want to marry anyone.

Well, I might want to live with someone someday. But not get married, not have babies."

"That's the new way." Spook nodded his head in approval. "That's how they do it now. They don't push them baby carriages. More power to them, that's all I have to say."

"Well, don't go living with someone. If you want to live with someone, marry them. I mean that, honey. I don't want you living with some boy." Daniel looked determined, began to butter toast. "Grandmother wants us for dinner tonight. Lynley and DeDe will be there and Winifred too. Then afterwards we'll all walk over to the club to watch the fireworks. Is that all right with you?"

"Sure, that's fine. That's why I'm here." Olivia sat down beside Spook and began to eat her scrambled eggs. She looked up at the black man and got tickled. He had a look on his face that said, Look here now, isn't this the funniest thing you ever witnessed? That was always Spook's manner in the early morning. It was only in the late afternoons that he got morose and decided the world was a terrible place and more trouble than it was worth.

CHAPTER 36

THE dinner party at the Hands' was festive. Mrs. Hand, Senior, had decided to make it festive, by which she meant having two maids work all day making fried chicken and potato salad and biscuits and carrot sticks and three different desserts, then gathering all of the family she could find into one room and making them sit at a table and eat the fried chicken with a fork. Lynley and Winifred and Kenny and Dede were there, the children of Helen Hand Abadie, and DeDe's husband, Kevin, and their father, Spencer Abadie, and Spencer's mother, Mrs. Delores Abadie, who was eighty-seven years old and still trying to make up for having been born in West Virginia, and Niall and Daniel and Olivia and James Hand, Junior, his family was at the beach, and Mr. Hand Senior's niece, Mary Lyle, and her husband, Edward Hill, and several other cousins. The idea was that they would eat an early dinner, then walk up the hill to the Charlotte Driving Club and watch the fireworks and think patriotic thoughts.

"How are things with your grandparents?" Mrs. Hand asked Olivia. If Daniel was afraid of his half-Indian daughter, Mrs. Hand was terrified. She had calmed down about the girl while she was in Charlotte and Chapel Hill, but now that she was back in Oklahoma she was worried again.

"They're fine," Olivia answered. "They found oil on their land. They're going to be rich. My granddaddy is very worried about it. He thinks all my uncles will quit their jobs."

"That's nice, Olivia. Well, that's a real surprise."

"Good for him," James Senior put in. "He's right to be worried. I'd like to meet that man."

"Who does he have taking care of his affairs?" James Junior put in. "I hope he has a lawyer handling things."

"He used to be in the council of chiefs." Olivia sat up very straight. "He knows more than most lawyers ever dream of knowing. He can read people's minds if he wants to do it. He's the strongest man his age you ever saw in all your life. He's so strong. I don't know how I stood being away from him that long. He taught me so much. He knows where the fox goes to hide, that's a saying that we have." I was supposed to watch, Olivia told herself. I wasn't supposed to be critical of them. They can't help how they are. They're just that way. They're afraid of everything.

"We can go into supper now," Mrs. Hand said. "I bet all you young people are starving."

Olivia got a plate and stood in line next to her cousins at the buffet. Lynley on one side and DeDe on the other. "So when's your baby coming?" Olivia asked.

"Too soon," DeDe answered. "I know what to do with it while it's still inside."

"Are we going to eat this chicken with a knife and fork?" Lynley laughed. He was always trying to impress Olivia. Trying to figure out what she wanted him to say. "I can't stand it when Grandmother does that."

"It's okay." Olivia turned her most brilliant smile on him. "You have to let people be themselves. They can't help it if they want to set the table three times a day. That's the life they lead. I kind of like it."

"We always did it," DeDe said. "Momma always set the table and made us eat very formally."

"Have you been up to see her yet?"

"No."

"She doesn't want us to," Lynley added. "She doesn't want anyone to come up there and bother her."

They filled their plates and sat at the table and said the blessing and ate the chicken and the potato salad and all the desserts. Then it was dark outside and they walked up the hill to the country club and lay around on blankets watching the fireworks go off. This is boring me to death, Olivia decided. If it was Bobby and me we'd be setting them off ourselves. We'd be blowing up every can in Green Country, and when it was over we'd go home and fuck.

"Are you having a good time, sweetie?" It was Daniel coming to sit beside her on the blanket. "It's so good to have you here. I wish you'd just stay. I wish you'd stay a few more days."

"I was thinking I ought to go back tomorrow," she said. But she could not resist the tenderness and she settled down beside her daddy and was happy then. No matter how boring the country club was and the fireworks and her careful cousins, he was her own wonderful father and for this night at least she had him all to herself.

"So why is this boy from a terrible family?" They were almost to the airport, taking Olivia to catch the plane back to Tahlequah. "Why is his family terrible?"

"It isn't terrible. Did I say that?"

"I thought you did."

"His mother's been gone since he was born. They don't know where she went. They think she's dead. His dad was a hero in Vietnam. He flew helicopters and was wounded. Bobby's just had a lot of different things happen to him. Well, wait till you meet him. When you meet him you can make up your mind. I'm not going to marry him, Dad. I'm not like Jessie. I don't want a house with flower gardens."

"What do you want?"

"I don't know yet. I'm trying to find out."

"What can I do to help you?" Daniel stopped the car and turned off the motor and got out and came around to get her bag out of the backseat. He was thinking as hard as he could. And he was sorry she was leaving but, on the other hand, he wanted to go sit down in his den and pour himself a drink and not think about daughters. Daughters, what a thing for a man to have. Girls going off and having boyfriends and letting them do God knows what. "Let's go on in the airport, honey. I don't want you to leave but if you're going to, let's don't go missing planes."

They walked together into the almost empty airport and checked the bag and walked down to the gate. Once or twice Olivia took hold of his arm. She had put on the other dress she had bought in Tulsa. This one was blue, with a white collar and a small white braided belt. She was trying to think of an answer to Daniel's question.

"Keep breathing," she said at last.

"What?"

"That's what you can do to help me. I love you, Dad. I'm glad I was here. I'll be back at the end of summer. I'm not deserting you."

"I've been thinking about this book I used to read when I was a kid. It was called *Wee Gillis*. It was about a Scots boy who was orphaned and his mother's folks were highlanders and his father's folks were lowlanders and they both wanted him to live with them. So he'd spend half his time in the highlands and half in the lowlands. Finally he ended up living halfway between the two countries and spent his life playing the bagpipes. My granddaddy used to read that book to me."

"Oh, Dad, that's wonderful. I wish I could read it. If you find it, will you send it to me?"

The ticket agent announced the flight and Olivia kissed her father and turned and walked away and onto the airplane. What a world, she decided, and settled down into her seat. All I do is leave people that I love. Like I'm practicing for when I die. Well, that's a morbid thought. She settled down into her seat and got out her Navajo grammar. She copied down some verbs, then copied a few sentences, then opened her notebook to a clean page and began to write a letter to her aunt Helen.

Dear Aunt Helen,

I hope everything is going all right in Boston. I just saw DeDe and
Lynley and Winifred and Kenny. They said Stacy is going to be a model
in L.A. Is that the truth? And DeDe looked great. You'd hardly know
she was going to have a baby if you only looked at her face. They all
looked great, to tell the truth. I thought you might want to know that,
in case you're worried about them. I really appreciate all the letters and
postcards that you wrote me. I really liked the postcard from the
museum. Mike's right. It does look like you. You turn your head like
that, when you think of something you forgot to say. If I come to see
you, you can take me there and we'll look at it together.

Olivia chewed her pencil for a while, then went on.

On another note, I met a woman I bet you'd like. She uses really
wild language but she's got so much life in her. She's teaching me
anthropology but she says it's a joke. She says anyone who can read
could pick it up. I don't know why I'm writing you but I thought
maybe you were lonely for your kids. They aren't mad at you even if
they act like they are. They just don't know what's going on and I
guess DeDe has a lot of conflict about this baby she's having. Give my
love to Mike.

I hope we see each other sometime soon.

Your loving niece,
Olivia.

The stewardess came through the cabin serving drinks and Olivia
folded up the letter and put it in her purse. It would be two weeks
before she thought to mail it.

CHAPTER 37

HELEN is at a party in a married student's apartment. She is sitting on an uncomfortable sofa biting her lip and thinking of answers to questions. It is five-thirty in the afternoon. The host of the party is a classics major who follows Mike around talking about the Etruscans. He has prepared all the food and is waiting on the guests. His wife is a second-year law student. She is standing in the dining area looking bored. She distrusts her husband's liberal arts friends and think they secretly accuse her of being a philistine. She likes to foster this whenever possible by declaring that she voted for George Bush. She is smiling in Helen's direction. She moves toward the sofa. She is hoping from the way Helen is dressed to have a conversation with a member of her social class. "So how does it feel to have a famous poet for a husband?" she asks.

"He isn't my husband," Helen answers, putting down the plastic plate on which she has three strawberries and a piece of cake. "We're the executors of my sister's estate. We're working on her papers."

"But you live together, don't you?"

"I guess you can call it that. I have a home in North Carolina. My children are there."

"How many children are there?"

"Five." Helen turned her face away. Took a deep breath. Don't panic, she told herself. This is only a child, a girl DeDe's age. She just wants to talk. It's not an interview. Through the doors of the dining area she could see Mike in the kitchen surrounded by his students. "I have five children I haven't seen in a long time and a grandchild on the way," she said finally. "I will be a grandmother in a few days or hours and I shouldn't even be here. I should be by the phone."

"Use ours," the hostess said. "Call and see what's going on."

"I tried to be a writer." They were joined by a tall dark-skinned girl with stringy hair. She moved in and sat on the arm of the sofa. The hostess took the other arm. "But I gave it up. American publishing is so corrupt. My father's an editor. He's a whore if there ever was one. Did you see that book they did last year about the China thing? They churned that out in six weeks. It's a religious tract for the far right. Print's dead anyway."

"Print's been dead." A boy had joined them now. "It was all over by the seventeenth century anyway. Except for Faulkner, Joyce, and a handful of poets."

"Are you in the English Department?" It was all Helen could think of to say to the boy, and if she stayed in this apartment she was going to have to make an effort to be nice to these ugly dull children.

"He's a deconstructionist," the girl explained. "He thinks his work is to unmask frauds, which is of course the biggest fraud of all. His specialty is southern women writers."

"Come on, Margo," he said. "That's not fair. I'm really interested in your sister, Anna." He turned his eyes on Helen. "She's one of the three women I'm doing my thesis on. Gloria Naylor, Anna, and Robb Forman Dew. Robb's a friend of my mother's. Her grandfather was John Crowe Ransom. Had there been other writers in your family before Anna became one? How many miscarriages were there? Are you sure none of them were abortions? The way I read that story called 'Grove of Yellow Dreams' I think it must have been an abortion or else the threat of having to have one."

"Excuse me." Helen stood up and brushed off the skirt of her dress. She handed the plate to the hostess. "I have to find Mike." She moved around the coffee table and started toward the kitchen.

"Where are your children living?" The boy had gotten up and was following her. "What do they all do?"

"I'm not sure." Helen turned to face him. "I went off and left them. I got tired of waiting for them to grow up."

"Like my mom." He smiled. "She's in Geneva with her lover. We haven't seen her in months. So, do you live with Mike? Are you two married?"

Helen shook her head. She walked into the kitchen and found Mike and pulled him out into the hall and began looking for her pocketbook in the jumble of possessions on a hall table. "I'm going to walk on home," she said. "I really have a bad headache. I can't stand the cigarette smoke in here. You stay if you like. I need to go call DeDe."

"Kundera," the voice of one of the female students echoed in the hall. "What a bunch of crap. It's just another example of a bad translation being passed off as genius. . . ."

"You're just pissed off because Mike Curtis sent back your story. If you weren't in such a bad mood . . . ," a male voice was answering.

"What's wrong, Helen?" Mike had her arm, he was pulling her out the door into the exterior hallway. He had her close to him. "Come here to me. Tell me what's wrong."

"Nothing. Nothing's wrong. Just let me go. I want to go home."

"No. Come on. Well, wait then. I'll take you."

"No. I want to walk."

"What happened?"

"Nothing happened."

"Yes it did. Tell me."

"I don't know what we do. To think, I've been sitting around being jealous of your female students. God, they're so ugly, so unattractive. They aren't even smart. You call that smart?"

"What happened?"

"This ugly girl with dirty hair asked me if we were married. I didn't know what to say. I don't know what we're doing."

"Okay." They were outside the apartment now, on the stone steps leading to a tree-lined street. "Okay, then say it. Tell me what you want."

"I don't want anything. I just want to walk home in the clean air. If I can find any clean air in Boston. At least today it isn't raining."

"Helen."

"Yes."

"I want you to marry me. To be my wife. Live with me and be my love. No, I mean it, don't turn away. Will you marry me?"

"If I can. I'm not divorced." She started crying. Laughing and crying. "Oh, yes. Oh, God, yes. More than anything in the world. Oh, yes, yes, yes, yes, yes." And the thing Mike liked remembering about that moment was that he knew she had never read Joyce.

"Would you like to go back inside and tell them?" he asked, when she had stopped crying and he had stopped kissing her. "I've never been engaged. I want to tell the students. I want to announce it to somone."

"Okay. If you really want to."

"You can snub the ugly girl."

"I don't want to snub her."

"You might want to. Come on. Let's go back to the party and see if you want to or not."

"Okay. I will." Helen wiped her face and combed her hair and they walked back into the building and up the stairs and went into the apartment and Mike got a glass and beat on it with a spoon and announced they were getting married at the end of the summer term. "Anyone who wants champagne can go with me to the store to procure it," he said, and began to collect some of his male students.

The girls surrounded Helen, congratulating her, seeming benign and almost cheerful in their enthusiasm for anyone's possible happiness. "Marriage is coming back in," the ugly girl decreed. "I've been thinking of writing an article about it for the *Crimson*. They've been begging me to do an op-ed piece."

"Mike is the best thing that's happened around here in my four years." A tall beaming girl was by Helen's side. "And you're the best thing that's happened to him. Everyone talks about how different he is this year. Last year he was so remorseful. Before he met you. Everyone in English knows all about your meeting. It's mythical now." The beaming girl was at least six feet tall, very fine and goddesslike. She led Helen to a pair of chairs and sat down beside her. She took Helen for her own. "You know, he never used to go out anywhere. He was always alone."

"He doesn't like to be alone." Helen moved into the comfort of the girl's kindness. "He's from a big family. So am I. We both come from very big families."

"You ought to see my husband." The girl laughed out loud. "He's Sicilian. He has nine sisters. He's never been alone in his life and he doesn't want to be. Well, this wedding is a wonderful idea. It will inspire some other people around here to believe in love. You might as well believe in it, I always say. What else is there with that much energy?"

"What is your name?" Helen leaned in close. This happy day. This happy, happy day.

"P.J.," the girl said. "I was named for a British actress. It's a joke. My parents were living in Stockholm. My parents thought having a baby was a joke."

The next afternoon Helen called Niall on the phone. "I want you there," she said. "I need you there."

"I can't perform the ceremony."

"Oh, I hadn't thought of that. Well, perhaps you could. But most of all, come here. Be here. Do you think I can be happy, Niall? Is this okay?"

"I'm happy. Why shouldn't you be?"

"Because it seems impossible. I don't know. I can't believe it goes on. That it doesn't stop. I keep thinking I should have a baby or something."

"Expiation?"

"I guess so."

"Well, don't have a baby. You don't need a baby, Helen. You can't have one, can you? Oh, God, I hope not."

"Well, theoretically I could, but I won't. I won't do that."

"Are you doing something against it?"

"I think so."

"You think so! Helen, you need to talk to a woman. Do you have any women friends up there?"

"Not really. I want to make them but Mike's friends are all married to these dreary women. They never get dressed. I know it's silly but I was raised to get dressed, to be pretty. I can't help it. I met a graduate student the other day who was nice. This tall girl with a beaming smile. I think she's some kind of journalist."

"I love you, Helen. I'm so glad you're happy. Call this girl if you liked her. Take her out to lunch. You know how to make friends. You always had the most friends of anyone."

"And you'll come, to the wedding?"

"Nothing could keep me away."

"It's August nineteenth. I don't know where yet but the reception will be at Favrot's. This little restaurant where we like to eat. Have you seen Lynley?"

"Quite a bit. He's in love, did you know that? The best thing you ever did for him was leaving town. Now he has to find another girl."

"Oh, Niall. I wish you wouldn't say things like that. You're worse than Anna was. Everyone doesn't have to have an Electra Complex or whatever you call it."

"Oedipus. Anyway, he's perfectly fine. He likes his work and the girl is nice. She lived in Europe for several years and has all sorts of lovely mannerisms. She's small and blond and very chic. You'd like her."

"He didn't write me about it. Maybe I should call him."

"Don't call him, Helen. He'll call if he needs you. He knows your number. Let him grow up."

"Oh, okay. Well, anyway, I have something I have to do so I better hang up. I have to read the new script for Anna's movie. I hope this one is better."

"You're a wonderful sister, Helen."

"I'm doing the best I can. It's fun, talking to these movie people. You don't have to do anything but let them call you on the phone. Mike makes me make all the decisions about it. He just tells me to be strong. He's teaching me to be strong. You just say yes and no and don't apologize. Well, I forget about not apologizing. I mean, I was taught to do that."

"I have to go to Daniel's for dinner. Can I call you later?"

"No. I just wanted to see if you'd come. August nineteenth. And bring a suit. I want it to be beautiful. I want Daniel too but I'll call him later."

"Are you going to ask the children?"

"I don't want to. It's my day, for Mike and me. I don't want them walking around frowning. Especially DeDe and Winifred. Stacy is nice to him but they'd just pout the whole time. Oh, well."

"It's okay, Helen. Spencer's taking care of the children. Let him do it. It's good for him. I think it's softening him up."

"Oh, well. Okay."

"I love you. Stay well."

"Love you too."

Niall hung up the phone and walked out onto the patio and began to water his roses. The American Beauties were in bloom, twelve plants in a circle, their huge red flowers so fragrant, so soft, so unbelievably delicate and rich. Velvet, Niall decided. The old comparisons are still the best. He worked the roots, watered the plants, powdered the leaves with insecticide, pulled off the dead leaves. He was smiling inside himself, laughing deep inside his heart at the divinity, the absurdity of it all, Helen and her poet, Lynley falling in love with a girl who looked more like Helen than her own daughters, Helen's annoyance with the most elemental psychological truths. *Nel mezzo del cammin di nostra vita* . . . , he was thinking. He picked three of the flowers and took them inside and put them in a vase. "In the middle of my life I came to my senses in a dark forest. . . ."

"He's coming," Helen called to Mike, following him into the bathroom where he was shaving. "Niall's coming to our wedding. Oh, Mike, we could get him to do the service. It doesn't have to be Catholic. It can be anything we want. You could write it." She put her hands around his naked waist, felt the lovely flesh of his stomach, ran her hands up and down the divine flesh of her lover's body. He smiled and kept on shaving, pulling the razor down across his cheek and chin. They were reflected in the mirror, two absolutely charmed and charming human beings in the best year of their lives. Striving, striving, striving.

"You write it," he said. "Why should I have to write everything?"

"What will I write?"

"Whatever you want it to say. Whatever you want to promise. What do you want me to promise you?"

"To love me forever."

"Then let it say that." He drew the razor down the last streak of shaving cream. Already the plot was forming in his mind, the characters beginning to fill his head. A family in the South, a dead sister, a sister who runs away, the men still caught in the net, the men left with the children, the women all gone away and the men and children still living the old forms, going to church on Sunday, having regular meals, living the dead past over and over again. The women plagued by guilt, marrying their lovers in churches they no longer believed in. The dead sister hovering over all of them, mementi mori. The martini shakers, the black servants, the wainscoting and expensive wallpaper and Doric pillars, the lawns and tennis courts and private schools and swimming pools. Patterns, forms, shapes, webs. She struggles against the web, Mike was writing. She looses a hand, looses a foot, the pattern closes, clutches, glued to her back. Because she is still breathing, she thinks she is free.

"My darling Helen." He goes to the bed and sits down beside her and begins to stroke her legs. "I wish to take you out for chowder tonight, madame. While you are still my mistress, I will treat you like one. You may not wish to exchange this for the married state."

"Are we doing enough to keep from having a baby?"

"What are we doing?"

"Well, I'm using jelly. And I sort of count the days."

"What day is today?" He put his face down on her thigh and began to kiss her legs.

"The day I'd ovulate if I still ovulate. I don't think I do anymore. I think I'm starting menopause but I'm not sure. I forget to think about it. It all seems so irrelevant now." She put her hands upon his head.

He parted her legs with his hands, began to kiss her stomach, put his tongue very gently into her navel. Where she is joined to the fields of time, he thought.

"Put it in me," Helen said. "I want to fuck you now." She imagined him bending over across the room, the great balls between his legs. She saw Spencer standing beside her as she pushed the babies out into the world, terrible searing pain, then release. "I love you," she said. "Oh, my baby, baby, baby, my love."

Anna could have told her what was happening. Or the tall beaming girl at the party who was writing a paper on sexual desire and release.

I must love violence, Helen had told herself a thousand times. Or else, why do I think such terrible things? Why would I mix up childbirth with making love? I must be a terrible person to think such nasty awful stuff. I think of Spencer watching the babies come and it makes me come. I still think this terrible stuff when I make love to Mike. Oh, God, if he knew what I was thinking he probably wouldn't want to make love to me anymore. All the sweet white nightgowns and Chanel Nineteen and little silver bedroom slippers in the world won't make up for thinking about blood all over the delivery room and me screaming and doctors cutting me. Oh, God, I am a terrible person and I will go to hell.

No you won't, the smiling girl could have told her. That's how we come. The sympathetic and the parasympathetic nervous systems. You overload one and it flips over into the other one. The intersection is orgasm. Fear overloads the circuits. Fear trips the spring. We go as far as we can go with one, then it flips over, voilà, orgasm. The other clicks in and stasis is restored.

CHAPTER 38

CHARLOTTE, North Carolina. Seven in the evening. "Spencer's plotting against her," Daniel is saying. He and Niall are seated on his patio, overlooking the leaf-strewn tennis court. Niall is nursing a gin and tonic. Daniel is on his third Scotch and water. Inside the house Daniel's old cook, Jade, is making shrimp gumbo.

"Oh, Dan, that doesn't sound right," Niall answers. "Why would Spencer plot against her? He's not vindictive."

"Yes he is. He'd like to take her for everything she's got. I want to see this divorce finished. I'm nervous about it. I talked to James the other day and he's nervous too. Spencer was supposed to sign the papers a month ago and nothing's happened. If she wants to shack up with the poet in Boston, she deserves it. What has Helen ever done but be everybody's doormat? She's never had a life. I couldn't believe she married Spencer when she did it. What a bore. He was a bore when he was sixteen."

"Well, he can't be vindictive enough to want Helen to be unhappy. He looks fine to me. I was over there the other night and he had out all his stamps and was talking about going to New York to buy some more. He's got plenty of money. Why would he want to take Helen's?"

"She cuckolded him, Niall. It looks bad. It makes him lose face with his insurance honchos. His friends know it."

"They have him out every night. Half the women in town are lined up trying to marry him. What's he got to complain about? And Helen isn't shacked up, baby brother. She's getting married in August. I guess I was supposed to let her tell you that. She called this afternoon. Well, act surprised when she calls you."

"She can't get married until she gets divorced."

"She said James promised her he'd get it done."

"That's not what he told me. Unless she's going to let Spencer have all the money. Surely James wouldn't let her do that."

"It belongs to the children one way or the other, doesn't it?"

"You could look at it that way. It's easy to talk about not needing it until it's gone. Not that I ever said I didn't need it."

"She'll always have the income from Anna's trust."

"That's not enough. No one could live on that."

"She'll be all right. She's happy, Daniel. She doesn't give a damn for anything but that."

"So Spencer gets the money? Grandmother's too?"

"She said he would always give it back if she needed it. She said that to me today."

"I'll shoot Spencer if he takes her money. I'm calling him right now."

"Don't do that, Dan. Please don't start something like that."

"This supper's ready," Jade called from the balcony off Daniel's library. "Come on and eat now. I got a bingo game at the church. I got to be there by eight."

"I ought to retire her," Daniel said, getting up, gesturing to Niall to precede him into the house. "She's getting worse every year."

"So are we," Niall said. "So are we all."

They went through the downstairs door and up the wide stairs which were lined with framed photographs of the Hand family. There were photographs of Anna Senior holding each one of them as they were born. Weddings, vacations, occasions, Anna receiving awards, Jessie and Olivia on horses; all of them in Paris the summer James Senior took everyone to discover Europe.

Niall stopped by a photograph of Helen with three of her children and pregnant with the fourth. She looked sixteen, and not a day older, wearing a white smock and sandals, DeDe, Lynley and Winifred lined up in front of her. Lynley holding a wooden rifle, DeDe holding a doll, Winifred holding the hem of Helen's smock and sucking her thumb. "Helen looks like a little girl," Niall said. "She must have been at least eight months pregnant with Stacy. You know, I always thought she kept having those babies to plague Anna."

"My God, Niall, you say the damnedest things. She had them because she wanted them. She liked being pregnant. Look at the expression on her face."

"Triumph is ecstatic. I'll admit that."

"I can remember her being pregnant, as young as I was. She'd sit on the porch swing and everyone would wait on her and the children would be all over the house. I built a barricade out of two-by-fours to keep them out of my room. Momma would let them tear up all my stuff. We ought to feel sorry for Spencer. By the time he was twenty-seven he had five kids to support. No wonder he had to spend his life slaving for his father in the insurance business. I can't remember ever seeing him without a tie, unless we were at the beach, and even then he looked like an insurance salesman."

"We lived in strange times," Niall said. "Well, come on, baby brother, let's don't keep Jade from her bingo game."

They went into the dining room and sat side by side at one end of the eighteen-foot-long table Daniel's interior decorator friend had bought for him in England. Jade served them salad and French bread, gumbo and rice and asparagus and baked squash. They finished up with coffee and brandy and sat at the table smoking Havana cigars Niall had brought over and continued talking about the family.

"Dad's been complaining to Spook about the way I keep the farm," Daniel said. "Goddammit, Niall, if it wasn't for me, there wouldn't be a farm. I saved it. I bought it and pay the taxes. To hell with it, if nobody appreciates it. I may have to sell it soon anyway. I don't know how I'm going to pay Olivia's tuition next year."

"You don't have to take care of everyone. That's an idea Daddy put in our heads. Children are better off if you leave them alone."

"I have to educate my daughters, Niall. And I'll help anyone who needs it. That's the way we do it. Just because you and Anna think a family ought to split up. Well, they're all you've got when the chips are down. As long as I live I'll help anyone who needs help." Daniel poured himself a second brandy. "Goddamn a lot of people going off and living all alone in their houses. Nobody having any responsibility for anyone else. I'm about to go nuts living in this house by myself. It smells funny when no one's here. Spook's going back to the farm. I can't stop him. Well, let him. To hell with him."

" 'Un homme seul est dans la compagnie mauvaise.' Paul Valery."

"What's that? What's all the frog talk?"

" 'A man alone is in bad company.' Paul Valery. A French Symbolist."

"Well, he goddamn well got that right. He got that one right on the nose."

Night fell on Charlotte, North Carolina. Outside the French doors of the dining room, the flowering shrubs unfurled their perfumes. A quarter moon rode the skies, stars appeared. Daniel and Niall drank brandy and smoked. Five blocks away, Helen's husband, Spencer Abadie, was entertaining a legal secretary by showing her photographs of his children. He almost desired her. For several hours he had been getting the stirrings of desire, but when she would meet his eye, he would lose the feeling.

I don't know if this one is going to be worth it, the woman was thinking. I'd probably have to suck his dick for an hour to get him to stay hard long enough to fuck me. I don't know what's happened to all the men. Look at these pictures of all these babies. She must have been some bitch. That supercilious look on her face. She looks like the cat that caught the mouse with all these babies. Boy, she got him where she wanted him, didn't she? Then ran off and left him. These rich southern dames are some shit.

"Where were you raised?" Spencer was asking.

"In southern Illinois. My mom had three of us. My dad had a dry cleaning store in Marion, Illinois. He died when she was pregnant with me. So after that Mom gave up on life and just ran the dry cleaning store. She died last year, of lung cancer. She smoked. When she quit getting laid she took up smoking. So . . ." She closed the photograph album and stood up beside him. She put her arms around his waist and squeezed his beige linen jacket. "So, you want to go to bed or not?"

"I don't know. I'm sorry. I'm not very good at that anymore. Have you ever read a book called *The Sun Also Rises*? Well, it's like that sometimes with me."

"Like what? Like you can't get it up because you think you'll get someone pregnant? I guess so. She saddled you with five children in six years and then left you? I guess you can't get it up. Well, listen, I'm on the pill and I've had two abortions and I'd have plenty more and not bat an eyelash. No babies for me, mister. But I like to cuddle. You got a bedroom in this mausoleum? Show me one. I want to get out of these panties and this bra."

She led him through the house and up the stairs and found a bedroom that looked as if it had belonged to a young boy and began to undress. "Take off your clothes, Spencer. It's summer, for God's sake. The sweet heart of summer and girls from southern Illinois don't take no for an answer when they get horny." She stripped down to a pair of purple crotchless bikini underpants and sat down on the edge of Lynley's old bunk bed. "Pretend I'm your childhood sweetheart," she said. "Don't worry. Nothing's going to go wrong. I won't let it. Trust me. Come on. Come here to me."

Spencer took off everything but his underpants and T-shirt and went over and let her have him.

The tall smiling girl named P.J. was going to become Helen's best friend in Boston, a companion on long walks, a confidante and keeper of secrets. Before the week was out they were exchanging life stories over lunch in a small restaurant near the campus.

"My dad's a molecular physicist," P.J. was saying. "He's totally nuts. He and my mom are still in love with each other. He comes home in the middle of the afternoon and fucks her. It's insane."

"It sounds divine to me. How do you think it happened?"

"God. I don't know. Neither of them believe in a thing. Except chaos, hazard, chance. Well, they believe in education. We lived on a sailboat when I was young and Mother taught us. I have two brothers and a sister. We lived on a boat in the British Virgin Islands and Daddy thought about the structure of the atom and Mother taught us. After a while, we took some tests and went to college. I came here when I was seventeen."

"How old are you now?"

"Twenty-two. I know. I look a lot older. It's from the sun. I love this restaurant. I know the guys that built it." The restaurant had been created by two of Mike's ex-students. It was in a house near the campus and had a waterfall made of recycled glass bottles. Red and green and blue and amber. Water poured over the bottles from plastic garden hoses and ended in a pool where carp swam lazily among water lilies.

"And you're in love with this Sicilian you married?"

"I met him the day I got to Harvard. I've been with him ever since. He's one of the men who went with Mike to get the champagne. The tall one with dark hair. He's a honey. He's studying to be a teacher. He wants to teach school. Fata Morgana. Who would I end up with?" She laughed delightedly and waved a glass of bottled water in the air. "Brave New World. We're already here if you have enough sense to know it."

"The new world is really new to me. I have daughters your age. I wish you could meet them. Or, maybe, we could just know each other." Helen looked down. It seemed a revolutionary idea. To have a friend and keep her to herself. "I'm beginning to love being selfish. I may not even invite my children to my wedding. Why should I? They don't want to come."

"I'm selfish. I'm going to arrange a life where I have time to write and it sure isn't going to include kids anytime soon. I want to write a book to remind the world of wonder. I want to write a book that contains the ten thousand beautiful things and the ten thousand horrific things. So I have to try to see all the great paintings and hear all the music and eat great foods and think about how they grow corn and grain and rice and where milk comes from and how it's processed and if we have a right to milk cows by machine. Not to mention veal. I want to put in everything. Of course, the writer who did that was Shakespeare. Everything was in, nothing left out. Thunder, lightning, love, baked chickens. I'm writing an article about orgasms now. About how to make it happen with your mind. How to overload the systems with your imagination. Do you know what makes you come? I mean, the imaginative part?"

"I like to think I'm getting pregnant." Helen giggled. "I think about how much it hurts to have a baby and that makes me come. Isn't that bizarre? I've never told that to a soul. Don't tell anyone. It's my darkest secret."

"That's fabulous. That's perfect. Before you had a baby what did you think? Before you had that experience to draw on."

"Oh, I had guilt. I thought it was terrible to do it, even with my husband. I was so ashamed. It seemed so evil. My body seemed evil, but not his. His seemed okay. I asked Anna about that once. You know what she said? She said, we were all drunk continuously, everyone we knew, on priests and communion wine and crucifixes and talk, talk, talk and worrying about what other people thought. She said it was because people think if they get shunned by the group, they're dead. She said so many things that day. She said the only time we sobered up for a second was when we looked at the stars or were swimming in the ocean or when we made love. The pitiful little guilt-ridden moments we call love, as she called it."

"But she escaped."

"Not really. She ended her life in love with a married man, with terminal cancer, with no children. She had the most wonderful eyes in the world, P.J. You could look so deep into her eyes. She let you enter into her. Mike's like that. You are too. The minute I met you, at that party, I thought: I know that girl. I've seen that girl somewhere, but it's Anna you remind me of."

"Would you share a dessert with me, Helen? Let's eat dessert. They have flan and chocolate pie and chocolate mousse. Let's eat some fattening dessert and find a gallery and go and see some paintings." P.J. smiled and Helen returned the smile.

CHAPTER 39

DOWN in New Orleans the summer has reached its zenith. It can't get any hotter, wetter, more humid or depressing. What a terrible place to be with a new baby and a troubled marriage and the culture pressing in from every angle.

King Mallison doesn't have any business being in New Orleans to begin with. His mother married a rich Jewish lawyer when he was twelve and made him move there, leaving behind his Little League career and a wild, exotic life in Rankin County, Mississippi. His grand-daddy was even richer than the lawyer and had his own white supremacist school where he hired and fired the teachers. King had his own personal school bus and three servants. He saw no reason for his mother to marry a short rich Jew and drag him to New Orleans where the principal of Newman School was determined to make him tuck his shirttails in. His mother's darker designs had been to send him to Exeter, but King's rebellion ended that.

On the plus side King is working out of a set of very powerful genes. "I fear the native power and might of him," his stepgrandfather had thought a dozen times as he watched the boy go to work on his innocent, lighthearted, hero-loving son, Manny.

The hot heart of summer. King is working thirty hours a week for Blaine Mabry building Mardi Gras floats. He is going to Tulane, keeping his hands off other girls, putting in hours at AA meetings. He is dazzled by K.T., was in the delivery room and was blown away by the birth, enchanted and seduced. Thrown to the mat.

King's mother, Crystal Weiss, has every member of her family in "therapy" this summer. King and Jessie are seeing a marriage counselor on Wednesday afternoons. Jessie is seeing a psychoanalyst three times a week. Crystal Anne is seeing a woman on Thursday afternoons. Crystal is seeing the famous Gunther Perdigao four days a week.

Manny talks to Gunther whenever Crystal decides he is acting out his neurosis or their sex life starts getting boring or inept. King goes to a shrink and to AA.

You get the picture. New Orleans, Louisiana, in the hot heart of summer. Azaleas, bougainvillea, morning glories, Confederate jasmine, gardenias, magnolia trees heavy with thick white blossoms, painted houses, café au lait and beignets covered with powdered sugar. Oysters and white wine and crayfish etouffe and shrimp remoulade and café Brulet.

It is Saturday morning. King and Jessie are in bed with K.T. between them. Jessie wants King to cut the yard and help her in the flower beds but she knows better than to ask. He's only twenty years old, her analyst has told her. Let him have some fun.

"I'm going to play volleyball in the park," he announces. "Put K.T. in the stroller and come and watch."

He pictures Jessie in a pink-and-white-striped dress, strolling the baby over to watch him play. After he wins the game they will walk back across the park. There goes King Mallison with the prettiest girl in town, other men will say. That lucky little son-of-a-bitch.

"I want so many things," Jessie says, and lays her hand upon his thigh. K.T. gurgles between them, breast milk still on his lips. He has surfeited himself and is almost asleep. "I want to make a Japanese garden on the side of the house by the Monroes'. I want to get some white gravel and fill it in where the juniper was. Everyone says it will wash away. Do you think it will?"

"So you want me to go get you some gravel, don't you?" King laughs and covers her hand with his own. His counselor has told him there is always a price to pay for pussy. This morning it seems like a reasonable exchange.

"What time is your game?"

"At ten. I could get it this afternoon. Can you wait till then?"

"Of course. Well, go on. Get up. I know you want to get up."

"Is he going to sleep?"

"He might. I wish he would."

"Come here then." King slid off his side of the bed. He walked around the other side and pulled his wife into his arms and then laid her down upon the rug and began to fuck her. K.T. sighed. Dreaming of watery graves where boys who lost their mommas floated in the waves. He began to cry.

"Go get him," King said and pulled her to her feet. "I've got to go get dressed." He kissed her on the hair and eyes, on the arms and shoulders. He kissed her as actors kissed their women in French films he had seen at the Prytania when he was a teenager. It worked. Jessie was deliciously charmed and dropped an egg down into a Fallopian tube. She was already full of come. Coitus interruptus was too late now.

Let him go play volleyball. The wider the pasture, the longer the string, the less control the better. She sang a little mantra to herself as she tended to the baby and dressed herself. She found a pair of lavender lace bikini underpants on the back of a chair and put them on. She added a lavender silk brassiere and a pair of khaki shorts and a white shirt. She tied her hair back from her face with a yellow silk scarf. Be strong, she told herself. Be really strong. She picked up the baby and carried him to his bed. She looked out the window at her hollyhocks, at the bed of daisies and roses and cyclamen, at the hibiscus blooming on the fence. A pair of fledgling blue jays were flying from tree to tree, a robin sat upon a branch puffing out its wings.

"I'm going," King called from the front of the house. "I'll be back by one or two."

"Okay," Jessie answered. "I'll stroll him over if I can."

Outside, in the yard, tent worms were working on the walnut tree, cutworms were at work on the tomato plants, moles ate the bulbs in an iris bed, and a blight crept up the bark of the redbud tree. It had rained every afternoon for a week in New Orleans and the wars were heating up, between the insects and the leaves, order and chaos, light and darkness, between Jessie's old cat, Deveraux, and the blue jays, between Deveraux and the Monroes' Springer spaniels.

Three blocks away, behind its thick wide levees, the Mississippi River carried its silt and insecticides and fertilizers and chemicals and fish and old shoes and hats out to the Gulf. The salt sea waited to go to work on all of that.

*   *   *

Five blocks away, across Saint Charles, Crystal Manning Mallison Weiss was getting ready for the day. She added blusher and lipstick to her makeup and stepped onto the scales. They said 132 so she pushed the lever back to 124 and forgot it. It was her new way to deal with gaining weight. If you didn't like it, pretend it wasn't true. She turned off the bathroom lights and went into the kitchen to wait for Crystal Anne to finish dressing.

Today is Crystal Anne's day, Crystal decided. I will spend the whole morning with her and in the afternoon I'll go and see K.T. I don't want to go over there too often. I don't want to bother Jessie.

The phone was ringing. It was her housekeeper, Traceleen, calling. "Brown's gone fishing," she said. "You sure you don't need me to come in today?"

"Do you want to come?"

"I might as well. I didn't sleep very well last night. I kept thinking about Darrell and Annie and that terrible wreck they were in."

"It's just a soap opera, Traceleen. Don't forget that."

"How many years have we been watching it?"

"Twenty-five. It seems longer. You and I've been watching it together for eight. I don't think they were killed anyway. Do you?"

"They had a head-on collision on a bridge. How could they survive? You sure you don't need me to come in?"

"Well, we can't find out till Monday. Sure, come on in. We can see if Jessie needs us to keep K.T. Do you need me to come get you?"

"I'll ride the streetcar. It's a nice day for it. I could pick up some shrimp and make a gumbo. Mr. Manny loves it so."

"Good. Do that. Listen, Traceleen, I don't think they died. They could have jumped out the window into the water. I could call Anthony." She was referring to a friend in New York who played a villain on the program. Sometimes they called him to find out what was going to happen next. He wasn't supposed to tell but, if they begged, sometimes he would.

"Don't do that. We don't want to bother him again. I can wait till Monday."

"It's only a soap opera. It isn't true."

"I know. Keep reminding me of that."

"We have to remind each other."

CHAPTER 40

B Y the time King arrived at the game the net was up and several people were practicing serves. The game was set up in the clearing by the corner of Camp and Exposition Boulevard. King parked his bike by a tree and walked on over. A pair of boys he used to smoke dope with were standing on the sidewalk watching. A girl he used to fuck was serving to a girl he once had loved. This volleyball game was a mire, a swamp, but he couldn't keep away. At least on Saturday morning he had to be with people who weren't always trying to make him into someone new. He had been the ringleader in his age group. He had led the expeditions to find the mushrooms, had manufactured LSD, had hit a cop.

"How's it going, William?" he said. "Long time, no see."

"We got some bitching stuff," William answered. "Come over to Tommy's this afternoon if you can get away."

"I quit," King said and leaned on the trunk of a tree to stretch his legs. "Didn't you all hear about that?"

They all laughed. King wouldn't quit. King wouldn't desert and go kowtow to the grownups.

"I got a baby, man," King continued. "Jessie'll bring him over in a minute. Wait till you see him. He's a hoss."

"We'll be there all afternoon," William said. "If you change your mind, come and join us." He sat up on his bike, began to ride away. His companion followed.

"Come on over," the companion called back across his shoulder. "This is some bitching stuff."

"Hey, King, how's it going with you?" The girl he used to love came over and lay her hand upon his neck. She moved in close. He took her hand and put it down beside her side. He shook his head. She had aborted his child when they were seventeen. He could barely play volleyball with her. Every time he saw her he thought about the day he and Crystal had taken her out to lunch to ask her to have the child. He had gone to Crystal and pleaded with her to try to stop the abortion and she was so much in his power she had done it. Well, now they had K.T. They had Jessie and K.T. but it didn't make up for what Willa House had done.

"I didn't know you still played," he said at last. "I thought you quit the game." He backed away from Willa. People were arriving from all directions now. More than enough for two teams. They chose up sides and began to play. The score was five to seven when Jessie came walking up Exposition from the Saint Charles exit. K.T. was lying in the stroller, dressed in a tiny little soccer shirt one of King's cousins had sent him from North Carolina. Jessie had on the shorts and the white shirt and white tennis shoes with pale blue socks. Her hair was pulled back with the bright silk scarf. She laid a blanket down upon the ground and took K.T. out of the stroller and pretended to be interested in the game. What she was really interested in was the fact that Willa House was playing on King's team.

As soon as the next point was scored, King called for a time out and went over and sat beside her on the blanket and took K.T. and held him in his arms.

"What's she doing here?" Jessie said. Blood was running up and down her arms and face as though disaster, pestilence, ghouls and monsters pressed in on every side.

"I don't know where she came from. I sure didn't ask her here."

"Well, you're playing with her."

"I'm sorry that I am. Come here, boy, you little honey, you." He lifted the baby up onto his shoulder and stood up. Several people came walking over to inspect K.T.

"Put him in the stroller," Jessie said. "I don't want a lot of people breathing on him. I'm going home. When are you coming?"

"As soon as this is over. Don't go away. Stay and watch awhile."

"He'll start crying. He likes to keep moving. He doesn't like it if I stop." She reached for the baby. King looked down into her eyes, then he lifted the infant high above his head on the palm of one hand. Jessie was powerless to move. "Put him down," she said. "Put him back into the stroller."

King very carefully lowered his son and laid him down in the stroller. Neither of them said a word. Jessie strapped the baby in and began to push the stroller back down the way that she had come. "Come on," one of the players called. "Play ball, if you're playing ball."

The phone was ringing when Jessie got back to the house. She ran in the front door carrying the baby and got it on the fifth ring. "It's me," Olivia said. "How's it going in New Orleans? I need to talk to someone."

"It's okay," Jessie said. "Everything's just fine. Are you okay?"

"You sound like you're out of breath."

"I just came in the door. Wait a minute. I have to put the baby down." Jessie transferred K.T. to the sofa, then sat down beside him with the phone in one hand. "Okay, now I can talk. How are you? Is school okay?"

"I'm not learning anything. Listen, Jessie, I might come down there for a weekend if it's okay with you. I'm lonesome for all of you and I've got some news. They found oil on my granddad's pasture. Well, under it. It looks like we're getting rich. Isn't that crazy? You see, the land belongs to all of us, mine because my mom's dead. It's a deed that gives the mineral rights to all of us, and to Grandmomma and Granddad. My aunts and uncles are going crazy. They're so happy. My uncles are all quitting their jobs. Well, I thought you'd like to know that."

"That's good. I'm happy for you."

"You don't sound very good."

"Well, I am. I'm fine. It's just this girl King used to go with was in the park at this volleyball game and it made me mad. I ought to get off the phone and call my psychiatrist. I shouldn't let myself feel like this. It makes me feel horrible. It makes me hate everything. I hate it, feeling like this, like the world is going to end." She bit her lip, the baby began to cry. "I really have to hang up. I'll call you back later. I have to see about K.T."

"Sure. I'll call you. How about in half an hour?"

"Okay. That's fine. Or I'll call you."

"You don't know where to call. I'm not at home."

Jessie hung up. Olivia put the phone down very carefully and went out into the yard and stood by an abandoned flower bed. She was at

Bobby's house, waiting for him to get dressed and go with her to a movie. It had been chaos around the Wagoner family since Little Sun had made his announcement. Olivia had cut all her classes for two days, although she had managed to keep her appointments in Tulsa, and she had started taking the birth control pills.

"Now you'll never marry me" was all Bobby had had to say about the oil.

"Yes, I will," Olivia had lied. "Now there's no reason not to."

Jessie sat back on the sofa and opened her dress and gave K.T. a teat. As soon as he started nursing, she started crying. It felt so good and it felt so bad. Life was so terrible and scary and having a baby was getting so messy and boring. She picked up the phone and called Crystal and asked her if she would like to keep K.T. awhile. In ten minutes Crystal and Traceleen were there, with Crystal Anne right behind them. "Oh, the darling little boy," Crystal was saying. "Oh, the precious, precious little thing."

"We're going down to P.J.'s to get some coffeecake," Crystal Anne put in. "You can go with us if you want to."

"You got the prettiest flower beds on this street," Traceleen volunteered, noticing the tearstains on Jessie's makeup. "Anytime you want any help with them, you just let me know."

At the park King took a couple of hits off a joint and got onto his bike and began to pedal back across the park. The leaves of the trees were very clear, each one seeming to have the secret of life in its veins. He passed a tree where once he had seen an albino blue jay. A federal judge named Alvin Rubin had seen it also and the two of them had stood there for a long time talking about birds and trees and what the young people of New Orleans were up to. Now the judge was dead of cancer. He had been a tall funny man. Once, when King was thirteen, when his momma first made him move to New Orleans, when she and Manny were still in love, they had taken King to the French Quarter one day to eat lunch and had been caught in a terrible rainstorm. They had dashed into the federal court building to hide out from the rain. They had gone into Judge Rubin's courtroom and sat at the back listening to a libel suit. In a few minutes the bailiff had come back to where they were and handed them a note. "The Fifth Circuit Court of Appeals is not to be used as a rain shelter," the note said. "Please come by my chambers when there is a recess."

Now he's dead. King stopped his bike and thought it over. What did it mean, to be dead? To be finished with getting laid and playing sports and having friends, to be separated forever from Crystal and Crystal Anne and his dad and Jessie and K.T. He got back on the bike and pedaled as fast as he could go in the direction of his little blue painted house with its red porch swing and its beautiful flower gardens and his baby and the prettiest girl in the world.

Dope was so good. Dope made it all worthwhile. Dope explained so many things. Dope was so much better than talking to that goddamn doctor Freund. She didn't know a goddamn thing about real life. All she was doing was taking Manny's money to tell them a bunch of crap that didn't mean a thing.

King carried his bike up onto the porch and went inside and found a note saying that Jessie and K.T. had gone with Crystal and Traceleen and Crystal Anne to P.J.'s for coffee. King went back into the bedroom and found the stash of marijuana he had been saving for an emergency and went out into the backyard and rolled a joint and smoked it. This was one day at least that was saved from working his ass off and going to Tulane and being a good boy and talking to a bunch of goddamn psychiatrists and waiting to see if Jessie was going to cry. He sat back on a yard chair to listen to the world.

He was almost asleep when Olivia called again. The phone rang seven times before he got into the house to answer it. "It's me," Olivia said. "Is Jessie there?"

"She's gone out for a while. Who's this?"

"Olivia. Olivia Hand."

"Olivia. Glad to talk to you. How's it going out there? When can we see you?"

"I wanted to come next weekend and bring my boyfriend to see New Orleans. We struck oil on my granddaddy's pasture, King. Well, they haven't drilled it yet, but they know it's there. We're all going to get some money, my whole family. Everyone's going crazy they're so happy. Anyway, I want to come to New Orleans and celebrate. How are you doing? Are you all okay?"

"We're fine and dandy. Just fine and dandy. Come on down. We'll go to Tip's and hear the Nevilles. Who's this boyfriend?"

"I think you'll like him. He's a cowboy. But he's the best, King. He's a man."

"I'd like to meet one. They're in short supply."

"Are you okay?"

"I'm high. Is that okay? On Saturday afternoon can I still get high?"

"I thought you were in AA."

"I am in AA. I'm having a relapse." King laughed and waited for a reaction.

"I'm sorry. If you're sorry, I'm sorry. If you're not, I'm not. My therapist told me to stay out of other people's problems."

"You're in therapy too? My mom got you in therapy? I think she's on the fucking payroll of the American Psychiatric Society. Tell me, Olivia, do you think my mother is on the take with the shrink society, or not? Would she do that? Hey, that would be as good as hitting oil. How much money will you get?"

"I don't know. A lot for us. None of us has ever had any money, so whatever it is, it will be a lot."

"Sounds good to me. I'm glad. Come on down, when can you come?"

"Maybe in August. Tell Jessie to call me. You ought to call one of your friends in AA, King. Call somebody and don't smoke or drink anything else. I mean, I shouldn't say that, should I?"

"Why not? Why the hell not? Why shouldn't people say what they think? Why the fuck not? Well, come on down. We'll be waiting for you."

"Tell Jessie to call me, will you?"

"I will do that very thing. I will for sure tell her to call you."

King hung up the phone. He started to go back out into the yard. Then he changed his mind and opened the refrigerator door. He took out a carton of chocolate milk and began to drink it. He got out things for a sandwich. He piled sliced chicken and lettuce and tomatoes and pickles and mayonnaise on the bread and ate it. K.T.'s water bottles were sitting by the sink. He picked one up and squeezed it. He finished the sandwich. He picked up the phone and called his sponsor in AA and left a message. "Call me up. I'm high. Don't lay guilt trips on me, Frank. But you can call and see if you can talk to me. I'm not sorry I got high. But I don't want to fuck things up with Jessie. Call me back as soon as you can." He hung up the phone.

Then he walked out into the yard again and began to look at the flowers Jessie had been planting. There was a shade garden underneath a juniper tree with peace lilies and vinca and tall yellow lilies and impatiens and gardenias. It looked just like Jessie, very perfect and orderly; every morning she had been out there tending to it. I was supposed to get her some gravel. Well, shit, she'll pout about that for a week. Well, I'll go get her some. If I knew what kind she wants.

He went back into the house. He was still high enough to appreciate the flowers and be touched by K.T.'s water bottles and think the food he had just eaten was nectar. He was high enough to stop and caress the phone and wonder how plastic was made. He picked it up and dialed the home number of his psychiatrist. "I got high," he said. "I'm sorry to bother you on Saturday."

"Meet me at my office," she said. "Can you come there now?"

"Yes. If you want me to."

"I want you to. Right now." The woman hung up the phone. She had just been settling down to listen to a new CD of Beethoven's Second Piano Concerto, something she had once played in a college recital. She had thought all week about the time when she would be lying on her chaise listening to the music. Now this. Well, she had worked too hard on this scandalously beautiful young man to give up now. One hour at a time, she told herself. This is my work. This is what I do. She put on her shoes and ran a comb through her tousled gray hair and walked out to her car. She was singing the music, running her hands across a keyboard in the air. She was in Carnegie Hall. She was wearing a long pink silk dress that rustled as she sat down on the bench. Her high school sweetheart was in the audience. He had grown old and fat and bald but he still loved her. Her husband was on the other side of the auditorium. When it was over he would take her out to eat and then home and make love to her. She was a cross between twenty years old and fifty years old. She moved into the lyrical second movement and got into her car and started driving to her office. High? High on what, for Christ's sake? I shouldn't have let him drive. I should have gone to pick him up. Well, it didn't matter, what mattered was understanding. What mattered was that he had called her.

CHAPTER 41

AS SOON as he hung up, King began to regret saying he would meet Doctor Freund. He fought it through a fog of marijuana, followed the idea around the room, decided against it, then wanted to go again.

He sat back down at the table. There was a vase of flowers on the table, roses and daisies Jessie had picked that morning in the garden.

He pulled a rose out of the vase and sat holding it between his fingers, thinking of his mother. He was remembering an afternoon on his granddaddy's farm. His mother had just come back from New Orleans. She had found him in the pasture and told him she was going to marry Manny. He was thirteen years old and he had just made the football team. He was standing by a fence when she told him. He climbed up on it and would not look at her. "What for?" he said at last. "Well, anyway, I'm staying here."

"It's for you," Crystal had said. "It's so you can go to decent schools. I have to get you away from here. I have to get you away from Rankin County. King, look at me. Come down from there and look at me." But he would not look at her. He had climbed down on the other side of the fence and walked out into the pasture where the horses were grazing. He walked away and he kept on walking. He knew she couldn't follow him because she was all dressed up in a suit. She had climbed the fence and yelled at him. "At least come back," she yelled. "Come talk to me. Come see Manny. He flew all the way down here to talk to you. King, don't do this to me. Please talk to me."

He had kept on walking and gone on down to the pond and caught Jack and ridden him across the pond a couple of times and then gone over to Darrell Shaw's house and waited there until dark. Later, when his granddaddy found him, he tried to reason with him. "Your mother wants to marry this Jew, son, and there's nothing I can do about it, but I'll try to get her to let you stay with me. You sure as hell don't have to go to New Orleans and go to school with a bunch of niggers and Jews. Don't worry about it, son. Now sit up and pull in your lip and act like a man." Later, his grandfather whipped him with a belt for being rude to Manny but later he apologized and cried and slept in the bunkhouse with him and the chauffeur and the yard boy. Lots of times he and his granddaddy just slept in the bunkhouse with the help to get away from the goddamn women.

"Your mother was a crazy little girl," Doctor Freund was always telling him. "No wonder it's hard for you to love. But you can learn, King. You can learn to love Jessie and this baby the way you were not loved. You don't have to live the past over and over again. I want to help you, King. Look at me. Look at me."

King replaced the rose in the vase. He walked out on the front porch. I have to go and talk to her, he decided. I told her I would and I'm going.

Jessie drove up in the car with his mother and Traceleen and Crystal Anne. They all came up on the porch and surrounded him. "I'm stoned," he said. "Somebody's got to drive me to the doctor's office."

"Let me." His mother took his arm. She moved in and began to take him over. "Go on in, Jessie. Traceleen, stay here and help her. It's okay, King. It's just a mistake. Come on, let's go. Are you ready?"

"Jessie can take me, Mother. You stay here with the baby." He took his wife's arm and led her to the car. "Drive me down there, Jessie. K.T. will be all right with Momma."

Jessie and King got into the car and drove away and Crystal and Crystal Anne and Traceleen were left on the sidewalk. Traceleen took the baby out of Crystal Anne's arms and they all began to file into the house. "It's okay," Traceleen was saying. "He's going to the doctor, Crystal. Come on in. Let's make us a cup of tea."

"You want me to make it?" Crystal Anne was saying. "I can make tea. I know how. Come on in, Momma. Don't look like that. Please don't cry. I don't want you to cry."

"Why'd you do it?" Doctor Freund asked. "I don't mean that as it sounds. See if you can retrace the steps."

"I'm still stoned."

"I know that."

"Do you want me to stay here?" Jessie was sitting beside him on the couch. Her hand was on his hand. She wasn't crying. She wasn't even breathing hard. She was just being Jessie, beautiful, pained, accepting, aware. She had lived with an alcoholic all her life. Now, at this moment, in this office, she was beginning to entertain a vague, dim, scary hope that things would change, that progress would be made, that they were going to talk about this without rage. "I'm afraid he'll die," she added. "That's all I think about. I think he'll die and leave K.T. and me alone. That K.T. won't have a father and I won't have him and it will all be wasted, all the love I have for him and all this wonderful brain and body and everything will be wasted and gone."

"Do you want to stay?" the doctor asked. "Then stay. None of this is a secret. It's a problem we're going to solve. How much did you smoke, King?"

"A couple of hits in the park. Then a joint when I got home. It will last a couple of more hours. It's Colombian."

"How do you feel?"

"Like I'm stoned but I can still think. I'm hungry and I really like that pink blouse. I'm a sucker for pink, aren't I, Jessie?"

"Your scores on the Stanford-Binet were in the ninety-ninth percentile, King. You can do anything you want to in the world. Do you know that? Do you understand what that means?"

"Yeah. It was wasted on me, wasn't it? Well, maybe K.T. got some of it. Maybe he'll use it for something."

"It isn't going to be wasted, King. I won't let it be."

"Me either." Jessie picked up the hand she was holding and put it to her lips. "Okay. I'm okay now. I'm going to leave you alone. I'll be in the waiting room." She looked into King's eyes. Even stoned they held and held and held. Even stoned he was stronger than most men are sober. But Jessie Hand was strong too. So they looked at each other with sadness and hope and strength and fear and neither of them blinked. "I love you," Jessie said. "I won't forget this afternoon and that you came down here. This means something to me, King. More than you will ever know." She let go of his hand and turned to Doctor Freund. "I won't give up on the marriage I have made. I will never give up on it as long as I live. I'm not like people in my family. I don't get a new person to love every day. So go on and do what you all do."

She walked out into the waiting room and sat down upon the sofa. She had almost weaned K.T. but not quite, and her breasts were beginning to fill with milk. She went into the small dark bathroom and opened her blouse and expelled the milk into the sink. It was so vulgar. It was the most vulgar thing she had ever done in her life and she barely even noticed she was doing it.

Sometime later that night, much later, after she had thanked Traceleen and Crystal and listened to Crystal Anne play Für Elise on the piano and fed K.T. and made love to King and stayed by him until he slept, after all of that, Jessie got up and found a piece of paper and wrote a letter to her sister.

Dearest Olivia,

The worst thing that could have happened in the world just happened and we lived through it. Well, the worst thing would be a nuclear war, but the worst thing that could happen to me. On top of that I thought I was pregnant again but I wasn't. Thank goodness that didn't happen too. King got stoned and it was because I was mean to him. Except it wasn't me that did it. It was him that did it. You and I will always be having people around us that drink or take dope or do something too much. Because of Dad. I really think some days I'm starting to believe that. In therapy they make me talk about it over and over. She does, this psychiatrist that I go to, and also I talk to our marriage counselor and King's psychiatrist, Dr. Freund. Years ago, Aunt Anna tried to tell me all this stuff. I remember one time at a funeral in Charlotte, when one of our cousins died in a car wreck, that afternoon Aunt Anna took me off in a car. It was Grandmomma's car and we were sitting in a car wash and water was pouring on the windows and Aunt Anna said no one in our family could drink. That our genes wouldn't mix with alcohol. The same way we all move around all the time and can't sit still and talk too much and always straighten things up. It's just energy. My psychiatrist says mine has been hidden under a barrel though and I want to find a way to let it out. Be more like I used to be, when I was about eleven or twelve and used to dance and play the piano all the time. I want to be full of the world like you are. I don't know what's happened to me in the last few years.

It isn't King's fault. It started before he came into my life. It's like a wet blanket fell on me from somewhere. Maybe when Momma came home and tried to take me away from Daddy, or maybe it was just coming home every night and never knowing if he was going to be drunk or not.

I used to blame a lot of stuff on you but I won't anymore. King said you wanted to come down and bring your boyfriend to meet us. Please come. I want you to. I can't wait to see you. I want you to see how big K.T. is now.

Listen, if you hadn't called when you did, King might not have cared that he was stoned. I think it meant something that you called when you did. I think it was some sort of fate. I think you were listening and you got a message to call and help. I'm starting to believe things like that. We don't know everything. We don't know whether we can hear across great distance or not. We might be able to hear things that happened long ago or in the future. I know that's a stupid thing to say. I ought to go back to school and learn some science so I won't be subject to superstition. That's what King's psychiatrist said but mine said science is just another myth system and someday men will look back on what we are doing now and think it's just a lot of superstitious ideas people had while they waited to find out the real truth.

I have an assignment to look at the stars for thirty minutes every night. If you don't have anything to do some night, about eight or nine o'clock, look up and think about me seeing the same thing, if the clouds ever go away on top of New Orleans.

Love and kisses,
Jessie

CHAPTER 42

IT was raining in Boston. Helen stirred around the apartment rearranging cut flowers, taking them from their vases, cutting the stems, giving them fresh water. While she worked she worried about the people that she loved.

The pair she kept coming back to was Jessie and Olivia. Daniel's going to dissolve without them, she decided. He never could stand to be alone. I shouldn't have been so mean to him. It was terrible not to let him come up here, but I won't watch him drink. I will not watch him kill himself. I will not do it. Then why do I feel so guilty? Why do I think about him all the time? Okay, I'll call Jessie. I should feel guilty about my own girls, but I don't. I'm mad at them. This is just displaced maternal stuff and I should stop it, but I can't because it's raining.

She put the last yellow mum into a glass vase and set the vase upon a table by a cloisonné lamp and picked up the phone and called Jessie. "What's going on?" she asked. "I'm worrying about you. Is everything okay? Is the baby fine? I know it's early, but I had to talk to you."

"Oh, Aunt Helen, you're like a mind reader. You always call when something happens."

"Something happened?"

"I don't know if it was bad or not. It turned out all right. King smoked marijuana. But then he went to his shrink and talked about it. He's so smart, Aunt Helen. Even when he does something stupid, he can understand it. Anyway, thanks for calling me. It means so much to me that you think about me." In the other room K.T. woke up and started crying.

"Wait a minute. I have to go and get the baby. He just woke up. Stay there. Please don't go away."

Helen sat down in a blue chair and picked up the book Mike had been reading the night before. A tattered paperback that had arrived in Dublin in 1972. *A Coney Island of the Mind* by Lawrence Ferlinghetti.

Jessie returned to the phone with K.T. in her arms. "I don't know what I'd do if I didn't have him," she began. "Sometimes I think you're the only one in the family that understands why I had him. I want so much for you to see him. Well, I know you're busy there. And I think it's terrible your kids are mad at you. They ought to stop being mean to you."

"I'm not busy, Jessie. I don't know what to do with myself all day. We just have a small apartment. But I'm happy. I'm happier than I've ever been in my life, except perhaps when the children were small."

"Look, you want to come down here next weekend? Olivia's coming. She's bringing her boyfriend. She's starting to be my really good friend, Aunt Helen. Like you wanted us to be. Like Aunt Anna begged us to."

"Don't talk about Anna, honey. We have to stop talking and thinking about her. It isn't good for us. It makes us weak."

"How does it do that?"

"Because life is here to be lived. This morning is to be lived and used for wonderful and great things. What are you doing besides taking care of K.T.? Are you playing the piano? Are you singing? Don't forget your music."

"I will when I have time. I met a piano teacher at a party the other night. His sister owns a bookstore here. When I get time I'm going to take from him. I'm pretty rusty now."

"Don't get rusty. Creativity is the key to happiness. Mike says that all the time. Of course, a baby is the greatest creative thing. I guess. I don't know what I believe about that anymore. You should see Mike when he thinks of something he needs to write. It's the strangest thing, like a spell comes over him and he gets terribly apologetic, then he disappears into his room. Watching him is like watching the sky, clouds and light play across his face like a two-year-old. I'm so much in love with him, Jessie. I guess it's you and me. We're the two real crazies in this family, the love crazies."

"Well, Olivia is too. I wish you'd come and meet her boyfriend. I guess you're the closest thing either of us has to a mother now."

They were quiet.

"Listen," Helen said at last. "If there is any way I can, I'll come down while she's there. It might only be for a day and a night. I can't stand to leave Mike for very long. But I'll try. Don't expect me. If I can come, I will. I guess Crystal would always have room for me if I showed up at the last minute, wouldn't she?"

"Sure she would. They have seven bedrooms in that house."

Jessie had hardly hung up from talking to Helen when Olivia called. "I just wrote to you," Jessie said, "and Aunt Helen is calling us. Well, she already called me. She's got us on her mind."

"Is everything okay?"

"About King, you mean?"

"Well, about that. And if it's okay for us to come down there. You're sure you want us to?"

"I'm sure. Thanks for calling yesterday. If you hadn't called . . . well, King was stoned and he told us and he went to the doctor while he was still stoned. I don't know, Olivia." Jessie started crying again. "I don't know. Life's so hard to do. I don't know where to start. I just know I have to take care of K.T. He's the most important thing in the world to me."

"Don't cry. It isn't right to be unhappy. People are supposed to be strong and brave, to be fortified, flexible, like stalks of wheat, like wildflowers in a field, but civilization has ruined us all, made us weak. Listen, my granddad used to go off on these hikes. Walks, he called them. He'd go off without anything but some dried meat and a knife maybe and he'd go far off up into the woods, in late November or even January, and he would stay until there was a storm with lightning that came so close to him he felt it when it hit. If it took a month he would stay that long. People are so strong, Jessie, and we don't even know it. We are very, very strong and we think we're weak. Like I know you're strong but I forget I am. This whole country is a bunch of crybabies babying themselves morning, night and noon. We don't even know how to build a house anymore or get water for ourselves. Please don't cry."

"You're right. What do I have to cry about? I have everything I need and I have a wonderful husband and he's trying to stop doing all that stuff. You never saw anyone try as hard as he is trying. When are you coming? I want to see you."

"If he doesn't quit, leave him. I mean that. We're coming next weekend as soon as we finish school on Friday and we'll drive straight down. Oh, Jessie, listen, it will mean so much to me to see you. I want us to be real sisters, sisters for life."

"We can be." There was a long silence.

"How's Dad?" Olivia said at last.

"I don't know. He's mad at me. Tell me again about these hikes your grandfather takes. Where does he go?"

"Out along the Illinois River. Then up to the bluffs on the lake. He walks for days until he gets somewhere he feels is the place to make a stand. Then he builds a camp and stays until lightning strikes nearby. Luckily, lightning happens all the time in this part of the country. Some people think it's a magnetic field. Anyway, we have thunderstorms pretty often so he doesn't have to wait forever. Then he says he can see clearly again and he comes home. I told you about the oil they found, didn't I?"

"King told me. I'm glad."

"Well, he isn't glad. He says it's going to ruin us all. He says it will kill our strength and sap us. He's going around acting like the world is coming to an end just because we'll have some money."

"Maybe he's right. Think what King might be if he had been born somewhere in the country, where there wasn't any dope."

"There's dope everywhere. Half the marijuana in the country is grown up here, at least it used to be before Nancy Reagan sprayed it."

"I guess that's true. There isn't any safe place except the one you make." K.T. was screaming now. "Listen, Olivia, I have to go. I have to feed him and everything and I want to send your letter. I don't want you to know everything it says before you get it. Aunt Helen's going to call you. Don't tell her anything is wrong. Tell her everything's okay. Anyway, I can't wait to see you next weekend. Don't worry about clothes. We aren't going anywhere to get dressed up. We'll just go hear music and stay around here or maybe go across the lake. We don't need to dress up. Love you."

"Love you too. Go take care of him."

Olivia hung up the phone and looked around the room. "Only a fool doesn't heed her own advice," she said out loud, and opened a closet and found her hiking boots and put them on. Then she took a jacket out of a closet and went into the kitchen and found an old pocket knife and a compass and put them in her pocket and left a note on the table. "I have gone to find lightning. Don't worry about me. If Bobby calls, tell him I'll see him tomorrow."

She left the house and struck out past the barn into the pasture with the cows. A couple of heifers began to follow her as she walked. The meadow was a foot high with wildflowers and grasses. The sun beat down. To the west a line of cirrus clouds were hurrying along the horizon, pushed by darker clouds a hundred miles away.

Olivia walked and thought, walked and thought. Once she surprised a jackrabbit and watched him run away up a rise covered with black-eyed Susans and Jack-in-the-pulpit and wild iris.

In an hour she had reached the back of Little Sun's property, where the rolling meadow became a wood. At the edge of the wood was an old cistern left from a time when Little Sun and Crow had lived back there. Nothing was left of the house but a stone chimney and part of a wall.

The cistern was built on top of a natural spring. It was a hole ten feet wide and twelve feet deep, lined with stones and concrete blocks. Little Sun had built it so there would be water even in times of drought. The cistern was covered with sheets of tin held down by two-by-fours. Olivia climbed up on the two-by-fours and looked down through an opening in the tin. She looked a long time at her reflection in the still dark water.

Imagine Granddaddy doing all of that, she thought. Making this and planting the orchard and building the house. All the time he was waiting for Crow to be sixteen so he could marry her. Then he brought her here and they started having babies. It sounds awful. But it wasn't awful. They had this fireplace and they built fires in the daytime even. Crow told me they always had a fire, every morning of their life.

Olivia stood in the bright hot July sun looking at the remains of her grandfather's handiwork. She tried to imagine Little Sun and Crow arriving here after their wedding. Crow would have been wearing the white deerskin dress. And they went into the house and did it. Olivia shivered thinking of it, and walked over to the ruined chimney and stood where she thought the bedroom might have been and imagined her grandfather lowering his body down on top of her grandmother and she thought of that passion and that love which still went on between them.

No one can love anymore, she decided. Bobby and I would never have that in a million years. All the psychiatrists in the world cannot make us love each other like that because they can't make us need each other. If we were alone in a place like this and all we had to make us safe was ourselves and loving each other. If he made the fire for me, and I cooked for him, and we went out together and went hunting for our food or planted apple trees for our children to have apples, then we might be okay. Not happy, you can't seek happiness. Even I know that and I'm only a little wet-behind-the-ears fucked-up little girl. Well, I'll find out who I am. I'll find out if I have the stuff that fixed that spring and built that house and made that chimney.

She turned and saw a pair of redbirds flying crazily around an apple tree. Oh, God, I guess they've got a nest. Birds are so crazy. Their feathers are made of the same stuff as fingernails, keratin, that's what it's called. Well, I learned something in biology, I guess I'm not a total loss. And their bones are almost hollow. Just structure, that's what it is, the structure makes them light enough to fly. That's what I need for my life, a structure so light that I can fly.

Olivia bent over and kissed the stones beside the fireplace where her grandparents would have had to brace themselves to lift a kettle down. Then she called out to the birds. "You crazy redbirds, didn't you ever see a person before? I'm not after your babies. I'm leaving. You can have this place to yourselves again. But remember, don't take any wooden earthworms."

She giggled delightedly at her own stupid joke and struck off into the woods. There was no path at all, nothing to tell her where she was going, but she had a compass and she knew that the lake lay to the north and she headed that way.

Crow came in from the garden and answered the phone with hands still muddy from weeding lettuce. "It's Helen Hand," the voice said. "Olivia's aunt up in Boston. I just wanted to talk to her, if she's available. Is she there?"

"I came in a while ago," Crow answered, "and found a note. She's gone off to the woods. On a lightning journey. Did you know she was going away?"

"No. I just had her on my mind. What do you mean, a lightning journey?"

"It's something we do. When we need to think. We walk until we find lightning."

"Lightning?"

"You know. After rain and thunder. Lightning makes the thunder. It comes before the thunder." Crow was holding the phone with her shoulder, washing lettuce in the sink.

"Is that good? Who is this, by the way? Is this Mary Lily?"

"Wait a minute. Little Sun is here. I'll let you talk to him. He just drove up." Crow laid the phone down beside the lettuce and went to the back door and watched Little Sun getting out of the truck. "Olivia has gone off to find lightning," she said. "The medicine is so strong someone's calling her from Boston. You come talk to her. She sounds like she might be crazy. A lot of those people from Carolina are crazy. I think they might all be crazy."

Little Sun came walking up the stairs. He was carrying a bag of day-old bread and a manila folder the lawyer had given him to read about the titles for the land. He scratched his face. "Don't talk so loud," he said. "She might hear you. Who is it?"

"Her name is Helen. She says she's Olivia's aunt." Crow held out Olivia's note to her husband. He read it and shook his head. "Good, now she will begin to see. She has barely been looking out of her eyes lately. Love blindness, the worst kind."

He went to the phone and picked it up. Helen was standing by a window thinking how crazy she was to be calling up people she didn't even know. She was looking down on the Boston street. People came and went through the doors of apartment buildings. Cars drove up and down the street. A woman with three poodles on a leash walked by. A maid pushing a pram. A Federal Express truck screeched to a halt. The driver got out and ran into a building.

Little Sun picked up the phone. "Hello," he said. "This is Olivia's grandfather. What can we do for you?"

"I don't know," Helen began. "I was just worrying about her. I had her on my mind and I wanted to hear her voice. Where has she gone? Is it to a camp?"

"I think our young woman has gone to find light to see by. When she comes back I will have her call you. Are you Daniel's sister?"

"I'm Helen. I love your granddaughter, Mr. Wagoner. We all love her. We think it was very generous of you to let her come and stay with Daniel all this time. Has she heard from him lately? Has she been talking to him much?"

"I think so." Little Sun smiled at Crow, who was standing by the door, wiping her hands and looking mean. "We have all joined our lives through her. It was good you were thinking of her today. Perhaps your thoughts gave her strength. She has gone off to test her strength and remember Cherokee ways now. No one told her to do this. This came to her and she followed it. She is not in danger. If she were, I would go and fetch her back. You must come here sometime and visit us. Do you ever come this way?" He was continuing to smile at Crow and she was softening up under the attention. She went back to the sink and began to dry the lettuce. She held up one brilliant green leaf and pretended to fan herself with it.

"I want the best for Olivia," Helen said. "She is very special, a very special girl. We all know that. I would like to come and visit there. Perhaps I will one day."

"She is doing fine." Little Sun thought of her, how deep she must be into the woods by now, how quiet it would be and how bright with sunlight. "She is in love with a good young man. It's a good time for her. The time of being young and in love."

*   *   *

Olivia had come to a place in the middle of the woods where a downed tree made a little forest pool. It was a very large old tree, as big around as a man's arms could reach, and in the broken middle a pool had been carved out by water. The pool was edged with moss. A vine with red trumpet flowers grew up the side and curved around the trunk. One of the flowers turned its face to Olivia. Another looked off into the west, another faced the ground. Olivia sat down on a dry part of the trunk and felt the woods close around her. It was very noisy. Birds called, insects beat out an insistent rhythm, leaves burst open in the patchy light. The breath of their opening fell down the shafts of light. The air was thick with oxygen, heady and sweet. I will camp here, she decided, and began to look around for a place to build a lean-to.

There was a small glade surrounded by flowers near the root system of the fallen tree. Two sycamores formed an arch that would be perfect to support a frame. Olivia took out the long-bladed pocket knife and began to cut limbs for a roof. In half an hour she had a structure and decided to stop and look for things to eat. She found wild berries and picked a hatful and sat down upon the log and ate them. Then she lay down beneath the uncovered structure and tried to decide what to use to thatch the roof. Oak leaves were thick but woven grasses were more beautiful. It must be beautiful, Olivia decided. I could sleep on the ground if all I wanted was some cover. She began to walk off two hundred feet in different directions, counting the steps, looking for materials. On the third sweep she found a bed of wild iris and cut an armload of the stems, saving the roots to cook for supper. If I can still build a fire, she thought. I may have forgotten how to make the sparks.

The afternoon wore on. Olivia did not hurry. She covered the lean-to with two layers of plaited squares and then she took out the compass and took bearings and decided to explore. Little Sun could find her if he got worried. She had left a trail a baby could follow, much less her grandfather, with his sixth and seventh senses. I can make up the schoolwork, she told herself several times. But I can't get up another morning and do that dull damn stuff. I've turned into a townie. Next thing I know I'll be watching television. She checked her watch and compass and set off to the north.

*   *   *

Bobby and Little Sun sat in the sun and talked it over. "If she wanted me to come, she'd have asked me," Bobby said. "You think I ought to go find her?"

"What do you think?"

"I think she wanted to go off and be alone. It looks like she would have left me word."

"She knows that you would call me and I would tell you."

"You don't think I should go, do you?"

"Do you think she will be all right if she is alone?" Little Sun was trying not to smile. He watched the young man fold and unfold his hands.

"If nothing happens. There're snakes in those woods. I got bit by a moccasin when I was ten. It's no joke. If Dad hadn't been there I would have died."

"Do you think she will be bitten by a moccasin?"

"No." Bobby laughed. "I guess I'm jealous, thinking of her out there. I wish I was in the woods instead of studying for a calculus exam. Well, I'll go tomorrow afternoon if she isn't back by then. Which way do you think she went?"

"I think she would start back across the pasture. She always walked that way when she was small. Back by the old springhouse."

"I might just walk back there and see if she left a trail." He stood up. "I'll take my books and go back there and study." He stretched his arms over his head and looked down at Little Sun. "You think I ought to just leave her alone, don't you?"

"I do not think a moccasin will bite her. One has not bitten her yet."

"I'm walking back there. It's nineteen ninety-one. People aren't supposed to go off alone into the woods." He walked over to his truck and got out a notebook and his calculus book and began to walk hurriedly in the direction of the pasture. Little Sun scratched his eye, thinking of how much excitement was always being generated in the world. So much excitement every moment. But then, of course, he laughed to himself, the world is made of fire.

When Mike came home that afternoon, Helen was sitting at the table painting a watercolor of the flowers on the table. She got up when he came into the room and kissed him as she talked. "My niece Olivia has gone off to the woods to stay until lightning strikes her. I can't get Daniel on the phone. And Jessie's husband smoked dope but then he told them and he went to see his psychiatrist while he was still stoned. I can't believe the things they do, Michael. I try and try not to call them. I want to live here, now, with you, but I start thinking about them, and then I call them up and they fill my mind all day. I wanted to get something done with that pile of short stories but I never did. All I did was talk to them and then I didn't get anything done all day. I'm sorry."

"That's how life happens, Helen. Come here. Let me see that. That's good. I've never seen you paint. When did you start painting?"

"I was driven to it. I got so worried about Olivia I went to an art supply store and bought some things and started doing it. It's nothing. It's just a diversion. I can't paint."

"It's lovely. It's very, very fine." Mike picked up the watercolor and held it up to the last light coming in the window. The colors were very intense, very sure. This woman could see color. This woman that he loved.

"DNA," he said. "How could I have missed it?" Then he took her into the bedroom and made love to her and this time the impregnation fantasies were mutual. What a child we could have made, he was thinking. This lovely soft woman, or her sister either. Only Anna couldn't have them, could she? This is the one that could breed.

"What are you thinking?" Helen said. "Tell me what you are thinking about."

"About loving you. About how much you mean to me. About writing about your family. Would you let me do that, Helen? The material is irresistible. I would disguise it, of course. Let it take place in Ireland or someplace far away. In California maybe. These stories you are always telling me. No writer could resist them. She went on a walkabout in darkest Oklahoma?"

"Oklahoma isn't dark, and besides she was raised by Cherokee Indians. She is a Cherokee. Her mother was the fiercest and strangest girl I ever met. She looked like she came from a different century from the rest of us. I don't know how Daniel ever met her or why she liked him except he was fierce and indomitable too. He was so hardheaded no one could make him do anything a day in his life. I guess it was a match. Matched pair, that's what the black people used to say."

"DNA," Mike repeated. Then he closed her mouth with kisses and fucked her for a while very gently. Then he lay her down upon the bed and began to kiss her body, kissing every crevice and bend and soft and hard place on her body and making her come again with his mouth, just for good measure, just to make up for the usurpation that was about to begin.

Olivia's plan was to walk in the direction of the river until six o'clock in the afternoon, then to turn and retrace her steps and arrive back at her camp by dark. Then I'll build a fire and cook whatever I can find. The less I eat the better. I've got plenty of fat. My body doesn't need to eat every day. Those monks Georgia told me about don't eat for days and days, then they can see very clearly and they know what to do.

But what do I want to know? She had stopped beside a stream that ran over limestone rocks and trickled down into a meadow. She stepped out onto a flat rock and stood poised above the water, knowing she would be dumb to get her feet wet but wanting to wade on in. Well, I want to know what to do next. I don't know about taking Bobby to North Carolina. What's he going to do there? No one will even know who he is. But if I stay here, I'll die. I don't want to live my whole life in Tahlequah. Okay, I came out here to think. So this is thinking. Thinking drives you nuts. That's why thinkers always sit around with their chin on their hand and their elbow on their knee. Thinking, what the hell, you think I ought to get my feet wet or not? I could take off my shoes and wade around barefoot and then put them back on. See what thinking does for you. It thinks of things you had forgotten.

Olivia stepped back on the side of the stream and leaned over and took off her shoes and socks and sat them in the crook of a tree and began to wade. As soon as the cold water touched her ankles she had another thought. We could go up to Montana and start all over. We could go out west and build a world no one knows of yet. We could pioneer up to the real mountains. He said they were so vast and tall I couldn't imagine them in a million years no matter how many pictures

or movies I saw about them. He's going with me to New Orleans. I
could go with him up there and see what that's about.

Olivia waded up and down the streambed, forgetting she was on a
quest for lightning. I think I've had about enough thinking for one day,
she decided. I'm going back. There isn't a cloud in the sky. It might not
storm for weeks. I can't stay out here for days waiting for lightning to
strike. And I sure as hell don't want to sleep in the woods all by myself.
I'll probably get about a hundred tick bites and chiggers if I don't
already have them. She sat down on a flat rock and put her shoes back
on and checked the watch and compass and began to march back to
her camp.

When she got back to the lean-to a snake was coiled above it in the
sycamore. A beautiful green and yellow and orange garden snake but it
seemed a sign and all the more reason to go home and sleep in bed.

She stopped by the pool in the tree trunk and took the water and
made the sign of the cross on her head and chest and started back the
way that she had come.

When she left the woods there was barely any light left in the sky.
Bobby was sitting on a blanket on the ground beside the springhouse,
pretending to read a book. He had seen her coming. He had known
she was walking his way by the way the birds flew up from the trees
along the edge of the woods.

"What are you doing here?" she asked.

"Studying math," he answered. "Looks like that's the only way a guy
can get laid anymore, is be a college student."

"You want to bet on that?" she answered. "I wouldn't bet on that if I
was you. If you're sexy you get laid, if you aren't you don't. You haven't
got anything to eat, have you? I'm about to starve to death."

He pulled a package of Oreos out of a bookpack and handed them
to her. "Come on," she said. "Let's get on home. I've had about enough
of this Indian bullshit."

"What's happening with your dad?" Olivia asked. It was later that
night, they were sitting on the corral fence with the stars spread out
above them. The old horse, Bess, nuzzled Olivia's leg. The cat, Desdemona, sat upon a fencepost listening for mice, a white owl was
above them in the tree. It was a still night and for a long time Olivia

and Bobby had been still. I have to ask it, she decided. I know it's what he's thinking about. "So how's your dad?"

"He's coaching a baseball team. He says it could be worse."

"You can't let it ruin your life."

"It isn't ruining my life. But I think about it. You would too."

"So you want to drive to Montana when school is out?"

"Do you want to? I'd sure like to see Tom and Sherrill."

"I can't see us going to North Carolina. The longer I stay away the more I hate the thought of going back."

"So you want to do that then, just drive west?"

"Yeah, I do. I hate that goddamn school. They're not teaching a single thing that's of use to anybody. If the lights went off, there aren't fifty people in that place who could figure out what to do. If the lights went off and the telephones quit and they ran out of gas, half of them would die in a couple of weeks. That's what I was thinking this afternoon. How lucky I am that I know how to live. I found some wild iris. Grandmother used to make soup out of them all the time. It's got every vitamin and mineral in the world in it. You could live on that if you killed a bird every now and then."

"Okay. We'll go then. As soon as school is over."

"I wish we could take Bess. I'd like to see her turned loose in a real wilderness." The mare rubbed its head against Olivia's leg. The constellations rode the night sky. The earth sailed on its appointed course.

"I'm going into town with you." Olivia reached over and touched Bobby's arm. "I'll tell them we're going to study for a test."

"It might be a test." He took her hand and held it against his chest. "To see if I can wait thirty minutes to get to fuck you."

AUGUST

CHAPTER 43

KING is dreaming he is dying. Crystal and her friends have turned into priests. They are standing in a circle wearing priestly garb. There is a tall white chair. They invite him to sit in it. It contains his death, a vial of poison he will drink. He has signed a paper or made an agreement to drink the poison, to sit upon the chair. Suddenly the idea of death dawns on King. The absolute nothingness of no existence, the no thing, and he stands up and knows he can overpower all of them and he says, No. I have changed my mind. I won't sit in the chair or drink the stuff. Fuck you, Momma. I'm out of here. He turns to leave. They all follow him. They say, Oh, King, you promised. You said you'd do it. I can't believe you won't keep your promise. He keeps on walking. I don't care, he answers. You're crazy. I'm out of here.

Jessie is writing down her dream.

I dreamed Olivia came with her suitcase to my school. She was going to embarrass me to death in front of my friends. Dad said I had to love her but I wanted her to die. I wanted to step on her and squash her like a bug. I was afraid she'd steal all my stuff. Steal my credit cards and checkbook and billfold. I thought she'd move into my room and take up all the closets. I can't love her no matter how I try. I think I just married King to get away from her and Dad. I hate to be in the room with the two of them together. They do such terrible things to each other with just the way they walk around the same room. They say such bad stuff to each other. He keeps asking her those questions and she keeps saying she's going to do it but she never does. Aunt Anna did this to us. She dumped Olivia on me because she didn't have any babies. Aunt

Helen said the central fact of Aunt Anna's life was all those miscarriages but no one who writes about her ever believes it.

Olivia is dreaming she is in a tent. She is wearing her grandmother's wedding dress and Bobby is coming to get her pregnant. It's raining on the fall leaves and water starts seeping in and turning the dress a dirty brown color and she is getting madder and madder and she can't move. She is tied down. She's tied down to an operating table and they are going to take somethi g out of her.

She burst from her bed and ran into the kitchen and threw open the refrigerator door and got out the milk and cut three pieces of banana nut bread and stood by the counter shaking and eating her food.

Georgia is writing down her dream.

> At four I waked, thinking I had made a breakthrough in understanding. I dreamed Zach and I were at camp. Everywhere I went, there he was, being a wet blanket, spoiling my natural spontaneity. The revelation is this. I'm afraid I'll have to take on his problems. He is afraid he'll be deserted by his momma (current Mother Figure, i.e., me). These are bonding issues. When we started talking about living together, the trouble started.
>
> He is pathologically unable to control the twins because he has to have their approval. His dad didn't pay much attention to him so he is always suing for approval everywhere. When he was sent off to school at age thirteen he found surrogates and found science. This explains why he likes meetings — groups of activists and cozy little meetings and love-ins and hate-ins and blanket parties and hikes. If he could only be at school forever. Well, he's a professor so he fixed that up but I am not good at Academia. Thought I would be. Am bored with it now. Want to see some ballet.

Zach is dreaming he is lying down beneath a tractor. No, you can't build the bomb here, he is saying. The tractor runs over him. The crowd cheers. He sinks down into the mud and is unharmed. When he rises from the mud he sees the twins by a roped-in area. They are selling his clothes to the crowd for souvenirs. I'm okay, he yells. They do not even turn their heads. Bonded in the womb, it says on the sign above their heads. Fuck you.

Bobby Tree is dreaming of his mother. He is four years old, standing by a door, waiting for her to come and pick him up. He is waiting all afternoon. The other children go out the door. Their mothers come for them and take them away. No one comes for him. After a while he is all alone beside the door and the rain begins to fall. He doesn't cry. He doesn't get mad. He doesn't want to make anybody mad at him.

I am only dreaming, a voice says to him, and he begins to fight his way to consciousness. If I wake up, it won't be true, he tells himself. Wake up, Bobby. Wake up, and it will go away. Wake up, no matter how hard it is, fight your way awake. He gasps for breath. He claws the pillow. He spread-eagles out across the bed and tries to climb the hall that leads to the light of day.

Doctor Coder is dreaming about Olivia. Memory is a vibrational dance, he tells her. Your mother is haunting you. Get out of Tahlequah. That's bullshit, Olivia answers. She is squirming around on her chair. My mother's dead and nobody's ever going to get me pregnant. No one's trying to get you pregnant. Doctor Coder moves in Olivia's direction. I want to make you well.

You want me to join the bourgeoisie, Olivia says. Good luck with that.

King's doctor is dreaming of a clear blue lake, a mountain lake. She is in the bow of a canoe. King is paddling it. They are going to pick up Jessie. The lake is very long and smooth, not a ripple on it. They will have to paddle for a very, very long time. You are strong enough to do it, she is telling him. You are a big strong boy. You won't fail in this. I'm here to guide you.

Can't I have any water? King says. I'm going to have to have a drink.

You can drink this water. She leans forward. She leans toward him with this wonderful information. *This isn't salt.*

I thought it would be salt, he says. *I thought it was salt.*

Little Sun is dreaming they are getting ready to go to war against the Sioux. The young braves think they are getting dressed for the pow-wow in Tulsa. They are thinking about the money they will get for the performance and what a good time they will have afterward getting drunk in bars. The elders know it is going to be a war. I think we should tell them the truth, Little Sun says. The council look at him with quiet faces. "We should tell them what's going on." They shake their heads no. "We should tell them," Little Sun insists.

CHAPTER 44

BOBBY was waking up every morning thinking about his father. Whether Olivia was there or not, whether he woke at dawn or slept late, as soon as he came to consciousness he was thinking about his dad. "If only they'd let me call him," he told Olivia. They were sitting on the porch swing at his house. School was over for the day and the sky was full of beautiful white clouds. The kind that make grand sunsets in the Cherokee Nation. "If I could hear his voice I wouldn't worry so much."

"You can't call him?"

"They transferred him to a different jail. The only time I can get him is seven to nine on Wednesday nights. Or he calls me."

"That's tonight." Olivia had been planning on getting Bobby to take her out to Baron Fork to watch the sunset.

"Yeah. Maybe I can get him tonight. The lines stay busy so I have to sort of wait around. You want to cook dinner here and stay with me?"

"No. I've got some stuff to do at home and I want to ride. I haven't ridden in a week. I was thinking Kayo'd lend me a horse."

"Sure he will. He's crazy about you. You got him around your little finger."

"Well, I'm going home then. You can listen for the phone." Olivia got up from the swing and started down the steps toward the car. She stopped and turned back to Bobby. "You think about him all the time, don't you?"

"I think he'll go to the pen. He isn't as strong as he used to be. I don't know. Well, what the hell, he's tough, isn't he?"

"It's too weird. A bunch of goddamn Mexicans and South Americans sending dope up here to kill everybody. It drives me crazy. I wish there was somewhere clean to be, with just land and horses and not any people around to fuck it up."

"Starcarbon is like that. Tom and Sherrill don't fuck anything up. Anything they touch gets better." He stood up straighter, thinking of the mountains. Then he took her arm and led her to the car. "Come back if you want to," he said. "I'll be here all night."

"I might." She got into the car, wondering why she was suddenly so old and mean. "Maybe I will. Call me when you get done talking to your dad." She drove off then and left him there and he was glad when she was gone. When Olivia got into a bad mood, the best thing to do was just leave her alone. She might be mad because I want to talk to Dad, he thought, then rejected the thought. No one could be angry with you for wanting to talk to your dad. Even Olivia on her worst day wouldn't come up with that.

It was five o'clock. Bobby went into the dining room and studied for a while, getting caught up in the math, moving the numbers around until they made perfect sense. Everything fit and everything returned to everything else and each thing proved the part before and was the groundwork for what would follow. When Bobby looked up from the papers it was ten to seven and he was starving. He took a casserole of macaroni and cheese that Mary Lily had sent over out of the refrigerator and put some on a plate with relish and brown bread and a sliced tomato. He put a placemat on the table and a napkin and a fork and sat down facing the window to the backyard. He could see the hollyhocks on the back fence and the morning glory vines that almost covered the garage. I need to drive up and see him, Bobby was thinking. If I left on a Friday afternoon and drove all night I could be there for

Sunday. I could miss a Monday. Hell, I could tell the teachers where I was going.

He cut off a piece of macaroni and ate it, thinking of Mary Lily and how she spoiled him every chance she got. I hope she keeps that guy she's going with, he decided. Hell, she deserves some happiness. Well, anybody does.

The phone was ringing. Bobby dropped the fork and ran for it.

"How's it going, son?" his dad said. "You doing okay down there? You got everything you need?"

"I'm okay, except for worrying about you. What's going on? You got a lawyer yet?"

"Yeah. They got me this big Iroquois named Roytame. He played football for Ohio State. He's okay. He says he can keep me out of the pen. I think they might let me out in a week or two. I might have to stay around here for a while, but they'll let me board around here and get a job. There's a stable near here where Roytame keeps a horse and he talked to them about me. Said they'd heard about me. How about that? So things are going good. How's the house holding up? You paid the rent for August?"

"Yeah. I might go to Montana when school's out. I hope you get back before I leave. I'd drive up there if it wasn't so far. You want me to come up there?"

"Hell, no. You stay there in school. I'm doing fine. At least it got rid of Sharrene. I'm glad she's gone. You can take over in the love department, Bobby. I'm getting too old for that game."

"That'll be the day." Bobby started laughing. "Goddamn, Daddy, goddamn, that's funny. I never saw you without a woman."

"You have a turn. All the time I've been in here, I've been thinking. This is okay. No one to bitch at you, no one to please, no one always asking you to do something. I'm getting good at it. Hell, I could have been a sailor. Gone to sea."

"I've been worried sick about you and you've been up there turning against women. You ought to see these math problems I've been solving. It's so clean. I lose track of time when I'm doing it."

"You were good at that when you were a little boy. Your teachers all said it was your cup of tea. Well, listen, son, I got to get off the phone.

There's four men behind me. You take care of yourself, you hear me. I'll call next Wednesday."

"I hope he gets you out."

"I think he will. I'll let you know. Take care of yourself. Keep the oil changed in that truck. Don't let it get low."

"I will. I'll check it tomorrow." Bobby hung up and went back to the table and ate all the food he had prepared and then opened a can of sardines and ate them. It was the first time he had been really hungry in a week. He called Olivia but Mary Lily said she was still at Baron Fork.

He took the math book back to his bedroom and lay down upon his bed and fell asleep reading theorems and slept until seven the next morning. In his dreams the figures turned into geometric designs. The big Iroquois named Roytame moved in and out of the triangles and rectangles and parallelograms. Without even lifting their legs, his dad and Roytame walked side by side through a field of designs, smiling and talking, coming in his direction.

Olivia is in Doctor Coder's office telling him about getting mad at Bobby for letting her go home so he could wait for his dad to call. "It made me so mad," she is saying. "I just got furious with him. I was up all night thinking terrible things about him. Then when I saw him the next morning I was mean to him. I hate it when I'm mean to him. I hate myself when I'm that way. I used to be that way to Dad. To Aunt Mary Lily too. I can't help it. It just comes over me."

"You feel abandoned," Doctor Coder said. It was a vein he had been mining for several weeks.

"Quit saying that." Olivia got up and started walking around the office. "Stop saying that. I had Mary Lily and Grandmomma and Granddaddy and lots of other people. I wasn't abandoned. Aunt Mary Lily took me the minute Momma died and she never put me down. I wasn't an orphan. I had plenty of folks to take care of me." Olivia moved across the room and sat down on a loveseat by a window. "Stop telling me about interrupted bonding. I'm sick of hearing it. It isn't true. That's not what's wrong with me. There's nothing wrong with me. Stop saying that there is."

"The body knows the difference between the mother and every other chemical system on the earth, Olivia. That doesn't mean there's something wrong with you. It just means you have problems around bonding issues. And that means that when you take off your clothes and get close to another human being you have problems letting go. If someone is allowed to get that close to you and then they let you go, you get enraged at them. All you have to do is understand it and then it can't rise up and blindside you. Don't get mad at me. I'm on your side."

"I was not an orphan. Dad didn't know where I was or he would have come to get me. Aunt Mary Lily picked me up the minute I was born and never let me go. She slept with me every night. She never even let me cry." Olivia was crying now, deep dark tears from the darkest reaches of the old hypothalamus, the oldest, darkest, most terrible part of the brain. She sat on Dr. Coder's floor and wept for many long minutes.

It was a day for the Hand sisters to make psychiatrists uneasy. In New Orleans Jessie's doctor was taking a chance. "I'm going to tell you what King's dream of dying means," she was saying. "Are you ready for this?"

"Yes. Go ahead."

"In all the old myth systems of the world the dream of dying doesn't mean death. It means the death of old ways or old beliefs. A person dies to the old ways and takes on new ways. Stops being a child and becomes a man. The myths and practices of all the major cultures use this imagery." She stopped and watched her. Jessie was very good at picking up on things and using them. She was so serious, so intent, such an endearing young woman. Doctor Kaplan had not been wrong in thinking Jessie would be worth teaching. She sighed. She perceived herself as teaching. Teaching what she had been taught. There was nothing else. Teach, teach, teach, keep your fingers crossed.

"So he's afraid to grow up?"

"No. He's just dragging his feet. Maybe this is his last defense. Give him time. Maybe this is how he's getting ready."

"He got stoned on Saturday. But you know what he did? He called someone in AA and then he went and talked to his psychiatrist and I went with him. He said it was because Olivia called and told him to. She's coming Friday. She's bringing her boyfriend with her."

"You went with him?"

"He wanted me to. Then we went home and finally the dope wore off and we went to bed. He kept making love to me but I couldn't stop thinking about him being stoned. But it's okay. We'll work it out. It's going to be all right." Jessie looked down at her hands. Thought of the stories she'd heard about her mother flying around Europe delivering cocaine to movie stars.

"Tell me your thoughts," the analyst said.

"It's all too terrible . . . there's nothing anyone can do. I never had a family, not a real one, but I keep trying to make one but it gets sabotaged. I don't think anybody's on my side. Crystal's always on King's side, no matter what happens. Manny's not. Manny's such an angel. I can't figure out why he wants to spend all his time with crazy Christians. His family are so good. They never get into trouble. They all do what they're supposed to do. Well, I guess he loves Crystal the way that I love King. Because they seem so fragile, like some old stained-glass windows so beautiful you think they will break at any moment. Like the windows in Sainte-Chappelle we saw when Dad took me to France."

"You think he'll break?"

"No. It's just everything seems so fragile. Everyone's in trouble. Traceleen's nephew, Richard, is terrorizing their whole family. I think they ought to kill drug dealers. Even if it includes my mother." Jessie was crying now and Doctor Kaplan felt tears in her own eyes. It was true. Every word of it was true. The dinosaurs reigned for millions of years. We have only been here fifty thousand.

"I'm glad your sister's coming," she said. "Try to love her. Give her a chance to love you."

"Thanks for helping me. Thank you for being here."

"It's what I do." She got up from behind her desk. Another hour had passed. Stay the course, she told herself. Pray for grace.

*   *   *

When Jessie got home that afternoon King was waiting on the porch, playing with K.T. "Come on," he said. "Let's go and get some gravel. I thought you wanted to make a garden underneath that juniper tree."

"Okay," she said, embarrassed to be so easily made happy.

"Come on, then. Hurry up. I owe you some gravel." He smiled up at her, holding their son around his waist. She was two days late and they both knew it. "I'm two days late," she had said at breakfast that morning.

"I know," King had answered. "I wondered about that."

Across town, in a little house on Athens Street, Traceleen Brown was on her knees beside her bed. "Bless Fairlie and Charles and Lula and Augustus and Blue and Terrance. Bless Miss Crystal and Crystal Anne and Manny and K.T. and Jessie and King. Bless Miss Noel and make her leg get well. If Richard comes over here, make me say what I think and not be afraid of him. Spread the love of your heart over the Desire Street project and don't let anyone die today. Don't let my back go out again and if it's all right, let the lawyers work out the contract for the house. Bless Andria and make her be more humble and understanding of others' failings and give Mandana the power to stop drinking, Lord. If King can stop taking dope there must be hope for Mandana. I don't know about my nephew Richard. For Thy name's sake, we pray. Amen."

Traceleen got up from her knees and gathered up her purse and went out onto Athens Street and started walking toward the streetcar stop. The little pregnant girl on the porch next door sat up on the swing and saluted. A black dog uncurled and stood up and sniffed the air. Her nephew Richard was walking her way, dressed up and looking sober. He was the youngest son of her second sister, Katie Blue, and was currently the blight and stigma of the family's life. He was the leader of the New Orleans branch of the Bloods. He had been one of its founders. That was after he was a star basketball player in junior high. He hadn't started getting in trouble until the ninth grade. The same year Katie Blue got cancer and turned her face to the wall and told her children to fend for themselves.

"Hey, Auntee Traceleen," he called out. "Long time, no see."

"I'm on my way to work, Richard. I got to catch the streetcar."

"You still working for the Weisses, Auntee?"

"I got my job and I'm happy with it." She stood on the sidewalk inspecting him. He wasn't wearing any of his gang symbols. He had on a shirt and tie. Either he had quit or he had come to ask a favor. He was in the habit of asking favors of Traceleen. He had lived with her after his mother got sick. He had lived with her until he joined the Bloods. Sometimes Traceleen blamed herself for Richard's getting into trouble. But that was always in the afternoons. In the morning she was too smart to blame herself for troubles people made for themselves.

"I just come by to tell you I was leaving town pretty soon."

"Where you going?"

"Oh, down to the Virgin Islands for a while, then to South America."

"What do you want, Richard? What are you up to?"

"I need a lawyer. I was wondering if you might ask Mr. Weiss if he'd talk to me this afternoon. You going over there now? Maybe I'll just come along."

"No. Don't do that. I'll ask him for you. What you need him for?"

"I just need some things looked into by a lawyer. Some deeds to property and some things. I might have to put a piece of real estate in your name. You wouldn't mind that, would you? Auntee Mandana said you were trying to get a new house. You could use it to get your loan."

"I don't want anything bought with dope money. I don't drink the blood of children. Come on, Richard. Don't stand in my way. I got to catch the trolley."

"Where can I find you later? So I can find out about Mr. Weiss." He stood there waiting. She opened her purse and took out a little pink notebook Crystal Anne had given her for a love present and wrote down a telephone number and an address. "I'll be here until noon. Then I'm going over to King's house to take care of the baby. King had a baby boy. He got married. Did I tell you that?"

"Yeah. You told me. Well, ladeedah. I guess that makes you and your white buddies happy, doesn't it? Now you got you a white baby to nurse."

"I nursed plenty of both colors. You're the only one that's broken my heart. Get out of my way, Richard. I'm going to the streetcar stop." She closed her purse and walked down the sidewalk. Richard was walking behind her. Don't let harm come to a human being on the earth today, Traceleen prayed. If it's got to be anyone, let it be me.

She turned and faced him. "Go over to my house and see your Uncle Brown and help him get off to work," she said. "Go be nice to people, son."

"I'll talk to you later, Auntee Traceleen. I'll call you in an hour or so." She walked on to the streetcar stop and Richard turned and went back down the street. So King Mallison got him a baby boy, he thought. He was remembering when Traceleen took him to the Weisses to visit one morning when he was fifteen years old and King was thirteen. King had taken him to his room and tried to sell him a joint. "I got this stuff yesterday in the park," King had said. "I'd give it to you if I could, but I owe this guy about thirty dollars. Sit down, have some M&M's." King shut the door to his room and sat down beside Richard on the bed. "This room's a mess but I'm going to get all this junk out of here as soon as I get a water bed. They made this place for me out of the basement. It's a dungeon." Richard looked around him. The room was full of hamster and gerbil cages and aquariums. There were three cages of hamsters and one of gerbils and an aquarium with two nasty-looking fish swimming around, chasing each other through a plastic castle. There was a yellow rug on the floor and the walls were painted blue. There were jars by the bed with M&M's and lollipops. King held out the M&M jar. He turned on a tape player and Bob Dylan started singing "Mr. Bojangles." Richard took the M&M's and started eating them, one by one.

"I don't smoke that shit," he said. "You better be careful with that shit, King. That shit can get you in a whole lot of trouble."

"I'm not worried." King lay back on the bed. He turned over on his stomach and brought a tin box out from underneath the bed. He sat up and opened it and began to get out paraphernalia.

"Richard." It was Traceleen calling from the stairs. "Come on back up here, honey. We got to go now."

"Let me know if you want to buy any." King stood in the doorway holding out the M&M's. "I'm right here if you change your mind. You know my phone number."

I might just have to go see old King, Richard decided. See how he's getting along now he's got himself a wife and baby. He's always been a friend to me. He always comes over and talks to me if I run into him at Tip's or down in the Quarter. I hadn't seen him around in a while though. He must be laying low since he got married.

He shook his head and started up the steps of the house Crystal and Manny had bought for Traceleen to get her out of the project. His uncle was in the kitchen making coffee and getting ready for the day. His uncle wasn't as kind to him as his aunt had been. "Well, the dope king done come by to see us," his uncle said. "The devil has come by to pay a visit. Howdy, devil. Have a seat. Tell me what you got to say."

"Nothing to you. That's for sure."

"What you come by for, Richard?"

"Auntee Traceleen said to come by and see how you were doing. So now I'll leave." Richard stared into his uncle's face, so unforgiving and so strong. So wide and deep and cold, like the Mississippi River, Richard decided. You could drown in there. "I hear the white folks are buying you another house. That so?"

"That's your auntee's doing. It's none of me." His uncle backed down. Whatever was coming next he didn't want to hear. He had worked all his life at a hard job, unloading cargoes on the docks, then bossing the crew that did. Still, the house was Traceleen's, a gift from her white people. He didn't want to hear about it and Richard was about to say it. "You gonna end up in Angola, Richard. Or dead. You better stop all that shit you're doing and let me help you get a job."

"I got a job." Richard looked around the room, at his uncle's union badge on the dresser, at his aunt's paintings her white friend in California had made for her, at the old bedspread where he had knelt to say his prayers when he lived with them. He softened up. He wasn't going to be mean to his uncle. It wasn't worth the trouble. "I got to get out of here," he added. "I got some work to do." He looked his uncle in the eye and waited, but his uncle did not move to touch him, did not deign to smile, did not care about or love him. "Goodbye, then," Richard said. "Tell Mandana's girls hello if you see them." He walked out of the room and down the front steps and across the yard. Leave the old people to themselves, he decided. Who needs them anyway?

CHAPTER 45

MISS those girls like my left arm," Daniel was saying. "Left and right arm." He was watching Spook, who was packing his clothes to move to the farm. An open suitcase was on the bed and Spook was slowly and deliberately folding shirts and putting them carefully into the suitcase. "You don't need to take them off the hangers. Just carry them out there on the hangers, Spook. Why are you folding them up?"

"You got to let them go," Spook said. "I'm getting tired of telling you that, Daniel. You act like they was some little wives you had that went off and left you for other men. Quit thinking about them. You need to get you a new wife and start you a life of your own. Mooning around here drinking whiskey every night. Letting everything go to pot."

"It's gone to pot. I'd sell that business this afternoon if I could come out even. But I can't. The economy's bust and I'm bust. You don't know a thing about children, because you never had any. You never invested your heart in a child. What do you know?"

"That's another thing. Getting out all them pictures of them when they was little and setting them up everywhere. Quit living in the past, Daniel. You're only forty-seven years old and you act like you're a hundred. Your granddaddy was the same way, the one you favor. You're turning into past people." Spook lay a white shirt down on top of a blue-and-white-striped one and looked Daniel in the eye. "Look at me, boss. If you got to come out here and stand around when I'm busy, at least act like you're listening when I talk."

"I'm listening. I was thinking maybe I'd move out to the farm too. Sell this goddamn house and clear on out if they won't even come and visit."

"Olivia came for the Fourth of July. Correct me if I'm mistaken. Did she or did she not come here for four days and scarcely left this house?"

"Four days out of a whole summer."

"You going back to work this afternoon, or not?"

"Yeah. I'm going back right now. If Margaret comes by to get the vacuum cleaner, let her in." Daniel turned and walked out onto the patio and lit a cigarette and stood underneath the walnut tree thinking over the conversation. Hell, maybe he'd charter a plane and fly down to New Orleans and apologize. Except it would cost at least a thousand dollars and that was half a month's payment on one of the loans. So that was out. Spook came up behind him.

"You got a cigarette, boss?"

"Sure. Have one of these." Daniel extended a package of Camels and Spook took one and lit it and went over and sat down on the stone steps.

"I'm sorry I'm leaving you. And I'm sorry for what I said in there. I know you're hurting."

"I am hurting. I'm hurting real bad." He went over and sat down beside the black man and they smoked in peace for a while. Then Daniel got up and put his hand on Spook's shoulder. "It's the lowest of the low for me," he said at last. "It's the worst summer I can remember."

After Daniel left, Spook went back into the guest house and began to take the shirts out of the suitcase. He couldn't leave him now. He was standing by his closet shaking his head and trying to get a train of thought going, when Margaret came walking out onto the patio from the kitchen calling to him.

"He's in a bad way," Spook said, coming out his door. "We got to do something about him if we love him. It's gone as far as I can let it go. Call Niall on the phone and tell him to get on over here and help us think."

"Good," Margaret said. "He's lost his spark, Spook. He won't even kiss me. I know I'm not Miss America, but at least he used to find some comfort in my arms."

An hour later Niall, Margaret, Spook, Daniel's nephew James, who was the Alcoholics Anonymous expert in the family, and Helen's ex-husband, Spencer Abadie, were in the kitchen planning a surprise. "It's called an intervention," James was saying. "We gang-bang him and break through his defenses. I think we ought to do it. We ought to do it tonight."

"He's getting so depressed," Margaret said. "I wouldn't put anything past him, the mood he's in."

"Okay," Niall put in. "I'm for it. I'll go along."

"We could bring Farley in from the farm," Spook said. "He'll tell him what it's like to never know from one day to the next what's going to get done."

"Okay," James said. "Tonight. Definitely tonight." He was excited. He had always wanted to be part of an intervention. He felt like his whole life had been moving toward this day. Now, on his slender young shoulders, the fate of his family would ride to victory or defeat.

"James?"

"Yes. Sir."

"Don't get carried away, you hear."

"We may need a straitjacket. Sometimes they try to run away. We have to have people stationed at the doors. We have to immobilize all vehicles. And we need to either tie him or get him in a jacket."

"We ain't putting him in no jacket." Spook stood up. "We get him in a room and we say our piece. I'm all for that. But we ain't going to tie him up or try to get a straitjacket on him. Not that any of us could do it anyway, if we really made him mad."

"Well, that's the recommended way. He'll leave when it gets painful if we don't restrain him."

"Restrain him, my ass. You ever try to restrain Daniel? He's six feet four inches tall. You couldn't restrain him if there were fourteen of you."

James put his arm on the mantelpiece. "You're supposed to have a hospital ready for them to go to. The police are supposed to be standing by. It's an intervention. There're supposed to be doctors and people standing by in the reception room. It isn't supposed to just be a lot of people going to talk to someone."

"You mean, you want us to arrest Daniel? That's what you're saying now? Think thou because thou art virtuous, there shall be no more cakes and ale," he added, just to see if James would catch on.

"We're not serving anything alcoholic tonight," James said. He sat down beside Niall and thought about how much he had always hated Spook. It was black people like Spook who made racial hatred. Spook was as bad as Jesse Jackson. Why did all the worst black people always have to come from the Carolinas? James had wondered that before. The most uppity, snottiest, ungrateful black people in the United States always came from right here. I think we got the meanest tribes, James decided, and sat back beside his uncle.

"At seven o'clock then," Margaret said. "Here, in this house, at seven."

"At seven," Niall agreed. "Try to get here early."

"What will we say we're doing? What do we say when he says, 'What are you all doing here?' "

"Coming to say we're worried about you and want to let you know it." Niall had taken over now. "We say, 'Daniel, we are moving in for a night or two. We are here because we love you.' "

"Good," everyone agreed. "Good. That's a good idea. A good, good plan."

At seven that night they were all gathered in the living room waiting for Daniel to appear. Spook stood by the door to the kitchen. He had made Jade get out things for soft drinks and had a pot of coffee going. "Don't guess we can offer anyone a drink?" he had told Niall, so the two of them sneaked a glass of brandy in the pantry, then locked the liquor cabinet door.

Margaret was seated on the sofa. She had her head bowed and her hands in her lap. She really loved Daniel Hand, and she figured after this she would never have another love of any kind, might even have to go to India to help Mother Teresa with her work.

Spencer Abadie sat on a blue chair leafing through a back issue of *Forbes* magazine. James marched back and forth in front of the picture windows memorizing his speech. The truth will make you free, he chanted to himself. One day at a time. We will help you. There are places to go. We are offering you your life. Sit down with us and start to talk.

"What in the hell is this?" Daniel said, coming into his living room. "Something happened? Something happened to my girls?"

"Nothing's wrong," Niall said. "We came to talk to you, Daniel. Sit down a minute. Let me have a minute. We came here because we're worried about you."

"Goddamn, Niall, give me a minute. Let me get a drink." Daniel started loosening his tie. He had had a very, very bad day, with creditors calling every hour and people that owed him money refusing to pay.

"No drinks, Uncle Daniel," James said. "We came to talk to you about drinking. We came to beg you to let us help you save your life."

"Oh, my God. Margaret, are you in this, too? You mixed up in this?"

"I'm mixed up in you. I love you. I won't stand by and watch you kill yourself."

"Sit down, Daniel." Niall went to him and took his arm. "Come sit by me. Let us have our say. I beg you, let us say what we came to say."

"Spook, get me a drink of Scotch." Daniel sat down on the sofa beside Margaret. She was twisting a scarf in her hands. She raised her eyes and looked at him and began to cry. Spook moved in from the door. Spencer moved his chair closer to the sofa. They encircled him. James began to make his plea. "There is a place in Atlanta you can go to," he began. "It's better than the one I went to. We are offering you our help, Uncle Daniel. We love you. We want to fight for you. Don't hate us. Don't get up. Don't fight back. For just a little while say you will listen."

"Start talking." Daniel sat back. Then, strangely, because she was so sad, he reached over and took Margaret's hand and held it. "Say what you came to say."

Many hours later Margaret and Daniel were upstairs in the master bedroom. They had made love for the first time in all the months they had fucked each other. Now they lay upon their backs and talked in whispers. "I'm not much of a catch," Daniel was saying. "But I could settle down if I ever got this business off my back. That's what you want, for me to settle down?"

"I want you to go to this place in Atlanta. If you still want me then, I want to live with you. You won't want me then. If you get well, you won't want me for a thing."

"I didn't say I'd go, Margaret. I said I'd think about it. Come on over here. Put your head on my shoulder. Let's go to sleep."

"I can't. It was so nice. If I got any closer I'd start crying."

"Well, don't do that. I never saw so many tears in my life. Goddamn. Niall crying. I never thought I'd live to see that. I tried to quit a few times," he added. "I had so much time on my hands. All I did was wait for the night to pass. Goddamn nights seemed to last forever."

"I could teach you how to read." She moved over closer and laid her head down in the hollow of his shoulder. "I bet you've forgotten how to read."

"Forgotten, hell. I never did learn how."

"If you knew what it would mean." Margaret kissed the muscle of his shoulder, kissed the shoulder bone. "It would make so many people happy. You could think of it as a mission. Like Pilgrim's Progress or the Lewis and Clark expedition. You like to do hard things."

"You think I ought to walk to Atlanta to this hospital?" Daniel turned over on his side and let his hands slide down to the soft fat sides of Margaret's rib cage. He was a master of tickling chubby girls into submission. He went to work on Margaret now. "Stop," she screamed. "Stop it, Daniel. Oh, God, please don't tickle me. I can't stand it. I'll do anything you want."

"Then go to sleep," he said at last, and patted her on the arm. "James the third's turning into a real prig," he added, taking a small piece of revenge. "He looks so much like Putty, it's scary. You'd never even know he was kin to James."

CHAPTER 46

THE day before they were supposed to leave for New Orleans, Bobby got a call from his uncle Kayo begging him to come out and help work a horse. "Bring the little girl if she can come. We're in trouble. We need all the help we can get."

"What's wrong?"

"That mare we sent to Enida won't work a cow. We paid Enida eight thousand dollars to train her and he said she was ready for the Futurity so we paid that entrance fee, that's two thousand more, and now she won't work a cow. Robert worked her yesterday and he says she's as green as a yearling. The boss has lost money on this operation four years in a row. One more year and we'll all be out of a job."

"I sure would like to help but I got to go to school all morning and I'm working on the Locust Grove exit in the afternoons. You know more about cutting than I do. Why do you need me? Well, hell, call Jimbo Reed and tell him to let me off this afternoon and I'll come. Hell, you always do things for me. We both owe you plenty."

"What's that?" Olivia asked, sitting up on the other side of the bed. "What's going on?"

"That mare we told you about. Boon Alto's colt. They had her up to Enida Grant's being trained and now she won't work a cow."

"She's supposed to be the best two-year-old in the country," Kayo was saying. "The boss is going to have a fit over this. He's got a bunch of buyers from Australia coming to the Futurity to see this mare. Come on out this afternoon, Bobby. There's two hundred dollars in it for you, just for trying. Tell the little girl there's a hundred for her for a consulting fee. She's got a touch as good as you."

"You want to make three hundred dollars this afternoon? It would pay for our trip." Bobby turned to her. "They're in trouble."

"Sure I do." Olivia got up and began to pull on her jeans and a T-shirt. She drew in her breath, felt her rib cage rise up out of the fat that had been settling on her body. Working a world-class horse and getting paid for it. That beat the hell out of another afternoon with a book of grammar. "Sure I will. What time does he want us there?"

"So what do you think is wrong with her?" Bobby had gone back to his conversation with his uncle. "What do you think happened?"

"Hell, I don't know. I think Enida burned her out. His colts been losing everywhere this year. Maybe he's lost his touch. Anyway, get on out here as soon as you can. I'll call Jimbo and make it all right."

"I'm making coffee," Olivia yelled from the kitchen. She pulled one of Bobby's plaid shirts over her T-shirt and tucked it in. She stuck bread in the toaster and threw some placemats on the table. Bobby's belt with his buckle from the year he won Best In State was hanging over a chair and she picked it up and put it around her waist. "Can I wear your belt?" she called. "God, I can't wait to see this mare. She's Alto's colt? That's a direct line to Boon San Sally. What's she called?"

"Allie's Dream. If Enida ruined this horse, there'll be hell to pay."

At twelve-thirty they were barreling down the highway in Daniel's Mercedes headed for Baron Fork. "I wrote this thing in Chapel Hill about how they put bits in horses' mouths," Olivia was saying. "When I was a kid my granddad made me ride every horse with only a bridle before I could use a bit on it. I bet somebody's hurt her mouth. You hurt their mouth real good one time and you've ruined a horse. The real horses don't forget. The sad ones let you keep on hurting them, but the horses that leave no tracks, the angel horses, they don't forget. I'll ride her without a bit, if Kayo'll let me."

"I'm the one that's supposed to be riding her. But, hell, baby, everyone knows you're better than I am. You've got the thing my dad's got. Like you can see into a horse's head. I used to think Dad could talk to them. The first time Dad saw you ride, in that little rodeo they had for the Special Olympics, he said I could give up the world for you and he wouldn't blame me."

He reached over and took her hand, thinking about Olivia on a horse, how she pulled her shoulders back and let her left arm hang, so elegant you'd think she was the queen of England. Nothing moving that didn't need to move. So that was how Little Sun had taught her, not letting her use a bit. The Wagoners were funny folks. They kept their secrets, most of them. Well, Olivia had that North Carolina blood and it had turned her into a talker.

"How's your dad doing?" she asked. "What'd he say when you talked to him?"

"He's got a new lawyer, a guy named Roytame who's an Iroquois. He might get out on bail pretty soon. It's looking better."

"He's a first offender. Georgia said the jails are so full they never put anyone in prison the first time they get caught."

"You told her about this?"

"She tells me everything she does. You wouldn't believe the things she tells me about her boyfriend. She was trying to break up with him last week because she hates his kids and you know what she said? She said she'd been masturbating twice a day so she wouldn't get in his power. We were having breakfast at The Shak and everybody at the next table heard her say it. You know how loud she talks. I thought they were all going to spit their coffee all over the table. Well, she's so blind and she never wears her glasses so she couldn't see them and she was just going on, in the voice she uses to lecture with, talking about masturbating to keep from being in love just like she was describing the mating habits of some tribe. She talks about herself like she wasn't even there. Like she is some kind of experiment she's running." Olivia started laughing. Bobby joined her and pretty soon they were laughing so hard they couldn't stop. They were still laughing when they went through the gate and entered the property of Baron Fork. The laughter cleared the air, made up for the jail cell in Iowa.

"My brother-in-law ought to be in jail," Olivia added. "He used to be the worst dope addict you ever saw. He was in trouble when he was fifteen years old for selling LSD. You aren't the only one with dope dealers in the family. It's big business. That's what Georgia says. The growth industry of the eighties. Either they ought to legalize it or they ought to sell stock. The way it's costing everyone so much. Well, it's not the first time people got a really bad idea and used it. They used to cut off people's hands for stealing bread when they were hungry. They did that in France not long ago. So don't tell me about high civilization. That's what Georgia always says. And the Cherokee weren't perfect either. We've got a lot to apologize for. And the Irish are still killing each other, so I don't guess I have a drop of peaceful blood."

"We weren't as bad as a lot of tribes. The Sioux. Goddamn, I can't think about the stuff they did. I wish people would stop making movies about the tribes."

"Sometimes I wish I was a horse."

"Then you'd have a bit in your mouth."

"People but the bits in. Horses don't hurt each other, unless they fight over a mare and that's only natural."

"If you say so, baby. There's Kayo and Robert. Well, let's go see about this mare."

*   *   *

Ten minutes later they were standing by the mare's stall. Kayo and two of the grooms and Bobby and Olivia, talking about the horse while the horse stood with her head over the stall gate and listened. "I think she's burned out," the groom named Robert said. He noticed Olivia watching him and took out his cigarette lighter and used it to burn off a string that was hanging from his worn denim jacket. He put the lighter away and ran his fingers through his hair. "Enida ruined her."

"Well, when the boss finds out about that entry fee, it's going to be my tail." Kayo put an arm around Bobby's shoulders. "Put a saddle on her, son. See what you think."

"Let Olivia ride her first. She says she can ride her without a bit. Let her try it, Kayo. She's got an intuition about her. You know that. You want to go first, baby?"

"Without a bit." Robert looked down at the ground. His jeans were so tight and his boots so old and his stomach so flat he looked like he had invented the idea of cowboy. "Well, if you get thrown, don't blame me. I worked her yesterday. She won't get on a cow. She don't want nothing to do with a cow."

"You got a Hackamore?" Olivia asked.

"Yeah, there's one by the sawhorse." Olivia picked it up, opened the gate to the stall and went inside and started talking to the mare. She removed the halter and slipped the Hackamore bridle over the mare's head and led her out into the passageway between the stalls. "Get out of the way," she said. "Dreamy wants some exercise before she goes to work." She heaved herself up on the horse's bare back and rode her out into the bright summer air. When they had cleared the barn she lay down against the mare and began to ride toward the yard of the Baron Fork manor house. The mare kicked up her heels and began to trot. "What happened to you up in Missouri?" Olivia was crooning. "What'd they do to you up there, Champion? That's what you are. Your momma was the greatest cutting horse in five states and your daddy wasn't any slouch. So maybe you don't want to show. Maybe you want to stay out in a pasture and be a brood mare. Is that what you want? You want to get laid and have colts and never go to Dallas–Fort Worth in the trailer? That's what you want?" Olivia rode the horse back to where the men were waiting. "Look at her ribs," she said. "This mare's been starved. Either she got mad and wouldn't eat or they didn't feed her.

I'd sue them if they sent me back a horse with ribs like this. Go find a couple of steers and turn them into the corral. I'll try her now. We'll see what she'll do."

"She won't do diddly without a bit." Robert was smoking now, starting to get his feelings hurt. "Except she might just dump you on top of a cow. Put a saddle and bridle on the horse, Kayo. Let's stop all this fooling around."

"She's okay," Bobby said. "Go on, Kayo, get her some cows."

Olivia rode the horse back into the barn and climbed down and saddled her and led her into the corral where Robert was waiting with the steers. Then, very gently, crooning a little song, Olivia began to work the steers. Cutting horses are bred and trained to zero in on a cow and bring it out of a herd. They have to be very sure. Horse and rider have to think and move as one. The mare Olivia was riding had not been treated badly. But she had been taken away from home and treated like a peasant when she considered herself a queen. She had been put in a corral with other horses and made to wait her turn in the ring. She had been ignored. Now, with Olivia light and sure on her back, she was ready to show her stuff. Subtly, Olivia signaled what to do and like a dancer the powerful small horse could do it.

The mare moved toward the first steer with small bright steps, then backed, then moved in again, cutting off the exits, turning the steer by small degrees, leading it to the chute, then running it away. She turned to the second steer and got rid of it in less than a minute, then backed across the open space with small pretty steps and began to trot around the ring. The men applauded and Olivia came to a halt beside Bobby and slid down off the side. "Here's your horse," she said. "Stay out of her way. If you want someone to ride in the Futurity, call me up."

"What are you doing over at that college?" Kayo sighed. "What do those college professors have to teach you that you don't know?"

"I thought I was going to learn to write Navajo, but it's so boring I'm about to flunk the class. This college professor talked me into trying to learn it. He said it would help me get a job on computers." She started laughing then and climbed up on the fence and sat on the top rail. "I had one in Carolina who had a sex-change operation. He had himself turned into a woman. We didn't know what to call him." She was laughing so hard now she could hardly stay on the rail of the corral. Her laughter rose to the top of the barn, a long golden laugh she had forgotten she possessed. A laugh that belonged to horses and barns and cowboys and wide open spaces.

"Goddamn," Robert said. "I'll be goddamned."

CHAPTER 47

BY one the next afternoon they were cruising down the highway headed for New Orleans, a tankful of gas, and three hundred dollars in twenty-dollar bills locked up in the glove compartment for spending money.

Bobby was driving. Olivia was settled down in the passenger seat reading a book Georgia had lent her for the trip. *Everyday Zen*, by Yoko Beck. There were strips of paper stuck in three pages, things Georgia wanted Olivia to read. "If she's so smart why is her life so messed up?" Bobby had been saying. "I like her. Don't get me wrong. I think she's a really funny lady, even if she doesn't let anybody else talk. But all the things you tell me that she says. If she can't even get along with her boyfriend, why do you want her to give you advice?"

"She teaches me things I don't know. She's interested in the same sort of stuff I'm interested in. I don't know. I like to be with her, that's all. She makes me think. Every time I've been around her I have to keep on thinking about things she said. Listen to this. In this book she lent me." Olivia began to read.

" 'Suppose that we talk about our life as though it were a house, and we live in this house, and life goes along as it goes along. We have our stormy days, our nice days; sometimes the house needs a little paint. And all the drama that goes on within the house between those who live there just goes on. We may be sick or well. We may be happy or unhappy. It's like this for most of us. We just live our life, we live in a house or an apartment and things take place as they take place. . . . We have this house, but it's as though it were encased in another house. It's as though we took a strawberry and we dipped it in chocolate; so we have our strawberry and it's covered with coating. We have our perfectly nice house, and on top of that house we have another house, encasing this basic house in which we live.

" 'Yet our life (this house) as we live it is perfectly fine. We don't usually think so, but there's nothing wrong with our life.' "

"That's good stuff," Bobby said. "Yeah, I like that. I might send a copy of that to Sherrill and Tom. Sherrill's always saying things like that. Trying to get Tom to be satisfied. He's a restless man. When he gets to writing a book nobody but Sherrill could live with him."

"I hope we have a good time in New Orleans. I don't know why I'm so nervous about it. I want you to know how beautiful my sister is, but don't fall in love with her."

"How could I? I'm in love with you. Don't you know that yet?"

"Yeah, I guess I do."

"I'm the one ought to be nervous. I think all the time you're going to dump me, especially now that you got that oil."

"Why do you always wait until you're driving to talk about things that are on your mind?"

"I don't know. Do I do that?"

"Yes. And I'm not going to dump you. God, I hope Dad doesn't show up in New Orleans. I want you to meet him. But not down there. I hope it doesn't happen down there."

"I'm looking forward to meeting him. And I can't wait to see New Orleans. Eleven more hours and we'll be cruising into town."

It was ten o'clock that night when they left the expressway and drove down the long ramp leading to Saint Charles Avenue at Lee Circle. They came down onto the avenue and Olivia began to point out landmarks to Bobby. "We could go to Tipitina's right now and I bet Andria would be there. She holds court at a corner table, she's got a crush on one of the players, a Baby Neville she calls him. Well, there'll be plenty of time for that tomorrow night. God, I hope Dad isn't here."

"You think he might be?"

"He might be, but I don't think he will." She scooted over very close to him and put her hand on his knee. "At least I can sleep with you at Jessie's house. At least she isn't going to make you sleep on the sofa."

"I could use a night's sleep. It's been a long day." He covered her hand with his own and they rolled down the windows and let the sweet night air come in. They drove past the Jewish Community Center and on down to Webster Street and turned and drove to Coliseum and stopped in front of Jessie and King's blue house. The lights were on and Jessie was sitting on the porch swing waiting. When they drove up she jumped up from the swing and ran out to the car. "I'm glad you came," she said. "I want to meet this Bobby."

Then he was standing up beside her and she got the kind of prickly excited feeling that only King could give her.

King came down the steps and shook hands with Bobby and they carried the bags inside and put them in the guest room. Then King walked Bobby out onto the porch. "I quit drinking," he said. "But I can get you something if you need it."

"I'm fine," Bobby answered. "The main thing I need is a night's sleep."

"My grandparents made him sleep on the sofa last night." Olivia laughed. "Well, I guess K.T. is asleep, isn't he?"

"You can look at him." Jessie smiled. "Come on in. I don't care if it wakes him up." She took her sister's hand and led her back to the child's room and Bobby and King went out and sat upon the steps.

"Jessie says you rodeo," King began. "I tried it once, when I was a kid in Mississippi. My granddad put me on a steer. That's a hard god-damn sport."

"It's what we do where I live." Bobby laughed. "It's mighty nice of you folks to have us here. Olivia's been a nervous wreck all day, hoping I'll pass muster."

"So how much dough is she going to get from this oil?"

"Too much. I guess I'll never see her again after that."

"It's a bitch. Figuring out what women want."

"That's what my dad always says. He says it's the hardest thing a man has to do."

"What does he do? He's a rodeo star?"

There was a long silence, then Bobby answered him. "He's a pilot. Right now he's in jail. He ran some dope."

"Hell, I've sold dope. Anyone can get into that. I'm sorry he got caught. Damn, that's hard to take."

"Yeah. Well, life's hard. No one ever wants to believe that, but that's the way it is."

Olivia and Jessie came out onto the porch and joined them and the conversation moved on to where they would eat dinner the next night and what bands were in town. At twelve-thirty they turned off the lights and went to bed. Jessie and King into the master bedroom and Olivia and Bobby into a smaller bedroom that joined the baby's room. The house was what is called in New Orleans a "shotgun house." A long rectangle turned on its side toward the street. A central hall ran from the front door to the back. If you shot a bullet through the front door it would exit at the back. The living room and dining room took up the front of the house, the master bedroom and kitchen were on the left of the central hall and the guest room and nursery on the right.

Way down deep in the Desire Street project Richard Brown was shooting cocaine with a couple of his old high school friends. He was staying away from his gang. His gang was mad at him and that was a very dangerous state of affairs. There was something his gang wanted that Richard didn't want to give. They weren't real mad about it. They were just starting to get mad. It would be another day or two before it became what Richard considered critical. It would be at least two days before he would have to leave town. For now, the gang still believed in Richard. They believed Richard would change his mind, which would be the best thing for everyone concerned. Only Richard couldn't change his mind because he no longer had the thing they thought they needed.

He should be doing something about leaving but he had run into two old buddies and started shooting up instead. It was nice, sitting on the stoop with his old friends, shooting up and thinking about King Mallison, Junior, and what a bad little boy he had been and now he had a baby. The cocaine was pretty low-grade shit. The whole deal was turning into a maudlin trip. Richard was getting sad for King. He decided King was like a lost prince in a tower, all closed around by the Jews his mother lived with and all their money and cars and perfect yards and all those goddamn hamsters and gerbils. I'd rather be me than that poor little kid, Richard was thinking. He was in a time warp now. He was fifteen and King was thirteen and he was going down to the Garden District and save the little kid and give him some dope and maybe get him laid. Only it was King who tried to give me some, he remembered. Sell me some. Well, he might have given it to me.

Richard wandered away from his friends. He wandered over to the edge of the project and got into his car and started driving. He had decided to go see King. He drove down Jackson Avenue to Prytania and turned and went on down to where there was a K&B and went in and got a Pepsi and a package of cigarettes and got back into the car and started driving aimlessly, trying to remember what it was he had set out to do.

Oh, yeah, he remembered. Go and see King's baby. Go and pay a call. He looked at the clock on the dashboard. It said two forty-five. Well, they might still be up. Hell, they'd want to get up and see him.

Richard had looked up the address earlier in the day in the telephone book: 1789 Webster Street. Coming for to carry me home. I looked over Jordan and what did I see, coming for to carry me home. Poor little old King. Fuck a bunch of white folks keeping a bunch of nasty rats in the basement, keeping little old white boys all locked up in a basement with a bunch of rats. He turned onto Webster from Magazine, which was the wrong way, as Webster runs from Saint Charles to the river. He drove slowly past Camp, Chestnut, Coliseum, and came to a stop behind Olivia's father's Mercedes. He took a .38 revolver out of the glove compartment and stuck it in his belt and walked up and knocked on the door.

Bobby heard the knocking before King did. He sat up, wondering where he had put his pants. The knocking grew louder. Then a doorbell began to ring. Olivia made a deep, irritated sound and pulled a pillow over her head. Bobby slipped out of bed and pulled on his jeans.

In his bedroom, King climbed out of bed and pulled on a pair of underpants and started walking down the dark hall. What the shit, he was thinking. What the hell is going on? He had thought at first he was in his old hippie commune in Buda, Texas. Someone was always beating on the door in the middle of the night in Buda.

King walked to the door and pulled it open. He was face to face with Richard. He had forgotten what Richard looked like and he didn't recognize him now. The two or three times he had run into him in bars, he had talked to him without really knowing who he was talking to.

"It's Richard Brown," Richard said. "I came to see the baby." King backed into the hall. Richard had the gun in his hand hanging loose at his side. "Want to see that little ole white baby. Auntee Traceleen told me you got you a baby and I come to see it." His eyes were everywhere. King kept on moving backward down the hall, trying to think. He was wide awake now and what he knew most was that he needed a weapon. He backed farther down the hall, past the open door to Olivia and Bobby's room, going to K.T. to protect him.

"I got to see that little baby," Richard was saying. "Got to see that little old baby of mine. Swing low, sweet chariot, coming for to carry me home."

K.T. started screaming. He had awakened to the sound of human voices and the static coursing through the house and he began to scream. King stopped dead still in the middle of the hall. "Get out of my way," Richard said. "Get out of my way and show me that little old baby."

Bobby stepped out into the hall and threw a T-shirt around Richard's neck and threw him to the floor. Richard pushed the trigger of the gun and the blast went through the wall of the baby's room and through a painting by the New Orleans landscape artist Katherine Sonlinga and out the door to the garden. Then Bobby was on top of Richard and King was holding the hand that held the gun. Jessie and Olivia were clutching each other in the baby's room.

"Call the police," Bobby was saying. "Get the cops over here."

"Oh, God, don't tell Daddy," Jessie was saying. "He's worried to death already about me living here."

"What the shit, Richard?" King added, having figured out at last whom he was dealing with. "What in the name of God are you up to?"

"I came to see the baby," Richard crooned. "Came to see that little old baby of mine."

Later, after Jessie had gotten the baby to stop screaming and Olivia had made a pot of coffee and they had tied Richard up with package string and the cords off the dining room drapes, they put him on the sofa in the living room and tried to decide what to do. Richard was crying now, coming down off a high and starting to be delirious. "We can't call the police," Jessie said. "They would send him to Angola. We have to wait until Manny and Crystal get up and ask Manny what to do. Richard, we are going to help you. I know you don't believe that."

"He didn't do anything I haven't done," King said. "Maybe we ought to let him go to jail. The three nights Dad left me in that jail in Florida were the beginning of wisdom to me."

"If we called the cops on Richard, we couldn't ever look Traceleen in the eye again. He isn't going anywhere, is he? Can't you hold him there, the two of you?"

"He's sick," Olivia said. "What he needs is a doctor."

"You want to give him something?" Bobby said. "Some kind of downer?"

"I don't have anything," King answered. He and Bobby were on either side of the sofa.

"We just need to sit here until about six o'clock and then call Manny. That's all we can do." Jessie had come and sat on the floor in front of Richard.

"I need a fix, man. I need a hit." Richard was starting to sweat. He was beginning to get sick.

"We should call Crystal now," Jessie said. "We need to get a doctor over here. Sitting up all night isn't going to do a thing."

"She's right. Can you hold him, Bobby? I'm going to call my mother."

In half an hour Manny was there. He was followed by his best friend from high school, a pediatric surgeon, who gave Richard a shot of Valium and Demerol and began to call around the country to find a place where they could dry him out.

"All the good places are voluntary," he said. "What do you think, Manny. Will he volunteer to go?"

"Richard's smart, Stuart. I've known him ever since he was a little kid. How much Demerol did you give him?"

"It will wear off by afternoon."

"We're breaking the law by not turning him in, you know that, don't you?"

"What do you want to do, then?"

"I can get him in a place in Dallas that's done miracles, but they won't lock him up against his will. He'll have to want to stay there."

"Call Traceleen," Manny said. "Get her over here. Call her up, King. Tell her what's going on."

Then Traceleen was there and people walked in and out of the house trying to decide what to do. Richard slept for several hours and woke up full of terror and remorse.

"Let's sit on him," King said. "Will you help me, Bobby? We'll keep him here and talk to him and try to get him to agree to treatment. I've done it before. If it works, it's the best way."

"You haven't got room here, in this little house."

"Yes, we do. Richard trusts me. He'll know I'm not going to call in the cops."

"He's got a gang. They'll come looking for him."

"Okay, then we'll take him to a hotel. Let's do it now. While the Demerol is still working on him."

"Where?" Jessie asked.

"The Pontchartrain," Manny suggested. "We can have the old suite upstairs where my grandmother used to live. Let me call and see. It's still early. We can go in the back way if we need to."

"Use our house," Crystal suggested. "Just use the basement of our house."

"No. I don't want to do that," King said. "Too many entrances to guard. How do you think I sneaked out all the time? No, a hotel is better. Okay, Bobby, get what you need. Let's do it."

Then Manny called the Pontchartrain Hotel and the manager met them at the back door and Bobby and King took Richard to a room and started working on him. For two days Bobby and King sat in the hotel room and ordered things from room service and watched old movies on television and tried to reason with Richard. "I got to go somewhere," Richard said several times. "I was planning on going to Florida. I got some money hid away. The trouble with my gang is that money. They found out I saved it and it's supposed to be share and share alike. I can't go out now. They think I've run out on them as it is."

"They'd never look for you in this place," King kept saying. "This is the richest dry-out center in the United States. Shit, man, they'll be so glad to see you. They never had a gang member there, I bet. You can tell them things they never get to hear. Besides that, you can save your life. Why you want to be dead, Richard? I've been there, man. I know what it's like to think your days are numbered, but they don't need to be. You can get well. You can start all over."

"And get me a little wife and baby and a job?"

"Don't knock it. It's not too bad. You can go to college and get an education and be a happy man. You don't have to hide out and be scared."

"Get Auntee Traceleen over here," Richard said at last. "I want to talk to her."

Then Traceleen came, and Andria, and they stayed shut up alone in a room with Richard for two and a half hours and at the end of that time Traceleen called Bobby and King into the bedroom. "I'll do it," Richard said. "How long does it take? How long do I have to be locked up?"

"Two or three months," King said. "It takes at least that long, but you're strong, man. Anybody strong enough to join a gang is strong enough to join the human race."

"Look at all the great people that have done it," Bobby said. "Hell, man, half the famous people in the United States have been in drug treatment centers. There's no telling who you might meet while you're there."

While King and Bobby were locked up in the hotel room with Richard, Olivia and Jessie worked on the Japanese garden. Traceleen's husband brought them a ton of gravel for a gift and hauled it around to the side of the house and Crystal took care of K.T. while they drew the pattern and smoothed the gravel into waves. It was almost dark on the second afternoon when they finished the pattern and set the stone markers to the east and west. Just as they were finishing, a soft rain began to fall. By the time they got inside it was pouring and they sat on the porch watching the rain fill the grooves in the pattern and run down into the yard. "I never thought about what it would look like in the rain," Jessie said. "I was just trying to copy the picture in the book."

"It's beautiful." Olivia slipped her arm around her sister's waist. "Nothing is ever what we plan. Everything is always a surprise."

Lightning played across the sky, so far away there was no sound of thunder. Inside the house the phone began to ring. "I bet it's Aunt Helen," Jessie said. "I was wondering when she'd call. She has a dowser's rod for trouble. She's worse than Grandmother."

"Are you going to tell her about Richard?"

"Sure. Why not. Who would she tell?" Jessie went into the house and picked up the phone. "Hello, Aunt Helen," she said. "I was wondering when you'd call."

"How did you know it would be me? Am I getting that predictable?"

"No, you're right on time. Wait till I tell you what's going on."

"Wait till you hear what happened in New Orleans," Helen said, when Mike came in that evening from class. "You won't believe what they're up to now."

"Oh, yes I will. Start talking. I can't wait to hear." Then Helen gave him an account of the events around Richard Brown's visit, stopping every now and then to say, "Oh, God, I bet this is boring you to death."

"Oh, no it's not," he insisted. "You can't imagine how much I like to hear about your family."

Helen did not call Daniel. No matter what anyone believes, Helen did not call Daniel or even mean to tell him. She had known Daniel all her life and she would have known better than to tell him that. She was sitting around knitting a blanket for DeDe's baby when Daniel called to talk to her about her divorce. Late in the conversation, just chatting, happy to be talking to her brother when it was clear he was sober, she just happened to mention the girls. "Your girls are doing fine," she said. "They've got hold of some real men."

"What makes you say that?"

"Oh, that thing down in New Orleans. The citizen's arrest and all that."

"What citizen's arrest?" Daniel's voice had grown quiet, but Helen chattered on, telling him the story as she had told it to Mike, putting in all the flourishes Mike had laughed at, saying several times how brave it was of them not to call the police and how young people were so understanding and forgiving.

"They let some black man go that broke into the house in the middle of the night? That's what you're telling me, sister?"

"It wasn't like that. Well, it's all over now. I guess I shouldn't have said anything about it. Well, never mind. Tell James to go on and get the divorce finished. You're sure he can do it without me being there?"

"If you're really going to settle for this offer Spencer made. I think you're a fool to do it, which is why I called you up. But whatever you want to do. It's up to you, Helen. It's your life. Well, I got to go now."

Daniel stayed up all night thinking about it. He started to call Jessie several times, then he would hang up the phone without finishing dialing. Finally, at noon the next day he went out to the airport and got on a plane and flew to New Orleans. He called Jessie from the airport and asked them to meet him for dinner at the Royal Orleans. Then he called Crystal and asked her and Manny to come and bring Crystal Anne. Then he checked into the hotel and lay down upon the bed and went to sleep. He had told everyone to meet him at six-thirty. At five forty-five he woke up and took a shower and put on a fresh seersucker suit and a white shirt and tie and went downstairs and had a shoeshine and then went into the bar and started drinking. By the time Jessie arrived he had had three double gin martinis. By the time the dinner party was gathered around a table he was slurring his words. By the time the waiter brought wine there was a chill around their end of the dining room so intense that Crystal Anne had started sneezing.

"What are you doing in town, Daniel," Manny said, trying to bring the evening back into some order. "Crystal said you came on business?"

"I came down here to talk to all of you," Daniel began.

"Well, great," Crystal said. "I was just thinking what to cook for dinner when you called. This is a real treat. An unexpected dinner party in the middle of the week."

Jessie closed her eyes. She knew the stages of Daniel's drinking like she knew the beating of her own heart. The most dangerous thing of all was when he grew quiet. It was the harbinger of disaster. The death of safety, the death of peace. I should get up and leave right now, she thought. I could say, King, take me out of here and he would. I can leave. All I have to do is stand up and walk away. She looked down into her lap. Folded and unfolded her hands.

"I hear you're trying to save the little son-of-a-bitch that broke into my daughter's house in the middle of the night and tried to kill your baby. Is that right, son?" Daniel leaned toward King. "I came down here to find out about that. You want to tell me that I'm wrong."

"I've known him for years, Daniel. Yes, I'm trying to help him. We all are. All he did was come to see K.T. He wanted to see the baby. He wasn't trying to kill anyone."

"He had a gun with him. Or was Helen wrong about that too?"

"Oh, please," Crystal said. "Let's talk about something else. Could we please just leave this alone. Tomorrow we'll explain it to you, Daniel. He's the nephew of our housekeeper. We couldn't call the police. They would have sent him to Angola."

"Angola is a terrible place." Crystal Anne was standing up. "I have to go to the bathroom, Daddy. Will you show me where it is?"

"I want you to see my new office anyway." Manny put his hand on Daniel's arm. "You come down in the morning and we'll explain it all to you. We have the young man in a clinic in Texas. It isn't whatever you think has happened."

"So you're trying to help this nigger that broke into my daughter's house and tried to kill her baby. That's the crap you got going on down here in New Orleans. Goddamn, Manny, I thought you had some sense. I wouldn't have let Jessie marry this boy and move down here except I thought you had enough sense to protect her. Letting her live in that little frame house on the edge of a black neighborhood. I wouldn't treat your daughter that way if you sent her to me. I want them out of that neighborhood tomorrow. That's what I came down here for, to buy my daughter a decent house." He waved his hand to the black waiter, who had been listening and would be very slow in waiting on this table. That was clear from the expression on *his* face. THE TYRANNY OF A DRUNK IN A RESTAURANT. Crystal Anne was standing up. She was facing Daniel. "You shouldn't yell so loud," she said, "and don't say racial things. You'll hurt somebody's feelings." She turned on her heels and walked toward the hall leading to the bathroom. Crystal jumped up and followed her. Manny was on his feet.

Don't move, King thought. Until you decide exactly what to do.

I think I'll kill myself, Jessie decided. Wherever I go, it's like this, someone is always getting drunk, always screaming, screaming, screaming.

"Daddy," she said. "Please don't do this. Don't do it here. Don't yell at anyone. Don't yell at King. Don't yell at me." She began to cry, very softly at first, then terrible sobs. King took her arm and pulled her up beside him. "I'm taking Jessie home," he said. "Daniel, don't say another word to her. If you say one more word, I'll kill you. I mean it, Daniel. You can trust me." Then the waiter was beside him and two more behind him and Manny held Daniel's arm and King and Jessie made their escape through the side door out onto Saint Ann Street.

At two that morning Jessie started bleeding. At four she started hemorrhaging and at four-fifteen the ambulance came and took her to Touro Infirmary and she bled away the fetus that would have been her daughter. "I'll be like Anna," she wept into King's arms. "I'll lose all my babies. I was probably lucky to have K.T. Go on home and take care of him. Don't leave him alone for a minute."

"He's with Momma," King said. "He's with Momma and Manny and Crystal Anne."

At ten the next morning Daniel showed up at the hospital with an armload of flowers but Jessie would not let him come into the room. "I lost my daughter," she said, when he appeared in the door. "I'm never speaking to you again, Daddy. Go away. I never want to see you again as long as I live. Doctor Kaplan said I don't have to do this anymore." As if on cue, Doctor Kaplan appeared behind Daniel in the door and came around him and went to the bed and sat beside it and took Jessie's hand. "Are you okay, honey?" she asked. "Are you doing all right now?"

"It was a girl," Jessie said. "It was my daughter. Now she's gone. I'll be like Aunt Anna. I'll bleed my daughters and sons away."

"Nonsense," Doctor Kaplan said. "It was a miscarriage. That's all. Nature knows what it's doing. There will be plenty more babies if you want them. You're a strong and healthy girl."

Then Jessie began to cry again and Daniel laid the flowers on a chair in the hall and walked down to the elevator and got on it and went down to the first floor and out onto the street. It was very bright and lively on Prytania Street in the hot summer morning light. Daniel stuck his hand into his pocket and felt his money clip. He felt his car keys and his hand brushed against his balls and he walked on down the street and stopped at a doughnut shop and bought a Coke for his hangover and thought about his life, now officially over, and went out to the airport and got on a plane and flew on home.

Back at Daniel's house, Spook was walking around the empty swimming pool picking up leaves and scraping mold off of corners and muttering to himself. Goddamn little kids, I'm not writing another check to that service until they come out here and get this thing right. We ought to fill the damn thing in and plant some flowers in it. Nobody's here anymore. Nobody swims in it. Nobody uses it for a goddamn thing.

Poor Daniel. He's finished now. Some days I wish he'd go on and shoot himself like his granddaddy did and get it over with. Spook climbed the steps from the shallow end and walked over and sat down in one of the four-hundred-dollar yard chairs by the bath house and thought about it. He lay back in the chair. Then he sat up and put his elbows on his knees and his head in his hands. "Father in heaven, it's a sinner pleading with you. Would you tell me what the hell I'm supposed to do here, please? Would you tell me where I'm supposed to start and don't tell me to clean out this goddamn swimming pool because I've already done that and if I hear any more about it I might get me some dynamite and blow it up."

*   *   *

The phone was ringing in the house. Spook could hear it but he wasn't going to answer it. It was Helen tuning in on the trauma. It was Helen, standing by a window in her living room looking out on the streets of Boston and biting her lower lip. She had on a white cotton blouse and a little red pleated skirt and a pair of white sandals and she was calling everybody up.

"We were prisoners," Crystal said, when Helen finally got her on the phone. After trying everyone in the family, she had finally gotten hold of Crystal. "If Jessie hadn't started crying. If Crystal Anne hadn't gotten up, I guess we would still be sitting there letting that drunken fool hold us hostage. Well, she lost the baby, I guess you know that. Is that why you're calling?"

"What baby? She was pregnant? What are you talking about?"

"She was three months pregnant. No one knew. King had only known a few days. She had menstruated twice so maybe it was inevitable. It might have been a bad pregnancy anyway. The doctor had said he wanted to do an amnio. She's pretty hysterical about it though. If you call her, be careful what you say. She thinks it was a girl."

"Crystal Anne was there? In the mêlée? God, I'm sorry about that. I feel responsible for this, Crystal. I shouldn't have said anything to Daniel. I didn't mean to. He called me about something and I was just rattling on. Oh, God, I'm so sorry. I think it was my fault."

"It wasn't your fault. It's Daniel's fault for being drunk. I don't think Jessie will ever forgive him."

"Where is he now?"

"He's in Charlotte. If you want my advice, leave him alone. He's got a nice woman who loves him. Let her deal with this. We have spoiled him to death all his life. Let him get away with murder."

"That's Daniel. He can always find a woman to tell him anything he does is all right. He was so beautiful to look at when he was young. Such a wonderful dancer."

"It's a curse, that kind of beauty."

"You should know."

"I know." They were silent then.

"Blessed and cursed," Crystal said finally. "All of us. Well, maybe things are looking up. For some of us. I don't give a damn what happens to Daniel now. I've had it with Daniel. That was the last straw."

"I think this was all my fault."

"Helen, it wasn't your fault. That's how alcoholics make people feel. Like they did something wrong. You didn't do anything wrong. You just said it to the wrong person, you said it to a drunk."

"Where did you learn all this, Crystal? You're getting so wise. I think of you dancing in that white dress at the Christmas cotillion that year you came to visit us in Charlotte and everyone fell in love with you. Anna said you were the prettiest girl who ever lived. I wish she could know you now. Anyway, that's embarrassing. I don't want to embarrass you."

"I'm going to a psychiatrist, Helen. I'm trying to find out what went wrong so I can fix it."

"What went wrong?"

"Good and bad. It isn't only me. It's the whole family. All of us. Starting with my father's mother and my great-grandfather's slaves and going back to when my father's father beat him and then he beat Phelan and turned Phelan into a killer. The way Phelan adores women, loves women to death. That's because Daddy was such a tyrant and Mother was the only hope he had. All those old bastards in north Alabama, those beautiful, powerful old Scots. They beat their sons and scared their daughters to death. It's worse than the Victorians and I had that too on Mother's side. It's the same for all of us. Why do you think Daniel drinks?"

"He had asthma when he was a child. He used to get sick before basketball games. He couldn't breathe."

"Did you hear what you just said?"

"What?"

"Before basketball games. I bet your daddy was standing over him expecting him to be a star."

"Yes."

"Helen. I have to go. The baby's crying. I'm taking care of K.T. He just woke up. But I'm glad you called. Come and see us. Come see Jessie. She really loves you. She misses you."

"Should I call her or not?"

"What will you tell her?"

"What Mike tells me. We live in a rich country and we have roofs over our heads and a Constitution that works and food to eat. This is not a tragedy no matter how much we want to believe it is. He always says that to me."

"He sounds wonderful."

"He is. He reads Yeats out loud to me. He knows most of it by heart."

"Food to eat and a poet to love. How'd you get so lucky, Helen?"

"I don't know. I think it's some sort of mistake but I don't want to give it back. Like someone gave you too much change and you feel good when you give it back. But this isn't like that, is it?"

"I'll ask my shrink. Love you, Helen. I have to go and get the baby."

Helen hung up the phone and went into the kitchen to see what she could cook for supper. There was a quotation stuck with tape on the refrigerator door. Every day Mike put a new one there. Yesterday it had said, "WRITE AS IF YOU WERE DYING." Today it was lines from a poem.

> *Though I am old with wandering*
> *Through hollow lands and hilly lands,*
> *I will find out where she has gone,*
> *And kiss her lips and take her hands,*
> *And pluck till time and times are done*
> *The silver apples of the moon*
> *The golden apples of the sun.*

Later that night, much much later, Helen lay in Mike's arms and tried to tell him the things Crystal had said. She tried to make him see the plantations in North Carolina and Alabama. Told him about the old wills that they had seen as children leaving the slaves to one another. Been cursed by seeing. Told him about the dogs and horses and the fox hunts and the field trials. The antiques and rings and chandeliers and the huge houses. "The niggers, as they were called," she ended. "All we ever heard anyone call black people, but my grandmother called them darkies. It's so complicated and it began so long ago and we have inherited so much sadness, but also, the sort of minds that made Anna a great writer. So I don't understand. But I want to understand. I want to be like Crystal and spend my life trying to understand."

"Have you ever been to Scotland?" Mike asked.

"No."

"Then you must go. The next time I go to Dublin I will take you. It started before you think it did, Helen. It started long ago in those Orkney Islands, if that's really where your people came from."

"They say it was. Half Irish, half Scots, part Welsh, you can't blame things on the past. That's the problem, blaming things on other things. We have to take our lives now, and do something with them now. I've been thinking about it all day and that's the main thing I believe."

"I thought you said you wanted to spend your life trying to understand the past."

"No. I didn't mean that. I want to spend my life like this, with you." She snuggled down into his chest, lay her hand upon his arm. What had she read that day? "We have some happy days and some unhappy days, some great loves and barren spaces. We have this life, this instantaneous blossoming. Will I ever learn not to choose among its moments, will I ever learn to walk its hollow lands and hilly lands?"

"You know that thing you put on the refrigerator today? About silver apples and golden apples?"

"Yes."

"It's very strange. I was reading some of Anna's essays. And she said that too, about hollow lands and hilly lands. I thought when I read it, I've seen that somewhere and there it was, on my refrigerator."

"It's from a famous poem. It's a vast metaphor for me, for the muse and also, the richness of life, the thing we overlook from day to day, the feast we forget to partake of."

"That's what the essay says. That's what Anna thought it was about. I want to see the rest of the poem. Will you show it to me tomorrow?"

"I will sing it to you while you go to sleep." And he did and she did and the night passed and it was another day.

CHAPTER 48

"A RMAGEDDON," Georgia said, when she heard the story of
Richard and the citizen's arrest and why Olivia had to spend
three extra days in New Orleans, causing her to miss an exam.
"Okay, write me a thousand-word essay on the incident and we'll call it
even. You're the only one in class who listens, much less knows what
I'm talking about. I don't think any of them can read."

"Armageddon?" Olivia rolled the word around in her mind.

"It's what Tolstoy said in *War and Peace*. When things got so bad for
the peasants that they lost all civilized sense, they became highway-
men. What's the difference between that and auto theft? Oh, well,
enough of that. Are you going to North Carolina in the fall? Is Bobby
registered? Can I help with that?"

"I don't think I'm going back. He wants to go to Montana and show
it to me. So I think I'll do that. Armageddon. Yeah, that's the word for
it. King showed us the project where Richard grew up. It looks like
someplace that was bombed in a war. And right in the middle of it are
these sweet little children with ribbons in their hair. I can't forget seeing that."

"You want to go for a walk. Let's chuck all this and walk awhile."

"We could walk out to the cemetery and see where my mother's
buried. It's out by the old Indian village, the Sah-Ke-Lah. You want to
see it?"

"Sure. Why not?" It was the sixth time Olivia had proposed going
to see her mother's grave.

They were in the school cafeteria. They put their trays on the con-
veyor belt and left the building and began to walk. "So how are things
with you and Zach?" Olivia asked. "Did you ever let him make you
come?"

"Yeah, the other night. I thought, What the hell. I'm only punishing myself. All that bullshit he believes about the twins getting better. He thinks he can make me like them. It's just a terrible pathology and I'm caught up in it. It's a tarbaby and I can't get loose. I get a hand free or a foot free, and then I get sucked back in. But it's better, it's getting better. Look at that cloud formation, will you? It's so good to be outside. People should stay outside. You don't get in trouble outside." Georgia laughed up into the air and began to walk faster. She had been a marathon runner in the 1970s. She was hard to keep up with when she had a theory forming in her mind.

CHAPTER 49

THIS TIME they were definitely going to kill her. "She's going to move in here and take up all the room," Taylor said. "All we have to do is fix the car. You fix it so the brakes go out."

"He doesn't really like her." Tucker had been all for killing her the week before. Now he was chickening out. "She isn't even here now."

"She's coming back. She's going to marry him and be our momma."

"Dallas Anne is our momma. I hate her too, Taylor, but we might get caught."

"I say we fix the car."

"It's Dad's MG. Why do we want to wreck his car?"

"We could wait till they switch. He said he was going to trade back with her this weekend."

"Is she coming this weekend?"

"She never comes when we're here. That's how much she hates us."

"We hate her too."

"That's why we have to kill her. Listen, Taylor, if we got rid of her Dad and Mom might get married again."

"No, they won't. Mom wouldn't do that. She says he's a workaholic. She doesn't like that. He won't ever have any fun."

"He has fun with us."

"When Georgia isn't here."

"Well, that's why."

"Okay. We'll do something. But not wreck the MG. There're other things. We could scare her to death."

"How?"

"I don't know yet. Let me think about it." Taylor handed the beer to Tucker. They only drank two beers in the daytime. One at ten o'clock and one at four o'clock. They had figured out that Zach didn't miss two, or, if he did, he overlooked two. He would raise a stink about three. But two he could tolerate. The twins were out on the back porch on the swing watching a blue jay fly around acting crazy. They had torn down his nest that morning after they found it in an apple tree. Taylor had wanted to shoot him with the 410, but Tucker talked him out of it. "Just watch him," Tucker said. "I love to watch them when they can't find the nest. I hate blue jays. I wish we had Momma's cat over here. Let's bring her the next time we come."

"Okay," Taylor answered. "We will. I'd love to bring her and see what she'd do up here."

CHAPTER 50

BUT what is love anyway?" Georgia asked. She and Olivia had finished their walk and were resting now beside a waterfall. The sun was past the horizon. The sky above the woods was celestial. Along the tops of the trees the clouds were pink and purple and azure, pale yellow and deep pure blue and amber and green and mauve and every subtle shade of white and gray. The sunset had been so spectacular that several times Georgia had thrown up her arms in abject worship.

"I don't know what love is," Olivia answered. "Maybe it's just sex. That's when you want to say it. Right after you come or if you're horny. Doctor Coder pointed that out to me."

"It can change your heartbeat." Georgia smiled at the seriousness of the girl. "It can cure disease. We know that. We know people get sick when someone they love dies."

"There's this woman in Eureka Springs that has this painting of the Virgin Mary. People touch it when they're sick and they get well. She painted it twenty years ago and she's taken it all over the world to get people to put love in it. She took it to Russia and all these peasants started worshiping it. There was this thing on television about it. I haven't seen it but Bobby has. He said it gave him a really spooky feeling."

"Maybe it's a catalyst."

"Doctor Coder says the joy of loving someone is in loving them, not in being loved. So a good way to get loved is to need love. He says I have to tell Bobby that I need him or let him know. I don't know. Then he turns around the next day and says I have to keep 'a proper distance,' he says that over and over. Are you still in love with Zach?"

"Not as much as I was. It's so bitter to have to back off from it, but the twins drive me nuts. I'm just not capable of loving them. I swear to God, I think they hate me."

"You could love them. Just try harder."

"I'm trying as hard as I can."

"Maybe you shouldn't have their dad's car. It would make me mad if Margaret was driving Dad's car."

"It's a practical thing. He wanted my Isuzu to haul things in and the MG is better on the road. You're right, though. Maybe it's the car. I'm going back to Memphis in October. I haven't told him yet. We could still see each other. He can come to Memphis on the weekends or maybe he could teach there if he ever got rid of Taylor and Tucker."

"You want him to get rid of his kids?"

"Someday they'll leave anyway."

"I think you better just find another boyfriend."

"Maybe I'll have to." They were silent, a long hard silence. "Okay, I'll try to love them. One more time I'll try as hard as I can, but they're really bad, Olivia. It isn't just my perception. They're bad boys."

"Try it." Olivia stood up. She felt very grand, giving advice to her older friend. "Well, I've got to be getting back. Bobby's waiting for me."

They stood up. Water was falling over the high granite bluffs behind them. The colors were fading from the sky. They started back down the path to the car.

When Georgia got home she called Zach and told him she was coming over the following night.

"The boys are here," he said.

"I know. I want to see them. I have something to tell you."

"What is that?"

"I'll tell you tomorrow. But first, let's take them out to dinner. Somewhere nice. Wash their faces."

"I miss you."

"I miss you too. Tomorrow night then. I'll be there by six. I want to trade cars while I'm there. So clean mine up. I mean, take things out of it."

"Okay. Fine. I'm not using it now anyway. I've been driving the old truck."

"Why?"

"I don't know. For the bumper stickers. I'm sorry, I didn't mean to push that button "

"Tomorrow night."

"Good, I'll see you then." She's going to leave me, he decided. Women always do. Well, at least she's going to be nice to the boys before she goes. She hurts them so much ignoring them that way. I hate her for being so ignoble to them. I hate women, to tell the truth. I hate the things they do to me. He walked across the room and picked up a bag of Doritos and ate a few. He opened the refrigerator and stood staring inside it. He was thinking about Georgia, but when the boys came in behind him they thought he was counting the beers.

"Oh, hello," Zach said. "Georgia wants to take you out to dinner tomorrow night. Is that all right? Would you like to do that?"

An hour later the twins were alone in the bedroom.

"Okay," Taylor said. "We fix the car. We fix the brakes so they fail."

"What if she kills some innocent person?"

"She won't. And she never wears a seat belt. She deserves it."

"Maybe it will just scare her."

"It's going to kill her, Tucker. Get that straight." Taylor finished off the beer and rolled off the bed. "Get dressed. He's going downtown to copy some stuff. While he's gone I'll show you on the Isuzu. You have to take the wheels off and work on the lining. It's all in that old Volkswagen book, but I know how to do it anyway." Tucker believed him. Taylor was a mechanical genius. Everyone knew that.

"Then what can we do?"

"Tonight?"

"Yeah."

"Let's go over to the cheerleader camp and pick up girls. Remember all those girls we met last year?"

"Okay. Yeah, that's a good idea. There he goes." The boys listened as Zach pulled out of the driveway in the old pickup truck. Then they walked out into the side yard and looked at the Isuzu. They rolled it into the garage and Taylor jacked it up and took off a wheel and showed Tucker what they were going to do. He pried up a piece of the lining to show Tucker how easy it would be to do.

"Put the wheel back on," Tucker kept saying. "He might come back."

"He won't come back. Did you see that pile he had to copy? He'll be over there for hours."

They replaced the wheel on the Isuzu and hammered the wheel cover back on and then they went into the house and began to eat potato chips and pretzels. There was a message from Georgia on the answering machine. "See you tomorrow night. I don't know why I called back. Just wanted to hear your voice, I guess. Call me if you come back before eleven."

"You want to erase it?" Taylor asked.

"No, we did that enough. Don't do anything suspicious."

Georgia was in a great mood driving to Fayetteville the next afternoon. She had sat in zazen for an hour concentrating on learning to love the twins. She fixed them in her mind and surrounded them with love, she smothered them with love, the more they hated her, the more she loved them. She would love them so hard it would make up for their having had the worst mother in the world, it would make up for the trauma of being two, it would make up for whatever needed to be made up for. She, Georgia Jones, Medical Doctor, could do it. She could do it with her will, her fantastic unbeatable will. Number seven in my goddamn class, she remembered. *Numero siete.* So I've had some setbacks since then. So what? It's an imperfect world. Where did I get that? Olivia. She has invaded my consciousness this summer, darling little hopeful child. God, I hope she gets what she wants.

Georgia drove bravely on, passing every car on the road, top down, no seat belt, tape player blaring out with the Rolling Stones, then Louis Armstrong singing "Cabaret." "Start by admitting from cradle to tomb, isn't that long a stay, come to the cabaret, old chum, come to the cabaret."

It's too short a stay to spend my time hating a pair of teenage boys. I love Tucker. I love Taylor. I do, I do, I do.

They were waiting on the porch when she arrived. The boys in matching pink polo shirts and Zach in a white shirt and a pair of chinos. If I didn't know better, I'd think this was a dream come true, Georgia decided, and turned off the motor and got out smiling. "Where do you want to go?" she asked. "This is my party. Where do you want to go, Taylor? You and Tucker choose. Anyplace in town."

"Anywhere?"

"Yes."

"The Old Post Office too?"

"That most of all. I love it. You want to go there?"

"Do you?" Taylor looked at Tucker.

"Sure."

"Okay. We do." They moved to the side of the porch, moved closer together, tried to compute the new material. She was being so nice, she didn't even look like a spy, which was what they had called her before they only called her She.

"I've been missing you," Zach put in. "I'm awfully glad you're here. This is nice of you, Georgia. To want the boys to go."

"Okay. You want to take the MG?"

"No, let's go in the Isuzu." They climbed into the Isuzu and Zach drove down Duncan Street. He came down the steep hill to the stoplight on the corner of Duncan and Center. Taylor and Tucker were strapped into the backseat. Georgia was riding shotgun. Taylor undid his seat belt and leaned over to pick up a quarter that was stuck under the floor mat.

"What did you want to tell me?" Zach asked. "I've been wondering what it is." Taylor leaned closer, trying to hear the conversation.

"Oh, it can wait," Georgia said. "It's just something we need to talk about. Let's go eat dinner. I found a waterfall the other day. Did I tell you about that? Up in the woods near Lake Tenkiller. Huge wide steps of granite right in the middle of the woods. Very, very nice. It's runoff from a change in the dam. It wasn't there a year ago. It made itself. A baby waterfall. Olivia and I found it. I told you about her scores on the Stanford-Binet, didn't I?"

Zach shifted into third gear and began to climb the hill toward Dickson Street.

The brakes held until they were almost to the top. The piece of lining that Taylor had loosened with the tire jack was torn and weakened anyway, and now it disintegrated. Zach stepped on the brake and the car slid sideways into a ditch by the local NPR studio and fell slowly onto its side. Georgia fell against Zach's shoulder. Taylor crashed into Tucker. Student radio announcers came pouring out of the building, one of them called 911, and from three blocks away a patrol car sped to the scene.

"You did it," Tucker was screaming. Taylor's blood was falling on Tucker's face. "You did it, you fucking asshole. You've killed us all, you crazy goddamn asshole. He did it, Dad. I didn't do it. I didn't even want to do it."

Two hours later Georgia and Zach and Tucker were released from the Emergency Room of Washington General Hospital but Taylor was being kept for a few days. He had a broken wrist and several broken ribs and a cut on the right shoulder.

"This is what I do for a living, Tucker," Georgia said. "I watch this go on every day. The dumb and stupid things people do to themselves by being stupid, uneducated, and careless."

"Let's go get something to eat," Zach said. "I'm starving. We're going to talk to you, Tucker. And you're going to come up with some answers."

The local taxi took them to Zach's house to get the MG and they got into that and put on their seat belts and drove to a Chinese restaurant, where the waiters were just off the boat and the paintings were authentic. Georgia propped her bruised hand up on the table and determined to watch the rest of the evening without making any judgments. If I don't live with them, it's an interesting problem in human behavior, she decided. If I live with them, it's my problem. Don't forget this, Georgia. Never forget this night.

"Taylor was messing with the brakes yesterday afternoon," Tucker began. "He wanted to show me how the brakes worked and he took off the front tire and messed with it."

"Why did he do that?" Georgia kept her hand propped up on the table. She looked around it at the boy. "Why did he mess with the brake linings of the tires?"

"I don't know. To show me how they work. I don't know why."

"Yes, you do." Georgia picked up the menu. It would do no good to hate the children for protecting the only security they had ever known. And what is my security? she wondered, and searched her lover's face and it was not there. She searched the tabletop and the blue porcelain pot of steaming tea. She raised her eyes to a wonderful painting that was the reason she came to the restaurant. A wonderful Chinese painting of ten people in a small boat on a stormy sea. They were dressed in many kinds of clothes. They leaned toward the bow of the boat, examining the waves which came up to the gunnels and threatened to capsize them. On their faces were expressions of mild interest.

The Chinese waiters came and went, serving rice and tea and huge steaming platters of food. Her hand ached. It was not hurt badly but it was sprained and bruised. It will heal by October, she thought. When I go back to work.

"What did you want to tell me?" Zach asked. "You said you had something to talk to me about."

"It can wait. Let's eat. Tell us why he took the tire off the truck, Tucker. Did he want someone to get hurt?"

"Oh, Georgia," Zach said. "That's going a bit too far."

"I'm going back to Memphis in the fall." Georgia poured the tea and ignored Tucker, who was looking down at his lap. "I hope that won't be the end of us loving each other. I have to go back to what I understand, Zach. I don't understand families. I like them and I wish them well, but I don't do them very well. I wasn't a very good mother to my own children. I'm not on the family track. On the other hand, I am a very good physician. So I'm going back to work. You're in the family dynamic whether you like it or not, however. We'll see each other. It isn't far to Memphis. An hour's flight. I don't want to lose you, to lose the love we have." She raised her eyes and looked at him and waited. He didn't even blink. He's relieved, she decided. My God, he's registering relief.

"I wouldn't want to lose you either," he said. "I'm sure we can work something out."

"You're going to live in Memphis?" Tucker said. "You're not going to be here?"

"I'm a medical doctor, Tucker. I do what that woman in the emergency room does. I got burned out on it but now it's time to go back."

"Drink your soup," Zach told his son. "We'll talk about this later. Let's get some food in our systems."

The waitress brought the rice and chicken and broccoli and shrimp chow mein. The passengers rode the waves. Zach and Tucker and Georgia picked up their chopsticks and began to eat.

Georgia and Olivia were having breakfast. It was two days after the wreck, the fifteenth of August. The semester was almost over. Summer was wearing down. "I want to tell you what I learned this week," Georgia was saying. "I want to tell you the wisest thing I know."

"Shoot."

"The great Zen master, Dogen Zengi, said relationships are with everything. Trees, rugs, mountains, rivers. The ones that give us difficulties are always with other people. They want to be themselves, but we want to meld them into ourselves so we'll never lose them. This is doomed to failure. In every relationship there is some genuine love and some false love. The false love is caused by thinking the lover will perfect us, will make us complete. But people are always changing, so no two people can maintain a perfect fit. If you are in a close relationship you will suffer part of the time. We have to learn to live with that if we are to have relationships with other people. We have to learn patience. We have to learn how to wait."

"You lost me."

"I was telling you the new wisdom I know. What did you think I said?"

"That you're going to Memphis to practice medicine and leaving him in Fayetteville to be his children's father."

"That isn't what I said."

"It's what you meant. Well, I don't know what Bobby and I are going to do. For right now, we're going to finish this semester and then we're going to drive up to Montana and visit his friends up there. He wants to show me those mountains. Also, he has to get ready to ride in the Futurity in Fort Worth. He might be riding against me. Kayo wants me to ride his mare. I know we have to get an education but it's driving us both crazy, sitting in classrooms listening to professors talk. Well, not you."

"You can miss a semester of school and it won't matter. If you have a chance to ride a champion horse in a race, go do it."

"It isn't a race, it's where they show off the bloodlines. It's a business."

"Do what you want to do. You're going to have money from the oil. The only point of money is to buy freedom. Maybe there'll be enough money for you to have a ranch of your own. How much will there be? Will you be rich?" Georgia giggled, raised her glass of Diet Coke.

"Well, not very rich. It sure has made my uncles happy though. My uncle Creek's making a sand painting for a celebration. He's been getting the materials together. Every color has to come from a sacred source. Like the charcoal has to come from a tree that has been struck by lightning. It isn't a Cherokee art. It's an idea he got from a book. Isn't that great? This grown man that used to be a mechanic suddenly decides he's an artist."

"What a fine idea. What a great idea. So, you think I feel guilty about leaving Zach?"

"Did I say that?"

"You implied it."

"Well, it might be true. Is it?"

"He's caught up in such messy stuff with those twins. They beat him up and he keeps coming back for more. He bribes them for attention. It's a reenactment of his developmental trauma. He had an indulgent mother and he's trying to re-create her. So he indulges the boys to get their approval and no one ever grows up. I can't live with that. I'd be in quicksand. Or I'd end up being his mother and then I'd never get laid. Good boys don't fuck their mothers. When he starts thinking he's my baby boy he starts making me come with his fingers instead of his dick. I can't live with that. Talk about getting in the quicksand. Well, eat your toast."

"Will I end up being Bobby's mother if I live with him?"

"It's the danger. And it's a pain in the ass to stay on guard all the time. There's no solution, Olivia. Just do the best you can and enjoy your life."

"Doctor Coder doesn't want me to live with Bobby. He says we should each have our own place and that way we can stay in love."

"Did you read that essay on Stone Age communities I passed out to the class?"

"Not yet."

"Read it. See if you can find the sources of the nuclear family. Of course, they were trying all the time to get food. It cuts down on the neuroses, when you have the problem of being hungry." Georgia drank her orange juice, ate part of her French toast. Blessed the earth and its bounty. Looked up into the bright young face beside her. Bless the young, she added. Bless their hope and beauty.

CHAPTER 51

DANIEL was depressed. He had promised to go to the treatment center on the first of September and he knew he had to keep the promise. Also, he had cut down to a jigger of Chivas before dinner and a brandy after dinner and, as a result, his dick was getting softer every day. The very thought of never having a toddy again made his dick softer than Jell-O. Margaret had been understanding. She believed him when he said it was caused by thinking about going to be locked up in Atlanta in the place where Sudie Macalester had climbed over a wall on bedsheets and tried to walk to the airport. Duck Macalester told him that story about a week after it got all over Charlotte that he had agreed to dry out.

So his dick was rebelling and he was having to live on blowjobs. His secretary had given him notice. Business was not picking up. They were barely bailing water, living off repair work and a few faithful customers from the good old days when Daniel could fly people to the Open in Augusta and pick up all the checks.

To top it off, Margaret had handed him an ultimatum. He had to marry her before he went to Atlanta or she was leaving and going to live in Washington, D.C.

"You couldn't have picked a worse time to start that," he had answered. "I quit drinking for you. Goddamn, Margaret Ann. What's wrong with you? You don't even act like yourself anymore."

"I'm sorry. I can't help it. It's how I feel. I'll be forty-one years old in October. I have to straighten out my life. I have to have something to depend upon."

"I can't get married right now. I have to go to Oklahoma and drive Olivia home. I promised her I'd come there. As soon as I get back from that I have to check into Atlanta. You want me to back out on that? Is that what you're driving at?"

"You don't need to drive her home. She's a grown girl."

"I want to drive her home. I want to meet her folks and see this boy that made the citizen's arrest at Jessie's. King says he's a man."

"So now you take King Mallison's advice on who to get for a son-in-law? Last month you wanted to kill him."

"Goddamn, Margaret, you're getting as bad as Helen. Have you been talking to my sister, is that what this is about?"

"What it's about is living by myself. It's about being married and living like normal people. If you don't want to, it's all right, but if you don't, I'm leaving. There's nothing in Charlotte for me but you. I could make twice as much money in Washington and see some opera occasionally." She moved back into the sofa. She began to look as though she might be about to cry. She had lost ten pounds this summer, she was getting thinner every day, and Daniel didn't like it. It wasn't the old Margaret. It was a new and scary Margaret and he didn't want her crying and he sure didn't want her moving to Washington, D.C.

"What are you thinking about? Say it out loud."

"I don't want you moving to Washington."

"So what do you want to do?"

"I don't know, Margaret. You just sprung this on me. I haven't had time to think."

"You've had five years. That's long enough."

"You might not like living here. I'm grouchy and I snore and I get up in the middle of the night."

"There are plenty of bedrooms. I could sleep in one of them."

"I might have to sell the house."

"Then I'll buy it from you and you can live with me." She began to gather up her clothes and put them on. They had been in bed having a nice afternoon, even if his dick wouldn't cooperate. She had made him come and he had made her come, and you can't beat that even under the worst of circumstances. She had moaned and groaned and hugged him and kissed him on the ear and seemed completely happy with the deal. Now this. She put on her slacks and her shirt. She put on her shoes. She picked up her jewelry from the table and dropped it in her pocketbook. "I'm going now," she said. "Call me when you make up your mind." Daniel got up from the bed and pulled on his pants and walked her downstairs to the door. "I wish you'd stay," he kept saying. "You don't need to go off like this."

"Yes, I do," she answered. "Call me when you make up your mind."

After she was gone, he wandered into the kitchen and ate some cold roast beef and drank a Coke and stood a long time staring into the whiskey cabinet. Giving up toddies to marry Margaret and spending all the money he had left building fences on a farm nobody gave a damn about anymore. What a deal.

Daniel walked out into the yard and sat down upon a rise of land and looked up at the stars. The constellations rode the moonless night. It was hard to believe the earth was a planet. Hard to believe a man could die. Hard to believe little girls would grow up and leave you and never even come home to visit. He sat for a long time thinking about all the women who had left him. Then he walked back into the house and called Olivia on the phone.

"I'll fly up there day after tomorrow and drive you home," he said. "Can you meet me in Tulsa?"

"The last day of classes is the nineteenth. I could come that afternoon."

"Okay. I'll make a reservation. How are things going, honey? You still got that boyfriend?"

"You can meet him when you come. I'll get him to drive me to Tulsa. He wants to meet you. He's dying to."

"Good, I want to meet him. I want to meet this young man." Daniel hung up the phone and walked back out into the yard and conferred again with the stars. "I got about twenty more good years and then maybe ten more," he told the heavens. "Hell, it's going to be a different life. Well, the one I had wasn't all that great. My dad looks pretty happy and old Mr. Faucette sure looks like a happy man. I'll model myself on him. Every day I see him jogging by here in the morning, putting in his miles. Maybe I'll take up jogging. Get myself a pair of those fancy running shoes and start running with Mr. Faucette. I guess I got to marry her. Once they get that idea in their heads, there's no living with them unless you do it. It will make Momma happy. Momma'll be right on top of that." He shook his head and stared deep and hard up into the night sky, trying to put his life into some kind of larger perspective, since it had grown unbearable on these two acres.

"All right," he said, when he called Margaret at eleven o'clock that night. "If you want to get married before I go to Atlanta, it's all right with me. I think we ought to wait till Christmas but if you want to get married now I'll do it. I haven't got a thing to offer you but a couple of rings that used to belong to my grandmother. We can go down to the bank tomorrow and take them out of the safe deposit box. You can see if you want them or not."

"Yes, Daniel, I will marry you."

"Which time? Now or Christmas?"

"I guess I'll wait until Christmas."

"I'd wait if I was you. I wouldn't go marrying someone that was on their way to Atlanta until I saw how it turned out. What time are you getting up tomorrow?"

"You're proposing to me?"

"I sure am."

"But you aren't going to come over here and sleep with me?"

"I don't sleep well at your house. I'll come get you and you can sleep over here with me."

"Do you want me to?"

"If you don't mind. Were you in bed already?"

"Come get me, Daniel. I'll be waiting for you." She turned from the phone and looked around the room where she had spent so many unhappy nights thinking about Daniel Hand. This doesn't feel like victory, she decided. I don't know what it feels like.

"Where you going, boss?" Spook had heard Daniel come out onto the patio and push open the doors to the garage. "Where you going this time of night?"

"Going to collect my bride-to-be. I asked her to marry me, Lucas. I popped the question. What do you think of that?"

"When did you do it?"

"Just now. I just called her. So I'm going to pick her up."

"On the phone? You asked her on the phone?"

"What's wrong with that?"

"It's good news, boss. I didn't mean to cavil." Spook stood in the doorway watching Daniel push open the garage door. "I mean it, boss. That's the best news I've heard all summer. She's a fine woman. She'll make you a mighty fine wife."

"What's that look on your face, Lucas? And don't call me boss."

"Yes, sir, boss. I mean Daniel. Well, I'll see you in the morning then."

He waited until Daniel had driven off down the street, then he went into the house and began to turn on lights and pick up newspapers. No sense in having Margaret coming in the middle of the night into a dark house. She might change her mind and then he'd never get back out to the farm where he could get some sleep.

CHAPTER 52

AUGUST 19, 1991. On the plains west of Tahlequah a tornado was forming. To be more exact, several tornados, gathering their winds, their stones, their sand, their insects and leaves and water, getting ready to head down Tornado Alley and clear some ground.

There was already enough excitement in the world. At six-forty that morning Georgia's radio alarm had turned itself on and the voice of Bob Edwards filled the air. "There is stunning news today from the Soviet Union. After six years in office . . . Mikhail Gorbachev has been removed from power in a coup . . . citizens of Moscow awoke to find the Soviet military mobilized on the streets. . . ."

Georgia sat up in bed, shook her dyed blond hair. That's great, she decided. The world is falling apart and I'm all alone in a rented house in this tacky little town. Where have I been? Where on earth have I been?

The phone was ringing. It was Zach. "Are you awake? Do you know what happened? Did you hear the news?"

"I just did. What does it mean, Zach? What's going on?"

"I don't know, but I'd sure like to know who's in charge of the arsenal."

"I woke up hearing it. I thought, What am I doing in this little town? But I know why. It was to escape your pathology." Georgia was waking up now. "That setup you've got going with the twins is pathological, Zach. You bribe them for attention because you feel guilty for not wanting them when they were born, for being sorry they messed up your life. All this concern with the universe is just your way of escaping your real problems."

"I just called to see how you were. I didn't want to hear a lecture."

"I'm sorry. I'm not awake enough to prevaricate this morning."

"Am I going to see you before you go to Memphis?"

"Of course. I have to come close up the house there."

"I want to make love to you, Georgia. That's the main thing."

"I want to, too, but I can't live with you. Come over here and spend the night if you want to fuck me."

"Tonight?"

"Yes."

"Okay. I will. I'll be there. There are storm warnings for tonight."

"Then hurry up. I'll be back from class by two. It's my last day."

"I love you. That much is true."

"I love you too. Come on over."

Georgia got out of bed and went into the bathroom and started brushing her teeth. The anxiety arises from the intimacy, she chanted to herself. Fear of dissolution. Disruptive bonding issues. If I go to bed with him, I rev up all the old bonding issues. Bond, bond, bond, the child is saying. Have a mother, be a mother, wah, wah, wah, feed me, love me, hold me, never let me go. Maria Louise Van Franz escaped. Why can't I?

"Dad's coming this afternoon." Olivia and Georgia were eating waffles at The Shak. They were seated at a table by the window.

"That's good. He's coming to meet Bobby?"

"To meet everyone. We're going to visit Mother's grave. He's been promising me he'd go with me. I guess you think that's morbid, don't you?"

"No. Just don't stay too long. Take him to that waterfall we found. That's better than a grave. I hope he and Bobby like each other."

"It doesn't matter if they do or not. I want Bobby to go with me to Tulsa to meet Dad's plane, but I'm not sure he can. He might not be able to get off from work."

"This has been a very special summer, Olivia. Because of you. More because of knowing you than any other thing. I'm going back to Memphis, I told you that. You can always find me there. I expect you to write and call me and keep up with me and come and visit me when you come back this way from wherever you end up."

"I just want to get settled and have a normal life."

"There isn't any normal life, Olivia. Not for people with brains like ours. The modern world's a mess. Find your work to do. That's the most important thing. Grow up. Get really grown up if you can. There aren't many grown people in the world in any age. Most of them are babies, sucking teat from the cradle to the grave. Go find the big boys and girls and play with them. Leave the babies to their drugged sleep." Georgia finished off her waffle. "God, I didn't know I knew all that. You've done that for me all summer, Olivia. Made me articulate things I didn't know I knew. It's been myself I was talking to."

"I want to see you again before you leave. Will you be going tomorrow? Maybe you can meet Dad."

"Good. I'll talk to you later today then. Call me when you get back from Tulsa."

They stood up, gathered their things, went off to the last day of classes.

CHAPTER 53

I N Charlotte, North Carolina, Daniel was packing a suitcase while Spook lounged in the doorway giving him advice. Spook had been spending the summer rereading the collected works of Louis L'Amour. He was on the last one now and wanted to get rid of Daniel so he could finish it and start on a set of mysteries he'd picked up at the secondhand bookstore the week before. He'd decided he needed to broaden his outlook and stop reading books with horses in them. With all the young black people getting into politics and law and being on television, Spook was ashamed to be so behind the times.

Daniel folded up a shirt and lay it on top of a pair of slacks in the suitcase. "I'm going up there to meet her folks and see this boy she's got herself involved with. Then I'm going to drive her home. It's as simple as that. Put her in the car and drive her home."

"Don't go trying to force her into anything, boss. She's like you. If you try to push her, she won't budge. Maybe you ought to take her a present. Call Margaret and tell her to go pick something out. Your plane doesn't leave till noon."

"Eleven. And Margaret's at work. Well, hell, I'll pick up something in the Atlanta airport. What do you think she wants?"

"Get her a bracelet or a necklace. They like that."

"You think so?"

"When you tell her you're going to Atlanta to dry out and getting married to Margaret, that's going to be a shock. You ought to have a present handy, just in case. Why you so nervous about this trip, anyway? I heard you up at dawn. You haven't been getting much sleep lately, have you?"

"I just want to make sure she comes on home. Hell, she's probably pregnant by now."

"Boss, they don't get pregnant now. If they do, they get rid of it."

"Like Jessie, yeah? Like Jessie a year ago? That was only a year ago, that's hard to believe."

"Well, that turned out all right. I thought you was so crazy about that little boy."

"I don't want to talk about it. Losing all the girls, whole damn family falling apart. You know what Crystal told me recently. You remember how I came home and I wasn't there when the baby was born. Well, he blew a hole in his lung when he was born. The first scream he let out blew a hole in his lung. They had him in an incubator for three days. Did anyone tell me about that? Hell, no. They decided not to tell me. Then months later Crystal tells it to me like it was some kind of a joke."

"Just go on up there then and collect your little girl and bring her home. It's your car, isn't it?"

"She didn't sound too enthusiastic when I told her I was coming. I think she's afraid to let me meet this boy."

"You just be careful, boss. Don't do anything you'll be sorry for. Most of all, stay off booze so you won't say anything you'll be sorry for."

"Okay. That's good. Okay. Here, put that suitcase down. I can carry it."

"I want to carry it. I got to do something. There's nothing to do around here anymore."

"You could clean out the pool and sweep off those tennis courts and get the weeds out of the flower beds. That's to do. If you didn't think doing it was beneath you."

"You never told me you was going to turn me into a yard man when you made me come stay here for the summer. You never said a word about I'm supposed to be somebody that weeds the flower beds."

"Then call someone and get them over here. You can call someone to come and weed the flowers, can't you? I guess that's not too much to do, now is it?"

"I want to go back out to the country and be there when they start working with the horses. The vet's coming this weekend. I hate to miss it when he's there."

"Then go on out there." Daniel was at the front door now. He took his suitcase from Spook and started down the front steps. "But you get it fixed up around here. I want it pretty when she gets home." He walked on down to his car and threw the suitcase in and got behind the wheel and started driving. He turned on the radio. "Soviet troops are on the streets of Moscow. Crowds, mobs, are all around the government buildings." That's about par, Daniel thought. You can't depend on a goddamn thing.

On the plane he ordered a Scotch and water, but when the stewardess brought it, he sent it back. "Get this out of here," he said. "Take this out of here."

He sat back. He opened a *Sports Illustrated* he had bought in the airport and began to read about John Daly's unbelievable win in the Indiana Open. He quit boozing, Daniel said to himself. Look what happened when he quit. Well, goddamn, this is one hell of a plane ride.

The plane was bucking up and down, then began to climb. "What's this wind all about?" he asked the stewardess. "Where's this coming from?"

"It's a front from Canada. It's been getting worse all day. This will make some weather for somebody before it's over."

CHAPTER 54

I N Boston, it was Mike and Helen's wedding day. Mike's brothers and his twelve-year-old nephew had arrived the day before from Dublin and were staying in the guest room of the apartment. They had awakened to the news from the Soviet Union and were huddled around the television set and a shortwave radio while Helen served them scrambled eggs and bacon and toast and tea.

"If the Lithuanians can do it, Ireland can too," Michael's youngest brother, Paul, was insisting.

"You're a hothead, Paul," his brother Devin put in. "It's not the same situation. This has been coming for a year. It doesn't surprise me."

"Who has their army?" the nephew, William, kept asking. "Who's got the bombs and the submarines?"

"I wish you'd drink some orange juice," Helen said. "We're going to have a long day ahead of us. We have to take the wine to the restaurant and I have to get my hair done and we need to clean up the apartment in case anyone comes here afterward."

"The Soviet slaves are rebelling." Mike reached over the sofa and pulled her into his lap and held her there. "Don't cook any more. We'll clean that up for you, won't we, boys? I won't have my bride cooking and cleaning on her wedding day. I love this woman, Devin. I pray every day that she keeps on being crazy enough to stay with me. Now she's going to marry me. Don't get up." He held her on his lap and kissed her hair where it grew around her ear and stroked her with his hand. "I'll have to go to the school for a while this morning. We have a lot of students from these countries. I imagine they'll be meeting sometime today. You can go with me, Paul. All three of you. It will be educational for William." He stroked Helen's leg. He kept her with him, feeling her heart beating like a captured bird. He had fallen in love with her the day he met her, in Anna's apartment a week after Anna's suicide. In a rainstorm, soaking wet, wind beating against the boards of the house. Helen had looked at him with those wide, sad eyes, standing before him holding sheafs of Anna's wild and lovely prose. "I don't know what to do with all of this," Helen had said. "I don't know where to begin." Within an hour they were in Anna's bed, on Anna's gray silk sheets, their bodies plastered against each other, love filling up the space that death had blown into their lives. Our relationship to nothingness and death, Mike thought now. That's what everything is about. He held Helen on his lap and would not let her go, while the people of Moscow vented their years of rage.

"Let go of me," she giggled. "I have to go get ready to get married."

"Look at that," Paul yelled. "They're tearing down the statue of Lenin. My God, who thought we'd live to see this happen. What a day for the world."

"Ireland's next," William said. "We'll be next. You wait and see."

Helen's wedding day wore on. The men turned on a second television set in the guest bedroom. The president of the United States held a press conference. Mike and Devin and William and Paul went to the university to talk to students. Niall came in from the hotel where he was staying and helped Helen straighten up the apartment. Helen went to the beauty parlor and had her hair done. The temperature reached eighty-seven degrees Fahrenheit. Then eighty-nine, then ninety. The men returned. A political scientist and his wife came over. A couple of journalists from South Africa. Helen began to hate the Soviet Union and its people. She went into her bedroom and shut the door and polished her fingernails and called two of her children and apologized for not inviting them to the wedding. "It's just a small ceremony," she told them. "Uncle Niall is here and Mike's brothers. It's really just a formality."

"I hope you have a good time, Momma," DeDe had answered. "I want you to know I really hope you're going to be happy."

"Dad's real sad about it," Winifred had not been able to resist reporting. "I don't think I've ever seen him so sad. He's lost about fifteen pounds."

At five in the afternoon, Mike sent all the political people away and everyone started getting ready for the wedding. At six o'clock they piled into two cars and started driving. They drove through the beautiful hot streets of Boston. Helen sat between Mike and Niall. She leaned her face into Mike's blue serge jacket. She laced her fingers into his and held on very tightly. This day, she reminded herself. This moment, this is what I wanted, this is mine.

She looked up and Niall was smiling at her, his face so like the face he had worn when he was a little boy. Beloved face of my brother, she told herself. The exact same face he wore when he was a scrawny, tanned Boy Scout, wearing his lanyards, going out into the garden to collect his specimens. The day he quit pinning them to cardboard. "They smell bad and it hurts them," he had said. "I've started feeling bad when I do it."

He wasn't pinning her now, only looking at her with the deepest love. I don't care what Anna said about the family, Helen decided. They love us. They are all we have to keep us from the dark.

"Are you okay?" Mike squeezed her hand and pulled it toward him.

"I'm fine. I'm happy. I really am."

"Want to back out?"

"No. Do you?"

"No."

"I can't believe this is me. Is this me, Niall?"

"It's you. Only you could have gotten me to Boston in this heat. Only you would look so pretty doing it."

"My hair looks terrible. It went limp the minute that they did it."

At six-fifteen they arrived at the church and went into the vestry and were met by the minister, a sweet-looking woman Helen's age who had been the first female Episcopal minister in the state of Massachusetts. She was wearing a black smock and a white lace surplice that was hanging haphazardly from one shoulder. Her smile was dazzling. Helen fell into the smile.

"I'm Sylvie MacArthur. Welcome. What a day for the world. Niall, I'm so glad to see you."

"You know Niall?" Helen asked.

"We've been at conferences together. I knew he was your brother. I kept forgetting to mention it when we talked. I'm getting so forgetful lately."

"Undifferentiated consciousness," Niall said. "Seventh chakra." He and the minister giggled and hugged each other until the already precarious lace surplice fell down the lady's arm.

"Our party is right behind us," Mike said. "Is there anything we should know? What do you want us to do?"

"Let's go in my office and talk. Then we'll go into the church and have a wedding. We'll tie your hands together. I'm a fan of yours. I might as well tell you that. 'The Moth on the Gate' is one of my favorite poems. Never a week goes by that I don't think of it."

"I'm glad. Thank you." His voice deepened as he considered his work. Helen took his arm.

"I try to forget he's famous," she said. "It makes me nervous."

"You might have been used to it, after your sister."

"That's what makes me nervous. She's gone, isn't she?" It was dark in the hall and fragrant, light came in the stained-glass windows from the far altar and from the portals above the doors. The smell of lilies and of prayerbooks, hope of the earth.

"This conversation is too serious," Sylvie said. She pushed open the door to the front lawn. Devin and William and Paul were walking up the stone path. "Here comes your party. Now the celebration can begin. Solemnity and celebration, prayers and vows." She held open the door with the arm on which the surplice had fallen down.

"My brothers," Mike said. "And my nephew."

"Handsome people," Sylvie answered. "Well, collect them and let's go into my office and talk about the ceremony, shall we?"

At six-forty-five they filed into the sanctuary and arranged themselves around the altar. Mike and Helen standing before Sylvie holding hands. Niall on Helen's right. Devin beside Mike, with Paul and William beside him. "Will you light the candles for us, William?" Sylvie handed him the matches and a taper. Very slowly the boy lit all the candles behind the altar, then handed the taper back to Sylvie and returned to his place. Sylvie opened the Book of Common Prayer and began, "Dearly Beloved, we are gathered together here in the sight of God and in the face of this company, to join together this man and this woman in Holy Matrimony. . . ."

By the strictest rules of the church she should not have been performing this marriage but Sylvie made her own rules. "Two people make a wider stream for life to flow through," she had told the bishop.

"I know this man's poetry. I want to marry him to this woman that he loves. Add to the store of goodness in the world. Say yes. They were both raised R.C.s. Someone has to make them feel like God is still in the world and on their side."

"Roman Catholics, Sylvie. Please. I wish you wouldn't do that. It sounds so haughty."

"I'm haughty. What's wrong with that? If I wasn't haughty, I wouldn't have to work so hard at being humble."

"Which is an honorable estate, instituted of God . . . ," she read, her beautiful voice falling upon the bowed heads of these hopeful people. ". . . and not to be entered into lightly, but soberly, reverently and in the fear of God . . ."

I should have told him I am pregnant, Helen thought. I have to tell him. I should have told him before we did this. I don't know how to tell him. Maybe I'll tell him tonight. She bowed her head even deeper into her chest, feeling so deeply, terribly embarrassed and guilty, so ashamed of her body and its endless cycles and how it always took her life away. Because I wanted it, she knew. Holy Mary, Mother of God, pray for us sinners now and at the hour of our death . . . Hail Mary, Mother of God.

Maybe now she'll be happy, Mike was thinking. Maybe she won't mind if I have to go to Ireland. Someone has to go. We have to begin the talks. There must be a beginning and an end to war.

"Signifying unto us the mystical union that is betwixt Christ and His Church; which holy estate Christ adorned and beautified with His presence and first miracle that He wrought in Cana of Galilee. . . ."

CHAPTER 55

HALF the stormclouds that were causing the bad weather in Tahlequah were blowing up from the Gulf of Mexico. The other half were in a jetstream moving across the Midwest. In that weather Bud Tree was riding the front seat of a Greyhound bus. He was sitting opposite the bus driver. He had a small suitcase on a rack above his head and a box beside him on the seat. It contained the belongings of a young man who had been in jail in Iowa City with him. Bud was going to deliver it to the young man's mother. Adair Wilson, it said on the box. Rural Route Three, Pine Bluff, Arkansas. "Let me take it to her," Bud had asked the jailer. "I'm going that way anyway. You don't want to be sending something like that in the mail." Now he had it on the seat beside him and he was sorry that he did.

"I'm going to have to stop before we get to Tulsa," the driver was saying. "I got caught out here in some winds one afternoon. I thought we were done for."

"I'd sure hate to stop in a field." Bud looked behind him. There were only four other passengers on the bus, two old people sleeping and a young couple reading a newspaper. "Still, you're the driver, what can I say?"

"There're tornado warnings out for half of Oklahoma. I'll have to stop in the next town. So tell me some more about this guy that shot himself. No one knows how he got the gun?"

"Not a clue. He was in the cell next to me. It was about five in the afternoon and a shot rang out. Then another and another. Hell, I was in Nam. I dove under the bed. I can only half remember it. The deputy was in the cell when he fired the third shot. He saw him do it. Three shots with an automatic pistol into his own heart. I think it's why they went on and let me out. It silenced everyone. Hell, I've seen some terrible things, I've seen kids blown apart, but I think it was the worst thing I ever witnessed. He was as sweet as a kid, he was a kid. No one knows how he got the gun and no one knows why he did it. He was only in for armed robbery. He held up a convenience store. He had these sweet eyes, this big sweet smile, and he was smart. Smart as a whip. So now I got to take these things to his mom. His boots are in here, and a Bible. Hell, I put that in. The sheriff and I decided there ought to be a Bible."

"Sounds more like a boarding school than a jail. Where was this?"

"Iowa City."

"We're going to have to stop. There's a town up here a few miles with a shed for the buses. We'll stop there and call for some weather. I can't get this set working." The bus driver tried the radio again but there was only static. Rain was pelting them now, turning into hail. Bud got up to stand by the driver. "There's nothing but flat land from here to Tulsa. What a country. Goddamnedest weather in the United States, but what can you do? It's where I live."

CHAPTER 56

AT one o'clock Zach started driving to Tahlequah. The skies were darkening and the wind was picking up but he had decided against turning on the radio. Concentrate on my girl, he decided. God, she's so excessive, excessive brilliance, excessive mess. Like the skies, one minute she's sweet as pie, the next she's cold as ice. Overeducated, that's the problem. What did Jung say? "There aren't any women psychiatrists because intellect isn't their long suit, and true love, which is, is invisible." He should have met Georgia before he wrote that down.

My God, wild weather. Electromagnetic fields. Well, it's all energy. Ch'i, prana. Just thinking about her makes me want her. Put that in your cosmic pipe and smoke it.

By the time he got to Tahlequah it was raining. By the time he got to Georgia's house it was pouring down. By the time he had taken off her blouse the wind was beating against the house. The cheap wooden walls seemed to pulsate with the rain. Georgia pulled the covers off the bed. She took off her clothes, talking the whole time she was undressing. "Did I ever tell you about the Bonobos, Zach? Pygmy chimpanzees in Africa. They're matriarchal. The males exhibit no aggression toward each other or any other living thing. They never kill. The mothers nurse the babies for four years. Even after they grow up the children can get milk any time they want it. They live on sugar cane in the forests of Zaire. All they do is eat sugar cane and fuck.

Even the little chimps do it. They climb on the adult females and have at it. The females stay in estrus most of the time and come back in a year after the babies are born." She pulled off her underpants and lay down beside him and began to touch him. "Listen, Zach, this is the missing link to heaven. These animals love each other. They never fight and they are fearless of other animals. The natives love them so much they have been known to go to war to keep anyone from harming them. A   matriarchal chimpanzee, Zach. Imagine it. If I wasn't going back to practicing medicine, I'd go join the research. They are just being studied. I saw some early photographs. A guy who works for *National Geographic* sent them to me. God, look at this weather. Is this perfect for fucking, or what, as Olivia would say."

"Come here, Georgia. Come here to me. Oh, honey, I've been missing you so much. Come to me. Come live with me. Stop all this madness about leaving me, all this nonsense, all this needing attention. That's the only reason you're doing this. To get attention. Well, you've got it."

"Pretend you're a regular chimpanzee," she said, "who wandered into a group of Bonobos. I'll be the Bonobos. Oh, Zach, I love you so much. I can't do without you." She was all over him now. In the kitchen the roof had started to leak onto the table, but neither of them was going to notice that.

"I have to go back to work," she said.

"You can work in Fayetteville. We have plenty of emergencies there."

Bobby and Olivia got to the airport just as the plane pulled in. Bobby let Olivia out at the door and she went running through the terminal while he parked the car. She made it to the gate just as her father came through the door. "This is some weather you're having, honey," he said, taking her hands. "I was worried about you driving in it."

"I know. It's a tornado watch. But don't worry about it. We're used to it. Bobby's parking the car. I want you to like him, Dad. But I'm going to live with him whether you do or not."

"Let's go get my bags." He took her arm and they began to walk down past the gates. "I rode out a hurricane once, in New Orleans. I guess I can stand a tornado watch." He looked up and saw a tall tanned boy coming toward them. Well, he looked like a man. At least he was a man.

"This is my boyfriend, Bobby Tree." Olivia stepped back. The men shook hands.

"Nice to meet you," Daniel said.

"It's good to meet you, sir. I've been looking forward to it."

"Olivia says you used to rodeo."

"I still rodeo if I need the money. It's a hell of a way to make a living. It's mostly cutting horses I'm interested in now. Raising them and training them."

"They're exciting animals. I've been on a few." The men walked along together, talking about horses. As if I wasn't even here, Olivia thought. As if I'm not the reason for all this.

They reached the baggage carousel. "You're looking mighty good, honey," Daniel said, turning to her, propping one foot up on the edge of the carousel. "You look like you're getting taller."

"It's the boots."

"We had to beat that weather all the way from Atlanta. That old DC-9 was bucking like a ship at sea."

"Soon as we get your bag we'll head on back. It's probably just a storm but it makes the roads slow."

"Granddaddy's been waiting for you for days." Olivia took hold of her father's arm. "He wants to talk to you about the oil. He wants you to tell him how to invest it."

"I'm the last one to ask about that." Daniel laughed his irresistible laugh. "Maybe he'll loan me some money." He picked his suitcase off the carousel and looked out toward the street. "It looks like it's clearing out there to me. What do you think, Bobby?"

"I think we better start driving if we want to get to Tahlequah."

They went out into the parking lot and put Daniel's bag in the trunk of the car. "You drive, Bobby," Daniel said. "I don't know where I'm going." Then Daniel got into the passenger seat by Bobby, and Olivia got in the backseat and they started on their way. The sun was out and the sky had cleared to the north and east, but by the time they were halfway to Tahlequah it clouded over and started raining again.

"We need to go straight to Grandmother's house," Olivia said, leaning up to touch her father's shoulder. "They're going to be worried about us."

"How's your Tulsa baseball team doing this year?" Daniel asked. "I used to follow the minors when I was in school. You've had some great players come out of the Drillers. Ivan Rodriguez went to Texas last year, didn't he?"

"I saw him play three or four times. We used to come up here all the time for the games."

"I think we ought to turn on the radio." Olivia was halfway into the front seat now. "It looks terrible out there. I've already been in one tornado this summer. I was driving home from seeing my psychiatrist. Well, they were called tornado-force winds, but it was terrible. It scared me to death. I was so glad I was in this heavy car. He's really a wonderful man, Dad. He's helped me so much. I love you for spending all that money for him. I think it's made a difference in my life. The other thing is this teacher I have, Ms. Georgia Jones. I really want you to meet her if you can. She's leaving tomorrow afternoon to go back to practicing medicine. She's a doctor, but she quit because she saw this little girl die and it was the last straw."

"That's nice, sweetie." Daniel reached over and turned on the radio. There was only static at first, then finally a station came on. "This is Green Country weather. The tornado watch has been upgraded to a tornado warning. Seek shelter immediately. Repeat, a tornado warning is in effect for Green Country and including the towns of Stillwater, Tahlequah, Regrade, Dumont, Dumas and Siloam Springs. A tornado has been sighted five miles east of Stillwater and moving to the southeast at a rate of two hundred miles an hour. . . ."

"That's toward Tahlequah," Bobby said. "It's coming our way."

"What should we do?" Daniel asked. "Should we stop or keep on going?"

"It's a crap shoot. There's a little town about five miles up this way."

"We have to see about them," Olivia was saying. "They might not be listening to the radio. They never watch TV. Granddaddy can't stand it."

"How far is it to the farm?"

"About twelve miles."

"There's a storm cellar," Olivia said. "We have to go there. We have to go see about them. They're old, Daddy. I'm going whether you go or not."

"We can make twelve miles, can't we?" Daniel was addressing Bobby.

"Sure. I think so. You want to try it?"

"Yeah. Start driving. Drive this goddamn German car. You got your seat belt on, honey? Sit back and put it on. Okay, son, drive the car." Daniel leaned back in his seat. Bobby leaned into the wheel and kept on driving. In six minutes they were within a mile of the house.

"It's right up here," Bobby said. "There's the turn to the road." The rain was harder now, pelting the car with hail. Bobby slowed the car and turned onto the gravel road and began to drive the last stretch to the house.

"This is where I was born," Olivia said. "Right here. Momma and me."

"Let's just make sure it isn't where we die." Bobby turned into the yard and parked the car in a cleared place by the barn and they got out and went running toward the house. Little Sun and Mary Lily and Crow were in mackintoshes, getting ready to make a run for the storm cellar. Crow had a basket in each hand and Mary Lily had a plastic sack filled with cookies and crackers. They handed flashlights and sweaters and coats and hats to the travelers, and then, with Little Sun leading, they filed out into the yard to a dirt embankment past the well. Bobby and Daniel pulled open the wooden cover and held it while Mary Lily and Crow and Little Sun and Olivia went down the stairs, carrying the folding chairs that were by the well. "I've got the bug spray," Mary Lily said. "There's no use in saving you from the storm if we all get bit by brown recluse spiders."

"I cleaned it out a month ago," Crow said. "After those winds that other time." They unfolded the chairs and set them up in the crowded passageway and Mary Lily lay a blanket down on the floor and spread the food out on it.

"Did you bring the radio?" Little Sun asked.

"I left it there. Oh, God, I left it in the kitchen."

"I'll go get it. We need to know what's going on." Bobby pushed open the cover and disappeared into the storm. The rain was coming in gusts now, the trees were whirling, the sky was black from horizon to horizon. In a few minutes Bobby returned with the radio wrapped in plastic and they turned it on and huddled around it. "A tornado has been sighted on a line two miles west and one mile north of Highway Sixty-five at Tahlequah, moving to the east-northeast with winds of two hundred miles an hour. Take cover. Repeat, a tornado is in the vicinity. Take cover immediately."

"That's us," Mary Lily said. "It's headed our way."

The shelter they were in had been built by an Irish stonemason in 1917. It was twelve feet long and six feet deep and four feet wide, with an even wider space just below the entrance. Wooden uprights a foot thick supported the walls. The floor was lined with large flat stones. "I used to play in here all the time when I was little," Olivia said. "We always kept it swept back then, didn't we, Aunt Lily?"

"I swept it just last month," Crow repeated. "When we had those winds."

"It sure is good to get to know you folks at last," Daniel said. "I been wanting to come and see you for a number of years."

"It wasn't your fault Summer died." Little Sun sat up very straight on his chair. "Come, move your seat over here by me. We will sit together while this storm passes."

"See if you can get a stronger station," Crow said. "We need to hear where it is." She and Bobby began to fiddle with the radio but before they could find a clear station, they heard the roar that heralded the twister. It sounded like it was a few feet away and it sounded like it was moving. Olivia threw herself into Bobby's arms. Mary Lily folded her arms around her chest and began to pray to all the gods of Roman Catholicism and the Cherokee. Daniel closed his eyes. Little Sun thought of his ancestors.

"What if it takes the barn?" Olivia said. "It might kill Bess."

"It would be a good way for an old mare to die," Crow answered. "She'd never know what hit her." Then, above the roar of the wind, they seemed to hear a mare whinny.

"I heard her," Olivia screamed. "I know I heard her. Was she tied up?"

"No, I let her out in the pasture hours ago," Little Sun said. "They know where to go."

"Arletti came in at four this afternoon and climbed into a closet," Mary Lily said. "She's still in it."

"I knew it was coming." Little Sun reached over and put his hand on Daniel's knee. "The birds and animals have known it all day. There hasn't been a sound out of a squirrel."

"He always watches the animals," Olivia put in. "That's how he knows what to do."

"I loved your daughter, Mr. Wagoner. I want you to know that. But I was a very young man. I had a bad temper. When she left me, I didn't know where she was going. I sure didn't know she was pregnant."

"She was very hardheaded," Mary Lily offered. "No one could ever budge her. We used to call her the stubborn mule, didn't we, Mother?"

"I'm glad to be here," Daniel said. "I'm mighty glad to be here with you folks."

The wind was even louder now and they pulled their chairs closer together and did not speak for several long minutes.

"Turn the radio back on," Little Sun said at last. "It sounds like it's moved away." Bobby fiddled with the radio and finally got a station.

"The storm struck first in MurMur Heights, moved across Highway Twenty-five, and headed into town," a voice was saying.

"The tornado seemed to gain intensity as it swept through Tahlequah," another said.

"It was moving with two-hundred-mile-an-hour winds. A tornado like that tears up trees. Trees are everywhere. I never saw so many trees lying on the streets."

"Three trees are on top of my truck," a fourth voice was saying. "It took the trailer and threw it across the yard."

"That was the voice of Lonnie Paterson," an announcer said. "Lonnie and Elaine's nineteen-foot trailer was picked up by the twister, thrown over the top of their van, then dumped upside down in the side yard of their house. The trailer is destroyed. This is station KIND, Tahlequah, Oklahoma. We are here on Muskogee Avenue where three stores have been gutted and a restaurant cleaned out by the wind. Carl

Crow of Tahlequah is standing by to tell us his story. Carl is the manager of Stone and Workman. Carl."

"I was in the store when I saw a dark funnel forming in the direction of the park. It was a dark, black-like thing. I thought, My God,
that's a tornado. It formed and ran down the street and was gone
before I could finish a thought. I felt the walls shake, but Jannette and
I, Jannette Sorel was here with me. We escaped death. It's a miracle we
are here."

"Let's go up now," Little Sun said. He stood up and stretched his
legs. "Let's go and see if we have a house."

"Let's see if we have a car," Mary Lily added.

"I wouldn't care if it was all swept away," Crow put in. "I been
thinking we should all move into town."

Georgia and Zach were asleep when the tornado hit. They woke up
and grabbed each other. "What was that?" Georgia asked, but they
both knew.

"Get in the hall," Zach said. He pushed her off the bed and grabbed
an armload of pillows and bedcovers and followed her out into the
small crowded hall. He shut the doors to the bedroom and to the bathroom and to the second bedroom. The entrance to the living room and
kitchen had no door. Outside the house the noise was deafening.
Getting louder every second.

"We should have left a window open," he said.

"Forget it," Georgia answered. "Get under these covers. Wait, there's
a closet here. Let's get in there." She pulled open the door to a small
linen closet that contained the heating and air-conditioning units and
squeezed herself into a corner. Zach squeezed in beside her and began
to try to shut the door. The noise was even louder now, a crescendo of
sound, thunder and a sound like a tunnel of wind. This is it, Georgia
decided. Ground zero. The end. "I love you so much," she said out
loud. "I'm sorry for all the pain I've caused you. Thank God you're
here. Thank God you're here with me." She buried her face in his chest
and pulled the blanket around them. The air conditioner hummed by
their shoulders.

Zach was still trying to get the door shut when the living room windows burst and glass flew everywhere. "Oh, God," Georgia screamed. "Oh, my God. Armageddon. The Bitter End."

Bobby and Daniel pushed open the door to the storm cellar and stepped up into the air. They looked around. The wind had dragged tree limbs and garbage cans and old harness and rocks and boards across the yard. The cars were covered with debris. Daniel stooped over and picked up an oak limb that had fallen across a wheelbarrow. "Look at the size of this. Well, son, I want you to know one thing. You can't live with my daughter unless you marry her. Aside from that, I'll stay out of your life."

"I've begged her to marry me, Mr. Hand. I offered my life to her, everything I have to give."

"Good. I'm glad to hear it. And I wish you luck with it, too. I've felt that way about women, not that it did me much good. Sometimes I think it was my fault. Other times I think I was doing everything a man could do, and they still left. What do women want? That's the question. Well, we're all still here. And the house is standing."

The others were coming up the stairs from the cellar, starting to survey the damage. The yard chairs were gone. Limbs were all over the roof of the house and, from the look of the power lines, there wouldn't be any electricity for a while.

Crow and Little Sun moved toward the house. Mary Lily walked toward her new Pontiac. Olivia started in the direction of the barn. A pygmy goat from a neighboring farm came out from under the hen house and nuzzled her hand. "I'm going to look for Bess," Olivia said. "When did you see her last?"

"She was here all afternoon. I turned her loose. They know where to go when it storms." Little Sun turned her way. "Come on into the house. If she isn't back in the morning, we'll go look for her."

Then they all went into the house and lit candles and Olivia and Mary Lily and Crow began to get out things for dinner. By eight-fifteen the phone started working again and they called the family members and a few friends and Roper and his brother Sam showed up and began to tell about the damage in the town. Olivia called Georgia first.

"Are you okay?" she asked.

"I'm back in love," Georgia answered. "I have the illusion that he saved my life. How about you? What happened out there?"

"I think Dad likes him. I haven't told him we're going to Montana yet. I guess he'll have a fit when he finds out I'm not going to drive home with him."

"When are you going to tell him?"

"I don't know. What do you suggest?"

"Tell the truth as fast as you can."

"Okay. Well, that's pretty hard advice."

"Try it and report back to me. I'll try a little on my end. I haven't told him yet I won't live with him. I mean, I haven't told him in a week or so. He's so insidious. He thinks if he doesn't react, I'll change my mind. Well, I have to get off the phone. Zach needs to make some calls."

Olivia hung up the phone and went back into the kitchen to tell her father she wasn't driving home with him in the morning. "Dad," she began, but he held up his hand. Roper was talking about turkey hunting.

"We got birds in these woods that have never smelled a man," Roper bragged. "But you have to know where to go. You come back up as soon as the leaves turn. We'll take you with us, won't we, Sam?"

"It will be a good fall for quail too," Little Sun put in. "This much rain makes fat quail in the fall."

"Dad, Bobby and I are going to Montana."

"That's fine, sugar. So where do you hunt these birds? It's all hills? Or you got some bottom land?" Daniel was sitting between the two young men. Drinking iced tea with sugar and lemon and watching Bobby. That's how it is, he was thinking. About the time your dick gets soft, somebody starts screwing your daughter. Well, he looks like a man. He acts like a man. They all say he was a man in New Orleans, even if he did agree to keep the dope addict there all night.

"I don't know where we're all going to sleep," Mary Lily was saying. "I guess Daniel can have my room and I'll sleep with Olivia, and Bobby can sleep on the sofa, if he wants to stay."

"I'm going to Montana," Olivia said again.

"That's good, sugar," Daniel said. "We'll talk about it later. So what do you use to hunt turkey with down here? I use a four-ten, but I

know a man who hunts them with a thirty-eight revolver. I been raising them for twenty years. I've gotten so attached to them I hardly
shoot them anymore. Just ride out in the truck and watch them walk
around. They come up on a rise like a flock of leaves, then scurry
across like the wind was blowing them. They're pretty birds, once you
get to know them."

At ten that night they blew out all the candles and left the windows
open to the cool night air and went to sleep.

As soon as she woke up, Olivia went out in the pasture to look for
Bess. She called and called, but there was no sign of her anywhere.
When she got back to the kitchen Bobby was up and her father was
sitting at the dining room table pulling on his boots. Mary Lily was
taking biscuits from the stove.

"So you're going to Montana and make me drive home all alone,"
Daniel began, "that's the plan now?"

"I can't find Bess," Olivia answered. "We've got to look for her."

"You go get a horse from Baron Fork," Bobby said. "I'll take your
dad and search the pastures. Go on. The sooner you leave, the sooner
you'll be back. The keys are in the truck. Take that."

Olivia ran down the stairs and Bobby and Daniel ate the biscuits
and then struck out to the pasture. "She's had that horse for sixteen
years," Bobby said. "She loves that horse so much."

"She used to talk about it. What does it look like?"

"Just a big red quarter horse with a white blaze on its face and four
white feet. You'll know her. She's the only horse on this place that I
know of. Olivia and I ride back here. This is where we ride unless we
go to Baron Fork. Did she tell you they want her to ride in the Futurity
in Fort Worth?"

"Nope. But she said she was going to Montana with you and let me
drive home by myself. What the hell. I've got a lot to think about. I
don't mind. As long as you come home soon."

Bobby turned his head away. Not wanting to promise anything.
Daniel was setting a good pace, his long legs stretching out before him.
He crossed the pasture like he had been there all his life, heading in
the direction of the spring. As they walked, Little Sun's small herd of
cattle began to gather and followed them at a distance. "She ought to

be showing by now," Bobby said, "unless she jumped a fence. I don't see how she could have done that as old and heavy as she is."

"Keep walking. She'll find us if she's used to people. The Futurity? That isn't until December, is it? How's she going to get out of school?"

"The prize is two hundred thousand dollars."

"I saw it once. Went with a gal from Arkansas. I love to watch those cow horses."

They had come to the top of a rise that looked down upon the spring. "If Bess got in that spring, she's dead," Bobby said. "Excuse me, Daniel. I'm going on ahead." He broke into a sprint. It was three times the length of a football field and downhill and Bobby ran at a dead heat all the way. Behind him, Daniel was running too. No twenty-year-old boy who was fucking his daughter was going to beat him in a race even if he was starting to like the kid.

Bobby could see Bess's head before he saw her body. The neck and head, barely above water. As he drew nearer he could see her front hooves pressed against the concrete blocks on the shallow end of the cistern. Beside the horse the pygmy goat stood like a sentinel. Bobby sprinted the rest of the way and edged his way out onto a two-by-four and lay down upon it and began to pet the horse and talk to it. "Brave horse, smart horse. Too smart to drown. You getting tired, old lady? Let me think a minute. I know how you got in, that's plain to see. But how in the hell will we get you out? You're a good girl, a good smart horse. We're here now. We're going to help."

"Is she alive?" It was Daniel coming panting up to the other side of the cistern. "Holy shit, this is a mess. How deep's that water?"

"She's barely holding her head up. I know her legs must be getting tired. How can we get this water out of here? Can we knock a hole in the wall? Can we break out one of those stones?"

"I need a crowbar," Daniel said. "Let me talk to her and you run get some tools."

"You don't think we can knock a hole in it with a stone? A brick or a stone?"

"The water won't go down anyway. We'll have to dig a trench. How far's the nearest tractor, do you think?"

"I don't know, but we'll find out. Let's go. One of us stay here and the other go."

"You go. You can run faster. Goddamn cigarettes have taken my wind. I could barely run down that hill. Get up and let me take your place." Then Bobby scrunched back down the length of the two-by-four and Daniel was just taking his place when Olivia appeared at the top of the hill, riding one of Kayo's work horses. Little Sun was behind her in the pickup truck.

In half an hour they had found a neighbor with a backhoe and Daniel was on top of it digging a trench to the cistern. Olivia and Bobby spelled each other lying by the horse talking to her. Once she pulled her legs down from the sides and seemed to give up but Olivia coaxed her back to strength and she placed her cut feet back on the cinder wall. "If we had an inflatable raft we could put it under her legs and help her out," Olivia said. "Or somebody find a bucket and start bailing. Do something else. How long's it going to take, Daddy?"

"He can't hear you," Little Sun said. "But we will bail. Get those feed buckets out of the truck, Bobby. Let's bail water." Then for forty minutes, while Daniel moved dirt, Little Sun and Bobby bailed water. By the time Daniel had come to the edge of the cistern and was getting ready to dig into the cinder blocks, both Bobby and Little Sun were soaking wet. "Get Olivia off that board," Daniel yelled. "I'm coming in." He ran the backhoe into the wall and the wall broke and water came pouring out. It lowered the water level to about half what it had been and in the midst of it the old red mare stood shaking. "I need a blanket," Olivia shouted. "Somebody get me a blanket." Bess shook herself several times, and then, very gingerly, stepped over the broken wall and trotted slowly up into the pasture and bent over and ate some grass.

"Let's put her in the barn," Daniel said, climbing down off the tractor. "She's cut. You need to put her up and let her rest until we can get a vet here and take care of those cuts." He walked up to the mare and began to pet her. Bobby and Olivia followed, but Little Sun stood by the broken cistern petting the pygmy goat and remembering the house he had built beside this spring and what it had been to be young and full of juice and work all day to make a woman love him.

* * *

"She's a brave horse," Daniel said, rubbing Bess's back, inspecting the line of cuts along her shins. "She'll heal in a week. Still, we better get a vet to look at these."

"I learned to ride on her." Olivia snuggled into the horse's neck. "She loves me to ride her. We're a team."

"I'll take Kayo's horse back," Bobby said. "Then I'll come back over."

"Wait a minute, son," Daniel said, getting ready to face the issue. He'd been getting his words ready while he dug the trench. "How long are you planning on staying in Montana? School starts in a few weeks."

"We might not get to North Carolina until winter." Olivia let go of the horse and faced him. "We may stay in Montana and work and study on our own. It won't cost you any money. Just don't get mad if you don't see me for a while. I have to go and find my life, Daddy. Go see what I can do." They were standing in a circle. Daniel with his back to the hill, wearing his old khaki shirt and a pair of handmade cotton trousers, so elegant, so endlessly kind and tall and funny and loveable and powerful and tortured and Daniel.

Bobby stood beside Olivia, young and vulnerable, strong from the work he had done and the horses he had broken and the lack of mothering he had endured. Needy too, and uncertain how much he could break into the circle of Olivia and her father.

Olivia faced her father, newly armed with jargon from the world of psychoanalysis, feet firmly planted on the ground, her hands on her hips.

"We're going up there, Daddy," she was saying. "I don't like to go to college. I can learn anything I want by reading it. Tom's going to read with us and Georgia's going to send me books. I'll learn more studying at night than listening to some college professor who hates his job. All they do is spout their opinions. The books they teach out of they either wrote themselves or some friend of theirs wrote them. I'm going to read Dante and all the Greeks and Shakespeare. Georgia said the first thing they should teach is Shakespeare since he made up half the language. Not some politically correct bullshit someone wrote down at the University of Texas. You ought to go to some college bookstore sometime and look around at what they make us read."

"It's pretty boring," Bobby added. "You can die of boredom listening to those guys."

"I want to make a living doing something I want to do," Olivia went on. "Somewhere where the air is clean and there aren't too many people and I can get up in the morning and see the mountains."

Daniel reached in his pocket for a cigarette, then remembered he had quit. "It's mighty cold up there in the winter," he said. "It's a desolate landscape. I used to hunt up there when it was cold as hell but I wouldn't want to spend a winter there." He sighed. "You going to be able to take care of her, son? You going to be careful not to get her pregnant? If you want to get pregnant, get married. Come on home and we'll have you a wedding and then you can go up there."

Bobby and Olivia looked at each other, then looked down and giggled. That's good, Daniel thought, at least they can still get embarrassed. He shook his head and stuck his hands deep down into his pockets so he wouldn't think about the missing cigarettes. He took a deep breath and waited for them to speak.

"I'd do it today," Bobby said. "She's the one who's dragging her feet. I'd change my name. I told her I would. Hand Tree, how's that for a brand? I won't always be penniless, Mr. Hand. It won't take me long to start buying some land."

"He can live on a handful of rice," Olivia said. "You never saw anyone save money like Bobby can."

"So you're just going to forget formal education? The biggest regret of my life is not getting a college diploma. I wanted that for you and Jessie."

"Dad, it isn't like it used to be. It's just a business now. The great things to learn are right there in the library. Unless I decided to go to medical school, which I am not. Georgia says it's the life of a slave. I might get a degree in veterinary medicine. I don't know. All we want to do is go up there for a couple of years and finish growing up and try some things."

Daniel shook his head. He imagined what would have happened if he and Summer had done that. He remembered suddenly a canoe trip he took with her and how she had picked up her half of the canoe and walked so fast he could barely keep up with her. He looked at Olivia and knew he really loved her, loved her the way he loved Jessie, without question, with wonder.

"I'll be all right, Dad," she was saying. "Nothing will happen to me. Look how tough and strong I am. I'm going to be all right. I really am."

Daniel reached out his hand and pulled her to him and hugged her to his chest, pouring out to her the kind of love he had been so famous for lavishing around when he was a little boy.

"Go on, then," he said. "What can I do to help you? You need to keep the car? You need anything I can give you?"

"Just your blessing. Just keep on loving me and write us some letters."

Then Bobby rode Kayo's horse and Little Sun started up the truck and Olivia and Daniel led the mare slowly back across the pasture. They walked a long time without talking.

Olivia didn't say, I heard you were going to a hospital and stop drinking and Daniel didn't say, You need to marry that boy if you're going to screw him and neither of them said what was moving in their hearts, which was, I love you more than I can say. I am sad to let you go. Will you be safe without me? Will you be there when I need you?

"That's a mighty nice boy," Daniel said at last. "He's a good man. I guess he will take care of you."

"I'll take care of myself." Olivia laughed out loud and the sadness dissolved in the August sun. "Who do you think I am, after all? Don't you recognize your DNA?"

When they got back to the house, Mary Lily served them iced tea and homemade cookies and Daniel called home to tell them when he was coming. He called Margaret first and left a message on her answering machine. "We're okay here. I'll tell you about it later. How about buying me a new tie in case we decide to have a wedding. I'll call you back when I get on the road."

Then he called Spook. "Everything okay there?" he asked.

"Helen's pregnant." Spook had been waiting all morning to get to tell it. He stuck his finger into page 198 of *Range Dreams* and said it again. "Your sister, Helen."

"You're kidding."

"No, I'm not. Niall's called three times looking for you. We got TV here, in case you forgot. We seen those storms you been having there. He tried to call the little girl's granddaddy's house last night but they said the phone was out."

"I'll call him. This is true about Helen?"

"Why would I make something like that up? Listen, Margaret came by a few times. I guess she can't find you either and that guy you got to reline the tennis court showed up but I sent him home. I don't think he was right in the head, boss. Looked like he was on dope or something to me. So when you getting home?"

"In a day or two. Well, call the family and tell them I'm okay. We got a sick horse here. I got to get off the phone."

"I don't see any point in my staying here any longer, boss. If it's okay with you I'll just pack on up and start moving to the country."

"Spook."

"Yes."

"Don't you leave that house until I get there. And get that court fixed up. You can't tell when somebody might want to play."

"What did he say?" Olivia asked. "Did they know we had a tornado?"

"He said your aunt Helen's pregnant."

"No."

"Oh, yes. The adventure continues, as Anna used to say." He hugged his daughter to him. Looked across the room at Bobby. "You going to take care of her for us?" he asked. "You going to bring her back in one piece?"

"If she'll let me," Bobby said. "If there is any way I can." Then Daniel hugged his daughter close into his side and thought biblical thoughts and held and relinquished, held and relinquished.

Later that afternoon, after the vet had come and Daniel had left, Bobby and Olivia rode into town to see what damage had been done.

When they got to Bobby's house, Bud Tree was standing on the porch. He was wearing a blue-and-white-checked shirt and clean blue jeans and a belt with one of his rodeo buckles. He looked younger than when he had left, thin and pale from not being constantly in the sun. As soon as he saw the truck, he began to smile. The closer they got, the wider he smiled. Inside the house was the box he was going to deliver to Pine Bluff later in the week. Because of that he was going to meet his last and truest love. He was going to have a romance that would be the envy of the gods, if there were any gods left in a world as crazy and scattered as the one that was making do in the United States of America in nineteen ninety-one.

But he didn't know that yet. All he knew was that his son was driving up with his girl riding shotgun in the truck and everyone was still breathing and the sun was shining and the storm had passed through.

"There's my dad," Bobby was saying. "Dad's here."

"We might as well do them both in one day," Olivia answered. "He looks great, Bobby. You'd never know he'd been in jail." She stuck her hand out the window and smiled and waved, getting ready to make yet another man love her and have a stake in keeping her alive.

CHAPTER 57

MIKE poured himself a mug of coffee and took it into his study and set it down beside the sheaf of fresh blank paper. The morning sun came in the window and laid a blade of light across the lilies from the florist. The faint fresh smell mixed with the smell of oil from the old Royal portable on which he had written poems for twenty years. A contract for a novel from an American publishing company lay in an open drawer. So much money. More money than a poet could imagine being paid for turning life into words. Not only words, Mike knew. Visions and revisions, sparks to make fire in the reader's brain. The only reader I want is the one with a brain like tinder. Call up an answering cry. Call up wonder, laughter, fear, pain. Evoke Dharma, son of Reason.

"I'm leaving," Helen called from the front room. "I'll be back at noon." He heard the door slam. She had said he could write it. She had said he could use it all, as long as he set it in Australia.

Mr. Marcus Octavius Lane, Senior, got out of his automobile and began to walk across the soccer field to the timber stands where his daughter-in-law waited. He kissed her on the cheek and took the baby from her arms and sat down to wait for his oldest granddaughter to come out onto the soccer field. His daughter-in-law chattered away beside him, the baby cooed in his arms. This is what a man does with his old age, Mr. Lane assured himself. Watch the genes re-create themselves, watch for the genius to reestablish itself, hope against hope it doesn't get lost in the careless breeding of my thoughtless careless brood.

She came out onto a field, a stout redheaded passionate little female thing, patting her teammates on the back, rallying them around her. Annie Winchester Lane. She listened intently to something the coach was telling her, shook her head, then shrugged and bit her lip. He saw himself fifty years ago, getting ready for a game, the quick intake of breath, the muscles tightening, then letting go. The clock ticking.

"I said, Jim is coming if he can," his daughter-in-law repeated. "He's had to work so late this week, so I'm glad you made it."

"Of course," he answered. "Wanted to be here. Wouldn't miss it." Annie's team took the field. She looked his way, saw him there, nodded. She threw her shoulders back. The game began.

He watched her as though angels had appeared, as though angels were being dropped upon the ground by celestial helicopters.

"She feeds my soul," he whispered to himself. "All else is prologue."